WHEN PLAN A FAILS

Other books by Diana Corbitt

An Izzy Santos Mystery

Dead Woman Walking

Ghosters

Ghosters 1: The Forbidden Attic
Ghosters 2: Revenge of the Library Ghost
Ghosters 3: Secrets of the Bloody Tower
Ghosters 4: Mysteries of Camp Spooky

an Izzy Santos Mystery

WHEN PLAN A FAILS

DIANA CORBITT

 Bink Books
Bedazzled Ink Publishing • Fairfield, California

978-1-960373-69-4 paperback

Cover Design
by

Sapling
Studio

Bink Books
a division of
Bedazzled Ink Publishing
Fairfield, California
http://www.bedazzledink.com

*I dedicate this book to my dear friends and writers
who have helped to make every book I have ever written better. Those
would be Gillian Hobbs, Maryvonne Fent, and Carrie Bedford.*

*I am also thankful for the help of my cousin Shiela Halloway, as well
as that of my dear friend Gloria Gomez. Both are good at finding my
mistakes, which I appreciate greatly.*

*Lastly, many thanks to my old friend Jane Leung, who even while
receiving chemotherapy, still volunteers to help.*

Chapter I

GABE

ATHERTON LAKE LAY far below them in all its scenic glory. But Gabe Fox had no interest in the view. What mattered to him was whether the fall would kill his wife, Angie. Never comfortable with heights, he turned his back to the toy-like picnic tables below. "Great view, huh, babe?"

"Hang on . . ." Unlike Gabe, who jogged several times a week, Angie was out of breath from the short hike up to the overlook. She bent at the waist, hands on knees. With her back to him, Gabe had a good look at his wife's spandex-covered ass. Ugh. Some wives aged like fine wine. Angie aged like milk. Eventually, the pile of blubber straightened. She puffed a wisp of auburn hair from her eyes and took in the landscape.

"You were right," she said grudgingly. "The view really is gorgeous."

"Go on, take some pictures."

Having recently maxed out the Visa card to buy herself a shiny new Pentax, Angie jumped at the idea. She unzipped her camera bag and beamed as she took out her new baby.

Geez, kiss it, why don't you? Gabe forced a smile. "Take all the shots you want. We've got lots of time."

Of course, Gabe had been planning Angie's death for months, but if he'd learned anything in his twenty years of police work, impatience got a man caught. His wife would be out of his life soon enough, so why not let her snap a few pictures first?

"Let's get one of you, now. Move over there." Angie pointed at the same knee-high bench-slash-barrier he intended to push her off.

"Sure." Thankful the thing was a good three-feet wide, he sat down. "How's this?"

"Boring. The picture would be so much cooler if you got up there."

"What? You know I've got acrophobia."

"Bla bla. Hop up there, you big crybaby."

"No way."

"Then rest your foot on the bench. Or is *that* too scary?"

"No, no. I can manage that." The bitch doesn't know what scary is, Gabe thought. But she's gonna real soon. Smiling through gritted teeth, he followed Angie's instructions. "Like this?"

"Yeah, but relax. Hiking up here was your idea, remember?"

Damned right it was. He adjusted his Yankees cap and—with the heart-pounding drop just inches behind him—managed to hold a stiff but toothy grin as his soon-to-be-dead wife snapped away.

"Okay, your turn." Angie passed him the camera. "So, where do you want me?"

How about dead and bleeding all over those rocks down there?

But Gabe couldn't say that. "You're the brave one. Why don't you stand on the bench?"

Always eager to show Gabe up, Angie trotted over and with a superior smirk, hoisted herself up onto the bench and struck a relaxed pose, unconcerned by the perilous drop behind her.

Was he really going to do this? Once done, it couldn't be undone, and his step kids, Kylie and Robby, would be devastated. He snapped three pictures, then, lowered the camera as Angie bounced on her toes, her arms outstretched. "See? No big deal."

Oh, what the hell. The kids would get over it.

"No, no, no!" Gabe dashed to stop her from hopping down. "I just got the best idea ever. Come on, baby, one more picture."

"What are you talking about?"

His entire being told him to throw her off the cliff, right then and there. Instead, he stuck with his plan and coaxed her, ever so gently, back into position. "Remember that motel room in Langston?" he began, pleased by his light, reminiscent tone. "It was right after we got married. Kylie had just turned seven, so Robby was only four. You took pictures of them jumping from one bed to the other, remember?"

"You want me to jump off the cliff?"

He chuckled. Actually, yeah. "No, sweetie. I just want you to stand on the bench and jump up. You know, so I can snap a picture of you in midair."

Angie looked over her shoulder at the open sky behind her. "I don't know . . ."

"Oh, so *you're* scared of heights, now? That bench is three feet wide. I mean *I* sure couldn't do it, but *you* . . ."

"Oh, all right, but if the lodge serves lobster, I'm getting it."

"Sure, sure." Gabe grinned, knowing that was one tab he would never have to pay. "Dessert too." Temples pounding, he positioned himself for the shot. "Okay, now, when I count to three, you jump as high as you can."

With a nod, Angie did a little half-squat, prompting a nervous giggle from Gabe.

"What's so funny?"

"Nothing," Gabe said, even though she looked like a fat toad ready to hop. His face flooded with heat as he adjusted the camera's focus. "One . . . two . . . three."

Angie sprang up, arms and legs forming a big X. Surprised by her agility, Gabe almost didn't click the button.

But he did.

"Okay, let's see what we've got." With surprisingly-steady hands, he brought up the image. "Hey, what's that?" He frowned up at Angie. "I hadn't noticed before, but there's something in your hair." A lie. Eyes on the top of her head, he moved in. "I think it's bird poop."

"Gross. Get it out." She pulled a tissue from her fanny pack, and as she passed it to him, a dog barked somewhere down the path.

Somebody was coming.

"Okay, lower your head." Amazed Angie hadn't commented on the tension in his voice, he swabbed the imaginary mess with now-shaky fingers.

"Didn't think you liked fooling with hair so much," she teased. "Maybe you should go to beauty school."

"Funny," he croaked. It was time. Angie was right where he wanted her, in fact, her ass was literally hanging over the edge.

He'd never get a better chance.

She raised her fat face to him. "Oh, come on, Gabe. I wanna go."

"And I want you gone." He pressed his palm to her forehead.

"Hey! What—?"

Gabe pushed.

Eyes like golf balls, a scream burst from Angie as good as any horror movie actress could produce. Arms and legs flailing, she fell.

There. He did it.

Legs suddenly boneless, Gabe slumped down on the bench as Angie half-bounced, half-slid down a steep rock wall, then caught some air for a few seconds before mashing down some baby pine trees. The last twenty or thirty feet was all free fall.

The breath he'd been holding whooshed out when Angie hit bottom. Nausea, either from guilt but more likely, the vertigo, tore him away. No, this definitely couldn't be undone. He dropped to his hands and knees, reveling in the safety of the hard-packed earth.

More barking. This time, closer. And now, voices. Well, if Gabe could hear them . . . he filled his lungs and screamed, "Annnnnn-geeeeee!" With any luck, they'd remember his agonized tone when making their statements to the local police.

Gabe got his feet under him as a young man toting a toddler in a kiddie backpack pulled to a stop in front of him.

"What happened?" The man panted. "We heard a scream."

"My wife . . . she . . ."

A leashed Irish setter tugged a woman past them both. The dog hopped onto the bench and peered over. The woman looked too. "Oh, God, Tyson, there's a body down there!"

Years of working in law enforcement had taught Gabe that, for some stupid reason, upon committing a murder, perfectly intelligent people tended to draw unwanted attention to themselves. Their dumbest behavior was not grieving.

"Angie . . ." he sputtered. "I was taking her picture and she . . ." For effect, he dropped to his knees. "Oh, my God, she's dead!"

The baby shrieked, reminding Gabe that he should be crying too. As planned, he went fetal, hands covering his face. They'd remember this. His anguish. His tears. Eyes open wide, he called up his saddest memory, and soon, he was ten years old, mowing the front lawn of the house he grew up in. His little sister had just opened the side gate, and his heart clenched as their little dachshund, Missy, ran out into the street. A few houses down, a huge black sedan turned the corner.

A lump swelled in the back of Gabe's throat as he recalled the roar of the car's engine . . . Missy bouncing off the fender . . . her yelp as she spun off into the gutter.

"Mister . . . ?"

A warm hand touched his shoulder.

Dog nuzzling his ear, Gabe sat up, tears dripping from his chin. He muttered some purposefully incoherent garbage and—even though the man was already placing a call for help—fumbled for his own cell phone.

"It's all right." Sobbing a bit herself, the woman crouched beside Gabe. "Tyson's already gotten hold of someone."

"Oh . . . okay," he said, pleased by the pained crackle he'd managed to put in his voice.

They were buying it.

"Here." The man passed Gabe his phone. "It's the 911 operator."

Gabe took it. "My wife!" He pressed the phone to his ear. "Angie fell off the cliff, and—oh my God—I—she needs an ambulance!"

"Someone will be there soon," a soothing female voice promised. "What's your name?"

"Gabe . . . Gabe Fox." He took several shallow breaths, hoping to hyperventilate.

"Try to stay calm," the woman told him. "You're at Atherton State Park, right?"

"Yeah, yeah. At the Overlook. She wanted me to take her picture, and—oh, God, please don't let her die!"

The woman—Sandy—asked him several more questions. Gabe responded with semi-incoherent blathering.

"They'll be there soon." Sandy's voice was filled with empathy. "Just hang on. Take some deep breaths."

Should he look down there again? Would people expect that?

Stomach twitching, he stole another peek.

What the hell?

Somebody was with Angie; a dark-skinned man with black hair.

So what? She was dead. Nobody could change that. He shoved the phone back at the man. "I have to go . . . my wife." Camera in hand, Gabe raced down to the picnic area.

Everything was going perfectly. And it was a beautiful day. Alone on the trail, he freed the grin that had been crowding his mouth ever since Angie went flying.

BY THE TIME Gabe reached the picnic area, an ambulance and sheriff's vehicle had already arrived. He shifted into high gear, ensuring he'd be winded and sweaty by the time he crossed the wide stretch of grass between them. Huffing and teary-eyed, he dodged through a crowd of picnickers, the grieving husband, rushing to the side of his dead wife.

Two EMTs had already loaded Angie onto a stretcher, the redness of her blood contrasting beautifully against the whiteness of the sheet one of the men was draping over her. It was all going perfectly. In a moment the guy would pull that sheet up over her head and break the unhappy news to Gabe. With Angie pronounced dead, the sheriff's deputy would take down Gabe's statement. Afterward, Gabe would request a ride to the river where he would complete the least enjoyable part of his plan, telling the kids.

The EMTs rolled the stretcher toward the ambulance. Eager for some drama, Gabe threw himself on the body. "Oh, Angie! My god, she fell so far."

One of the EMTs pulled him away, leaving the other free to slide the stretcher into the ambulance. Silly, since there was really no rush with Angie dead.

"Sir, are you the husband?" It was the guy who'd draped the sheet over Angie—and why hadn't he covered her face?

"Yes, my name is Gabe Fox." Cheeks wet with a fresh crop of tears, he begged the man with his eyes. "Please . . . tell me she isn't dead!"

"She's not dead. But she *is* in bad shape. We're leaving for Moresby Memorial, right now." The EMT pointed toward a drinking fountain where a sheriff's deputy was talking to the dark-skinned man Gabe had seen from up at the overlook. "See that guy washing his hands in the fountain? If it wasn't for his quick thinking . . ." He patted Gabe's shoulder, then helped his partner push the stretcher into the vehicle.

Tears flowed down Gabe's cheeks as the ambulance pulled away. What the fuck was he going to do now?

Although he'd rather pound Mr. Nosy-helper's face in, Gabe stepped to him and offered the man his hand. "You saved my wife's life. Thank you."

"No thanks are necessary." The man dried his hands on his pants before accepting Gabe's. "Dr. Avani Singh."

"A-a doctor . . . ?"

The deputy grinned. "Lucky you, right? Your wife wasn't breathing, so Dr. Singh performed a"—He referred to his notepad—"a cricothyroidotomy."

Gabe blinked back, suddenly lightheaded. "A . . . a what?"

"A small incision, here." The doctor pointed to his throat. "I made it with my pocketknife, then widened the airway by inserting a section of straw from my soda cup. She'd have died otherwise."

"Isn't that something?" the still-grinning deputy said. "And this guy just happened to be walking by."

Chapter 2

IZZY

DETECTIVE ISABEL SANTOS raced into the Emergency Room. Breathing heavily, she scanned the faces of a half-dozen people, finally locating Sean Fulton seated on the far side of the room, his suit coat draped across the back of the seat beside him. Calling his name, she rushed to the man who over the last year had become more family than boss.

"Izzy." Looking a little rattled, Fulton stood. He opened his arms, and she fell into them.

"You okay?" She pulled back to see his face.

"I think I'm in shock. This is all so . . . so crazy."

"No kidding." Izzy hugged him tighter. "I don't get it. Maggie was grocery shopping?"

"She was."

A woman with two small children were about to sit down nearby. Fulton collected his jacket and found them seats on the far end of the room, away from other people.

"The responding officer interviewed the witnesses, and they all said the same thing. Maggie had parked her car and was walking toward the store entrance when she was hit." His voice quavered. "It was all just a stupid accident. Some old man named Alvin something-or-other started backing out of his parking spot at the same time Maggie was walking by. When he noticed her, he hit the gas instead of the brake."

It sounded serious, but surely not fatal. Izzy had lost both parents by the time she was twenty-three. Her aunt was the closest thing she had to a mother, and now that Maggie and Fulton were married, it was almost like having parents again.

"So, have you learned anything new since you called me?" she asked. "What's her condition?"

"One of the ER doctors came out here a few minutes ago." Fulton slumped against the chair's vinyl backrest. "According to him, your aunt's got a concussion and huge impact bruise on her hip."

"That doesn't sound so bad."

"Well, no . . ." Fulton shrugged. "But that bruise means there's a good chance a bone was broken. They're taking x-rays now, and will probably do an MRI after that." He pulled his loosened necktie off with a frustrated tug.

Izzy allowed herself to relax a little. "So worse scenario, she's got a broken hip?"

Fulton nodded halfheartedly. "Or leg."

"Sorry, I'm late."

Izzy looked up at her boyfriend, his green eyes filled with concern. "Hi, Brody. That's okay." She accepted his embrace and pressed her cheek to his chest, reassured by the familiar scent of hamburgers emanating from the graphic tee shirt he and his employees regularly wore. "Did you close Salty's early?"

"Yeah, finally, after I made the folks who'd already ordered to-go bags." He stroked her hair. "Now, what happened to Maggie, exactly?"

They sat down, and Fulton filled him in.

"Sounds bad, but it also could have been a lot worse." With Izzy's hand in his, Brody turned to Fulton. "Did that doctor say how long all those tests were going to take?"

"No." Fulton stood. The operating rooms were somewhere behind the double doors on the far wall. He stared at them with the intensity of a man trying to fire lasers from his eyes.

"Help me! Please!" A man's voice, thick with fear, echoed down the corridor.

Izzy peered over her shoulder and was surprised to find Gabe Fox, an officer she didn't know well, had pushed his way past the half-dozen people in line to the reception desk. Ignoring their complaints, he leaned across the counter.

"They . . . they just brought my wife in." Fox's voice cracked. "Her name's Angie Fox."

For a moment, the receptionist, a ruddy-faced woman rounding sixty, seemed ready to tell him off, but her anger vanished as two teenagers joined Fox, the boy almost as tall as his dad. Like Fox, the kids cheeks were streaked with tears. The crowd behind them quieted, their shared expression having shifted from angry to compassionate.

The receptionist nodded. "Okay . . . let me see what I can find out."

"Please hurry," the boy urged. "She fell really far."

After a few keystrokes, the woman raised her gaze. "They just took her into surgery."

"What kind of surgery?" the girl asked.

Izzy could only see the side of her head, but she looked familiar.

The woman apologized for not having that information yet, then slid a box of Kleenex across the counter toward them. "Have a seat. I'll call you over as soon as I know something."

Izzy shared concerned looks with Fulton and Brody who lowered his lips to her ear. "I've seen that guy at Salty's. He's a cop, isn't he?"

"Yeah, his name's Gabe Fox," Izzy said. "I don't really know the guy, but he seems nice. His little sister's Tonya Fox. Remember her?"

"Sure, I do. Back in high school, you two were tight."

They watched Fox guide the teary-eyed teenagers across the waiting room to seats two rows over.

"You and Tonya still in contact?" Brody asked.

"She lives up in Seattle now." How long had it been since they'd spoken? A year? Two? Izzy vowed to get in contact.

"Hey." Fulton tapped Izzy's arm. "Think we should go over?"

Izzy understood Fulton's reluctance. The kids seemed to be hanging on by a thread, and Fox? She peered over the row of empty seats between them at the man—the officer—she'd often heard referred to as one of the boldest and most self-assured on the force. "God . . . he looks so . . ."

"Broken?" Fulton suggested.

Izzy moved her gaze from the boy's green high-topped shoes to Fox, now hunched forward, his head in hands. "I suppose it would be weird if we didn't go over," she murmured. "I mean, we are right here."

Chapter 3

GABE

GABE SAT FORWARD in his waiting-room chair, hands clasped between his knees, trying to absorb what he was dealing with. On the downside, Angie wasn't dead—but she had to have been knocked around a lot. With any luck, she might die on the operating table. It would sure make things a lot simpler.

This was her own fault, really. The Angie he first met was fun, slim, and great in bed. So much so that when he knocked her up, he hadn't argued when she refused to have an abortion. No, he'd overlooked the two kids and married her anyway. Stupid, considering she lost that baby a month later. Hell, for all he knew, Angie invented that pregnancy to trick him into marrying her.

He sat back. Baby or no baby, things were good for at least two years. And then, after a few drinks with the guys, he'd come home late and noticed Darcy standing in her open front doorway. Although just a silhouette, he could tell she was naked. Well aware that Darcy's truck driver husband had left for a cross-country trip the day before, he'd paid his hot-as-hell neighbor a visit.

For a while, they'd hooked up once a week—not that it meant anything. Then, Angie found out and Darcy moved away. Understandable, considering Darcy was Angie's best friend and often watched the kids for them. With one woman pissed and the other history, sex became a rare commodity.

It just wasn't fair, Gabe thought as he recalled the way Angie had tumbled down the steep embankment. At least two people had fallen to their deaths from that very spot. He should be collecting insurance money, not wondering if she was a vegetable. And how much of this would his health insurance cover?

An even worse scenario was Angie waking up. Of course, the first words out of her mouth would be that he, the man everybody thought was so torn up with worry, had shoved her off that cliff *on purpose*. What would he do then? Run? For that, a guy needed money.

Too antsy to sit, Gabe stood and stretched. Beside him, eighteen-year-old Kylie and fifteen-year-old Robby sat zombie-like, their arms wrapped around each other, an intimacy they only shared in photographs. Well, if it took their mom's "accident" for them to realize how much they loved each other, then he'd done them a favor.

Not that the kids were bad, really, but they were definitely money pits. A senior in high school, Kylie was already dropping hints about needing a car for college, and paying for Robby's new braces had forced Gabe to work even more double shifts than normal. He checked his watch, then sat back down. No, regardless of what happened, pushing Angie had been the sensible way to go. He didn't have much, and a divorce would take half of it.

And how long was all this surgery crap going to take? His stomach rumbled. No wonder, since he hadn't eaten anything since breakfast. He opened his mouth to suggest he and the kids head over to the cafeteria. A familiar voice drew his attention. God, what was *he* doing here?

Gabe looked up to find not just Chief Fulton walking over but also Izzy Santos, the hot little rookie detective Chief Garver had given Fulton's position to before he retired. Sure, she'd solved two murder cases last year, fresh out of the police academy, but didn't his twenty years on the job count for anything?

His heart froze. Had Angie regained consciousness? Is that why these two were here? To arrest him? "Sir?" He pulled himself up on rubbery legs, focusing on the chief. "Wh-what are you doing here?"

"My wife, Izzy's aunt, was hit by a car," Fulton explained. "We're waiting for news from her doctor."

"Maggie?" Gabe said, trying to look more stunned than relieved. "That's rough."

Fulton nodded to the kids who were now standing and following the conversation.

"We couldn't help but overhear," Izzy said. "So, your wife had an accident? I'm so sorry."

"Poor Angie." Fulton rested his hand on Gabe's shoulder. "If there's anything I can do, just tell me."

"Thanks. Yeah, my poor sweet Angie." Gabe pinched his face as he retold his tale, sprinkling in a few pauses and voice cracks for effect. The act seemed to go over well, especially with all the background sobs from Kylie and Robby.

"Oh, honey." Santos pulled Kylie to her, and they shared whispers Gabe couldn't make out.

Great, a hugger. Expecting Santos might move on to him, Gabe took a step back. Thankfully, nobody seemed to notice.

You're probably wondering how we know each other," Santos said, one arm still around Kylie's waist. "Your daughter is my inside connection at the local library."

Smiling, Kylie nodded. "The Inspector Gamache books are super hard to get, so when a book Detective Santos wants becomes available, I set it aside and shoot her a text."

"Oh." Gabe smiled. "Nice."

To his relief, the doors leading to the surgery area swung open. He didn't recognize the lady doctor who appeared, but Fulton seemed to.

Eyes on the new arrival, Fulton rested a hand on Gabe's shoulder. "Sorry, man. That's my wife's doctor. We should . . ."

"Go," Gabe said. "I understand."

Thankful he didn't have to speak to them anymore. He watched Fulton make a beeline for the doctor. Santos went too, but not before motioning for a familiar-looking man sitting two rows over to follow her.

About the same age as Santos, the guy was tall, good-looking, and familiar. Not a cop—at least not one here in town. But he did look familiar.

Chapter 4

IZZY

FULTON INTRODUCED IZZY and Brody to Dr. Hong, Maggie's orthopedic surgeon. The petite, young Asian woman escorted them to an area similar to the main waiting room but a fourth the size, suggested they all sit on the sofa, then dragged one of the single chairs to in front of them and sat down in it.

"Mrs. Fulton suffered what's known as a femoral shaft fracture." Dr. Hong rested her hand on her upper thigh. "In this area here. It's also called a displaced fracture. That's because the two sections of bone have separated and are out of alignment."

"Okay." Fulton ran one hand through his mop of dark-brown hair, mussing it. "So, how do you get them back in alignment?"

"It's a long process." Dr. Hong tapped the tablet in her hand and turned it for them to see. "The first step, which we'll begin once Mrs. Fulton is anesthetized, is skeletal traction."

The image showed a simple ink drawing of a man in a hospital bed. Thigh bone obviously broken in two, his leg was raised and suspended at both knee and calf by cables.

"See this?" Dr. Hong pointed to the knee area. "We're going to insert a metal pin here."

She went on to describe the traction process and how once Maggie's bones were aligned, she would then need surgery.

"And how long will she be in traction?" Brody asked.

"That depends on several factors," Dr. Hong said. "But in Maggie's situation, I'm thinking a week to ten days."

"Then, you'll operate?" Izzy asked.

"That's right. The procedure is called intramedullary nailing. That's when a specially designed rod is inserted into the canal of the femur to keep the bone stabilized." Dr. Hong next showed them an animated simulation.

"How big of a scar will it leave?" Fulton asked.

"I won't know until I get in there, but probably five inches. Maybe six."

Fulton grunted. "Good thing Maggie only wears jeans."

He was right. Dresses were taboo to her aunt, and dress pants were normally reserved for weddings and funerals.

"But . . ." Fulton eyed the doctor warily. "Will she recover completely?"

Izzy held her breath, comforted by Brody's large warm hand taking hers.

"That's mostly up to Maggie." Dr. Hong turned off her tablet. "We're talking about a lot of physical therapy."

SUNDAY, 3:28 PM

Chapter 5

GABE

HOURS LATER, ANGIE'S doctor finally stepped into the waiting room. Clad in aqua-colored scrubs, white, and about the same age as Gabe, he introduced himself as Dr. Jennings, then suggested they'd all be more comfortable down the hall in a smaller, more private area. Gabe took it as a sign that Angie was either dead or so messed up he expected at least one of them to freak out. Good.

Besides a round table and several chairs, the room was empty. Jennings closed the door and waved them over to the table. Stone-faced, he stood by as they each took a seat.

Please-please-please—Gabe's prayer played on a loop in his head—tell-me-she's-dead. Please-tell-me-she's dead—

"Angie survived her surgery," Jennings began. "She's being moved to the intensive care unit as we speak."

Sonofabitch. No, wait. She could still be a vegetable. "But"—He pinned the doctor with his eyes—"is . . . is she going to be okay?"

Jennings remained unreadable. "Your wife has incurred substantial injuries, all of which we've addressed."

"That's good," Robby said.

Jennings nodded. "Let me tell you what we've done for Mrs. Fox."

Gabe didn't care if they'd given her new boobs and a tummy tuck. What he wanted to hear was that the man had removed a small tree branch from Angie's brain.

Sadly, Angie's long list of surgeries didn't include a pine tree lobotomy, but it was more than enough to get the kids crying again.

God, what a mess. Gabe passed around a nearby tissue box and took one himself. Screw Angie. What about *his* future? He dabbed his tears which were born from frustration. "That's a lot to recover from, Doc. But it's all physical stuff, arms . . . legs. What about her head? Is Angie's brain going to function . . . you know, normally?"

"Honestly, only time will tell. As they were bringing her in, she had a seizure, due to the severity of her head injuries. The neurologist found some swelling on Angie's brain, and after careful consideration, we decided it best if we induced a coma." Jennings looked at each of them in turn. "It sounds scary, but it's a common procedure. Keeping her unconscious for a while will allow her brain to heal properly."

"See, guys? They've got it all under control," Kylie said, surprising Gabe that she hadn't fallen to pieces. Robby responded with a hopeful nod, so Gabe went the other direction. "Oh, God, a coma." He dragged his hands across his face.

"But it's an induced coma," Kylie said. "They can take her out of it whenever they want."

And then, what? She tells everyone Gabe pushed her? Feeling like he might throw up, Gabe pinched his eyes shut and swallowed hard. "So, like in a day or two you'll take her out of it and she'll wake up?" Say-no-say-no-say-no.

"I wish it were that simple."

Oh? Was this be the light at the end of Gabe's tunnel? He opened his eyes and found Jennings staring back.

"We have to monitor her progress," Jennings continued. "If things go well, we'll stop giving her the coma medication after about a week. Then, either she wakes up by herself . . . or she doesn't."

"A week!" Gabe didn't have to cover his eyes because, this time, the tears were already flowing.

Chapter 6

IZZY

FULTON, IZZY AND Brody were allowed to enter Maggie's hospital room by midafternoon. Although Maggie was obviously still groggy, her dark, Moorish eyes brightened as they trailed in.

Weighing just over a hundred pounds and barely an inch taller than Izzy's five-one, Maggie didn't just look helpless in the bed, she looked tortured. To keep the bones from shifting, her left leg sported a fresh new cast. Bad enough, but what really bothered Izzy was the stainless-steel pin protruding from each side of her aunt's lower thigh, right above the knee. A metal device had been attached to both ends of the pin, sort of a down-facing horseshoe with a rope threaded through the curve. That rope extended up over a pulley, then down over the foot of the bed where a ten-pound weight kept the leg elevated and immobilized as the ends of Maggie's broken femur were slowly pulled back into alignment.

Izzy's first impulse was to cover her precious Tita Maggie with kisses, but she let Fulton approach first. He took Maggie's hand and kissed her softly.

"What's this?" Maggie murmured. She pressed her thumb to his furrowed brow. "Sean . . . *Cariño*. It's okay. I'll be fine . . . eventually."

"Yeah, eventually." He tipped his head to the side as he took her in. "Look at you. Still beautiful, even when you're trussed up like a Thanksgiving turkey." With a crooked smile, Fulton signaled for Izzy to take her turn.

Eyes welling with tears, Izzy stepped forward.

"*Ay, hija*, you too?" Maggie opened her arms, and Izzy kissed her cheek. "It looks worse than it feels."

"Now." Izzy combed Maggie's dark curly hair with her fingers. "You're still doped up."

She responded with a sleepy smile that widened when she noticed Brody standing in the doorway. "Hey, you." She gestured at her odd new accessories. "What do you think?"

"What I think"—Brody crossed his arms and smiled back—"is that I'm looking at one tough little Spanish woman." He strode to the bed and kissed Maggie's hand. "Do you remember what happened?"

"Mostly." She closed her eyes for a few moments. "I was walking through the Safeway parking lot when this big white car rammed into me. After that . . . nothing." Maggie stared through Brody with unfocused eyes. "Oh, man, I . . ." She looked at Fulton. "Do the police know who hit me? I mean, it wasn't a hit-and-run, was it?"

"No way," Fulton said. "We've got a dozen witnesses. Like I told these two, the driver got flustered, he hit the gas instead of the brake, and here you are."

"Okay . . . good. That's good."

What was that look on her aunt's face, because it sure wasn't relief.

"Something bothering you?" Izzy asked.

"I'm not sure." Eyes closed, Maggie pinched the ridge of her nose. "I saw something . . . but then I didn't." She offered a weak smile. "Guess the concussion made me a little goofy. What time is it, anyway?"

"Half past three," Brody said.

"Oh my gosh. You didn't skip lunch, did you?" Stifling a yawn, she waved them out of the room. "Go. Eat."

"She's right." Fulton flapped his hand at Izzy and Brody. "Go."

"You need to eat too." Maggie pushed Fulton weakly. "Go. I need more sleep." Already fading, she grabbed his sleeve. "And don't forget to feed my *gatito* when you get home. You know how upset Diego gets when he's hungry."

Chapter 7

GABE

SINCE THE INTENSIVE Care Unit only permitted two visitors at a time, the nurse suggested Gabe see Angie first. He waved goodbye to Kylie and Robby then followed the woman down the hallway to the nurses' station where she picked up a small brown paper bag and held it out for him to take.

"Those are your wife's personal effects."

He cast an unseeing glance inside.

"We couldn't save the clothes," the nurse continued. "What you've got there is her fanny pack, earrings, locket, stuff like that."

"I get it." Since it seemed like the right thing to do, Gabe clutched the bag to his chest. "Where . . . where is she?"

"Right behind you." The woman gestured toward Angie's room, just a few steps from where two nurses sat working at their computer stations and another stood preparing some type of meds.

Great, if you want your wife to get lots of attention. Terrible, if you don't want to get caught while you're finishing her off. Feeling like a kid forced to tell his mom he'd broken her favorite vase, he shuffled into the room where the woman he'd tried to kill lay at the mercy of tubes and wires, a sleeping cyborg. They'd even stuffed one down her throat. Gabe grimaced.

From what he could see, they'd done a good job of cleaning her up. One arm was in a cast, but the other didn't look that bad, considering. Her face was a different story. Gabe would definitely have to prep Kylie and Robby. He groaned at the thought. The day had gone badly enough without having to deal with screaming kids.

According to her doctor, Angie would be this way for at least a week, but once they took her off the meds . . . he licked his suddenly dry lips. No, he had to finish her. But how? A pillow wouldn't work, not with that respirator. He looked the device over and found the on/off button. But didn't these things have alarms? He imagined himself pulling Angie's plug and an army of nurses bursting in and tackling him to the ground.

Ugh. No, suffocation was off the table. With one look at Angie's eyes, even a half-ass doctor would spot the telltale broken blood vessels. Those things just screamed suffocation.

But what about the IV drip? He followed the tube up to a plastic bag filled with clear liquid. Saline, probably. But how hard would it be to add something lethal?

He traced the IV line back to Angie's hand and the little port thingy taped onto it. Nurses injected medication into them. But how? He squeezed the paper bag, annoyed by his own ignorance. Where did people get poisons, and which should he use? The last thing he wanted was Angie foaming at the mouth or dying while he was still in the room. Well, he'd just have to do some research.

He turned to leave as a nurse holding a clipboard entered the room. At the sight of him, her brow furrowed sympathetically. "I can't imagine how overwhelming this whole situation must be for you."

"You're right. You can't."

Chapter 8

IZZY

A YEAR HAD passed since Izzy first heard that the elderly owner of Rocky Harbor Marina was planning to sell his fifty-foot 1929 Elco cabin cruiser. She'd moved onto the boat a month later, causing her morning rituals to change dramatically. The bed, although still double sized, was now enclosed on three sides by ceiling-high mahogany cabinets, a snugness she adored. Nearly a foot taller than Izzy, Brody wasn't quite as enthusiastic, but he couldn't deny the soothing effect of the water's gentle but constant movement. For Izzy, the only downside of the bunk was that it was three feet high. Happily, the cabin also came with a matching mahogany step ladder.

As was their custom on days when Izzy had no major cases to deal with, Brody had slept over, and they had dressed for a morning run. That was another change to her life, this one definitely for the better. Accustomed to jogging past houses and apartment buildings, that unimpressive scenery had been upgraded to soft sandy beaches, sea gulls, and colorful fishing boats hurrying out to sea.

Finished with their four-mile jog, Izzy and Brody returned to the boat, ready for a shower.

"You go ahead," Brody said, and as he often did, began gathering up his things.

"Yeah, yeah. Great boat. Tiny shower." Izzy chuckled.

"You're very understanding." The morning sun streamed through the porthole onto Brody as he collected his wallet and keys. He was sweaty and a little musky, but Izzy didn't care. In that light, he was a Viking. She surprised him by pulling him to her, and they shared a deep and sensual kiss. Izzy had just lured Brody back onto the bunk when her cell phone rang. Seeing it was Fulton, Brody passed it to Izzy and climbed down off the bed.

"Hold that thought," he said, his honey tone intensifying the heat that had risen within her. Green eyes laughing, he pulled his shirt back on, kissed her forehead, and climbed the five-step ladder to the galley.

"You hold that thought," she called after him. Irritated by Fulton's timing, she poked the button on her still ringing phone. "Morning, Boss."

"What took you so long? Is Brody there again?"

"Not your business. How did Maggie spend the night?"

Fulton chuckled. "Good, considering. Apparently, they're keeping her well medicated."

"I'm glad she's managing the pain." She knew he'd slept on the pullout bed in Maggie's hospital room. "How'd you sleep?"

"Let's just say my back wouldn't turn down one of your aunt's pain pills. If you're thinking of stopping over for a visit, there's no rush. Maggie just had her breakfast, and she's ready for a nap."

"That's fine," Izzy said, relieved her aunt was doing well. "You go home and get cleaned up. I'll head over to the hospital as soon as I'm dressed." After a quick shower, she pulled on her usual detective clothes: a charcoal gray pantsuit and fitted, white collared shirt. She'd just finished French braiding her hair when a familiar engine sound warned her that every boat in her part of the marina would soon rock violently. Malcom Dillbeck was going fishing.

Thankful she wasn't still in the shower, Izzy tottered over to the already open porthole as the cabin door banged against the wall. Like every other time she'd caught the eighty-something-year-old leaving the marina, the old goat was pushing his Boston Whaler like he was late for his own funeral.

"Damn it, Malcom, slow down!" The surrounding vessels bobbed and sloshed in their moorings as Izzy shouted after him through the tiny porthole. "The next time I see you speeding through here I'm going to write you a ticket!"

As she expected, Malcom responded by raising his middle finger.

She should crank up her boat and chase the old criminal down. Right. And how realistic was that? Especially with no first mate to help her cast off. She tracked down her second shoe and her phone rang.

"Good morning," Rhonda Pinteaux said, Rocky Harbor PD's day shift dispatcher. "I'm so sorry about your aunt, Detective Santos. She doing okay?"

"I haven't seen her since last night, Rhonda, but the chief just told me she's as good as can be expected. Thanks for asking."

"Oh, what a relief. I'm calling because there was a vehicle burglary about two blocks north of the marina. You interested, or are you headed for the hospital? I could send over a uniformed officer, if you'd rather not."

Izzy thought it over. "No, I'll take it." Maggie was probably sleeping, anyway. She took down the details and grabbed her jacket.

Chapter 9

GABE

COFFEE IN HAND, Gabe stepped onto the front porch of his two-story craftsman-style house where Kylie waited for her best friend, Addison, to pick her up.

Kylie heaved a dramatic sigh. "This is stupid. I should be at the hospital with—"

"Look, kiddo." Gabe smiled over his coffee cup. "You can quit shooting eye daggers at me, because my mind is set. Your mom would want you kids to keep your grades up. Did you forget all those scholarships you applied for?"

Kylie grumbled. She checked her watch. "If Addison doesn't get here soon, we'll have to run across the entire school if we're going to be dressed and ready for PE on time."

She should take her mom's car, Gabe mused. Angie sure didn't need it. As he wondered whether the suggestion would help or hurt him, he looked in the direction of the familiar rumble of Addison's 1965 Mustang. With a screech of tires, the car stopped in front of the house. He followed Kylie down to the curb where she gave his cheek a goodbye peck and quickly climbed into the car.

Since the girls had spent two hours on the phone last night, Addison knew everything Kylie did about Angie's accident. A sassy little brunette, she waved him closer and reached across Kylie for his hand. "Hi, Mr. Fox. I'm sorry about what happened to Mrs. Fox. I've been praying for her."

"Thanks, Addison." Smiling sadly, he squeezed Addison's hand and shut the car door. Ugh. Would this be his world, now? Gloomy faces and pitying stares?

He wouldn't mind so much if Angie were dead.

He watched the Mustang pull away and turned back to the house in time to see Robby riding his bike down the driveway toward him.

"Bye, Gabe. See you this afternoon."

"See you." Gabe waved and sipped his coffee as Robby peddled off down the street. Of course, his big fatherly spiel about keeping the family boat on course had all been bullshit. If the kids were in school, they were also out of his hair.

Happy to finally get the house to himself, he took a quick shower then headed straight to the Dalton City Library. Of course, Rocky Harbor had a library too, but a prominent police officer dropping by to use one of the computers would likely raise several eyebrows, especially since Kylie worked at that library part-time. Dalton was another story. A one-hour drive, there, nobody would give him a second look.

Since the last time he set foot in a library was his senior year in high school, Gabe remembered little more than the place held books and computers, and anyone could use them.

He found several tall circular computer carrels scattered throughout the Dalton City Library, each with three stations. He continued his tour until he found a carrel with all three seats empty. Even better, it was in the far back corner where nobody could peek over his shoulder.

Although these county-owned computers were probably ten years old, doing his research here was smart. Why leave evidence on his home computer if he could avoid it? Not that there was any reason for the CSI guys to be geeking around with *his* search history, but it was always better to be safe than sorry, especially when you're researching poisons.

He climbed onto the stool, and with a quick mouse jiggle, the screen came to life. Dalton County Public Library, it said above two large buttons. The one on the left took him to the Internet. The other to the book catalog. Well, what was wrong with books?

Chapter 10

IZZY

IZZY ARRIVED AT 557 Parker Street and found what looked like a brand-new Honda Civic sitting in the caller's driveway. She easily spotted the basketball-sized hole in the car's driver's-side window and bent to peer through the opening. The garage door rumbled upward, and an apple-shaped man wearing jeans and a quilted flannel jacket stepped out to greet her. Izzy showed him her badge.

"You're here fast," the man said.

"Yeah, I was close," Izzy said. "You Eric Sherman?"

"That's right. I was heading off to work when I found that. Bastards took my stereo system."

"Sorry to hear it. Okay if I take a closer look?"

Sherman agreed, and Izzy tugged on a pair of nitrile gloves. She opened the door and poked her head in. As she expected, she found more glass beads, a gaping hole in the dashboard and one item she didn't expect.

"My insurance guy said I should report it," Sherman said. "But it's probably a big waste of time, isn't it?"

"Not necessarily." Izzy walked around the car and opened the passenger-side door. "What color's your wallet?"

"Black, why?"

She picked up something on the passenger-side floorboard; A tattered, brown leather billfold. "Any idea who this belongs to?"

Sherwood shook his head as she flipped the wallet open. Inside, she found fourteen dollars, but most importantly, a driver's license. "Jerry Greene. You know this guy?"

"Nope." Sherman grinned. "This is fantastic. Looks like the dummy served himself up on a silver platter."

"Maybe." Izzy dropped the wallet into an evidence bag, which she pocketed. It seemed like a slam-dunk arrest, but a thief with criminal smarts could claim his wallet had been stolen and the thief had dropped it there to frame him. She shared those concerns with Sherman.

"You're kidding." Sherman rolled his eyes. "What if you had video evidence?" He pointed at the house across the street. "There's a porch camera over at Benny's house. Maybe it caught something."

Izzy peered across the street at the gray-stucco two story. "I don't see it."

"It's right above the . . ." Sherman's jaw fell limp. "It's gone."

They crossed the street to the neighbor's front porch. "Now, where was it, exactly?"

"There." Sherman pointed out three screw holes right above the front door. "At least Benny got it free. His brother put in a whole new system last month and gave Benny his old stuff, but the footage would have been clear. I was there when they tested it."

Nodding, Izzy lifted her hand to knock on the door.

"Don't bother, Detective," Sherman said. ""Benny's visiting his mom in the Philippines and won't be back until the seventeenth."

"That's . . ." Izzy counted. "Friday. You okay with waiting that long?"

"To tell Benny they stole his camera?"

"Well, that, but I was talking about getting this Jerry Greene guy arrested. He probably took that camera because he believed the footage came with it."

For a moment, Sherman seemed confused, but then a look of happy realization spread across his face. "Oh, yeah, the recorder. It's on a shelf back in the house. Benny showed it to me."

"Perfect." She slipped one of her business cards into the doorjamb and handed another to Sherman. "I'll run a check on Greene. When Benny gets home, have him call me."

IZZY STRODE INTO her aunt's hospital room, expecting to find Maggie still snoozing. Instead, she found the TV playing softly and her aunt squinting up at the ceiling. "Hey, Tita Maggie." She bent down and kissed her aunt's cheek. "How's the leg?"

"The leg is okay." Maggie rubbed her forehead with the heel of her hand, then looked up at Izzy, her substantial dark eyebrows gathered. "There's something you should know."

Oh, God. Did Maggie have another one of her supernatural visions? "What's going on?" Chest tightening, Izzy smiled nervously as Maggie opened and shut her eyes a few times.

"That concussion seems to have scrambled my brain," Maggie began slowly. "This morning I didn't remember a thing about the accident, but after I woke up from my nap . . ." She shook her head as if trying to sort her jumbled thoughts. "I saw something, Izzy. When that car hit me, I saw something."

Izzy straightened. "Like what, Tita?"

"Like . . ." She kneaded the sheets with her hands. "I don't know . . . an animal . . . no . . . it was a person. It had to be."

"I don't understand."

"Before the car hit me, it struck someone else, and I think they might be dead—I mean, that's what I see, right? *Violencia*?"

"You mean, like before that car hit you, the driver ran somebody else over . . . on purpose?"

Still kneading her covers, Maggie shrugged. "That, I don't know. Some of it's still fuzzy." She shook her head again.

"Should you be doing that? I mean your head already bounced off the pavement once. Maybe you should . . . I don't know . . . not move it so much."

"I'm just trying to understand what I see, Izzy. You must look into this."

"And what do you suggest I do?"

"You're the detective. Examine the car. You don't need a warrant to look at the outside, do you?"

"No, as long as what I find is in plain sight."

"Then, what are you waiting for? If there is evidence, it won't be there forever. Rain could wash away blood, and if the guy decides to get it washed or, *ay Dios,* fixed . . ."

"I'll be screwed." Izzy thought it over. "Okay, well, that shouldn't be too hard. If he's getting it fixed, Rocky Harbor only has three places that do body work." She took out her phone.

As soon as she confirmed the vehicle she was looking for was at South Bay Body Work, Izzy drove over in what once was Fulton's unmarked vehicle when he was a detective, a slight upgrade from the well-marked SUV Izzy had driven. She parked in the lot out front and went inside to speak to the owner, Big Sheila Murkowski.

Dressed in her usual postman's-blue overalls, Big Sheila reminded Izzy of a large, human globe with no continents. With some effort, the big woman rose from behind her ancient desk, which, like the last time Izzy had visited, was stacked with files and various-sized boxes of auto parts. "Detective Santos, what can I do for you?"

"Hi, Sheila. I'd like to take a look at that Chrysler 300-S you got in yesterday."

"Sure. You got a warrant, or are we just talking about the vehicle's exterior?"

"Just the exterior."

"Okay, let's have a look." Long gray hair streaming down her back, Sheila lumbered over to a wired safety glass window beside a door that opened onto the main garage area. High ceilinged like a warehouse, the place had six parking bays with three mechanics moving about the four occupied spots. "That's it on the end."

They strode past a pick-up truck with no windshield followed by a red convertible where two men were installing a new black-canvas top. The next car was a big white sedan. Izzy pulled out her notebook and recited what she'd written there. "So, this is the car owned and driven by Alvin Griswold, age seventy-three?"

"It is."

"And what sort of work does he want done?"

"We're replacing this for sure." Sheila patted the trunk door and lumbered toward the front of the vehicle. "Also, the windshield and the hood." Hands on hips, she studied the front of the car. "The grille and front bumper too. Obviously."

Since Maggie had been backed into, Izzy expected the trunk door to be replaced, but the hood? She walked around to look at the front of the car. "Dang. What caused all that?"

Sheila eyed the long cracks in the windshield and the plate-sized dent in car's hood. "Apparently, the owner hit a deer last week but didn't get around to reporting it until now." She puffed her cheeks and looked at Izzy as if saying, "Hey, I just work here."

"Is that what it looks like to you?"

"Not a big buck, but yeah. Dent pullers are cheap. My guess is the owner thought he could live with the windshield crack and tried to fix the hood damage by himself."

"And that didn't work."

"Let's just say my people would do a better job." Sheila chuckled. "Anyway, now he's got trunk damage, and since he can't fix that, he's decided to report what the deer did." Sheila lumbered back toward her office. "Just remember," she told Izzy over her shoulder. "It's only fair game if you can see it from the outside."

"Got it, Sheila. And thank you." Izzy stared at the car. Even if the damage to the front had really been caused by a deer, that made two accidents in one week. Did Griswold need glasses? And how did Maggie's vision fit in?

She started by examining the front grille, which was missing a section about the size of her hand. Although not interested in dead insects, Izzy expected them, but the black-plastic honeycomb of 4x2 inch rectangles was surprisingly bug free. Okay, so the deer bled a lot, and Griswold decided to wash it. Nothing nefarious there . . . if what he hit was really a deer.

She took a few photos then moved around to the back of the car where she took more pictures of the damage caused by running into Maggie. Higher than most, the trunk door turned down at a sharp, almost ninety-degree angle, the center of which was now pushed in a good three inches, misaligning the latch which had been tied down.

Bending closer, Izzy discovered a tiny smear of what looked like blood. Of that, she took a picture and a sample. The area below the trunk door appeared clean, so she examined the two back corners, both of which had dents and scrapes.

Izzy straightened. Nothing criminal yet, but Alvin Griswold could definitely benefit from installing a backup camera. She decided to speak to Big Sheila again.

Chapter 11

GABE

BETTER INFORMED BUT frustrated, Gabe left the Dalton Library. The books he'd flipped through, and the websites he'd looked at had all told him the same thing. Poisons were part of nature. Hemlock . . . arsenic, hell, even those big bushes growing wild in the middle of the freeway, and if used properly, every one of them would kill. The problem was, he didn't want Angie puking her lungs out before she died. What he needed was something deadly, but low-key. Botox seemed his best bet, a real shocker since women paid big bucks to get the stuff jabbed into their faces.

His second choice was Aconite. Knocked out the way she was, Angie wouldn't complain about the stomachache it gave her. There was no stopping the monitors from picking up her breathing and heart problems, but Gabe would be long gone when those symptoms kicked in. Happily, Aconite wasn't normally tested for in autopsies, but what would the nurses think if their intubated coma patient suddenly threw up? With a sigh, he decided he'd worry about that once he found the stuff.

As Gabe returned to Rocky Harbor, his cell phone rang. It was the high school nurse. Somehow, Kylie had gotten banged in the head with a volleyball. She might even have a concussion, and since Angie was out of commission, it was Gabe's responsibility to pick her up. Wasn't it just like the bitch? Unconscious and still sticking him with chores.

What with work and looking for safe ways to end Angie, Gabe had enough to do. Of course, he could have accepted Fulton's offer to take a week off, but then, he'd be expected to spend his days at the hospital, and he sure didn't want that. So, he'd told the kids that they needed the money. "Lucky for me, the hospital's right in the center of town," he'd explained, and had vowed to visit their mom every chance he got.

And now, since Kylie expected Gabe to be working, he would have to stop by the house and change into his uniform before heading over to the school. Bad enough, but, he didn't have his patrol car. He called his boss.

"Sure, take a car out anytime you want," Fulton said. "If anybody knows how frustrating it can be to see their loved one in a hospital bed, it's me."

So, two hours after receiving the call, Gabe strolled into the nurse's office, and less than a minute later, Kylie came bounding around the corner, backpack slung over her shoulder. Just as he thought. She was fine.

KYLIE HAD BARELY buckled her seatbelt when Gabe started his interrogation.

"So, some girl served the ball into the back of your head?"

"Yeah, and hard, too. I saw stars."

He started the police cruiser and backed out of the parking spot. "And this was on purpose?"

"Well, I can't prove it, but I've seen Lexi play in tournaments, and she's the best server on the team."

"Well, why would she do a thing like that?" he asked, guiding his police cruiser out of the crowded lot. "Did you do something to piss her off?"

"I wasn't trying to. Jade Su and Eden Hendrix saw me talking to Lexi's ex-boyfriend. I guess they told her I was hitting on him."

"Wait a minute. Is this Lexi *Siegel*? A cute blonde, but kinda skanky?"

"Yeah, how do you know Lexi?"

"I shouldn't be telling you this"—Gabe smirked—"but I caught her and her crew drinking beer out at Stafford Park a few weeks back."

"Seriously? Please, tell me you arrested her."

"Naaaah." He flapped a hand dismissively. "Too much paperwork. I just radioed Mathis. Between the two of us, we piled them all into our cruisers and handed them over to their parents. That girl sure has an attitude problem. Anyway, if it helps, her folks were really pissed."

"Good."

So, Kylie was looking at boys. Well, she was eighteen—and he wasn't blind. The girl was full grown and had developed well. He also remembered how sex-starved he'd been at that age.

"Okay, back to the skank's ex. Were you . . ?" he asked, wondering if girls were built the same.

"Was I what?"

"Hitting on him?" Stopped at a light, he turned to her and made one of those stupid buggy-eyed faces that always seemed to annoy the heck out of her.

"Ugh, do you have any idea how dorky you look when you do that? And by the way, the light's green."

"That's me." He hit the gas. "King of the Dorks. Anyway, since when do you hit on boys?"

"I was *not* hitting on him." As he expected, Kylie's cheeks reddened. "He caught me walking into the gym this morning and asked if I would tutor him in math. Plus, Ryan broke up with Lexi like two weeks ago."

"Ooooh, Ryan, huh? Ryan what?"

"Ryan Lanister."

"Lanister? Is his mom Patsy Lanister?"

"I guess."

"Yeah, your third-grade teacher, if I remember right. Well, that's interesting. He's cute, isn't he?"

"It wasn't like that. And if I'd known the way Lexi would react, I'd have told him no."

"So, you did say yes. And Lexi's friends heard you guys flirting?" He smirked. "No wonder she conked you."

"I told you, it wasn't like that. And like I said, Ryan had already broken up with Lexi." Kylie stared out the window for a while. "They gave her a week of detention for hitting me. Addison told me when she brought my stuff to the nurse's office."

Gabe chuckled. "Oh, that seals it." Seeing there weren't any cars behind him, he paused at the stop sign and took a closer look at her head. "So, where's the lump?"

She touched a raised area in the back.

"I don't see anything."

Kylie unfolded the piece of paper in her hand and read, "List of concussion symptoms: Vomiting . . . none. Nausea . . . none. Vision . . . fine. Mind . . . clear, and I don't have any headaches. So, according to this check sheet, I do not have a concussion."

"That's good enough for me." He drove a few more minutes. "So, are you still going to do it?"

"Do what?"

"Tutor that Rolly kid."

"His name's Ryan." She shrugged. "I haven't decided yet."

"Well"—Eyes still on the road, he smiled slyly—"the skank won't like it if you do."

"That's what scares me." Kylie slouched down in her seat. "Have you been over to see Mom today?"

"Just for an hour or so," he lied. "Why? Want to stop by?"

"Yeah. I know she's asleep, but I miss her, you know?"

Well, it would give him a chance to figure out that IV port. "Sure, I was just going to suggest it."

KYLIE STARTED THE waterworks the moment Gabe opened the hospital room door. Not that it surprised him. A swollen mass of scabs and bruises, Angie's appearance hadn't really changed since yesterday. Tube down her throat and, with any luck, brain damaged, his wife wheezed away on her stupid respirator as they approached the bed. Since Gabe would rather clean ten gas station toilets than spend one minute looking at Angie's lumpy meatball face, he put on his angry, tortured act and prowled the room, ending his tour in front of Angie's IV stand.

Two bags of liquid hung there, plastic tubes dangling. He did his best to ignore the relentless whisper-wheeze of the machine and traced the tubes to their destination. One, a milky, white solution, went straight to Angie's mouth and presumably, down her throat, but the other ended at a little plastic device taped to the back of her hand. Okay, so where did the nurses jab their syringes? Was it that little blue thing there by the main tube? It couldn't be that hard to stick a needle in there, but why worry about that until he'd gotten his hands on some Botox?

With Kylie busy mumbling away at her mother, Gabe stepped to the window, barely noticing the row of leafy green elms on the far side of the parking lot. Where did a person get Botox, if not from a plastic surgeon? He supposed he could start with Yelp, then run some background searches. If he found one that looked dirty . . .

There was a knock on the already open door. Gabe turned to find Fulton standing in the doorway.

"Hey, Gabe, how's it going?" Dressed in his usual dark suit and holding a paper coffee cup in each hand, Fulton passed one to Gabe. "I saw your car out front, so—" He noticed Kylie. "I'm sorry, honey. I should have realized you might be here. Would you like me to bring you a soda? I've got gum."

"That's okay."

Fulton gave her shoulder an I'm-with-you squeeze, then offered his hand to Gabe. "Guess we shouldn't expect any changes, huh? You holding up okay?"

"Yessir," Gabe muttered his thanks, amazed by Fulton's visit. But then, he remembered Fulton's wife also had a room on this floor. "How's Maggie doing?"

"Ehhh." Fulton made a little seesaw motion with his free hand. "She'll be here for at least two weeks, but it's nothing like what you guys are dealing with." He eyed the thing in the bed, then turned quickly back to Gabe.

Yeah, Gabe thought. He didn't like looking at her either.

"I should leave you to your family," Fulton said, shaking his head. "Let me know if you need anything."

"I will." Duplicating Fulton's Droopy-Dog expression, Gabe followed Fulton to the door. "Thanks for the coffee." He took a sip and waited until Fulton disappeared into Maggie's room before stepping back inside.

"I'm ready to go too," Kylie said.

Oh, thank God.

"Think maybe we could stop for something to eat?" she asked. "I missed lunch, sitting in the nurse's office all morning."

"Sure." Gabe was eager to get out of there, himself. Knowing the girl would expect it, he went to her mother's bedside, disgusted by the thought of pressing his lips to her scabby ones. Inspired, he kissed his fingertips and pressed them to Angie's cheek. "Okay, let's go." Having spent the morning researching poisons, Gabe had also missed lunch, but you didn't hear him whining about it.

Chapter 12

GABE

SINCE HE WAS already dressed for work, Gabe told the kids he was too wound up for sitting at home. And that was true. So, he took a night shift—or, at least, that's what he told the kids. What he was dying for was the freedom to do whatever he wanted. And that was to fuck a woman whose name wasn't Angie.

"Here, get yourselves some takeout for dinner." He handed Kylie a twenty, then trotted upstairs, showered, threw on a fresh uniform, and left the house carrying a duffel bag containing the outfit he would later change into.

Gabe wasn't stupid. He would look for sex, (possibly his last, if Angie had any say in the matter) but like his field trip to the library, he wouldn't do his looking in Rocky Harbor. With Angie still breathing, the one-hour drive to Dalton was well worth the effort. Once there, he searched for a place to eat, and after wolfing down a quarter-pounder with cheese and medium fries, stole into the men's room to change into his "dating outfit."

He started his evening at a bar named Sideways where he soon discovered he was the right age, but way overdressed in his leather jacket, collared shirt, and dress slacks. At Sideways' the uniform of choice was jeans and a tee shirt with the dressier fellows sporting polos. Well, he'd know better next time.

Seeing the dance floor and most tables empty, he also realized that seven-thirty in the evening was probably too early for barhopping. So, what now? A movie? Ice cream? No way. He climbed onto one of the many open barstools and asked for a martini, a pack of cigarettes, and some matches.

But as Gabe stubbed out his first cigarette in ten years, a woman walked in. A real hot ticket. Immediately heads turned. All decked out in soaring stiletto heels and a skin tight red dress, her intentions could not have been more obvious if she had walked in wearing a sandwich board reading, "Looking for Sex? Inquire Within." She took a spot at the bar a few seats down from him.

Now that was some prime real-estate. He called the bartender over and tipped his head toward the raven-haired beauty.

"Let me guess. You want to buy her a drink."

"Yeah, I do." If Angie was sending him to prison, he might as well go out with a bang. Gabe chuckled at his own joke. "What's she drinking?"

"Hell, what she always orders. Sex on the Beach."

"Okay, send her one of those." Gabe glanced down the bar and frowned. A smarmy looking guy with a shaved head had already taken the empty seat beside her. Although annoyed, he couldn't blame the guy. Men were dogs. A hot bitch shows up and they all come sniffing.

He grabbed a cocktail napkin and blotted the sweat trickling down the sides of his face. Why had he worn this stupid jacket? Worried there'd be armpit stains on his shirt, he toughed it out and looked over at the bartender who was stirring some sort of pinkish-orange concoction with a long metal spoon.

All shiny white teeth and heaving cleavage, the woman seemed to be into whatever garbage the bald guy was serving her. Finally, the drink was delivered and the bartender pointed in Gabe's direction. To his surprise, a mischievous smile lit up the woman's face, and without a moment's hesitation she picked up the drink and brushed past her confused suitor.

"Well, hello, stranger." She set her drink alongside his and slid onto the empty barstool beside him. With a warm hand on his thigh, she leaned over and whispered, "Wow, I sure didn't expect to see you here."

"Me? How—I mean, do we know each other?"

"Hell, yeah, we do." Bright blue eyes twinkled up at him through wispy black bangs. She leaned closer. "It's me, Gabe. Darcy." Her warm breath tickled his ear.

"Darcy?" He pulled back and studied her face. The lips were fuller. The eyes were bluer, but the tiny mole on the corner of her mouth was right where he remembered it. "Darcy Prescott?"

"Shhh." She slapped his shoulder playfully. "Keep it down. And it's Callahan, now."

His gaze moved over the mass of black curls and drifted down to her chest. Those had sure as hell improved. Pushing his lips through her thick mane, he found her ear. "What are you doing here, and why are you wearing that wig?"

She giggled. "I'm in disguise."

Disguise? "What the hell for?"

"For the same reason you should be." She eyed his ring hand and the wedding band he'd forgotten to take off.

"Let's not talk about Angie." He pointed out her own huge wedding ring. "If you're really in disguise, why are you still wearing that?"

"I can't get it off." Giggling, she rested her ring hand on his thigh. "And don't think I didn't try."

"So, where's your new husband? What's his name . . . ? Malcolm?"

She giggled. "*Patrick* is away on business, and honestly, I'm not sure where this time . . . Bloomington . . . Chicago. He travels a lot, poor baby. Gone days at a time." She took a sip of her drink, then wagged a long, manicured nail at the cigarette pack. "I see you've started smoking again. Can I have one?"

Chapter 13

GABE

THE FEELING OF falling jolted Gabe awake. He rubbed his eyes and looked around. Above him, the three bulbs on the ceiling fan lit up the room like a dentist's office. He blinked a few times, then smiled. He was in Darcy Callahan's bedroom, and he was naked in Darcy Callahan's bed.

Although all the curtains had been drawn, a round window high on the opposite wall told him it was still dark out. He rolled onto his side. Except for the sheet covering her from the waist down, Darcy was naked, and his gaze immediately went to her more than generous breasts. He'd been right about them being implants. Drunken memories of kinky sex made him ready for another go. He ran his finger lightly across the tip of her right nipple.

No reaction. Gabe assumed she was still drunk and raised his gaze. The black wig was long gone, and Darcy's straight blonde hair was strewn across her face and neck. He brushed it aside and gasped. His belt was wrapped around her neck.

"Darcy?" He nudged her with his foot.

No reaction.

"Hey, stop fooling around." He gave her shoulder a hard shove.

Still no reaction.

Hands shaking, Gabe unclasped the belt, revealing an ugly purple band. "Oh, no . . . no." He searched in vain for a pulse as more memories flashed. The belt had been Darcy's idea. She'd giggled as he looped it around her neck.

Ironic, wasn't it? The woman Gabe truly wanted dead was still breathing, and somehow, he'd managed to kill one of the few people he really liked. Hands gripping his suddenly throbbing temples, he lurched off the bed. It was all coming back to him.

"Come on, it's fun." Darcy's speech had been slow and sloppy. "You do me, and then I'll do you. You'll love it, I promise."

And she was right. Too right. It came back in bursts . . . her naked body straddling him, rocking, moaning . . . and all the while, he'd kept tightening that damned belt, applying more and more pressure. Yes, it *had* been fun. A real rush. He remembered getting behind her. Pumping. Grinding. Tightening the belt.

Even shitty drunk, Darcy's instructions had been clear. Let up as soon as she passed out.

But Gabe hadn't. Sloshed on tequila as well as a newly-acquired power of life and death, it wasn't Darcy's face he'd seen as he was pulling on that belt. It was Angie's.

He had squeezed Darcy's throat long after his own orgasm, and, more importantly, long after the light had left her eyes. And now, Gabe was standing in his dead lover's bedroom, naked except for his socks, and—what time was it?

On the nightstand, big green numbers on the clock radio glared one-sixteen a.m. They'd left the bar just after ten o'clock. Luckily, Darcy had suggested they leave separately. "We don't want to give people anything to gossip about," she'd whispered just before she waved goodbye for everyone in the bar to see. Considering the present situation, that had been awfully considerate of her. It might even be the difference between freedom and an eight-by-six prison cell.

He dragged the bed sheet up over her face. Well, she'd brought it on herself. "Sorry, Darcy, but I'm not getting locked up over this."

GABE ARRIVED AT home just as the sun was rising. Finding Kylie and Robby still fast asleep, he popped a couple of Tylenol, took a quick shower, and crawled into bed, still amazed by what he'd just done. He looked over at the clock-radio and grinned. On any other Wednesday, he'd be getting up in two hours, but because of the situation with Angie, Chief Fulton had given him the freedom to work whenever he pleased. Thanking God for his police training, he drifted into unconsciousness.

ROUSED FROM A deep sleep, Gabe sat up, groggy and confused by the sound of shouting. Had they come to arrest him? Realizing it was only Robby and Kylie quarreling downstairs, he threw back the covers and shambled down to the kitchen where he found them wrestling over a box of cereal. His first instinct was to clunk their stupid heads together. Instead, he gave his throat an exaggerated clearing.

As one, they let go of the box, and it fell, spilling whatever cereal was left on the floor. Kylie shoved her brother. "Great Robby. Now nobody gets to eat."

"I had it first." Robby looked at Gabe as if asking for judgment.

Exhausted, Gabe slouched against the door frame, only half listening as they blathered on about frozen waffles and not having groceries. With a sigh, he raised both hands, quelling the racket. "Okay, okay. Just make me a list. I'll go to the market this afternoon."

"Thank you!" Robby boomed, throwing both arms up dramatically. He snaked past Gabe and bolted up the stairs, leaving Kylie with the mess.

"Yeah, thanks, Gabe, and I'm sorry we woke you." She pulled the broom from the closet and started sweeping. "It's not even seven-thirty yet. Maybe you should go back to bed. You look kind of rough."

"Yeah, I uh . . . stopped off at the hospital earlier." He kissed her forehead and headed back upstairs, wondering just how understanding Kylie would be if she knew what he'd really been up to. He flicked on the bathroom light and squinted into the mirror. Puffy red eyes stared back.

Kylie wasn't kidding. He needed some Visine.

Gabe opened the medicine cabinet and stopped to look at his hands, half expecting them to still be covered with yellow kitchen gloves. He put some drops in his eyes and shuffled back into the bedroom, and as he climbed back into bed, pressure turned to pain in his chest. He let out the breath he hadn't known he'd been holding and filled his lungs with a loud gasp. He had to stop torturing himself. Darcy's death was an accident. That said, he prayed he'd never have to sell that idea to his fellow police officers.

As he tugged the covers up around him, he froze at the sight of his empty left wrist. Where was his damned watch? Seeing it wasn't on the nightstand, he sat up to check the dresser. But the watch wasn't there either. Grumbling, he marched into the bathroom. No watch.

Okay, the last time he saw it was—oh God.

Suddenly lightheaded, Gabe staggered back into the bedroom and sat down. Darcy's husband was flying in sometime this morning, but when, Gabe didn't know. Any normal husband would dial 911 the moment he found the body, and once the CSI guys took over, Gabe was screwed. He had to retrieve his watch before that. But how?

At Darcy's request, he had parked more than a block away from her house. Her fear of gossiping neighbors had been a lucky break. But inside the house, his DNA was everywhere, and what he couldn't wipe clean had to be disposed of. Retrieving his own car was out of the question, so Gabe had packed the trunk of Darcy's with everything from the bedding they'd rolled around in to the many towels he'd used to wash things down with, as well as the five-gallon container of gasoline he would later use to burn it all. Even if one of Darcy's neighbors had seen him, they probably couldn't identify him. And they sure wouldn't expect Darcy's killer to come back driving a squad car.

That settled, he threw on his uniform and headed to the station. And as he hustled past coworkers pledging prayers and casseroles, he repeated the same BS he'd used on the kids: that Angie's suffering was too painful in large doses. He had to work.

Once outside, Gabe all but ran to his vehicle, and for the next hour, his heart leaped into his throat every time the radio crackled. Surprisingly, the call came through just after nine. Even more surprising, a woman had made it.

Gabe took the call, and, sirens blaring, arrived at Darcy's five minutes later. An older woman he'd never seen before was sitting on one of the two white wicker chairs on the front porch. Spotting the police cruiser, she sprang up as if electrocuted and raced toward him, arms raised and flapping.

Gabe was pretty wired himself. He was responding to his own crime scene, and how many cops could say *that?* Teeth gritted, he ignored the urge to shove the woman aside and dash into the house. Instead, he met her in the middle of the driveway. "Good morning. Are you Monica Curtis?"

Huge owl-sized eyes fixed on him, puffy and rimmed with red. "Yes, I live right over there." Her voice was as shaky as her hands, which she unclasped just long enough to poke one knobby-jointed finger at the ranch-styled house across the street.

"How'd you happen to discover the body, Mrs. Curtis?" My guess is because you're a nosy old bat.

Mrs. Curtis sniffed. "Darcy and I have coffee together every morning at nine." She wiped her nose with a balled-up tissue. "It's been our custom the last few years. Usually, she leaves the door unlocked for me, but today, it wasn't, so I knocked. When she didn't answer, I let myself in."

"And then, wh—?" He stumbled back as the old bag threw herself against his chest, weeping uncontrollably. What the hell? "Mrs. Curtis?" He tapped her shoulder. "Monica? You okay?"

"Who could have done such a thing?" she groaned.

Since she probably expected a hug, Gabe lifted his arms and—as loosely as possible—wrapped them around the woman as she blubbered, her jaw moving against his chest. Great, that made two snot-covered shirts in one week. Although he knew the answer better than anyone, Gabe peeled her off him and asked what she had seen.

"The first thing . . ." She stuffed the old tissue into the left sleeve of her sweater and reached into the right sleeve for a fresh one. "The first thing I saw was her cell phone. It was lying in the middle of the entryway, all smashed as if someone had stomped on it."

Yeah, me.

Gabe did his best to look concerned, and with a quick frown at his soiled shirtfront, said, "And how about Ms. Callahan? Where'd you find her?"

To his dismay, the question only brought on another sobbing fit.

Christ on a cracker, I do not have time for this.

Knowing backup might arrive any moment, Gabe grasped her arms. "Where is she?" He fought an urge to shake the woman. "The kitchen? How about the bedroom?"

With a sniff, the owl-eyed woman bobbed her head.

"Okay, the bedroom. I'm going in."

But as he headed for the front door, Mrs. Curtis grabbed his arm. "Don't you want to know how I got inside?"

Realizing he was about to punch the woman in the face, he drew a deep breath and relaxed his already fisted hands. "Okay, how'd you get in?"

She fished a potato-sized decorative rock out of a potted plant next to the front door and cracked it open, revealing a shiny silver key.

Jesus, that thing wouldn't fool Helen Keller.

For dramatic effect, Gabe turned the knob slowly, and the door swung open, revealing the grey tiled entryway where he'd stockpiled his evidence just a few hours ago. Now, the only thing out of place was Darcy's stomped-on phone.

"Well, that's not a good sign," he told Mrs. Curtis. "And that was there when you came in?"

She nodded.

Knowing he couldn't look for his watch with Old Owl-Eyes glued to his hip, he lowered his lips to her ear and whispered, "I doubt the killer's still in there, but just in case . . ." He waved her over to the far side of the porch where she perched on one of the wicker chairs, her fingers kneading a balled-up tissue. "Perfect. Stay right there."

"The bedroom is down at the end of the hall. She's . . . in the tub."

Gabe nodded and drew his gun for effect. As he expected, the place was silent. Leaving the door open, he marched down the freshly vacuumed hallway with Monica Curtis's footprints leading the way.

Grasping the irony, Gabe couldn't help but smile. He'd vacuumed the whole house leaving the carpet smooth and pristine, only to come back now and stomp all over it. He slid the gun back into its holster as soon as he entered the bedroom. So far, everything looked the same as he'd last seen it. The bed was still stripped down to the mattress, the fan in the bathroom was still whirring away. So, where was that damned wristwatch?

He checked the nightstand first. Finding no watch there, he pressed his ear to the wall and peered behind. No damned watch.

Angie had given it to him during their first anniversary party so many years back. The stupid bitch had even had it engraved. *"Gabe + Angie."* Crap, if they found that, they'd lock him up and throw away the key.

Realizing he'd totally forgotten to clean under the bed, Gabe dropped to his knees, and as he took out his flashlight, the sound of Mrs. Curtis voice made his gut flutter. She was talking to someone, a voice Gabe didn't recognize.

Running out of time, he swept the beam back and forth beneath the bed. All he found was a sock.

It's a freaking watch, he told himself. How far could it have—there. A glimmer. He leaped to his feet. Tears glazed his eyes as he scrambled across the bare mattress and squeezed his entire arm between it and the headboard. A few moments later, he slipped his prize onto his left wrist. Grinning, he hopped off the bed. Now, they could bring in all the CSI assholes they wanted. He turned to find Isabel Santos standing in the bedroom doorway.

"Why the grin?" she asked.

Like Ebenezer Scrooge after a night with the ghosts, Gabe could have danced the little detective around the room. Instead, he shrugged. "Found a sock. But, considering how they cleaned the place, it probably belongs to the husband." He waved his watch hand at the mattress. "See that? The guy took the bedclothes with him."

"Yeah, and it looks like he vacuumed too." Santos cast a somber glance at the bathroom door. "Neighbor lady said the body's in there."

"Yeah. Pretty gruesome—and be careful with those fumes. She's been scrubbed down with something. The stink will scorch your nose hairs off."

Santos nodded and stepped into the small room, returning moments later, her peaches-and-cream skin now pale and bloodless. "I could have lived my whole life without seeing that."

"I know, right?" Gabe stepped to her, shaking his head in mock disgust. "What kind of person does a thing like that?" With Santos looking like she might puke, Gabe placed a hand on her shoulder. "Let's get you out of here." He escorted her out of the room, down the hallway, and out the open front door. "There, the fresh air will do you good."

Although a great weight had been lifted from Gabe's shoulders, finding his wristwatch didn't mean he could kick back. As first on the scene, his duties were to seal the area and interview the neighbors. Santo knew that too. After a few deep breaths, she was well enough to give orders and sent Gabe off to begin his interviews.

"Sure thing," he said, even though it gnawed his gut to take orders from a woman just a few years older than his own stepdaughter. As he was leaving, an equally wet-behind-the-ears officer named Adrian Vega showed up. Santos set him to stringing the police tape.

Fine, Gabe thought. Let Santos take over. He wondered if she would put Vega in charge of the crime scene log—not that Gabe wanted the job. What mattered now was whether his fellow officers remembered his near breakup with Angie, and who had caused it.

Chapter 14

IZZY

THE CSI TEAM'S inability to find evidence at Darcy Callahan's house irritated Izzy. She stood in the living room, wondering how soon Fulton would get there when Officer Vega poked his head in. "Detective. The chief just pulled in."

She headed outside. Not much older than Vega, the young rookie's enthusiasm reminded Izzy of herself, It felt like forever at times, but really, only a year had passed since her promotion. She thanked Vega for the heads up and walked down the driveway to meet her boss, who had parked behind the big CSI truck that now blocked in her and Fox's cars.

Dapper as usual in his dark blue suit, Fulton looked at Izzy. "Well?"

Across the street, a woman with very large eyes studied them from her front window.

"Let's go inside," Izzy said. She led him up to the porch where Vega met them with the log sheet.

"Morning, Chief." The young rookie held the clipboard for Fulton to sign. "Folks sure do terrible things, don't they?"

"Some do, yeah." Fulton took a moment to look the rookie over. "You doing all right, Adrian? I know this is your first murder."

"Yessir, I'm fine." He took back the clipboard and handed Fulton a pair of disposable shoe covers. "Any news on Mrs. Fulton? I hear her leg was broken pretty bad."

"Thank you, and you heard right." Fulton sat down on the nearby wicker chair to put on the paper booties. "She'll be in traction for a couple of weeks, but I think she'll come out okay."

"That's good news, sir." Vega offered a pair to Izzy.

She almost turned them down, then realized she'd stepped out of the murder scene. "Thank you." She slipped on a new pair and escorted Fulton inside.

"What happened there?" He pointed down at evidence marker #1 and the crushed cell phone lying on the floor beside it.

"No idea," Izzy told him. "Gabe Fox said it was there when he first walked in."

"Oh, Fox was first officer on the scene?"

"That's right."

"And what's the victim's name again?"

"Darcy Callahan."

Fulton seemed to mull the information over for a few moments. Then his attention turned to the fresh vacuum tracks zigzagging their way across the living room rug. "So, the CSI team vacuumed this room then moved on?"

"No, the killer did that." Even though the last thing Izzy wanted was to see Darcy Callahan's body again, she waved him toward the hallway. "You ain't seen nothin' yet."

"I got hold of the husband," she told Fulton as he stopped to peek into what appeared to be an office. "The woman who found the body gave me his cell number. As you'd expect, he was shocked—or at least he sounded shocked." She checked her watch. "If his plane is on time, he should get back to town around three."

"Good." Fulton continued walking. "It probably won't come to anything, but find out what hotel he was staying at, and get his cell phone records. The wife's too—and find out who that phone in the entryway belongs to."

"It's already on my to-do list," Izzy told him.

They entered the master bedroom where they found the windows wide open and one CSI dusting the closet door for fingerprints. She explained that the others were in the bathroom and headed for the open doorway. The bathroom window was also open, the fan running full blast, and the relatively small area was crowded with equipment and people covered head to toe with the mint-green polyethylene coveralls, their speech made robotic by respirators. Regardless, the ME was easily identifiable by her angular form and thick round glasses. Busy talking to one of her team, Andrea acknowledged their existence with a raised finger.

"Is that stink why they're all wearing respirators?" Fulton's nose crinkled. "What is that, anyway?"

"Drain cleaner. He put her in the tub and poured it all over. Pretty gross, actually."

From the look on Fulton's face, he'd already imagined it. He turned his attention to the bare mattress in the bedroom behind them. "Any luck with the bedclothes?"

"No, that's just another example of the lengths this guy is willing to go."

"Are you saying the killer took the bedding with him?"

"Yup. This guy is super thorough." She stepped over to the fingerprint guy. "You haven't found one print, have you?"

The man shook his head. "Probably won't either."

Izzy turned back to Fulton. "The washer and dryer are empty, so unless the guy took the time to fold and stack those bedclothes in the linen closet, they're gone, and the same goes for whatever Mrs. Callahan was wearing last night. I suppose we could assign some people to sort through her wardrobe, but I doubt this guy would simply hide evidence and hope we didn't find it."

"Yeah, you're probably right." Fulton handed her a stick of Juicy Fruit. "So, she's in the tub, huh?" He popped the gum in his mouth, and Izzy did the same.

The fingerprint tech stepped into the bathroom and asked Andrea a question, but between the fan and the respirator, Izzy only caught the odd word. Dismissed, the tech left, and Andrea stepped out to meet them.

She pulled off her mask and gloves. "Pretty smelly in there."

"No kidding," Fulton said. "So, what have you got?"

"Ugh." Andrea ran her fingers through her short gray hair. "The victim was strangled, and from the markings on her neck, I'd say with a belt."

"Like sex games gone bad?" Izzy asked.

Andrea shrugged. "Well, he did take the bedding."

Fulton peered past Andrea into the bathroom. "Sounds like a guy intent on not leaving any DNA behind."

"So intent that he scrubbed the body down with drain cleaner—outside *and* in. Caused a whole lot of nasty chemical burns too."

Reminded of what she'd seen, Izzy grimaced.

Fulton worked his chewing gum. "Is that everything?"

"No, there's definitely something else." Andrea walked back to the bathtub. "Have a look."

Like Izzy, Fulton appeared to steel himself. He covered his face with a handkerchief and, with long determined strides, crossed the room, and stopped abruptly a few feet from the tub. "Oh . . . my . . . Lord."

The image was already embedded in Izzy's brain. She didn't need a second look. The monster who did this hadn't been satisfied with blistering every inch of his victim's skin, they had also sawed both of the woman's hands off. But why? It couldn't be the fingerprints. Feeling no urge to linger, she glanced back at the bedroom where the techs stood waiting with an empty gurney.

"Boss?" She tapped Fulton. "Maybe we should leave."

"Yes, please," Andrea said. "They'll be needing the space."

Izzy followed Fulton back to the living room where they found Gabe Fox talking to Adrian Vega.

"Finished with your interviews?" Izzy asked Fox.

Chapter 15

GABE

PRAYING HE HADN'T missed anything, Gabe tried to read Fulton and Santos as they stepped into the living room, its hard surfaces now grimy with fingerprint dust. He stepped over to Fulton. "Hi, boss. Muncy find anything helpful?"

"Not really. How about you? Learn anything from those interviews?"

"In a word, no. The woman across the street didn't hear or see anything—at least not until she peeked into that bathtub this morning. As far as she could tell, except for the bed being stripped down, everything looked normal."

"And the other neighbors?"

"Same thing. One house down at the end of the cul-de-sac has a camera. I rewound it and saw a car leave the Callahans' garage at about four-thirty, but don't ask me who was driving it."

As Gabe was speaking, Christine LeBlanc, a drab-looking blonde and possible lesbian, stepped out of the kitchen carrying a large plastic case similar to a toolbox. With a nod, she continued past them. "Afternoon, Chief. I'm all done in there, if you want a look-see."

Although he already knew the answer, Gabe just had to ask, "Hey, LeBlanc. Find anything good in the vacuum cleaner?"

"Never looked," she said as she was signing out on Vega's clipboard.

"Seriously?" Struggling to keep his face straight, Gabe pushed. "But the cannister might have all sorts of stuff in it, and the roller brush . . ."

LeBlanc nodded her agreement. "And I'd have loved to check those things . . . but there's no vacuum cleaner in this place."

"Oh, man." Shoulders slumped, Gabe tried to look stunned.

But he knew exactly where the vacuum was. At the abandoned quarry, along with everything else he'd stuffed into Darcy's car. He had saturated the whole mess with gasoline, then put a match to it and watched it burn. With any luck, all that evidence was now a giant blob of metal and plastic dusted with cinders.

As if reading his mind, Santos, who had been standing in the foyer admiring Darcy's crushed cell phone, noticed the door behind her and opened it. "It's the garage," she told Fulton over her shoulder. She poked her head in for a few moments then closed it. "No cars."

"No surprise there," Gabe said.

"The husband's is at the airport, and someone drove off with the other." Santos scribbled something down. "I'll check on what Mrs. Callahan drives."

Scowling, Fulton swung his attention to the closest CSI, the one currently dusting the coffee table. "What about you, Gonzalez? Find any prints?"

"Not a one, sir."

Fulton raked both hands through his dark hair, making the part stand out in spikes. "Well, vacuum the place again. We might just get lucky." He strode off toward the kitchen. "Come on. Let's see the rest of the place."

The country style kitchen table was decorated with two bright yellow place settings and an arrangement of fresh pink, white, and yellow tulips.

"Hard to believe the woman that arranged these flowers is lying dead in her own bathtub," Chief Fulton muttered.

Gabe couldn't agree more.

All the appliances and countertops were covered with LeBlanc's latent print powders, making the kitchen he'd left spotless appear grimy. Fulton paced around the large central island, running his hand through the fingerprint dust as he surveyed the rest of the room. "So, Vega secured the outside?"

"That's right," Santos said.

"Call him in here, would you, Gabe?"

"Sure thing, Chief."

After a few moments, the young man followed Gabe into the kitchen looking a bit like a pup that had just been caught whizzing on the rug. He eyed the chief. "Anything wrong, sir?"

"No, Adrian. Not if you followed proper procedure when securing the area."

"Oh, I did, sir. First, I strung up the tape. Then I did a walk-around, checking all the doors and windows."

"Find anything unusual? Any jimmy marks?"

"No, sir. Nothing that would suggest a break-in."

"So, there's a good chance the victim knew her killer." Frowning, Fulton worked his gum, then focused on Gabe. "And you were first on the scene?"

"Uh, yessir." He stared back, reminding himself to blink. He had to relax. Fulton couldn't possibly have connected him to Darcy that fast, and even if he had—

"Then, you know how the neighbor lady got in?" Fulton asked.

"I do." Gabe shared what the old woman had told him about coffee dates and Darcy's hidden key.

Fulton rolled his eyes, and even though they all chuckled, Gabe still didn't feel safe. He spotted a three-foot section of closet rod standing in the corner near the sliding glass door. "Hey, there's something about that door I hadn't noticed before."

"It's locked tight," Vega said. "Try it if you don't believe me."

"Oh, I believe you. But I just might have figured out how the killer got inside." Gabe picked up the closet rod and laid it in the track of the sliding glass door. As he expected, it fit perfectly. "These houses were built forty-fifty years ago. And, as you can see, the kitchen's been remodeled. But this door looks old. Like it came with the place." He returned the dowel to its spot in the corner, then unlocked the door and grabbed the still-locked panel with both hands. With a bit of jiggling, the entire door rose from its track, disengaging easily from the lock.

"Now, how in the hell did you know that?" Vega asked.

Gabe winked and set the door back into position. "My first apartment had a door just like this. Came with a dowel too. Without it, I might as well not have bothered locking the place."

"Well, that changes everything," Vega said. "I was thinking the killer was somebody she knew. But now, with this, and that stupid fake rock . . . it could be anyone."

"Sure looks that way," Fulton said.

Gabe nodded his agreement. That's it, Chief. Follow that path, because it sure won't lead you to me.

Santos slid the door back and forth a few times, then opened it wide, and the four of them stepped out onto a large back patio. Fat pots full of new spring flowers lined the wall, competing for attention with the bright yellow cushions on a new-looking sectional sofa. A fountain with four levels of green copper bowls trickled peacefully in the corner next to a foot-tall cast-iron frog.

Sure, Darcy's decorations were pretty, but just like the crap decorating their own pool, it was all totally useless. He took it all in. Yeah, Angie would love all this crap, especially that stupid frog. He followed the others out into the yard.

Beyond the patio a six-foot-wide waterfall highlighted a walk-in lagoon style swimming pool surrounded by a stamped concrete deck. On the far side stood two chaise lounges. Always the decorator, Darcy's floral cushions picked up the colors in the patio.

The thick hedges were at least eight feet tall and framed the lot on both sides of the house, giving a feeling of privacy. But on the back side, about one hundred feet from the pool deck, freshly cut grass butted up against a shallow creek and a few feet beyond that the ancient pines of Moresby Forest.

"Oh, man," Santos said. "The killer could have come out of the woods, seen the lights on, and . . ." They all looked at the sliding door.

She was way off, but wasn't that what Gabe wanted? He went with it. "And with these tall hedges, nobody would have seen a thing."

"True," Santos said. "We should get the crime scene guys out here."

Nodding, Fulton pulled an old gum wrapper from his right pocket and unfolded it. Nothing different there. Santos and Vega seemed normal too. But what if the CSI bunch had found something incriminating while Gabe was out doing interviews?

"Should I move the tape further into the forest?" Vega asked, shoulders back.

Fulton spit his gum into his Juicy Fruit wrapper. "I think that would be wise."

Chapter 16

GABE

AS FIRST TO arrive at the crime scene, it was Gabe's responsibility to stay at Darcy's until the CSI team had wrapped everything up midafternoon. The sky had filled with dark clouds, creating the perfect backdrop for the mess he'd created for himself. As he drove, Gabe pictured the living corpse he was about to visit with and groaned. Getting a root canal would be preferable to hanging out with that beat-up lump. But he had to go. Staying away was as good as admitting he'd pushed her.

Thankfully, Gabe's I-don't-want-to-be-here face looked a lot like his grieving husband face. He sulked past the nurses' station to Angie's room. Eyes glued to the linoleum, he flopped into the visitor's chair, exhausted.

It had been a long stressful day, but he'd still rather hang out at Darcy's than this dump. He stretched out his legs. Maybe he could take a quick nap. Angie sure wouldn't mind, and it was definitely quiet enough. Of course, her respirator was still pumping away, but even that had its own hypnotic rhythm. He checked his watch and found it was almost four. Fine. He'd stay there an hour or so, then head home to eat, something he hadn't done since he'd stopped at McDonald's the day before.

He closed his eyes, wondering where he might search for Aconite next. Maybe out behind Stafford Park. But what about Botox? That stuff sure didn't grow wild, and weren't plastic surgeons the only people who kept it? Probably under lock and key, too. Was he ready to break into a doctor's office or run a background check? These were things he should look into, and soon. It wouldn't be long before they took Angie off her coma meds.

"Hi, Gabe."

He opened his eyes to find Kylie standing in the doorway. So much for sleeping.

"Oh, hi, honey. Come on in."

With a nod, Kylie shuffled straight to the bed, her already tear-glazed eyes locked on Angie's bruised and battered face. "Any changes?"

Changes? Like maybe she'd had died from a heart attack? Wishing he could say that, he stood and stretched as if he'd been sitting there all day. "Now, Kylie . . ." He took her hands in each of his and gave them a quick squeeze. "You know there's no way she can wake until they stop giving her the coma meds. Hang in there. Sunday's only four days away."

"Yeah, four little days, and then, she'll wake up." Kylie's puppy-like eyes begged him to agree.

"Yup." Nodding, he made himself look at his sleeping wife, thankful he didn't have to meet her eyes. "So . . . how was school?"

"It was all right."

Remembering how uncomfortable Kylie had been when they'd discussed that boy, Gabe brought him up again. "Hey, you tutored that Ryan kid last night after work. Why don't you tell your mom about it? I'm sure she'd be interested."

Her cheeks reddened. "Okay." She picked up the cheap hospital hairbrush lying on the bed table. Of course, brushing her mom's hair gave the kid a good excuse to keep her back to Gabe while she spoke, but how would she manage with Angie's head looking like a mummified soccer ball? She seemed to realize her stupidity and put the brush down.

"Angie, Kylie's been tutoring a boy," Gabe said, moving things along.

"Yeah, remember that boy who asked me to tutor him?" Kylie carefully squeezed up onto the bed beside her mother. "We got together at the library last night. He said I was super helpful, and I agreed to meet him there again, tonight, but I've got that Spanish test Friday." She stroked her mom's cheek—at least the little purple patches that stuck out between the bandages. "Is that stupid?" She chuckled. "It's just one hour at the library. I mean, I can't study all the time, right? And Ryan is really . . ." As if remembering Gabe was there, she peered over her shoulder at him, cheeks flushed with color. "Sh-should I have said no, Gabe? Am I screwing up? That test is super important."

Although Gabe couldn't care less about her grades, he did have to keep up appearances. "You're smart. And if she could, your mom would say the same. Hell, you've been at that Spanish book every night for a week. A little time off won't kill you."

Nodding thoughtfully, Kylie stood, straightened her mom's covers and turned to him. "Gabe, would you come out in the hall for a minute?"

"Oh, okay." Gabe assumed Kylie wanted to discuss Angie's injuries and followed her out, closing the door behind him.

"I heard about Darcy," Kylie said.

"Darcy?" Blindsided, he blinked back stupidly.

"All my friends know she was murdered, so you must too."

"Of course, I know. But it hasn't even been on the news yet. How the heck did a bunch of high schoolers find out?"

"Jeff forgot his lunch, and when he texted his mom to bring him something, she told him."

That red-headed bag of gristle? The woman spent so much time at the gym he was surprised she'd leave her Zoomba classes long enough to answer a text, never mind making her son a sandwich. "And how did Lisa know about it?"

"She just got a police scanner installed in her car. Her husband bought it for her."

"Smart, considering how many speeding tickets she's gotten since Carl got her that Porsche Boxster."

"How can you joke about speeding tickets at a time like this?" Again, her eyes filled with tears.

"I'm sorry, honey. What do you want to know?"

"I want to know what happened. Lisa said the killer cut off Darcy's hands and . . . and . . ."

He pulled her too him, another uniform shirt ready for the dry cleaners. "I'm sorry," he whispered, "but that's actually true."

"But what kind of sicko cuts a person's hands off?"

"I don't know." The kind that doesn't want his DNA found under the woman's fingernail?" He stroked her short coppery hair. "Honey, the department's doing everything they can to catch this guy." And Gabe was doing everything in his power to not get caught. He pried her off of him and looked into her eyes. "That said, I'm a little surprised at your reaction. I mean, you haven't seen Darcy since you were a little girl."

"I know, but she was sweet to me and Robby. Like an aunt or even a second mom. Then, all of a sudden, she just took off, and we never saw her again. Why was that? All I remember is the moving van pulling away. No reasons. No goodbyes . . ."

That's because Angie wanted to scratch Darcy's eyes out, Gabe mused. "Yeah, that surprised me too."

"Luke thinks it's another serial killer like that Coates guy last year."

"Luke Manetti's a goof. Coates killed six people, but he wasn't a serial killer."

"He wasn't?"

"Nah, Coates killed most of those people just to keep himself out of jail, not because he enjoyed it. Honestly, I cannot understand what Addison sees in that boy."

"Who told you about Addison's crush on Luke?"

"It's obvious—another example of what a dope that boy is. And his buddy Jeff is only slightly better. Kid looks like Shaggy from those Scooby Doo cartoons—but at least he had the good sense to ask Chelsea out." Gabe wasn't into hair extensions, but the girl had a decent rack and an even better ass.

"Hey!" She shoved him playfully. "Lighten up. All my friends have been really supportive—and protective too. When Ryan asked me to tutor him, Luke practically interrogated him. He even asked Ryan what his intentions were. You know, embarrassing stuff. Like you would ask."

"Like I'd ask?"

"Yeah. And Chelsea researched people who fell from huge heights and lived. She sent me like five links."

A surprise, since Gabe had always considered Chelsea a female version of Jeff, just half-black and with hair extensions. "So, you're tutoring Rolly tonight, huh?" he asked through a yawn.

"His name's Ryan, and yeah, at eight."

"Okay, Ryan. But what about Lexi Siegel? If she knows you work at the library, she and her friends might decide to jump you in the parking lot. If I were you, I'd look around before getting out of the car."

"No, Ryan spoke to her. She promised to leave me alone."

"Ha." He opened the door to Angie's room. "Well, what people say and what they do aren't always the same thing."

And who knew that better than Gabe?

Chapter 17

LEXI

LEXI SIEGEL WAS proud of the volleyball serve she'd bashed into the back of Kylie McKenna's head. The bitch deserved it for trying to steal Lexi's man. But the week of after-school detention that stupid chrome-dome principal had assigned her was a real pain. Not only was she expected to sit and work quietly for ninety whole minutes, but she was missing volleyball practice. And no practice meant no game. Like Ryan, Peabody had told her she should learn to accept responsibility for her own actions. What a laugh. As far as Lexi was concerned, it was all Kylie's fault, and with the help of social media, everyone would know it.

Along with a handful of other kids, she stepped from the detention room onto the asphalt path, astonished at how gloomy the sky had become in the short time since she'd entered the classroom. The sun had been shining then, with just a few puffy clouds in the otherwise blue sky. Now, the whole thing was an ominous grey, closing on black. Rain was coming for sure, but hopefully, she'd make it home before the hard stuff came down. She tightened the straps on her purple backpack and started walking.

As Lexi tramped across the near-empty school grounds, her thoughts returned to the events that had brought her there. Of course, she'd hit Kylie with the ball on purpose, but how could that bitch PE teacher know that? She couldn't. All she had was her suspicions—and a lousy opinion of Lexi. That wasn't justice, and it sure wasn't due process. It was like . . . like Nazi Germany. She should find out what kind of cars those detention monitors drive. That bitch of a PE teacher too.

Her mom's advice had been to stop whining and spend her detention time doing homework, but who could sit still that long?

A few fat raindrops stained the pavement as she passed the music building. Another struck her forehead and trickled down her nose. Lexi zipped her sweat jacket and walked faster. Since Mom and her stepdad both worked, calling for a ride was not an option. Her friend, Lance Harper had also served detention. If the detention Nazis had let her, Lexi would have asked him for a ride, but now, Lance was gone. Of her two best friends, Eden had no access to a car, but Jade might be able to borrow her mom's. Frowning up at the all-but-black sky, she stepped under the breezeway in front of the science classes and placed a call.

"Answer the freaking phone, Jade." Lexi shifted her weight from one foot to the other as the dial tone droned on. It went to voicemail, and she hung up without leaving a message.

"Damn it!" She watched the raindrops darken the pavement, unsure what to do.

"No ride for you?" It was that weird Mexican custodian, Mr. Juarez, or whatever. Grinning like some kind of child molester, the old guy rolled his mop and bucket down the hall toward her, brown water sloshing. "I hope you don't get too wet. De rain, she gonna come down pretty hard, I think."

What a perv. As it turned out, the old janitor's weather forecast had been accurate, and after walking for less than fifteen minutes, the cold and damp reached right into Lexi's bones. She pulled the already soggy hood of her jacket up over her head and tied the strings beneath her chin. It probably looked stupid, but at least the wind wasn't whipping her hair into her eyes anymore.

With her house on the outskirts of town, Lexi would be walking for at least twenty more minutes. She slogged down the shoulder of the two-lane road, eyes lowered to the path in front of her. Few cars passed, but when they did, she looked up to see the driver hunched over the steering wheel, windshield wipers flapping madly. Once, an unmarked police SUV zoomed past. Another time, a big truck splashed by, spewing water onto her legs. Even with those tortures, there was no way she would consider hitchhiking.

Well, maybe with someone she knew. Or a cop.

Chapter 18

IZZY

THE NEXT MORNING, Patrick Callahan arrived at the police station for his interview. With his wife, Darcy, in her late thirties, Izzy expected someone in the same general age group. What she got was a man in his fifties. But as unexpected as their age difference was, what stunned Izzy most was his attitude toward Darcy's infidelity.

"I didn't ask, and she didn't tell," the man croaked. Hair thinning and paunchy in his nice blue suit, Callahan's eyes welled with tears. "She cheated on her first husband, but I didn't care. We had an unspoken agreement. While I was home, she was the perfect wife, but when I was away on business . . ."

"Would you be okay with the department examining your phone records and those of your wife?" Izzy asked. "It's standard procedure and will help eliminate you as a suspect."

"Whatever it takes," Callahan answered. "I . . . I want you to catch this guy."

Izzy promised she would do her best. The man really did seem heartbroken, and a hotel manager two-thousand miles away in Dallas had assured her he had spoken to Callahan himself that morning at check out. But what if the don't-ask-don't-tell story was all BS? Most people wouldn't tolerate an unfaithful spouse, but those marriages usually ended in divorce, not murder.

But in those rare cases people did pay to have their spouse killed, the usual method was to shoot their victim, then make things look like a burglary gone bad. The killer definitely didn't preface the assassination by having sex with them, although the damage to Darcy's body made it impossible to tell if she'd been raped.

After asking Callahan for names of friends and coworkers she could speak to, Izzy then interviewed the woman who discovered his wife's body. In Mrs. Curtis's opinion, the Callahans got along fine, but as the husband had also stated, he did travel quite a bit, and Darcy didn't have many friends.

"As far as I know," the woman began, "they only associated with his people. You know, business associates . . . old college friends."

"And what about Darcy's sex partners? Were they just one-night stands, or did she try to develop relationships?"

A flush crept across Mrs. Curtis's cheeks. "I'm sorry?"

"You saw Darcy's bedroom, Mrs. Curtis. The bed was stripped. Darcy was naked. She brought someone home last night, and according to her husband, this wasn't the first time. In fact, she cheated on her first husband too. It's understandable you not wanting to speak ill of the dead, but in this situation, secrets only benefit the killer. If you know anything about Darcy's lovers or saw something . . . I mean, your front window has a pretty good view of her house."

"I wish I could help, Detective, but if Darcy brought anyone home, it was late, and I'm in bed by ten most nights."

"Okay, well, surely she must have said something."

Eyes glued to her clasped hands, Mrs. Curtis shook her head. "We discussed other topics. You know, gardening, cooking. If she was seeing other men, she never mentioned it. She did say something about her first husband passing away about a year back. Some sort of hunting accident."

Finished with her interviews, Izzy then arranged to collect the Callahans' telephone records. When the phone company rep asked for a couple hours to get everything together, she took the opportunity to run background checks on Alvin Griswold, the man who had put Maggie in the hospital and Jerry Greene, the man who had left his wallet inside the car he'd just burgled.

As she expected, Jerry had been arrested more than once for burglarizing houses and breaking into cars, and was now on probation for a crime a lot like the one he appeared to have just committed. She phoned his probation officer to give him a heads up and find out where she could find Jerry when she was ready to arrest him.

"He's a dishwasher at Mary's Diner," the probation officer told her. He also provided her with Jerry's current address and promised to keep Izzy updated if anything should change.

Alvin Griswold was a different story. After a DUI arrest twenty years ago, the guy became a model citizen with not even a parking ticket until a month ago when he was pulled over one night after leaving a bar. According to the report, the cop who pulled Griswold over was her dad's good friend Lester Mathis. To her surprise, Lester had given the man a break and allowed him to call a friend to come pick him up.

So, Griswold had started drinking again, but why? The responding officer at Maggie's accident also hadn't arrested him. In fact, he hadn't even bothered to test the man. Was it just too early in the day for drinking, or was that stop at The Captain's Anchor just a blip on the radar?

It was going on four o'clock. Since Lester worked the day shift, he'd already been gone for two hours. Maybe she'd give him a call later, once they'd all had their dinner.

Eager to share what she'd learned about Alvin Griswold with Maggie, Izzy decided to drop by the hospital again, then pick the Callahans' phone records up after that. Having spent most of her day indoors, the darkened sky surprised her. It started sprinkling as she climbed into her SUV, and by the time she passed the high school five minutes later, the rain was coming down in sheets.

Never comfortable with driving through hard rain, she turned her windshield wipers up full blast and was wondering what Maggie might make of Alvin Griswold's background check when she spotted someone trudging down the side of the road near the new housing tract that had recently begun construction.

"Dang, that sucks," Izzy muttered.

Totally underdressed for this weather, the poor soul was trudging down a mud path dressed in nothing but a sodden purple hoodie and equally wet jeans. Feeling a little guilty for being so warm and dry, Izzy was about to stop and offer them a ride when her phone rang. It was Brody. She picked up immediately.

"You heard we have another murder, didn't you?"

"I sure did," Brody said. "Look, I know you're busy, but I was wondering how Maggie's doing. I called earlier, but she didn't answer."

"Oh, that's nice of you. Maybe she was sleeping. When I stopped by this morning, she was doing okay. I mean, as well as could be expected." Izzy paused. "Babe, she remembered something."

"Well, that's good."

She noted the positivity in his voice. "Yeah, well, don't get too excited. Apparently, she thinks the guy who hit her also hit someone else."

Brody gasped. "So, she had a vision when the car hit her?"

"Yeah, I'm going to see her right now. If she remembers anything else, I'll share over dinner."

"Excellent. What are you making me?"

Izzy chuckled. "You do recall that I'm working an active murder case."

They continued their banter until Izzy reached the hospital. Since neither wind nor rain had lost their intensity, she left her umbrella behind and settled for zipping up her jacket. As she pulled the hood up over her head, she remembered the person she'd seen walking down the road earlier.

Oh, man. I hope they don't get sick.

Chapter 19

GABE

AFTER JUST THREE days of hospital visits, Angie's face still reminded Gabe of one of those weird, ornamental gourds. The scabby lumps and bumps disgusted him, but if he wanted folks to believe he was actually rooting for Angie's survival, he had to play the part. Eager to get out into the forest and find some Aconite, he'd made his morning visit quick and headed out. Sadly, he'd had no success. And now, he was back looking at Gourd Face again.

Like yesterday, Kylie had also stopped by, and this time, she'd even dragged Robby along, something she probably regretted, since all the boy did was slump against the wall and sulk. Since Angie was nothing but a wheezing mass of scabby flesh, Gabe didn't blame him.

After ten minutes of intolerable boredom, he said, "Well, kids, your mom is doing as well as can be expected, but since there won't be any change until Sunday, let's call it a day, huh?"

Robby jumped on his suggestion, and they parted ways in the parking lot.

"Here." A drop of rain fell on Gabe's debt card as he handed it to Kylie. "Go pick up some burgers while I head back to the station and drop off the cruiser."

Naturally, Kylie agreed immediately since she wouldn't have to cook.

The light rain intensified as Gabe drove to the station, and by the time he had the car parked, it was coming down pretty hard. Never one to mind a little water, he entered the building on the off chance there was something good to munch on at the coffee station. Hell, why not eat a donut? If Angie woke up, he'd be eating bologna sandwiches for the rest of his life. He was trying to decide what sort of pastry he would choose when a fellow officer fell into step beside him.

"How you doing there, Gabe?" It was Gordy Lytle, a guy he'd known since high school.

"Good. How about you?" Gabe asked, even though he didn't care.

"Eh . . ." A good fifty pounds heavier and three inches shorter, Gordy seesawed his stubby-fingered hand. "Guts been bothering me on and off."

His expression brightened as they reached the coffee station and the recently arrived large pink box. He flipped it open.

"Did you hear about the big drug bust last night?" Gordy asked.

Seeing Gordy eyeballing a pair of fat apple fritters, Gabe snatched the biggest and dug in. "Drug bust? You talking meth or oxy?"

"Neither." Gordy picked up the other donut. "Botox."

Gabe choked on his fritter. "Really?" he managed between coughs. "Who got the bust?"

"Lester Mathis." Gordy eyed Gabe, took a bite of his own fritter, then eyed him again. "Hey, you okay?"

Gabe nodded. "What? Like a Botox drug ring?"

"More like a Botox party. See, some nurse from Dalton was coming to town on weekends. She'd stay over with a girlfriend who was gathering all these women together at her house for a wine and cheese party. They'd drink some chardonnay while the nurse went through her spiel, and then the ones who were still interested got their faces shot up with the Botox at a discounted rate. All totally unlicensed, of course."

"Yeah, but Lester at a Botox party?" He imagined the sixty-four-year-old squashed between squawking women as he sipped white wine and balanced a paper plate of brie cheese and water crackers on his knee. "Hell, that's just weird."

Gordy took a second bite and chewed deliberately, as if demonstrating safe eating practices. "Lester's wife showed him the invitation, so he decided to check things out. Dumb move inviting a cop's wife."

Gabe couldn't believe his luck. The Botox was right there in the building. All he had to do was figure out a way to get his hands on it. Not an easy task, but not impossible either, considering how starved for conversation Gordy always was.

"It was a decent sized bust, too," Gordy went on. "Not as big as the one back in ninety-eight, and definitely nothing like what Jimmy and his guys hauled out of that meth lab up at Thompson's farm, but significant, you know?"

"Well, I'm sure I'll hear all about it at tomorrow's staff meeting."

Gordy nodded, and, ignoring the fact that his shirt buttons were already holding on for dear life, shoved a good part of his fritter into his mouth.

Of course, the Botox was locked up in the drug room, and if the haul was as big as Gordy claimed, then a few bottles might not be missed, but how would he wrangle a peek inside?

Asking Gordy was out. Locked in the basement most of his day, the guy would talk the ears off anyone who stepped through the door. But if all or part of the stuff suddenly went missing, did Gabe really want the guy remembering their little interview.

"Oh, man . . ." Gordy cut loose with a loud burp and dropped what was left of his fritter. "Not again." One hand already unclasping his belt, he dashed off toward the men's room, nearly knocking over the janitor's trash cart.

The man was definitely a mess. Gabe decided to stop off at the evidence room tomorrow to check on him . . . and that Botox.

Chapter 20

IZZY

WITH THE DOOR to Maggie's room wide open, Izzy could hear her aunt's voice as she approached. She sounded good, strong. Smiling, Izzy entered the hospital room expecting someone to be standing by the bed. Fulton, maybe a doctor. But there was no one.

"Tita?" Izzy eyed the empty corner of the room where her aunt had been looking. "Who were you talking to?"

Gaze still focused on the corner of the room, Maggie gestured for Izzy to come in. "Okay," she told her invisible friend. "I'll try, but I can't promise he'll believe me." She turned back to Izzy. "*Hola, guapa*. Have you looked at the car yet?"

"Yes, but what was all that about?" She tipped her head at the corner.

"*Ay, sí*." Maggie's dark eyes brightened. "Guess what? This hospital is full of spirits. That one was Dr. Pierce's father. Apparently, when Mitchell was twelve, he challenged his father to swim across the river. Mitchell made it, but sadly, his dad didn't."

"And Mitchell is your doctor's first name?"

"Yes."

"So, what's Dad's problem? Does he blame Mitchell?"

"The opposite. Mitchell blames himself for his father's death, and Dad wants him to stop."

"And the dad wants you to speak to him."

"Well, *he* can't do it." She shrugged. "I can."

"Hmmm." Izzy imagined the average person's reaction to being told such a story. "Good luck with that."

"Oh, I'm not worried. By the way, how is my Bennie?"

Izzy smiled at the thought of Maggie's orange, football-shaped cat. "I haven't been over to see him, but I'm sure he's fine."

"Sean says he misses me."

"I'm sure he does." She filled Maggie in on what she'd learned at Big Sheila's Body Shop.

"See." Maggie pointed one finger at Izzy. "I told you I'm not the first person to be hit by that car." She filled her hands with her long black curls. "This is so frustrating. If I could touch that dented car hood I could describe the person he hit, maybe even give you a name. Now, all I can say is that the guy had a gray beard."

"You never told me that."

"No?" Maggie squinted up at the ceiling for a few moments. "Well, he did. That helps, doesn't it?"

Chapter 21

LEXI

AS A KID, her brother Frankie had scared the hell out of her with tales of female hitchhikers who'd been raped and murdered after accepting a ride from some kindly looking driver. And where had her brother come by that information? YouTube, most likely. The kid sure didn't read the paper or watch the news on TV.

She trudged past the same billboard she'd read every day for the last two months. *Future Home of Dawn View Estates,* the ten-inch letters proclaimed. *Models Available Soon.* A fat red arrow pointed at the housing tract's main entrance. Like her family would ever live there. She cast a weary glance at the partially finished buildings to her left.

Sidewalks hadn't been poured in this area yet, and Lexi shivered as she plodded through the mud, thankful the recently installed streetlights were there to keep her from falling into the drainage ditch that paralleled the trail. Near to overflowing, its cloudy surface boiled with a million raindrops.

If it looked like rain, tomorrow, she would skip detention. What could Principal Peabody do? Kill her?

Lexi was still trudging along when a sedan barreled past. No big deal there, but then, the car suddenly braked, its red taillights reflecting on the road as it fishtailed to a stop.

What the hell?

Lexi blinked in surprise as the car backed up, swerving across the opposite lane and onto the muddy shoulder a few steps in front of her.

Oh, great. It's him. Wishing it were Jade or—anyone but this guy—she stepped up to the driver's side window. It slid down, and warm air rose up to meet her.

"Hey, I thought that was you." He looked her over. "Damn, girl. You look like a drowned rat."

"Gee, thanks." Scowling at the irony of the situation, she crossed her arms over her chest, hoping it would stop the shivering.

"Well, I can give you a ride if you want."

Yeah, he'd like that, wouldn't he? With a glance up the road, she said, "That's okay. I'm almost—" A huge gust of wind struck her. She staggered and grabbed hold of the side-view mirror, pulling it out of position.

"Fine with me." He watched her try to straighten it. "The heater's not working right, so actually, it's too warm in here." He plucked at the front of his rain slicker. "But, hey . . . you do what's right for you."

Warm air continued to waft out at her. He was right. It was like a sauna in there. "No thanks. I don't hitchhike."

"That's good, and you shouldn't . . . with strangers."

"Yeah, well, like I said, I'm almost home."

"Okie-doke." With a hum, the window motored back up, taking the heat with it.

"Wait!" She tapped on the window.

The glass slid back down, but this time, the gap was barely wide enough to speak through.

"You're right," she told him. "I'm being ridiculous."

The door locks clicked open, and Lexi couldn't help but smile as she jogged to the other side and opened the door. Warm air kissing her face, she tossed her backpack onto the floorboards and climbed in. "Oh, I'm sorry. I'm getting your seat all wet."

"That's okay. It's had lots worse things than water on it."

"Thanks." She raised her eyes to his. "To be honest, I doubt if I'd done the same."

"Buckle up." Smiling, he put the car in gear, and as the automatic door locks clicked shut, Lexi fastened her seatbelt and slumped back in her seat.

"When I get home, I'm gonna take a super-hot shower."

"Good idea." But her rescuer didn't pull out onto the road. Instead, he aimed the car into the housing development.

Lexi stiffened. "What are you doing?"

"Oh, I'm sorry. Did I scare you? It's just that my neighbor's dog ran off this morning, and I think I just spotted it."

"Here? In these half-built houses?"

"Yeah, well maybe she was chasing a cat." He winked. "Don't worry, this won't take long."

Lexi stared out the window as the car rumbled into the heart of the empty subdivision.

She wasn't joking about the houses being half built. Only a handful were finished, and those were models, dark and unoccupied. The rest were either concrete foundations or wooden frames waiting for cement to be poured. Several lots showed even less progress with nothing but scraps of wood and rebar lying around. The rain had chased away all the workers, and the lateness of the day gave the place a sinister abandoned look.

"I don't see it," she said, wishing Eden and Jade were sitting in the back seat. "What kind is it?"

"What?" He looked both ways as they crossed another vacant street. "Oh, yeah, the dog. She's a uh, kind of a lab. That's it. A yellow lab puppy." He turned right onto the last street and pointed. "There she goes, behind that house up there."

"I don't see anything."

"Boy, the Swansons will be so relieved." He parked behind a battered grey dumpster, grabbed a fat tactical flashlight from the glove box, and climbed out.

Ding, ding, ding.

As the chime warned the key had been left in the ignition, another alarm went off, this one inside of Lexi's head. She leaned across the bench seat, and called out into the rain, "Hey! Can't you just phone the Swansons? I mean, why do *you* have to catch their stupid dog?"

He lowered his head and peered in at her, the hood of his slicker now raised. "I know you think I'm a dork, and maybe I am. But Bill just turned eighty and Linda's got a bad hip. Come on, Lexi, it'll be easier with the two of us—unless, of course, you're too scared. I mean, it is kind of dark."

He was mocking her. If she refused, he'd tell the world what a big chicken she'd been, and tomorrow, everyone at school would know, and they'd all think it was so funny.

Maybe she *was* better off outside. She never did feel right around the guy. She pushed the door open, and the wind flung it wide as if in agreement. She would help him with the dog, but she was also taking her backpack, because she wasn't getting back in. That settled, Lexi climbed out and shut the door. "So, what's the plan?"

He tipped his head at the house across the street. "Okay, you circle around the right side, I'll take the left. There's a fence in the back, so, with any luck, we'll trap Daisy between us."

"Daisy, right." She hoisted the pack onto one shoulder and picked her way across the muddy street toward the house. More like the skeleton of a house, since half of the tar paper was now flapping in the wind. She glanced to her left as the self-proclaimed dork disappeared behind the building. A chill that had nothing to do with the storm ran up her back.

Run, said the little voice in her head. That's what a smart person would do.

Yeah, and how would that look?

Doing her best to not fall on her butt, Lexi minced her way through the muddy lot to the back corner of the house. She peeked around it.

Damn. The big two-story cast a long shadow leaving a backyard so dark Lexi would have a hard time spotting a bull mastiff, least ways the lab puppy she was looking for.

Why hadn't she asked for a flashlight?

A sudden gust iced her wet clothes, making her shudder. She squinted into the darkness. "D-daisy?" Her voice trembled as she called out. "Hey, puppy, w-where are you?"

And even more importantly, where was *he*?

Something moved above her. She looked up as the thing wrapped itself around her head. Screaming, she tore at it but slipped and fell, just as another blast carried the tar paper sheet away, leaving her panting.

That's it. I'm out of here.

Furious, she rolled onto her hands and knees. "Screw Daisy and screw—"

"Lexi, are you okay?"

She looked up just as a powerful shaft of light struck her face.

"Ugh. Stop that."

He tilted the flashlight downward. "I caught Daisy. She's in the car now, if you're interested." He chuckled. "And she's almost as muddy as you are."

Even though the little voice told her not to believe him, Lexi muttered, "Good," and raised a muddy hand, afraid she'd fall on her face if she tried to get up on her own. "A little help?"

"Not this time." Again, he pointed the light directly into her eyes. "So, screw Daisy and screw me, huh?"

"Oh, you heard." She shaded her eyes with her forearm. "I didn't mean it. I was just frustrated."

"Oh, I understand. I get frustrated too, especially when people hurt someone I love." Rain spattered off his arm as he swung something long and thin up over his head, a ghastly silhouette in the flashlight's beam.

Whatever it was, Lexi didn't see it come down. She had already closed her eyes.

Chapter 22

IZZY

HAVING RECEIVED A phone invitation from Principal Peabody, Izzy arrived at the high school for her nine a.m. appointment with Lexi Siegel's parents. Apparently, the Peytons recognized the need to speak to the police, but since the idea of stepping inside the station was as unpleasant as having cops inside their house, they settled on a neutral zone with Peabody as their go-between.

She entered the administration office and was quickly greeted by Principal Peabody, a middle-aged man with a horseshoe of closely clipped hair. They were still shaking hands when a couple in their early forties also arrived. Both wore faded jeans and a hoodie. The woman looked fragile and confused, unlike her skinny long-haired husband, who stared at Izzy with flinty eyed distrust.

Peabody made his introductions with the somberness of a mortician. "Mr. and Mrs. Peyton, this is Detective Santos."

"Santos?" Mr. Peyton looked Izzy up and down. "Let me guess. Your daddy was Andy Santos."

"That's right." Izzy took Peyton in, too. Her dad had patrolled the streets of Rocky Harbor for thirty-odd years. Had he arrested this man? "Mr. Peyton. Let me get this straight. So, Lexi Siegel is your stepdaughter?"

"So what? You saying I don't love the girl cause she ain't my blood?"

"Quit your crap," his wife scolded. "I don't care who her daddy was, as long as she finds my Lexi."

"Why don't we step into my office?" Peabody waved them around the counter to a nearby open door. "Go right on in," he told Mrs. Peyton.

By the time Izzy made it inside, she found the woman crumpled into one of the three chairs in front of Peabody's desk and her husband hovering over her.

"You still wanna do this?" he asked, his tone now more concerned than defensive.

Nodding, she plucked a tissue from the box Peabody offered her. "Go ahead." She nodded at him. "Say what you gotta say."

"Sure." Looking like he'd rather be anywhere else, Peabody dropped into his own chair and looked up at Izzy, his eyes begging her to take the empty seat beside Mr. Peyton. She did. "Officer Santos." He paused, as if choosing his words carefully. "As you know, the Peytons' daughter, Lexi, left school yesterday . . . and she hasn't been seen since."

Izzy nodded somberly. Since Peabody had guaranteed she would get an earful if she suggested Lexi may have gone off voluntarily, she reached into her jacket pocket and pulled out her pad and pen. "And who was the last person who saw Lexi?"

"That would be Mr. Jimenez, our afternoon custodian." Peabody leaned back in his chair. "Detention gets out at three-thirty, so it was probably a little after that. Around the time it started raining."

Izzy turned to the Peytons. "You live on Winston Court. Does that mean Lexi walked down Jefferson Avenue all the way until she got to Hendricks?"

"Well, it's the shortest way, so yeah," Peyton grumbled, looking surly.

Man, what a jerk. Izzy had driven down Jefferson Avenue herself yesterday, and it was raining pretty hard. Had that been Lexi she'd seen slogging down the side of the road? "Mrs. Peyton, when did you discover Lexi was missing?"

"How come you didn't ask why Lexi never called one of us to come get her?"

"Okay, why didn't she?"

"'Cause we have jobs," she said angrily.

Her eyes dared Izzy to comment. Izzy didn't bite.

"I got home at six, and when I saw Lexi wasn't there, I called her. She didn't answer, so I called her friends Eden and Jade. Neither of them picked her up. Hell, Jade didn't even notice Lexi had phoned her until I told her to check for messages."

"Is there anyone else Lexi might have called for a ride?"

Mrs. Peyton seemed to consider Izzy's question then came up with two names: Lance Harper and Jesse Ortiz. Then she suggested Izzy add Ryan Lanister to the list. "But I ain't got their phone numbers."

"No worries," Izzy told her. "You know, if Lexi's still got her phone on, we could track her with GPS. All I need is the number and your permission."

Chapter 23

GABE

GABE WASN'T THIRSTY, but he bent over the drinking fountain anyway. From there, he could look in both directions without appearing to be loitering around the police station's lobby. He let the water brush his lips until the coast was clear, then trotted down the nearby staircase to the basement.

Covered in worn, brownish-gray linoleum, the dimly lit staircase led to a similarly decorated, yet even gloomier t-shaped hallway. To the left was a scuffed wooden door leading to a storage area used for office supplies. To the right, a similar door labeled *EVIDENCE*. Although Gabe had no need for office supplies, he pushed open the storage room door and, not bothering to turn on a light, grabbed whatever lay on the closest shelf.

Armed with a ream of photo copy paper, his excuse for being downstairs, he strolled across the hall to the evidence room, hoping Gordy Lytle was still suffering from the trots like yesterday.

A chain-link fence divided the room into two parts: the twenty-foot-wide, five-feet-deep entry area and the much larger storage space behind it. "Sorry, gotta go," Gordy all but shouted. Looking like he had a timebomb in his pants, the man frantically waved Gabe out the door with his free hand, keys clinking against the heavy galvanized rolling gate he was struggling to pull shut.

From the pained look on Gordy's face, the man's health had not improved in the last twenty-four hours. Gabe dropped the copy paper and dashed over. "Gimme those." Before Gordy could argue, Gabe was already holding the keys. "Get to the john. I'll lock up and bring these to you." To his relief, Gordy didn't argue. He threw the exit door wide and dashed off, his footsteps heavy on the wooden staircase.

Knowing he didn't have much time, Gabe secured the door to the hall before nipping back to the cage gate, which he intentionally hadn't locked. But as he was pulling on his first nitrile glove, he froze.

Three Arrows Security Company.

Gordy had requested a CCTV system every year. Lucky for Gabe, they'd never had the funding, but about two weeks ago, Fulton had announced that Three Arrows, a local security company, would be donating a system to the department. Heart leaping like a fish, Gabe jerked his head up, eyes aimed at the nearest corner. Empty. He spun round and found nothing looking at him from the other three.

Relax, he told himself. Nobody can see you . . . yet.

Hands gloved and veins surging with adrenaline, he shoved the big gate open with one easy thrust. The Cage Room, as Gordy liked to call it, reminded Gabe of a weird sort of convenience store. Designed by Gordy himself, the space was lined with four parallel rows of floor-to-ceiling shelves, eighty percent of which were filled with blue plastic tubs, each labeled with a three-inch-long barcode sticker. Above each sticker, Gordy had also taped a three-by-five card with a handwritten description of the tub's contents as well as the date it had been checked in and the name of the officer who'd done it. Scattered amongst these tubs sat the items that didn't conform to standard container dimensions. On one shelf, a prosthetic leg wearing a mud-stained Nike shoe lay on its side. Up near the ceiling, a dusty stuffed tortoise glared down at him suspiciously.

Since no one but the officer in charge was allowed, Gabe had never entered the pen. He would have loved to do some exploring, but there just wasn't time. He strode past a three-foot ceramic monkey-waiter holding a silver tray in one hand, anxious to get to the back of the room and the three doors he'd been told existed but had never actually seen. The ones labeled WEAPONS and MONEY looked a lot like bank vaults. Although Gordy's keys probably gave him access, he headed straight for the door labeled DRUG ROOM. Like the other two, this door was also made of metal and the lock sturdy looking. Thankfully, the keys on Gordy's ring were labeled. After a few clinks and clanks, he heaved the door open and stepped inside.

Finding no video cameras there either, Gabe scanned the shelves of the much smaller room.

Now, how did Gordy say this was organized? Recalling a department picnic from five years ago during which Gordy had spent at least ten minutes rambling on about his precious evidence room, Gabe studied the small handwritten signs thumbtacked to the shelves' ends, then nipped down the aisle reading the little cards Gordy had taped to the tubs. After a few moments, he found one labeled *Botox and Syringes*. Inside he found a shrink-wrapped carton holding more than half of the hundred syringes it once contained and a second shrink-wrapped carton labeled Botox. That box was supposed to hold thirty-six hundred-unit vials, a few of which were missing. No big deal there.

Gabe decided four vials would be enough, then cut into the package of syringes and stuffed some into his back pocket.

Now, to cover his tracks.

He couldn't leave the two packages torn open, so he carried them out of the room to Gordy's worktable and found the shrink-wrap machine was cold. Knowing he couldn't wait for it to warm up, he located a roll of clear packing tape and tore off a foot-long strip. *This ought to do it.* Satisfied with his patch job on the syringe package, he did the same with the Botox.

It took him less than a minute to return the bundles to their tub, lock up the drug room, then pull the gate shut and secure it. Now, all he had to do was lock the door to the evidence room behind him, preferably with no witnesses. He opened the door a crack and peeked into the hall. No one was there, so he slipped outside and jammed the key into the lock. Seconds later he reached the top of the stairs, struggling to force back the giant grin erupting on his face.

I did it, he mused. What a rush. This has got to be what shoplifters feel like.

Afraid he must look like the cat that ate the canary, he shoved his tongue between his teeth and bit down as he strode across the lobby to the men's room.

Damn, Gordy must still be crapping his lungs out.

He waited outside and barely began checking his text messages when Gordy appeared, still zipping his pants.

Chapter 24
IZZY

ALTHOUGH NEITHER PARENT could remember what Lexi had been wearing yesterday, they did give Izzy a good description of Lexi and permission to track her cell phone. Izzy left the high school with a copy of Lexi's last yearbook photo and drove to the station. She sat down at her computer as Fulton walked in.

"What are you doing?" he asked.

Izzy looked up from her computer. "I was about to track Lexi Siegel's cell phone, why?"

"Don't bother. They just found a body over at that new housing tract down past the high school. It's a teenaged girl. Blonde."

Lexi.

Izzy grabbed her jacket.

THE SKY WAS clear and blue when Izzy and Fulton arrived at the crime scene, the air crisp and fresh smelling. They found veteran officer Lester Mathis already there and hard at work. On his own, the older man had already encircled three lots with police tape, interviewed the half-dozen workers that had come in that morning and sent them all home after being cautioned not to share.

"The body's behind this house, here." Mathis nodded toward the one in the middle. "I heard you were looking for Lexi Siegel, and this might be her, but I can't say for sure. Was a bit of a shock, you know."

Izzy and Fulton peered past the yellow tape and down the long fifteen-foot-wide strip of bare ground between the center house and its neighbor.

"Show us," Fulton said.

With a less-than-enthusiastic nod, Mathis lifted the yellow tape and led them down the long tarpapered wall and around the corner of the house to where the body lay face up in the mud.

"See what I mean about not knowing?" he murmured.

Izzy did.

Surrounded by mud the way she was, the young woman was wet but relatively spotless. Her blonde hair lay matted against her head and what remained of her face in tangled clumps. Hours of rain had washed away all the blood, making the girl's cause of death obvious. Someone had beaten her face in.

"My God, and she's missing her hands, too," Fulton said.

Yeah, just like Darcy Callahan. Izzy reached into her jacket pocket for the photo Principal Peabody had printed out for her. She showed it to Fulton. "What do you think?"

Fulton shrugged.

"Okay." She took a few photos, then slipped on gloves and brushed some hair away the woman's face. "Boss?" Again, they compared the photo to what lay before them.

"Probably, but I still want a DNA comparison." Fulton frowned up at the clear blue sky. "Too bad it wasn't this nice yesterday."

"I know. Assuming this really is Lexi, her body has been exposed to at least twelve hours of rain, making the chance of collecting trace evidence or shoe prints slim." As if drawn, Izzy returned her gaze to the dead girl's face. Whoever she was, she sure didn't deserve that.

"Did Lexi's parents tell you what she was wearing yesterday?" Fulton asked.

"No, but who else could this be? She's the right size and weight, and the hair and skin color match up." She searched the girl's pockets.

THERE WEREN'T MANY murders in Rocky Harbor, so when Gabe heard the radio call, his ears perked. The body of a young woman had been discovered at Dawnview Estates, and hadn't Kylie and her girlfriend Addison been talking about the Siegel girl not coming home last night?

Curious, he stopped searching for Aconite and drove to Dawnview Estates, which was eerily empty for the middle of a weekday. Not sure where to go, he drove up and down the streets in search of official vehicles. It was too early to expect the CSI truck to be there, but he soon found Izzy Santos' black SUV Along with Lester Mathis' patrol car, the only two vehicles in the tract. He got out of the car and looked around at the empty houses, many of which were just bare frames. What sort of girl would be dumb enough to walk through a place like this alone, especially during a rainstorm? He spotted some yellow police tape strung between two houses, and as he schlepped across the muddy ground, the familiar sound of Chief Fulton's voice told him he was headed in the right direction.

Careful not to fall, Gabe picked his way along the house's long tarpapered wall. He turned the corner and found the chief and Lester Mathis standing by as Izzy Santos went through the victim's pockets. Like her boss and semi-stepdaddy, Santos looked sharp in her form-fitted suit, especially with that dark hair pulled back and braided.

"Is it Lexi Siegel?" he asked.

They all turned.

"What makes you think it might be?" Santos asked.

Man, was he *trying* to sound suspicious? Gabe smiled, happy he didn't blush easily. "I overheard Kylie talking about Lexi on the phone last night. Something about her folks calling around trying to find her." He stepped closer and froze. The girl's face had been bashed in, but that wasn't what got him. "Crap, they took her hands?" Shaken, he turned around. Was the killer taunting him? Why cut a young girl's hands off?

He must have said the last bit out loud because Mathis squeezed his shoulder. "Hey, if you're worried about Kylie, don't. She's got a good head on her shoulders, so there's no way she'll end up like this one. I don't like to speak ill of the dead, but Lexi *was* one of those kids we caught drinking out at the park a few months back—and it wasn't the first time."

"True," Gabe murmured, not sure what to think. "Good point."

As he stood there trying to make sense of things, the sound of a large vehicle approaching, drew their attention. The CSI truck had arrived, accompanied by Andrea Muncy's unmarked black van. Four techs piled out of the truck just as another vehicle pulled up behind it. Yellow with huge blue lettering, the KDMC News van was unmistakable. The four of them watched as an attractive woman wearing high-heeled shoes and a tight-fitting red business suit climbed out. It was on-the-scene reporter, Gloria Gomez.

"Oh, Christ," Fulton said.

A string bean of a cameraman trailed behind Gomez as she hobbled across the ground, spiked heels sinking into the soggy ground with every step. On any other day, Gabe would have chuckled at the sight, but this murder scene had him rattled.

Looking freshly highlighted, Gloria's ash-blonde hair flowed in the breeze as she hustled past the jumble of cars, microphone in hand.

Frowning, Fulton looked from Gabe to Mathis.

"We're on it." Gabe tapped Mathis's shoulder, and the two marched over to cut Gomez off. Of course, they couldn't let Gomez or the cameraman anywhere near the body.

"This crime scene tape's here for a reason," Gabe said.

Gloria Gomez came to a hard stop just outside the yellow tape, looking irritated yet still pretty sexy. Rolling her eyes, she blew an upward breath, poofing her wispy bangs. "Geez, like we were really going to duck the tape." She looked past Gabe. "So, what's going on over there?"

"A body was found," Mathis answered.

Another eye roll. "Yeah, we know that. But who is it? Were they murdered?"

She peered past Gabe at Fulton and Santos, who, at the moment, were doing their best to block Gomez's view of the dead girl's red sneakers, still partially visible.

"I heard it was a teenaged girl," Gomez continued. "Is that right?"

Having gathered their equipment, the forensics people were now heading their way, so Gabe ordered Gomez to step aside as the medical examiner and four techs carried their expandable tent and several other containers past them to the back of the house. As instructed by Gomez, the cameraman filmed it all, and as his focus turned back toward Santos and the chief, Gomez shouted, "Chief Fulton! Sources tell me that body belongs to a girl who went missing yesterday. A Lexi Siegel. Can you confirm this information?"

Busy talking to the ME, Fulton didn't respond. But Gomez was right. Lexi was dead and right around the corner, face up in the mud. But who would do such a thing? And why copy Gabe by cutting off the girl's hands?

"Sorry. What?" Gabe blinked at Gomez, who had asked him something.

"I asked if that skinny woman with the round glasses who just passed by was the Medical Examiner."

"Yeah, that's right. Andrea Muncy."

She elbowed her cameraman. "I'd love to interview *her*."

"Will you settle for me?" Chief Fulton strode over. Looking less than thrilled, he lifted the tape and stepped under. "What can I do for you, Miss Gomez?"

Gomez signaled for her companion to start recording and raised the microphone to her lips. "I'm here at Dawnview Estates with the head of the Rocky Harbor Police Department, Sean Fulton. Chief, we've received information that the body discovered here this morning is that of Lexi Siegel, a seventeen-year-old girl missing since yesterday afternoon. Can you confirm that? Who discovered the body, and what else can you tell us?"

Lips drawn back into a grimace, Fulton set his feet. "The body of a young woman *was* discovered by construction workers here this morning. We have a pretty good idea who it is, but the identification process hasn't been completed yet, therefore, next of kin hasn't been notified."

"I see."

"One more thing." He jutted his head at the camera. "As you just stated, Lexi Siegel is a minor. So, do you really want her family learning about this on TV?"

The skinny guy lowered his camera. "Gloria, we're not really going to air that, are we?"

"Before the family's been notified? Hell, no." Her flawlessly-manicured hands clamped onto her hips. "Keep rolling. We'll edit the name out later." She returned her attention to Fulton. "Chief, isn't it true that both of the young woman's hands were completely severed and have yet to be located?"

"What? Who told you that?"

Like Fulton, Gabe was also caught off guard. Who was this broad talking to?

Gloria turned back to the camera. "Chief, people are calling this a serial killing. They believe this young woman was killed by the same person who killed Darcy Callahan, the Rocky Harbor woman who was found strangled in her home just three days ago. A valid concern since that woman's hands were also severed. In fact, some people have begun referring to this killer as 'The Taker.' What do you think about that, Chief? Care to comment?"

Nostrils flaring, Fulton scowled down at Gomez, his already thin lips pressed into a slit.

Izzy stood by helplessly as Gloria Gomez went on about "The Taker" and how inept the Rocky Harbor PD was at solving Darcy Callahan's murder. She'd never seen Fulton blow up at anyone before, and the possibility seemed imminent.

Thankfully, his expression softened. He took a deep breath and looked into the camera. "The department is exploring every avenue in both investigations. But considering these new remains were discovered less than an hour ago, I don't feel comfortable confirming a connection between the two cases."

"What if he's planning to take someone else's hands?" Gloria asked. "Is there a plan in place?"

Where was this woman getting her information? And who came up with The Taker? Her? For a moment, Fulton looked at Gomez as if she were a fly that wouldn't stop landing on his potato salad. Then, just as quickly, the expression was replaced by one of professional confidence. "Our department is ready for any situation, and the public has no reason to think otherwise. We're on this." He took a step back and clasped his hands behind him, as if signaling that he had said everything he was going to say. Gloria took the hint.

"That was Chief Sean Fulton," Gloria told the camera sternly. "And as you've just heard, the Rocky Harbor PD refuses to share any information about either of these two heinous murders. But rest assured. When new information comes to light, you'll hear it here first. This is Gloria Gomez, your KDMC on the scene reporter."

A statue, Fulton didn't move until the camera was lowered and Gloria had hobbled to the front of the house. As her van pulled away, she stopped and rolled down her window. "You never told me what you thought of the name, Chief. The Taker is only a working title, so if you have any better ideas, feel free to run them past me. I'm nothing if not flexible."

Santos cracked a smile. "Don't worry, boss. She's way too smart to air that recording unedited."

"I know—"Fulton's jaw worked his gum like a piston—"but it pisses me off just the same. What I want to know is who told her all that."

"Not me," Mathis said. "But there were at least a dozen construction guys here earlier. Any one of them could have called the TV station. Everybody knows she pays for tips."

"True." Gabe Fox shrugged. "But only us cops knew about the missing hands." He turned the conversation away from himself. "Hey, that reporter could be getting her information from one of the crime scene techs."

"That's right," Mathis said. "Or the woman who discovered the first body."

Fulton stopped chewing his gum. "I suppose both are possible. For all we know, the neighbor woman blabbed the Callahan woman's details to her Facebook buddies while she was sitting on the porch waiting for the police to show. People, we have to put a lid on this thing. Now, before it blows up. I shouldn't have to say it, but don't discuss anything with anybody. You got that?"

They all nodded.

"So far, we have very few leads on either case," Fulton continued. "Except for the hands, this one doesn't have a lot in common with the Callahan case. Different victim type, location, even the MO."

"What *was* the MO on this one?" Fox asked.

"Of course, we'll have to see what the ME decides, but from what I can see, this girl died from blunt force trauma. I mean, look what he did to her face. The hands were cut off too, but probably postmortem. So far, that's the only similarity we've found." Fulton added a second piece of gum to the one he was already chewing. "These two killings don't match up perfectly, but that reporter might be right about this not being the last."

Chapter 25

IZZY

AS FOX CHATTED with Fulton about method, Izzy wondered why the killer had chosen Lexi in the first place. That sort of violence meant the killer was likely angry at the victim. But why?

She watched the news van drive away from the crime scene, then pulled Lester Mathis aside. "I need to ask you something. About something totally unrelated to this case. Do you remember pulling over an older gentleman for DUI last month? Last name Griswold? It's the guy who backed into my aunt Maggie."

"Yeah, Alvin Griswold." Mathis scratched his thinning scalp. "You want to know why I didn't arrest him, don't you?"

Izzy nodded.

"Well, it's like this." Mathis started a slow stroll back toward the patrol cars, and Izzy followed. "I spotted Alvin about ten that night. Yes, he had been drinking, but he'd also just buried his wife of nearly sixty years a few hours earlier. As you might expect, the guy was pretty torn up, so he'd decided to visit The Captain's Anchor, one of his old haunts. I was driving by and saw him stumbling through the parking lot. He was just starting his car when I got to him. Since he hadn't driven anywhere yet, I offered him a ride, and he agreed never to drink and drive again." Mathis tipped his head to the side, his eye narrowed. "Hey, he wasn't drunk when he hit your aunt, was he?"

"I don't think so. Nobody felt the need to test him." She thought a few moments. "But at his age, they'll probably take away his license anyway."

"Yeah, getting old's a bitch." Mathis nodded thoughtfully. "You'll see."

HAVING SEEN EVERYTHING she needed to see at Lexi Siegel's murder scene, Izzy headed over to Dalton. The one-hour drive was a pain, but necessary. Rocky Harbor PD was too small to have its own CSI unit, so they exported much of their forensics concerns to the Dalton Police Department where her good friend Erina worked upstairs in Forensics. She crept into the crime scene technician's lab hoping to find Erina so absorbed in her work that Izzy could sneak up and "tag" her, a game they'd invented back when they were roommates at the police academy. Finding Erina's computer station empty, Izzy walked around the room, looking at the various forms of equipment, but other than refrigerators and microscopes, there were few she could identify.

A sudden shoulder squeeze accompanied by Erina's gleeful shout of, "Tag!" and Izzy was doing the screaming. She spun around to find Erina stifling her laughter with a brilliant blue hijab.

"My God!" Weak-kneed, Izzy braced herself on the nearest counter. "I think that was the best one yet."

"Agreed," Erina said, still chuckling. She looked at the doorway where two clerks and one police officer stood gawking as Izzy caught her breath. "A mouse frightened her. It ran right between her feet."

"She's joking." Izzy straightened and waited until her little audience had gone. "Okay, let's get down to business. Have you got *any* physical evidence on these murders?"

"Not really. Whoever killed Darcy Callahan should teach a workshop on how to clean a crime scene." She rolled an empty computer chair over beside her own, and they sat down. "No fibers, hairs, fluids, or DNA. How do you say nothing in Spanish? *Nada*?"

"Yeah, nada. But the lack of evidence in that second murder might be more because of the rain than anything the killer may have done. So, was the Callahan woman's cause of death strangulation?"

"Uh-huh. There was a good amount of alcohol in her blood, but not enough to kill her. The belt was one-and-a-half inches wide, if that helps."

"Not really. How about Lexi's head wounds? Does Andrea know what made them yet?"

Erina checked her watch. "Actually, she just started the autopsy five minutes ago, but I believe she was leaning toward tire iron."

"Ughhhh!" Izzy slumped down in her chair. "If Lexi's hands hadn't been cut off, I'd be looking for someone with impulse control problems. You know, like the killer saw Lexi walking along through the rain as he was driving by and thought, 'Maybe I should kill her. But with what?' And then, he remembered there was a tire iron in the trunk."

"I can see that happening," Erina said. "Because we all carry tire irons. But you can't say the same about a hacksaw."

"No, you cannot." Izzy thought for a few moments. "Darcy's murder seems kind of spur-of-the-moment too. Like they were having sex—or maybe trying to. If the guy got frustrated, he could have lost his temper and grabbed the first thing he saw, which was his belt."

"But where did he get the saw?" Erina asked. "The garage?"

"Probably. His truck, if he's a carpenter."

"Electricians use hacksaws too. Also plumbers."

"Seriously? I had no idea."

"Neither did I, until I Googled it." Erina sighed, "Andrea says we'll never know for certain if the killer used a hacksaw on Darcy because the chemical burns damaged the skin around the wound, but it is likely. Maybe you should look into your local plumbers, electricians, and construction workers."

"Good idea." Wondering how many people that would involve, Izzy made herself a note then handed Erina the evidence bag containing Lexi Siegel's cell phone. "You already mentioned Darcy's toxicology results. Too early for Lexi's?"

"Yes, sorry." Erina looked at the device and smiled. "Well, at least Lexi's phone is all in one piece. She placed the bag beside her computer then gave her forehead a slap. "That reminds me. I found a dating app on the smashed cell phone. It's called . . ." She picked up her tablet and scrolled through it. "Between You and Me. An even sleazier version of ashleymadison.com." She crinkled her nose. "Not my thing."

"I would think not." Izzy chuckled. "But that app might be the break we need. If cheating on her husband was a regular thing for Darcy, Between You and Me could give us a whole list of suspects."

Erina grinned. "All I need is time and a warrant."

"Which I will get you. What else is on that phone?"

"I'm not finished looking, but does Candy Crush help?"

Chapter 26

GABE

GABE LEFT LEXI'S crime scene shaken—but not about the girl's death. What upset him were the missing hands. Why go to all that trouble? Gabe's purpose for taking Darcy's hands was simple. To keep the police from finding his DNA under her fingernails. Did Lexi's killer share the same concerns, or was his motive more sinister?

With no way of knowing, he focused on the problem of the moment, his wife. Pockets filled with Botox, he drove to the hospital, ready to use it—not that killing Angie would solve all his problems. He'd still have to deal with the kids. Also, the funeral. Yes, life would suck for a while, but it would suck a lot worse if Angie woke up.

Excited yet terrified, Gabe crossed the hospital lobby and went straight to the elevators. This is it," he mused and pushed the UP button. Angie's time had come. All he had to do was shoot some Botox into her.

And then, something occurred to him. Did hospital rooms have locks? If they did, it would sure keep people from catching him in the act. As Gabe pushed the UP button a second time, he imagined a nurse trying to get inside Angie's room. That nurse was soon joined by others, all shouting angrily. No, locking the door was out. He just had to be careful.

Finally, the elevator opened, and thankfully, it was empty. Gabe stepped inside, thinking about the YouTube video he'd watched on how to fill a syringe. The doors opened to a good-looking surfer-type guy with golden hair. Hadn't he been with Izzy Santos that day in the emergency room? In no mood for chit chat, Gabe brushed past, ignoring the man's greeting.

After five days, the sight of him strolling down the hospital hallway in full uniform no longer drew the nursing staff's attention. Far too occupied with their own responsibilities, they barely made eye contact. And since Gabe was on his way to murdering his wife, that was fine with him.

He was still working through his plans as he reached the door to Angie's room. Normally open wide, it now stood half open. Adrenaline flooded through him as he stepped into the dimly lit room, the half-closed blinds creating a calm and mellow atmosphere for his sleeping wife. But Angie wasn't alone. A big male nurse was changing what Gabe called "the bags" which, most of the time, were hidden under the bedclothes.

"Almost finished, Officer Fox." With a smile, the man pulled the bed curtain closed with one practiced tug.

Always grossed out by such things, Gabe announced he would wait outside and backed into the empty hallway, shutting the door behind him.

Oh, man. His entire body misted with sweat as he leaned against the wall. Breathe. Look sad. Look frustrated. Just don't look creepy. He surely didn't want the big nurse commenting to the police on how weird the husband had acted right before his wife died. Knees weak, Gabe slid down the wall until his butt hit the floor.

Maybe he should wait. He checked that no one was watching before wiping his forehead with his sleeve. Well, at least nobody had seen this little freak out. He had to rally. He got to his feet as Angie's door opened wide.

"All yours," the nurse told him.

Afraid his voice might crack, he nodded, and once inside the room, turned his back to the thing on the bed. Ten deep breaths later, he opened the door just wide enough to see if the nurse was really gone. He was.

Gabe turned toward his sleeping wife, careful not to focus on her still-swollen face. As always, the IV stand was just to the right of the bed. From it hung a fresh bag of saline and some white milky stuff. "Okay, let's do this." He unsnapped one of the pouches on his duty belt and took out one of the small glass vials.

"Excuse me," came the deep male voice.

If a heart could fold into a fetal position, that's what Gabe's did. He spun around. The big male nurse stood in the doorway. At first, he was smiling guiltily, but at the sight of Gabe's face said, "I'm sorry. Did I startle you? It's just that I've misplaced my reading glasses. Have you seen them?"

Gabe wrapped his fingers around the vial. "Huh? Uh, no. I . . . I don't think so."

"Oh, well, again, I apologize for—oh, hey. There they are."

Gabe followed the man's gaze to a pair of tortoiseshell glasses lying between the two lumps of Angie's blanketed feet. "Oh, yeah, huh."

"Sorry." He brushed past Gabe and grabbed his glasses. "I must have set them there when I was straightening the bedding. I'll leave you two alone now."

Gabe nodded, hoping the smile on his face wasn't half as ghastly as it felt.

Holy shit. The door clicked shut. What if that guy had come in while he was shooting her up? He imagined how stunned they'd both be if the nurse had walked in while Gabe was jamming a needle into Angie's IV port.

Not a good image. But the one with Angie waking up and telling the world he had pushed her off that mountain intentionally was even worse. Feeling like ripping his hair out, he glared back at Angie, the source of all his difficulties and so oblivious to the drama playing out in front of her.

I should be loading these things in the bathroom.

Angry for not thinking of it sooner, he stepped into the room and closed the door behind him. If someone else stopped by, he'd be safely out of sight. He flicked on the light and found himself face to face with the mirror above the sink.

Yeah, you're safe now, he told the haunted-looking policeman before him. But if you want Angie dead, you'll have to take that syringe out there where anyone who pushes the door open will see you shooting her up—and how much Botox does it take to kill a person? Google never had given him a clear answer.

With no better options, Gabe reached into his back pocket and pulled out a plastic-wrapped syringe. Disposable, the thing was long, thin, and flimsy.

Over the years, he'd shaken down a few junkies, but he'd never paid much attention to the syringes, other than making sure they didn't poke him. Heart in his throat, he tore the wrapper off and dropped it into the trash, then dug it out in the same motion.

"Jesus. How stupid was that?" Heat flooded his cheeks at the words echoed off the four tiled walls. "He placed the wrapper on the sink. When he left, he would stick the syringe back in the wrapper and dispose of them both in the trash can outside.

Having watched a YouTube video on his phone, Gabe had a pretty good idea of how to fill the syringe. With the plunger pushed all the way in, he stabbed the needle through the end of the vile then watched the syringe's little chamber fill as he pulled the plunger back out.

Easy enough. Syringe full and safely capped, Gabe tucked it up the sleeve of his jacket and stepped back into the room.

Chapter 27

IZZY

NOW THAT HER new investigation had upgraded from a missing person to murder, Izzy needed to interview Lexi's friends as soon as possible. But by the time she had driven back to Rocky Harbor from Dalton, it was way too late to catch them at the high school. Since Brody had texted he would be stopping by the hospital to see Maggie, she decided she would too, hoping they might spend a few minutes together before tracking the kids down at their homes.

Izzy waited for one of the hospital elevators and turned at a tap on the shoulder. For a moment, she didn't recognize the young woman dressed in a dark pantsuit similar to her own. And then, she knew. "Tonya."

"Izzy. I thought that was you." A thinner, black-haired version of her older sister, Angie, Tonya let go of the suitcase she'd been towing and pulled Izzy into her customary boa constrictor embrace.

"Oh, that's right." Izzy managed once she was able to breathe freely. "You're here for your sister. That poor thing. I was here when the ambulance brought her in."

"Are you visiting Angie, too?" Tonya asked.

"Actually, no. My aunt Maggie had an accident."

"Oh, no. I hope it's not serious." Tonya went in for another squeeze, and as Izzy steeled herself, the elevator doors slid open.

"Hey, who's that crushing my girl?"

Tonya gasped. "Your what?" She let Izzy go and grabbed hold of Brody.

Having experienced a few Tonya hugs himself, Brody trapped her arms beneath his own and lifted her off her feet. "Girl, you look great." After a quick cheek peck, he returned Tonya to Earth, then settled a more substantial kiss on Izzy's lips. "What's it been? Five years?" he asked Tonya.

"You tell me. You're the one who left town first." She looked back and forth between them. "Are you two really . . . ?"

"We are." Grinning, Brody pulled Izzy to him. "We've been dating for just about a year, now." His green eyes softened. "I guess you're here to see your big sister, huh?"

"Yeah." Tonya winced. "I should probably find out which room she's in."

"I know," Brody told her. "It's 301. Izzy's aunt Maggie is two doors down. In fact, I just crossed paths with your brother-in-law. He was getting out of the elevator as I got on."

"Oh, great," Tonya said. "How'd he look?"

"Overwhelmed," Brody told her. "Or at least that's the impression I got."

"Aw, poor guy," Tonya said.

Izzy took Brody's hand. "Where are you off to? I thought we were going to hang out a little."

"Maggie asked me to do something for her."

"Oh? Like what?"

He glanced at Tonya. "Let's just say it's got to do with one of those new friends Maggie's been making."

New friends? As Izzy realized Brody had been talking about ghosts, he turned back to Tonya. "You staying in town for a while?"

"Until they take Angie off the coma meds, so Sunday, at least."

"Good. Make Izzy bring you over to Salty's. I'll buy you lunch."

Brody left them with a wave and a smile, and as Izzy watched him walk away, she noticed Tonya was also watching. "See anything you like?"

"Everything." Tonya giggled. "Girl, I hate you."

"That's fair. I'd hate me too." She pushed the elevator button again. "Come on. "I'll take you to your sister's room."

Chapter 28

GABE

HAVING FILLED A syringe with Botox, Gabe crept over to the door and checked the hallway. Seeing no one, he turned back to Angie. But where would he stick the needle? He followed the tube attached to the saline bag down to Angie's hand. The thing was taped down six ways to Sunday, but it did have that blue plastic thing on top. Was that where the nursed injected the meds?

Idiot. Why hadn't he paid more attention?

He examined the needle. Compared to others he'd seen, it was shorter and also thinner, making it likely to snap off if he messed up. And what if he couldn't get the broken piece out? With the IV port blocked, anyone who tried to use it would see. No, he would inject the Botox into one of Angie's injuries and hope the needle track would blend in. She certainly had enough scabs to choose from.

Hands trembling, he pushed the sleeve of her faded blue gown up and selected a thick patch on her right upper shoulder.

Just jam it in and push down on the plunger. Angie won't complain.

He touched his fingers to the palm-sized scab, smooth, shell-like, and dark, dark red. Could the needle break off there, too?

With a quick glance at the door, he picked a spot at the edge of a scab and pushed, surprised at how easily the needle sank into the flesh. He then pressed down on the plunger. Not hard, but steadily. Of course, the stuff was traceable, but even if they did have an autopsy, who tested for Botox poisoning?

Heart beating like a chipmunk's, he stepped back into the bathroom, eager to reload. The YouTube video had warned not to reuse needles, but Angie wouldn't mind, and as far as Gabe was concerned, the more germs the better.

Confidence growing, he soon had the refilled syringe capped and safely tucked up his sleeve. After another quick check of the hallway, he strode back to the bed where he immediately inserted the needle into the exact same spot. He did the same with the third and fourth doses.

Okay, but how many shots did he have to give her? Every injection left him vulnerable to discovery, and Angie sure didn't seem bothered by it. He frowned over at the monitor, still beeping and booping, the little zig-zaggy lines on the screen doing what they always did.

Chapter 29

IZZY

"I CAN SEE why we haven't talked much," Tonya said as she and Izzy rode the elevator up to the third floor. "A police detective with two murder cases. You must be so busy."

"That's true, but it's not like people are getting killed here every day. Can you come see my boat before you leave? It's got two extra bunks, so you're welcome to stay there."

"Thanks, but I should probably stay with Angie. Plus, boats and me don't get along."

"What? Even when they're tied to the dock?"

"Don't you remember that big boat regatta I bailed out on back in junior year? Just walking on the dock made me woozy. You look great in that suit, by the way."

Although her friend's appraising look proved she was serious, Izzy couldn't help but feel embarrassed. "Knock it off, already. You look pretty svelte yourself, and I'm sure lawyers make tons more money than small-town detectives."

"Yeah, but you finally got Brody." Her grin widened. "I haven't forgotten how much you mooned over him back in high school." Hands pressed to her chest, she heaved an exaggerated sigh. "Those shoulders, that wavy blond hair, those sparkly green eyes . . . mmm-mmm-MMM."

"I did say that, didn't I?" Izzy couldn't help but smile. "Well, it's still true, isn't it?"

Chapter 30

GABE

AGAIN, GABE MARCHED himself back into Angie's bathroom. Having only emptied one vial of Botox, there was no danger of running out of the stuff anytime soon. He would empty the other vials, then go home and hope for the hospital to call.

Then someone knocked on the door.

"Hello?" This time the voice was female.

Gabe's first instinct was to tuck the empty syringe up his sleeve, but where was the cap that went over the needle? Flustered, he dropped the syringe in the sink, put on the face he imagined would be expected of him, and stepped out into the room. Oh, crap.

"Oh-my-gosh, Tonya." He offered his hand, hoping Angie's sister would take it.

She didn't.

"Gabe, my God." Angie's only sibling, Tonya threw herself at him, her all but non-existent breasts pressed to his chest. A sinewy, even more bitchy version of Angie, her lanky arms quickly enclosed him. Shoulders heaving, she sobbed into his shirtfront. Tonya's clinches were always long and uncomfortable, and Gabe was about to start peeling her off when someone else stepped through the doorway. "Detective Santos. I forgot you two were friends." He patted Tonya's back and said words that were expected.

After a while, Tonya pulled back. "I caught a flight as soon as I heard. Why didn't you call me?"

Why? Because the last thing he needed was Angie's nosy-bitch sister looking over his shoulder.

He substituted the truth with a tortured glance. Having never bothered with tissues on these visits, he searched the room for a box. Tonya found them first. She plucked out two.

"That's okay. I understand." Dabbing her eyes, Tonya edged over to look at Angie. "My God, Gabe. How did this happen? Donna Hendricks told me about it on Facebook. She said Angie fell off the overlook . . . by *accident?*"

Donna Hendricks? The pharmacy clerk? "Yeah, well. Sort of." He stood beside Angie and, even though he'd rather hold a dead rat, clutched her scabby hand as he shared the details of the story he'd concocted.

When he got to the part where Angie jumped up in the air, Tonya's expression flip-flopped between anger and horror. "That's crazy. Isn't that crazy, Izzy?"

Santos agreed.

With Angie apparently no worse for wear after pumping all those shots into her shoulder, he huffed out a frustrated breath. "I begged her not to, but you know Angie."

"I do." Tonya looked her sister over for a few moments then turned back to Gabe. "Mind if I . . . ?" She tipped her head at the bathroom.

"Sure . . . go ahead." Gabe's heart clenched. The syringe. How would he explain the thing lying there right in the open? Mind racing, he smiled over at Santos, hoping he didn't look as nervous as he felt. "So . . . how's your aunt doing?"

"As good as you can expect with her leg up in that traction harness."

"Sounds pretty rough." Their eyes locked. Was she staring or was he? He fiddled with Angie's covers a little and listened for the toilet to flush. There. In a moment, Tonya would walk to the sink and—

"So . . ." Santos began. "I hear Sunday, they stop giving Angie the coma meds?"

"Huh? Oh, yeah. Sunday." Was this an interrogation? He adjusted Angie's pillow, ears perked for the sound of running water.

"And, uh . . ." Santos asked. "Is she supposed to wake up right then, or . . . ?"

"I don't really know." Jesus, woman, enough with the questions. Gabe turned to Santos and shrugged. "I hope so."

Behind the bathroom door, the paper towel dispenser whirled a couple of times, but no water. Why would she . . . ?

The door swung open, and there stood Tonya, white and green wrapper in one hand, syringe in the other. "Do you believe this?"

"Oh, wow." Gabe stared. "Where'd you find that?"

Tonya pointed with the syringe. "Right there in the sink. Probably left there by"—She marched past him to the little whiteboard screwed to the wall by the door—"Nurse Janice."

Of course, it was great Tonya hadn't connected the syringe to him, but if she confronted that nurse about it . . . "Hang on, now." He took her arm as she reached for the door.

"No, Gabe. They can't be leaving things like this lying around. It's . . . it's a biohazard."

"Please. Let's give Janice a break on this one." Gabe gently removed both items from Tonya's hand. "There was a code red just as I was walking up, and a nurse—probably Janice—came running out of here. I'm sure she meant to come back for it, but . . . you know." He glanced back at Angie, who, after four days, was only slightly less hideous than the day he'd pushed her. "No harm done, right?"

Tonya seemed to relax. "Right."

"Hey, where you staying? I'm sure Kylie wouldn't mind if you—" he said, knowing it was expected.

"I wouldn't think of it. Kylie has enough to worry about without being kicked out of her own bed. Robby too."

"I offered her a bunk on my boat," Santos said, "but the goof wouldn't take it."

Tonya shook her head. "No, I'll stay until Sunday when they take her off the meds, but not at either of your places. The fold-out bed will do me just fine."

"What fold-out bed?" Gabe looked around, confused.

"Seriously?" Tonya chuckled. "That thing there." She pointed at the little four-foot-wide bench in the corner. "Didn't you know those things pull out? Or haven't you been staying here?"

Chapter 31

IZZY

SINCE TONYA HADN'T eaten since breakfast, Izzy suggested they take Brody up on his offer and headed over to Salty's, Brody's newly remodeled and very popular burger joint. Compared to five years ago, which was the last time Tonya had visited, the place was a palace, and she was thoroughly impressed. Izzy next drove her over to the marina to show off her boat.

"That's her on the end," Izzy said proudly. "I still have a lot of work to do, but . . ."

"Yeah, but she's gorgeous right now." Tonya stood at the top of the ramp. "I can see why you want to live here."

"Well, come on down. I'll make coffee."

"If I'd taken some Dramamine, I'd say yes." Tonya looked at the ramp and grimaced.

"Maybe tomorrow. The only way my boss agreed to let me go on such short notice was if I promised to work from here." She eyed the ramp again and shuddered. "Plus, if I step one toe on that . . ." Eyes crossed, she puffed her cheeks.

"Okay, let's go." Izzy led Tonya back to the parking lot. "I've got work to do too. There's a bunch of teenagers who need interviewing."

AFTER DROPPING TONYA off at the hospital, Izzy spent the next two hours questioning Lexi Siegel's friends. Eden Hendrix was eager to help, as were Lance Harper and Jesse Greene, but none of them knew anything. Like Jade Su, they *thought* Kylie McKenna was involved somehow. How? None could say, but Izzy thought she knew. After Lexi's parents left Principal Peabody's office yesterday, he told Izzy that Lexie—and therefore, the others, had it in for Kylie. Some crazy story about stolen boyfriends and volleyball serves.

"Teenaged girls." Peabody smiled. "You gotta love 'em."

Did she? Glad her high school years were behind her, Izzy decided to speak to Ryan Lancaster, the inspiration for Lexi's war on Kylie. Ryan wasn't home, but with his father's help, she tracked him down at Seaside Market, where he worked part time. Ryan seemed nice enough, and with his big blue eyes and blond highlights, Izzy could understand Lexi's attachment.

Since Izzy wanted to speak privately, Ryan suggested the loading dock out back. With the store manager's permission, he guided Izzy through the stockroom to a big roll-up door which rumbled upward with the touch of a button, revealing an elevated concrete platform and beyond, a thick wall of oleander bushes separated from the store by garbage dumpsters and a paved driveway.

"Sorry there aren't any chairs out here." Ryan toed the edge of the platform. "We usually sit here on the edge."

"Then, let's do that," Izzy said.

Looking a bit surprised, Ryan offered his hand. Ignoring her tough-cop instincts, Izzy took it, and soon, she and Ryan were seated side by side on the pavement, legs dangling. "I know you're on the job, so let's start with why you and Lexi broke up."

"Do we really have to talk about that?" Ryan asked. "It feels . . . I don't know, wrong or something. Like speaking ill of the dead." He shook his head as if confirming his reality.

"I know it's hard," Izzy told him. "But if I'm going to find Lexi's killer, I have to understand Lexi herself. What kind of person she was."

Ryan nodded. "Actually, I've been thinking about it a lot. Ever since she disappeared." He leaned back on his elbows. "Lexi was really sweet at first, but then she started getting all . . . I don't know . . . clingy. Girls couldn't look at me without Lexi wanting to fight them over it." He grimaced. "I swear, if she could have put a burka over me, she would have."

"And do you have any idea why she behaved this way?"

Ryan's chin dropped to his chest for a few moments, as if deep in thought. "Maybe." He kicked one leg back and forth. "Lexi didn't think much of herself." He looked at Izzy sideways. "You've met her mom and stepdad, right?"

Izzy nodded. Add a biological jailbird dad to that mix, and anyone would have issues. "Okay, how long have you known Kylie?"

At that, Ryan smiled. "Just since Monday. I always thought she was cute, but the first time we spoke was when I approached her about helping me with math. Oh. Crap." He pinched his eyes shut. "That must have been when Jade and Eden saw us talking." He looked at Izzy with pained eyes. "Don't believe Lexi's bunch, Detective. Kylie's a good person. She's got nothing to do with these murders. And just so you know, we've started dating."

"Thank you for your honesty." Izzy wasn't surprised. She'd gotten the same vibe from Kylie.

Through further questioning, Ryan explained that, like every other Wednesday, he was working the afternoon Lexi disappeared. He'd learned of Lexi's fate from friends and had first heard of Darcy Callahan's murder from the local news.

Izzy thanked Ryan for his time and drove over to the school custodian's house, but Mr. Juarez only repeated what the principal had told her: that he'd seen Lexi making phone calls then watched her walk off into the rain.

Around nine-thirty, Izzy completed her interview of Mr. Juarez. She hadn't spoken to Kylie McKenna yet, but it was far too late for that. Exhausted and frustrated, she drove back to the marina, wondering when her luck would turn. Hopefully, there was something useful on Lexi's cell phone, because at this point, she was miles from solving either of her two cases. At this point, the only glimmer of hope was the dating app Erina had found on Darcy's phone. If Between You and Me panned out, they wouldn't just have the names of the men Darcy Callahan had hooked up with, but the dates and times too.

With her police vehicle parked and locked, Izzy trudged down the ramp to the dock where she kept her boat moored. In daylight hours, the marina was a cheerful, active place with boats coming and going, and the nearby fish processing plant guarantying a never-ending supply of cawing gulls in search of scraps. But nighttime was a different story, and tonight, the silence and gloom matched Izzy's mood.

Since it was low tide, the ramp was badly lit and steep enough that Izzy felt the need to grip both railings as she made her way down it. Besides herself, only two other people lived at the marina. One was a bartender, and the other was Malcom Dillbeck, the old guy who was always buzzing around the marina making waves big enough to slosh the coffee out of Izzy's cup. She strode past his ancient cabin cruiser and turned. Was that snoring?

She eyed the two cobwebbed ropes securing Dillbeck's boat in place and imagined herself unwinding them from their cleats and gently guiding the boat out of its slip. It would serve the old guy right if he woke up five miles offshore. A lovely image, but of course she couldn't do that.

Chapter 32

IZZY

IZZY WAS DISAPPOINTED when she ended her phone conversation with Erina. Having worked most of the previous day on getting Darcy Callahan's dating records for *Between You and Me*, Erina had compiled a list of five men Darcy Callahan had dated during the last six months. Problem was, the app showed no record of Darcy seeing any of them the night she was killed.

Working with the possibility of some "off the books" arrangement, Izzy spent her morning at the station researching the men's criminal records. Finding no red flags, she had moved on to analyzing Darcy Callahan's phone records. Around midafternoon, Brody called.

"Meet me at the hospital," he suggested.

"Does this have something to do with that secret mission Maggie sent you on?"

"It does."

"I don't know," she said as she checked the time. "The high school got out a few minutes ago. There's a kid I need to speak to, and I was about to head out."

"Ohh-kaay . . ." He drew the word out enticingly. "But if what Maggie thinks is gonna happen does happen, I'll be there to see it and you won't."

Intrigued, Izzy decided Kylie McKenna's interview could wait. She met Brody in the hospital lobby, and they headed for the elevator. "So, that's it?" Izzy reached for the brown paper grocery bag Brody was carrying.

"Stop that." Brody clutched it to his chest. "You'll see it when Maggie sees it."

Grumbling, she followed him into the elevator. "It's in a grocery bag. How amazing can it be?"

She tried to look hurt as they rode up to the third floor, but Brody's green-eyed smile made it impossible to hold her frown for more than a few seconds. Arms linked, they strolled down the third-floor hallway past Angie Fox's room, where a nurse had just pulled the privacy curtain around the bed.

"I don't see Tonya," Brody said. "You were there when she saw her sister. How'd she do?"

"As well as you can expect. She and her brother-in-law didn't seem all that tight."

"Well…" Brody squeezed her arm with his. "Families can be complicated."

"I suppose."

A few doors down, they found Fulton and Maggie, now wearing a *Don't Pick Me, Pick My Cat* tee shirt and watching *The Price Is Right*. At the sight of them, Maggie turned the TV off. "Perfect. My nurse just told me Dr. Pierce would be stopping by any minute." She eyed the grocery bag. "Is that it?"

Brody nodded. Grinning, he reached into the bag and pulled out a dirt-encrusted mayonnaise jar.

"And you're showing that to your doctor?" Izzy took the jar from Brody and peered through the dirty glass. "I see a Ninja Turtle, a Lego Spaceman, a green sticky hand from a gumball machine, and is that a"—she gave the jar a shake—"yup, a monster finger puppet."

"My time capsule!" Dr. Pierce strode toward her across the room, eyes bright and hands reaching. "I forgot all about that thing."

Amazed, Izzy passed the jar to him. From the smile on Maggie's face, Brody's secret mission had definitely been a success. They watched as the doctor, a tall dark-haired man maybe ten years older than Izzy, tried to unscrew the jar's rusty lid.

"But how on Earth did you find it?" he asked Izzy. Unable to get the lid off, he held the jar up and peered through the glass.

"She didn't," Maggie told him. "Brody dug it up, but I'm the one who told him where to dig."

From the look on Dr. Pierce's face, he was just as confused as Izzy. "Only my dad and I knew where this jar was buried, and Dad's been dead since . . ."

"Since a week after you and he buried it." Maggie gave Izzy a wink, then held the man's gaze.

Dr. Pierce groaned. "Okay, I know you said you see ghosts, but surely, you don't expect me to believe . . ." He looked from Brody to Izzy, who, having been there herself, felt for the man.

"If you're expecting us to back you up, don't," Izzy told him softly. "This isn't a joke."

"But . . ." Dr. Pierce's tipped his head to the side as he turned back to Maggie. "But that's just . . ."

"How else would I have known?" Maggie shared a smile with Fulton. "Try opening it again. I want you to read what's on the little piece of paper inside there."

"There's a paper?" He turned the jar over and looked through the bottom. "Oh, yeah, I forgot I stuck that in there."

"Well, it's been more than twenty-five years." Maggie relaxed back on her pillows, watching calmly as Dr. Pierce worked the lid off. "There, now shake all that stuff out here." She rolled her little over-the-bed table toward him, and they all watched young Ethan Pierce's toys spill out on onto the table, along with an inch-square piece of folded paper.

Looking simultaneously excited and wary, Dr. Pierce picked up the paper.

"Hang on." Maggie lifted her head. "Before you unfold that, do you believe you're the first person to open that jar since it was buried?"

Dr. Pierce gave a nearly imperceptible nod.

"Okay, then, let me tell you what you wrote." She glanced at the empty corner. "It says . . . Ethan Pierce buried this time capsule on June thirteenth . . . 1991."

Dr. Pierce followed Maggie's gaze. Mouth slightly open, he unfolded the paper. "That's exactly what it says." His cheeks flushed as he eyed the corner of the room. "Are you saying my dad's ghost is over there?"

Maggie nodded.

"But why's my dad even here? Surely, not to reunite me with some old toys."

"No," Maggie said. "But it was his idea to dig up your time capsule. Ethan, your dad has never stopped watching over you and wants you to know that he's very proud of the man you've become. But he's also worried about you."

"About me?" He dropped the paper on the table. "Why? I'm fine."

"Well, physically, maybe, but not emotionally."

"I don't understand."

"The guilt, Ethan. Your dad drowned because he'd been drinking and didn't appreciate how fast the river was moving that day. Accepting your challenge to swim across that river was a stupid idea—his words, not mine." She looked at the corner for a few moments, then turned back to Dr. Pierce, smiling. "He says he was the adult. He should have acted like one and refused. So, forget the guilt, already."

Chapter 33

GABE

HAVING DOSED ANGIE with a hundred units of Botox the previous afternoon, Gabe hadn't slept a wink all night. But the hospital never called. For that matter, neither had Tonya. Around three, Gabe was tired of staring at the ceiling and grabbed the landline on the nightstand beside him. He would call the duty nurse on Angie's floor. Tell her he'd had a nightmare and needed to know if Angie was all right.

"I just peeked in," the woman told him. "Your wife's condition is stable, but unchanged."

"Thank you." He hung up the phone, then put a pillow over his face and screamed until his throat was raw.

Still fuming, Gabe showered, dressed, and drove back to Dalton. In fact, he was so angry that halfway there, he rolled down the car window and heaved the remaining three vials of Botox into the forest.

He arrived at the Dalton library just as it was opening. By that time, he had calmed down some, but his peacefulness didn't last. Thirty minutes after he walked in, Gabe returned to Rocky Harbor angrier than when he arrived. And for two very good reasons. As it turned out, Botox was definitely toxic, but to make Angie dead, it would have taken at least three vials of the stuff— and he'd tossed them out the window.

Now, all he could do was search the forest for aconite, which, apparently, was a ton harder to find than he expected. But even if he did find a plant, how was he going to get around guard-dog-Tonya?

Well, whatever happens, happens. Resigned to his destiny, at least for today, he decided to skip his daily hospital visit and drive home.

Rest. That's what he needed. To just kick back and do something non-Angie. Tomorrow, he would feed Tonya some tearful BS story about why he hadn't stopped by yesterday, thereby cementing himself in Tonya's heart as the most dedicated husband who'd ever lived. But the meat of his day would be spent searching for the damned poison.

The thought of not having to look at that hideous Angie-lump again raised Gabe's spirits. He would spend the afternoon by the pool. Of course, the water was probably still too chilly to swim in, but there was no reason he couldn't lie in the sun and toss back a few beers.

Chapter 34

IZZY

IZZY AND BRODY left Maggie in her hospital bed and went their separate ways, Brody back to Salty's to help with the lunch rush. Izzy intended to go back to the station, but as she was getting into her car, she received a text from Eric Sherman, the man whose car stereo had been stolen. Sherman's across-the-street neighbor had just gotten back from vacation, and they were both eager for Izzy to see the surveillance video. She drove over. A few minutes later, she'd pocketed a very damning recording of Jerry Greene, not just breaking into Eric Sherman's car and stealing his stereo, but also trotting across the street to pilfer the neighbor's surveillance camera.

Ready to make an arrest, Izzy called the thief's parole officer who informed her that Greene was living with an elderly gentleman named Earl Benson, who Greene had met while working as a dishwasher at Mary's Diner. Apparently, Benson had allowed Jerry the use of a spare room in exchange for some cooking and cleaning.

She radioed Vega for backup and parked a few houses down from the Benson place, hoping not to spook her target. Although Benson's house was small, his yard was well tended with the lawn recently cut and edged and the shrubs well-manicured. As Izzy wondered whether those chores were also Jerry's responsibility, Vega pulled up behind her. She sent him around to Benson's back door while she knocked on the front. Jerry Greene opened the door.

Introducing herself, Izzy showed him her badge. "Are you Jerry Greene?"

"That's right." Greene eyed her through the screen door. "What's this about?"

"Your wallet, Mr. Greene. You lost it, right? Well, lucky you. Somebody turned it in."

"Oh?" Greene scratched the back of his neck as Izzy held the wallet open for his inspection.

"This is yours, right?"

"It is." He pushed open the screen door.

Greene reached for the wallet, Izzy pulled back. "Pardon my curiosity, but why didn't you report it lost?"

"I dunno." Greene shrugged. "Seemed like a waste of time. There wasn't much in it."

"I see. So, not because you lost this wallet while committing a felony?"

"No way." Greene snapped his hand back, and the screen door banged shut. "They left it in that Honda to frame me."

Izzy chuckled. "I never said anything about a Honda."

Greene muttered something to himself, then spun round and sprinted for the back of the house.

"Here he comes!" Izzy shouted to Vega. She drew her service weapon and listened. After a few moments, Vega informed her that Greene had been arrested. Weapon holstered, Izzy returned to her vehicle. Soon, Vega and a handcuffed Jerry Greene stepped around the side of the house.

"Where's Earl?" she asked Greene.

Seeming to have accepted his situation as par for the course, Greene shrugged. "Lady, I went to work Sunday morning, and that's the last time I seen him. He's probably staying at his hunting shack out on Gibson Road."

"So, he's hunting?" Vega asked.

Jerry chuckled. "Hell, no. Earl stays out there when he wants to tie one on. Rudy's Tavern is just up the road."

She stepped aside as Vega tucked Jerry into the back of her SUV. "Oh, like he walks to the bar, gets wasted, then staggers back to the hunting shack?"

"That's right."

"But he's been gone for nearly a week. Is that normal?"

"Actually, no." Jerry looked thoughtful, then shrugged away his brief concern. "But I'm not worried. Earl's like a cat. He always comes back."

Armed with directions to Earl's hunting shack, Izzy drove Jerry to the station for processing while Vega searched the house for Benson as well as the stolen car stereo and camera. When he found them, Vega would then lock the place up and head over to the shack and inform Benson of Jerry's arrest.

As Greene was getting his mug shots taken, Izzy informed Mary's Diner that they should look for a new dishwasher.

Then, Vega called.

"I found the stuff Greene stole," he told Izzy. "I also found the hunting shack. Benson's truck is out front, but I couldn't find him."

As Izzy took in Vega's words, her stomach fluttered. "Something happened to him." She blurted it out like a statement of fact, the same way she'd told Kylie McKenna that everything would work out for them. But why say either?

"See what you can find out at Rudy's Tavern. I'll be over as soon as I take care of a few things." Izzy hung up and, once she'd turned Greene over for fingerprinting, headed back to her desk where she called Erina. "Hey, anything on Lexi Siegel's phone?"

"Not really." Erina sighed. "Sorry I didn't call you earlier. As for photos, none had been taken for two days. And any phone calls she made that day were to people on that list of close friends you gave me."

"Any downloads or texts I should know about?"

"No, they were mostly silly things. Making fun of teachers. Angry texts about having to serve detention—oh, and she had a lot of negative things to say about some girl named Kylie."

"Yeah, that seems to be a theme."

After a little chitchat, Izzy thanked Erina and hung up. She stared at her empty computer screen, not sure what to do.

Thankfully, Vega checked in again. "I'm at Rudy's. The bartender said Earl Benson was definitely here last Saturday night, and four regulars confirmed that, but they haven't seen him since."

"Did they remember what time he left the place?"

"That, they didn't agree on. But it was late. After the baseball game ended for sure."

"Great, and does the parking lot have a working security camera?"

"Hang on." After a few moments, Vega came back. "Bartender says yes."

"Okay, I'm heading over."

Chapter 35

GABE

GABE HADN'T PLANNED his pool party very well. He'd finished his second beer at noon, made himself a sandwich, and was now enjoying his fourth and final. That was it. Of course, he could probably have more beer delivered, but how would that look? Plus, the pool water was way too cold for swimming and, considering his situation, playing music out there was totally out of the question.

Seeing no better alternative, he went inside and took a nap.

Chapter 36

IZZY

BY THE TIME Izzy arrived at Rudy's Tavern, Officer Vega had already tracked down the security video from Saturday night and had isolated a brief clip in which Earl Benson is seen exiting the building. Benson then shambles across the parking lot and waits at the two-lane road for a truck to pass. He then crosses over and strides down the gravel shoulder.

"That's it." Vega hits pause once Benson is absorbed by the darkness. "It was boring as hell, but I fast-forwarded through the next three hours, and that man does not come back."

"Good job, Adrian." Izzy turned away from Benson's ghost-like image to the bartender, a beefy-armed man in his fifties. "Sir, were you working Saturday night?"

"No, that would have been Eddie, but when Earl's spending time at his cabin, every recording's gonna look like that."

"Why's that?"

"Man loves two things: beer and baseball. He shows up a few minutes before the game starts and leaves when it ends."

"Always walking?"

"Rain or shine."

Izzy nodded. "And do you know if Mr. Benson has any family living in the area?"

"Not here in town, but I think he's got kids over in Dalton."

IZZY PACED THE parking lot of Rudy's Tavern. "I tracked down Benson's son in Dalton," she told Fulton over the phone. "He said he calls his dad every Saturday morning at nine, and had just spoken to him the day of his disappearance."

"That explains why nobody reported him missing," Fulton said. "The roommate thought the old guy was at the hunting shack, and the son thought he was safe at home."

Izzy agreed. "So, Earl Benson disappeared somewhere between the bar and the shack."

"Right. Want me to send some men out to search the area?"

SINCE JERRY GREENE had told her the walk from Rudy's to Earl Benson's hunting shack only took ten minutes, Izzy decided to make the trek herself. The shack was on the opposite side, so, like Earl, she crossed the road and started walking, her gaze focused on the gravel shoulder and the area beside it, a five-foot deep drainage ditch and the few feet of grass and weeds separating public land from private.

Like a cat, Greene had described the missing man. He always came back.

Izzy hoped so, but Greene had also admitted that, as far as he knew, Benson had never stayed at the cabin for more than three nights. She remembered her own cat when she was a girl. Like Earl Benson, Mittens often disappeared from time to time, and he always came back until he didn't. She'd found his body by accident a month later—or at least she thought it was Mittens. Hidden by tall grass, the small well-decomposed body seemed to have the same markings.

So, had Earl Benson met the same fate as Mittens? Well, the little voice in her head sure seemed to think so.

She continued slowly up the winding country road, her focus rarely leaving the ground. If not the man himself, maybe she would find some clue to show he had passed this way. But what? A cigarette butt? There were plenty, and did Benson even smoke?

At such a slow deliberate pace, it took Izzy twenty minutes to reach the hunting shack. Like Vega, she knocked on the door, and when Benson didn't answer, peeked through every window. Finding no signs of life or violence, she toured the rest of the property. No Earl Benson.

Frustrated, Izzy headed back to Rudy's Tavern. There was no doubt the man had left the place. She'd seen the videos. But somewhere along the way, something had happened. If he'd hitched a ride with someone, where had they taken him? Not the hunting shack. She considered whether Jerry Greene might be involved. The man was a low-level crook, but Izzy had seen no history of violence in his background, and until his recent arrest, Jerry had a pretty good setup. Why kill the hand that feeds you?

Izzy froze. At first, she thought she was looking at a branch sticking out of a mud puddle at the bottom of the ditch. But she quickly realized it was a hand, or more accurately, fingers. Earl Benson's fingers? Feeling like she'd just chugged three triple cappuccinos, she sidestepped her way down the mud-slicked embankment to the bottom, a miniature swamp of water, ferns, mud and grass, happy California didn't have alligators.

No wonder she hadn't spotted him on her first pass. From the chest down, he was completely submerged in brown water, and his top half was covered with mud and hidden beneath a patch of large ferns. As she bent to pull the ferns aside, she remembered what Maggie told her the day after Alvin Griswold backed over her in that parking lot. That at the moment the car hit her, she'd had a vision of someone else being hit by that same car; a man with a gray beard.

Izzy took out her phone and pulled up Earl Benson's driver's license photo. No beard there, gray or otherwise. She pulled aside the ferns.

Chapter 37
GABE

STARTLED AWAKE BY the sound of voices, Gabe's first thought was that Angie had woken up, and the police were at his door. Then, he recognized Robby's voice. But who was that with him? He pulled on a tee shirt and jeans, and as he made his way down the stairs, heard some very familiar sofa springs creaking. He turned into the living room and found a cute mussy-haired girl standing in front of the sofa alongside one very sheepish-looking stepson.

Robby and a girl? Had it really come to this?

And then, he remembered what a sex-starved idiot he'd been at fifteen.

"Hey, Robby. Who's your friend?" Gabe offered his hand to the girl, whose name turned out to be Rebecca. Supposedly, she'd come to help Robby study for his biology test.

"So, you've been up there sleeping all this time?" Robby asked.

"No," Gabe lied. "Just the last hour or so."

Certain the boy wanted him gone, he excused himself and headed for the backyard, but to do what? He sat down in one of Angie's patio chairs and looked around. It really was a nice setup. Great pool. Great yard. The house was no big deal, but home values had gone up. After all the fees, he could possibly end up with a couple of hundred thousand—if he ever got the chance to sell.

Gabe got up and strolled the aggregate pathway surrounding the pool. No, he would sell the place. Keeping the pool clean was a hassle and—a sharp pain shot through his bare big toe. Gabe stumbled backward. What the hell? He looked down and found a large, brightly painted cast-iron turtle staring back at him.

"Damned thing." He rubbed his throbbing toe, then hobbled over to the sliding glass door and threw it open. "Robby. What's that turtle doing out here?"

"The one by the pool?" Robby trotted into the kitchen. "One of those Amazon guys dropped it off. It was addressed to Mom, so I stuck it out there. Something wrong?"

"No," Gabe muttered. "Just warn me next time."

He dropped back into his chair. And then his gaze drifted up to the combination patio cover/balcony. Nice at first sight, yet after six months, Angie still wasn't satisfied with it and neither was he. It was time to get the tools out again.

Since Robby and Rebecca probably weren't studying, Gabe made his presence known by banging the sliding glass door shut behind him and did the same when entering and leaving the garage. Confident he'd given the little horndogs enough time to put some space between them, he strode out of the kitchen, level in one hand, tool belt in the other. As he expected, Robby and the girl—whose hair was now twice as mussed as it was fifteen minutes ago—were sitting on the sofa. This time, with books on their laps.

Gabe smirked. "Working hard, huh? What are you studying? Biology?"

Chuckling, he marched upstairs to the master bedroom. The French doors he'd installed swung open perfectly and closed behind him just as well. The deck's floor was sturdy enough too. But, for some reason, the railing had a wobble he just couldn't get rid of. Like the pool, the balcony had been Angie's idea. She knew Gabe hated heights, but she'd still insisted he build her a deck outside their upstairs bedroom. "I want to look down at my pool while I drink my morning coffee," she'd explained.

Both projects had sparked more than one argument, but now that the deck was finished, he liked it—except for the stupid railing which continued to drive him nuts, no matter what he did. "Just like Angie," he grumbled. He set the level on top and bent to look at the bubble. Level. Just like every other time he'd checked. He tapped in a nail that wasn't quite flush. Did that help?

He was seriously considering the pros and cons of tearing the whole thing down and starting over when the garage door's familiar rumble told him Kylie was home. He looked at his watch, surprised to find it was already past six. No wonder his stomach was growling. Sure, Kylie. Stop for coffee with your new boyfriend. Spend time with your yogurt-headed mom and your bigmouth aunt. So what if your stepdad starves.

Thankfully, she'd promised to bring home pizza. Ready for a mouthful of stringy mozzarella, he pulled open the French doors and groaned. Even from upstairs, he could hear Kylie and Robby arguing. Preferring to stay out of it, he stayed put. But he also listened. After a few moments, the front door opened and closed again. Robby's girlfriend had gone home.

Good. More pizza for me. As Gabe expected, angry feet pounded up the stairs and soon, a grumpy-looking Kylie stepped into the bedroom, her mother's locket strung around her neck, a talisman she'd kept close ever since he'd given her the bag with Angie's effects.

"Hi, Gabe. Aunt Tonya says hi, and I got the pizza you asked for."

"Good, I'm starved."

"Sorry I'm late, but you know how Tonya loves to talk. And there was this big birthday party going on at the pizza place, so . . ."

It was all BS Gabe had no interest in, but of course, he couldn't show that. "That's okay." He looked at Kylie hopefully. "Any news on your mom?"

"No, but I guess we shouldn't expect any until Sunday. Only two days to go, thank God."

"Yeah, thank God." As always, his shoulders tightened as he envisioned Angie glaring at him from her hospital bed, surrounded by friends and family. At the sight of him, her arm would fly up, fat pointer finger stabbing the air between them.

Enough of that. "Hey, uh . . . how'd you do on that Spanish test?" The subject bored him, but anything was better than thinking about his wife.

"Pretty good." She shrugged. "We'll probably find out Monday."

"Oh . . . well, then, fingers crossed, huh?" He waved Kylie out onto the balcony.

Seeing he'd brought his tools, she rested both hands on the railing and looked at him hopefully. "So . . . ? Any better?"

Chapter 38

IZZY

IZZY COMPARED BENSON'S driver's license photo to the half-submerged body lying in the ditch. The upper half of the body was slathered in mud, but not enough to hide that this was the man she'd been looking for. Disturbing for sure, but even more so was the beard the dead man was sporting.

Was this the man Maggie had seen run down by Griswold's Cadillac? The beard was gray enough. Pulse surging in her temples, Izzy phoned Fulton, then Andrea Muncy.

Once the crime scene people arrived, she retrieved her SUV from the tavern and came back. By the time Benson's body was removed from the ditch, it was just starting to get dark. Izzy was about to call it a day when she remembered she hadn't interviewed Kylie McKenna about the Siegel murder. Tired and hungry, she drove over to the Fox house, hoping to finish quickly. An annoyed-looking teenaged boy with shaggy auburn hair answered the front door. Was his name Robby? Richie? She'd never know until she tried.

"Hi . . . Robby. Remember me from the hospital?" Since he didn't correct her, she continued. "I'm Detective Izzy Santos. Is your sister home?"

"Yeah, she's upstairs talking to Gabe." Wearing the same green high-topped shoes Izzy had noticed back in the hospital emergency room, he waved her into the living room. "Have a seat. I'll call her down."

Izzy thanked Robby and watched him climb the stairs. Could *he* have been involved with Lexi's murder? The boy seemed nice enough, but might he have killed Lexi—or helped Kylie kill Lexi—in some warped effort to protect his sister from bullying? The boy was big for his age.

Before Izzy could work it all out, Kylie appeared at the top of the stairs, but she didn't come down directly. From the look on her face, her stepfather was continuing a conversation that Kylie would rather be finished with.

"Well, heck." Chuckling, Kylie turned around to face Fox. "You asked for my honest opinion, and I gave it."

"I know, but I just worked on that railing for more than an hour. How can it not be stronger?"

"I didn't say there was no improvement," Kylie told him. "I said it's still wobbly."

Fox said something Izzy didn't catch, then sidestepped his stepdaughter and as he started down the stairs, noticed Izzy standing there. He came to a halt halfway. "Detective Santos. I guess you're here about Lexi Siegel."

"That's right. Sorry about the timing."

Mouth twisted grimly, Kylie pushed past Fox and trotted down the rest of the steps. She stopped in front of Izzy. "I don't mean to be rude, but why are you here?"

"Just doing my job." Izzy kept her tone gentle. "I've already spoken to Lexi's friends. You don't fall into that category, but I still need to ask you a few questions. That all right? It would really help with the investigation."

"Sure, yeah."

They headed into the living room and found Robby standing alone in front of the TV. The huge Breaking News font filled the screen: Rocky Harbor Girl Found Dead. Cut to the on-the-scene reporter, Gloria Gomez standing at the front of the house where Lexi's body was found.

"My God, this is so weird." Kylie paused the TV. Eyes glazed with tears, she looked from the screen to Izzy. "Look." She pointed at the TV. "That's you . . . standing at the back of the house."

"And there's Gabe," Robby all but shouted. He turned toward the stairs just as Fox reached the last step.

"Why are you crying?" Robby eyed his sister. "You told me you hated that girl."

"Not hate," Kylie said defensively.

"Then why are you so upset?"

Yeah, why? Izzy wondered.

Kylie grabbed a nearby throw pillow and hugged it. "Because Lexi hating me made her friends hate me. Her dying is my third strike."

"What do you mean?" Izzy asked, even though she thought she knew.

"Strike one was daring to associate with Ryan Lanister in the first place," Kylie explained, eyes filled with tears. "Strike two was for kidnapping Lexi."

Fox snorted. "Those morons actually accused you of that?"

"Or something similar," Izzy said. "During their interviews, every one of them thought Kylie was involved—although none could explain how she'd managed it."

"Holy crap." Grinning, Robby dropped onto the sofa beside his sister. "You knew an actual murder victim?" He eyed Kylie appreciatively. "Let's hear what else that reporter has to say."

Robby picked up the remote, and Gloria Gomez continued her dramatic narration. The camera slowly zoomed in on Izzy and Fulton as they stared down at something just around the corner of the house. "And this"—Gomez continued—"is where—by the grace of God—Lexi Siegel's body was discovered earlier today."

The video then cut to Gloria's interview with Chief Fulton, and, of course, Gloria mentioned the girl's missing hands. Naturally, she compared Lexi's murder to Darcy Callahan's. But both of those juicy little tidbits were supposed to be classified information, so who blabbed?

"Darcy Callahan," Robby repeated. "That name sounds really familiar. Anybody else feel that way?"

Kylie stared at Fox, who paused the TV for the third time.

"That's because she used to live across the street from us," he told Robby.

"Here? Seriously?"

"You were too little to remember," Kylie said, "but Darcy watched us sometimes when Mom and Gabe went out."

At first, Robby looked at his sister thoughtfully. Then, one corner of his mouth turned up. "That means *you* knew both victims." As if realizing what he'd implied, He looked at Izzy, eyes wide. "N-not that I think Kylie killed Darcy—or that other girl, for that matter."

Until now, the possibility hadn't really occurred to Izzy. So, Darcy lived across the street? Why didn't Fox say something about that? She turned to him. "Hey, uh . . . got a minute?"

"We were about to eat dinner, but sure. Let's go out on the patio."

Izzy followed Fox into the kitchen where the smell of pepperoni pizza made her mouth water. On the table lay a huge pizza box and three plates. She turned to Fox. "Sorry I'm interrupting dinner. Hopefully, your pizza doesn't get cold."

"No worries." Fox flipped open the pizza box. "I can microwave it." He slid the patio door open, Izzy stepped outside, and shut the door behind him. "Okay, you want to know why I didn't tell anybody I knew Darcy Callahan."

"Hell, yeah, I do. What's the matter with you?"

"I know, I know." Shoulders slumped, Fox shoved both hands into his front pockets. "This is so embarrassing. But the truth is, I . . . I didn't recognize her at first. You saw her. Remember how messed up her body was?"

Of course, Izzy did. The images were burned into her brain. "Okay, that's true, but didn't her name ring a bell?"

"Not really. When I knew Darcy, her last name was Prescott. When the truth finally dawned on me, I was too embarrassed to speak up." Fox shook his head. "And since I hadn't seen her for years, I figured, what the hell?"

Although technically wrong, it did make sense. "Okay, I get it."

Fox offered Izzy his hand. "We good?"

Izzy shook it. "We're good. Now, all I need is a few minutes with Kylie."

"Sure, I'll send her out."

With that out of the way, Izzy looked around. The patio was nice. In fact, it was a lot like Darcy Callahan's with all the potted plants and cushioned patio furniture.

Kylie stepped outside and motioned at two floral-patterned chairs. "There okay?"

"Perfect." Izzy dropped into one of the chairs and once Kylie had taken the other, asked her the same questions she'd asked the other kids: How she knew Lexi, where she was at the time Lexi was killed, and who she thought might have had it in for Lexi.

"Okay, so you were at home studying," Izzy said as she jotted the information down in her notebook. "And is there anyone who can vouch for that? Your stepdad?"

"Robby can. He came home right after school and we both stayed there all night." Her eye widened. "I'm in trouble, aren't I?"

Izzy was honest. "Robby's family. A stronger alibi would have helped with public opinion."

"Oh, God." Sobbing, Kylie covered her face with her hands.

"I'm sorry how this is all working out for you," Izzy said as Kylie gathered herself. "Things are probably going to be rough until we find Lexi's real killer. So, if you can manage, I'd like to hear your version of what started all this."

"You mean why Lexi hit me with the volleyball?" After a few sniffles and eye wipes, Kylie finished her story.

As Izzy expected, Kylie's matched up better with what Ryan Lanister had told her than any of the crazy tales she'd heard from the dead girl's friends. According to those kids, it was always Kylie who'd gone after Ryan. But in his version, Ryan had only asked Kylie for tutoring help because his math teacher recommended her, a fact Izzy had already verified.

"I agreed, and met him at the library," Kylie explained. "We'd never even spoken before, but just so you know, he did buy me a coffee and a scone afterward. Plus, he joined me and my friends at lunch a couple of times."

"That's exactly what Ryan told me."

Nodding, Kylie peered out at the pool, now bathed in shadow. When her gaze returned to Izzy, she was smiling. "I like him a lot, and I think he likes me too."

"Aw, good for you." Izzy couldn't help but smile back. "Ryan seems like a nice guy."

Stop it, she told herself. She had to stay objective. Because, in a way, Robby was right. Kylie really did know both murder victims, and besides, maybe the killer, who else could say that?

"So, Darcy Callahan used to take care of you and Robby, huh?"

"Yeah." As if reminded a person she once loved was dead, Kylie's chin trembled. "Her and Mom were friends, so we saw her all the time."

"And all that ended when she moved away?"

Kylee nodded.

"And when did that happen?" Izzy asked.

"I'm not really sure. I think I was eight, so . . . ten years? I don't even know why."

"And you never saw her again?"

"No, never." A worried expression crossed Kylie's face as she watched the solar lights around the pool pop on. Was that worried look a murderer's fear of being caught, or just Kylie wondering how Lexi's crew would react to the news of her death?

Izzy hoped for the latter. What kind of person murders someone they haven't seen since they were little? She consulted her notes again. "You know, Darcy was killed some time Tuesday, late. Where were you Tuesday night?"

"With Ryan," Kylie answered quickly. "We met at the library and had coffee afterward. But I was home in bed by eleven, so, if it happened after that . . ." She looked at Izzy with fearful eyes. "You aren't going to arrest me, are you? I mean, I barely remember what Darcy looks like."

"I'm not going to lie, Kylie. A better alibi would be helpful, not just for me, but for Lexi's people. That said, I need actual evidence to make an arrest." Izzy took in Kylie's large green eyes and pixie-cut copper hair. Not the look of a murderer, but she'd thought the same of Dylan Coates last year, and by the time she figured out what he was up to, the guy had already murdered six people.

She thanked Kylie and spoke to Robby, who corroborated Kylie's story that the two had spent the rest of the day home together.

Chapter 39
GABE

BY THE TIME Izzy Santos had finished questioning Kylie, Gabe and Robby had finished eating. That was another perk of Angie's "accident." With the kids grown and eating more, he'd been feeling a little shortchanged the last few times they'd ordered pizza, even when they got a super-sized thick-crust from Santini's. But with Angie out of the picture, he and Robby had eaten their fill, and there were still three slices left for Kylie.

Bellies full, Robby headed upstairs and Gabe headed to the living room, proud of how fast he'd spun that BS for Santos—and she'd bought it. Chuckling, he turned on the TV, more concerned with finding a good movie than of Santos locking up his stepdaughter. The idea of Kylie running around killing people was a joke, but as long as Santos wasn't looking at him, Gabe was fine with it.

Remote in hand, he settled back in his recliner and scrolled through the TV guide where he found one of his favorite movies, *The Searchers*. But just as a dust-covered John Wayne rode up to his brother's house somewhere in post-Civil-War Texas, Kylie entered the room, carrying a plate loaded with the leftover pizza slices.

"Good movie?" She asked and took her usual spot on the sofa.

"One of his best."

Gabe was just starting to believe she'd actually come to eat and watch TV when she heaved a great noisy sigh.

"Something wrong?" he asked, hoping to move things along.

"No . . . I'm fine." She picked up a slice, then dropped it back on the plate.

God, what did this twat want now? He stopped John Wayne halfway off his horse and rolled his head to look at her. "Okay, spill it."

Tears spurting, the words exploded from her. "Darcy's dead. Lexi's dead. Isn't that enough?"

It would be if she'd listed Angie. Gabe held back a smirk and nodded.

"And if that's not enough," Kylie sniveled. "Robby made sure Detective Santos knows my relationship with both victims. How could he be so stupid?"

Christ on a cross. "Don't you think she'd have found out on her own? She *is* a detective."

Chin tucked, Kylie's sad puppy expression shifted to one of disgust. "Well, it's still a jerky thing to do."

"Yeah, well, that's what little brothers are for. What did Santos ask you, anyway?"

Lashes spiked with tears, she seemed to think it over. "The basic stuff about Lexi and Darcy, like how I knew them and where I was at the time they were murdered." She sniffed. "Apparently, I don't have an alibi for either." Eyes pinched shut, she flopped back on the sofa.

Oh, boo hoo. He was the one who might be going to jail Sunday, but, of course, he couldn't say that. "Don't worry, honey. Santos is a great detective. She'll close these cases." Hopefully, by pinning Darcy on Lexi's killer— whoever that was. "All this will go away. Stay positive."

"Yeah, positive." She drew in a deep breath and once she'd blown it out said, "Mom's going to wake up Sunday, and my Spanish test is going to have a big fat A on it."

Gabe chuckled. "That's my girl." Now, if she would just shut up and let him watch his movie.

At that moment Kylie's phone buzzed. Never without it, she drew it from her pocket and gave it a few taps. "Chelsea wants me to go to the movies with her and Addison."

"You going?" Gabe hoped she would. With Robby upstairs on his computer, Gabe would almost have the place to himself.

Before she could decide, the phone buzzed again. Another text. "Now, Luke and Jeff are going." Another buzz. This message got a smile out of her. "And Ryan."

That did the trick.

Chapter 40

GABE

HAVING WASTED THE previous day searching the forest for aconite and not finding any, Gabe strode into the hospital lobby Sunday morning, feeling like he was going to his own execution. The time had come. Angie was going to be taken off the coma meds, and he had no way to stop it. Accompanied by Kylie and Robby, he found Tonya waiting for them in the lobby. She doled out the usual bear hugs.

"I am so nervous," Robby said as they crowded into the nearest elevator. His eyes darted from face to face. "You guys too, from the looks of you."

"Yeah, we're all uptight," Gabe told him. And they were. Just for totally different reasons.

Since Tonya was now living in Angie's hospital room 24/7, she updated the group as they strode down the hallway, Gabe beside her, Kylie and Robby behind. "A nurse came in at three this morning. And when I asked what she was up to, she said she'd been tasked to ween Angie off her coma meds. She also told me she would be coming back for another adjustment every thirty minutes."

"And how many times did she come back?" Gabe asked her.

"Like I said, she started at three." Tonya stifled a yawn. "And about thirty minutes ago, they took her off the respirator, so . . ." She smiled over her shoulder at the kids. "Your mom's breathing on her own now."

Oh, crap. Gabe licked his lips. "That's . . . that's good news." Feeling like his knees might go out on him, he locked arms with Tonya as they entered Angie's hospital room, which, if he didn't count the thing in the bed, was empty. With no more respirator, the silence was nerve-wracking. He stared at Angie's puffy-bruised eyes, expecting them to spring open at any moment.

"Good morning. I'm Dr. Kendall." Some lady-doctor Gabe had never met swept into the room and over to Angie's bedside, carrying an iPad. She did some tapping on the tablet, then checked Angie's vitals. She even lifted her eyelids.

This was it. He'd screwed things up with the Botox, and if there was any aconite growing in the forest, he sure hadn't found it. He hid his shakiness by gripping the foot of Angie's bed with his free hand. Tonya squeezed the other. Get ready, he told himself. You might have to run.

"So, how long before she wakes up?" Tonya asked the doctor. "Minutes? Hours?"

"I'm sorry." The woman looked surprised. "Dr. Assani didn't go over that with you?"

"Go over what?" Kylie asked. "All he said was that she'd be taken off her meds in a week and that hopefully, she'd wake up."

"I see. My apologies for the misunderstanding." The doctor looked from Kylie to Tonya and back again. "It could take days for Mrs. Fox to reach full consciousness. Possibly a week or more."

"A week?" Legs suddenly boneless, Gabe shook free of Tonya and grabbed the footboard with both hands. Was he laughing or crying? He couldn't tell.

Chapter 41

IZZY

IZZY'S PLAN SUNDAY morning was for her and Brody to meet Fulton at the Chart House for breakfast. Afterward, they would all head over to the hospital and spend some time with Maggie. They entered the hospital lobby as one of the elevators opened and out stepped Gabe Fox, his kids, and Tonya. None of them looked happy.

"Gabe, hey." Fulton offered Fox his hand. "So, did the doctors . . . ?"

Looking like a hound that had lost its rabbit, Fox nodded. "Yeah, but it's not like we expected. It could take days or weeks for Angie to come to. Then again, she might never wake up."

"Come on, Gabe." Tonya wrapped an arm loosely around Fox's waist. "We have to stay positive."

"I know, but it's hard, you know?" Fox's voice cracked. He raised his gaze to Fulton. "Boss, this is my sister-in-law, Tonya Milburn. Tonya, this is my boss, Chief Fulton."

"Nice to meet you," Fulton said. "Tonya, this is—"

Izzy wrapped her arms around Tonya. "Damn, girl. I'm so sorry for you guys. I can't even grasp how hard this is for you all." She gave Tonya a final squeeze and answered Fulton's raised eyebrows with an apologetic shrug. "We've been friends for years."

"I figured." Fulton chuckled.

Seeing the kids close to tears, Izzy rested a hand on each of their shoulders. "Hang in there, guys. Everything's going to work out the way it should. For all of you."

After some more small talk, the two groups parted ways.

"I'm sure you wanted to make the girl feel better, but I don't know if it was it wise to say that," Brody said, once the elevator doors closed behind them.

Already wondering the same herself, Izzy looked up at him. "It just came out. But now that I think about it . . ."

ONCE IN MAGGIE'S room, the first topic of conversation was how great she looked.

"I am far from well," she'd told Izzy yesterday, "But close enough to start caring about my appearance."

Ready to put her best face forward, Maggie had tasked Izzy with bringing her all her makeup and "Hair Doodads," the classification she'd given her brushes and plug-in stuff.

"Aren't you the hot babe." Brody stood back, taking in Maggie's new/improved appearance. "Gorgeous hair . . . makeup. And I love what you're wearing. That Gucci?" He fingered the fabric of her powder-blue *Cats, Not Drugs* tee shirt.

"Oh, you." Maggie pulled Brody in for a hug. "If I had my way, I'd be wearing jeans too, but . . ." She gestured in frustration at her still pinned and elevated leg. "So, what's new?"

Fulton caught Maggie up on Angie Fox's situation, and that led the conversation to what Izzy had told Kylie down in the lobby.

"You said that, huh?" Maggie looked quizzically at Izzy, who climbed onto the bed beside her.

"I really meant it," Izzy said, feeling a little defensive. She looked up at Brody. "And I still do."

"*Seguro.*" Maggie patted Izzy's hand. "Sure. Like mother like daughter."

"Don't you mean, 'Like mother like Auntie?'" Fulton suggested.

"No, my sister was also gifted. Just . . . differently."

"What?" Izzy was stunned. "Mom never told me that."

Maggie smiled. "Because, like me, she'd been raised to keep it a secret. Our parents considered such things *una vergüenza*. An embarrassment to the family. I told you what happened at that birthday party when I was little. How upset the little girl's parents got when I relayed her dead grandfather's birthday wishes?" She looked at Brody. "I never even saw the cake, they kicked me out so fast. When I told my sister—Izzy's mom, she vowed to never tell a soul what she could do—especially our parents."

"So"—Brody looked from Izzy to Maggie—"Izzy really *can* see the future?"

"Not exactly," Izzy said. "I've got no idea what will happen to Fox's family. I just feel like things are going to work out for them."

Fulton chuckled. "Whatever that means."

"Exactly." Izzy groaned, leading to a well-appreciated hug from Brody.

"Okay," Brody said, loosening his grip on Izzy. "Let's talk about something else. Maggie, today makes one week you've been in this bed. How's that leg doing? Any pain?"

"No, thanks to the pain pills." She frowned down the bed at her casted leg and the weights and cables attached to it. "Mostly, I'm just bored. Oh, and Teddy Beckett called. She offered to open the gallery for me."

"Really, Tita? That was nice of her." Familiar with Teddy's creations from her displays at Maggie's gallery, Izzy met her aunt's longtime friend last year while investigating the disappearance of Teddy's daughter. "Are her ceramics piling up? I know how busy she keeps herself these days."

"*Claro que si.* Her studio is overflowing. I told her to drop by this afternoon so we can discuss it. *Bueno, hija.*" Hands in front of her, Maggie arched one substantial eyebrow at Izzy. "What's going on with the man who ran me over?"

"Funny you should ask."

HAVING PARTED WAYS with Brody and Fulton, Izzy drove over to South Bay Body Work, where she found Andrea Muncy sitting in her car, waiting for her. A few moments later, Big Sheila Murkowski arrived driving a big red GMC tow truck. Izzy introduced them, and they all went into the building.

"It's exactly as you left it Monday," Sheila told Izzy as she flipped on the overhead lighting.

Izzy thanked Sheila, then led Andrea down the spotless concrete walkway to Griswold's big white Chrysler 300-S.

"So, this is the car that hit your aunt?" Andrea asked. "I hope she's going to be okay."

"She's just starting her second week of traction," Izzy told her. "So, hopefully. You know, the minute Maggie woke up from her surgery, she knew she wasn't the only person this car had hit."

Oh, I believe it. Remember? I was there when Maggie answered the door to my grandpa's ghost at that birthday party she was kicked out of."

"Wasn't it your cousin's party?"

"That's right." Andrea grinned. "Grandpa asked Maggie to relay his birthday wishes to Tina, and when she did, the grownups flipped out."

Izzy chuckled. "You know what they say, no good deed goes unpunished."

Andrea had completed the autopsy of Earl Benson the previous afternoon, and Izzy had already been filled in on her findings. As Izzy expected, Benson had been struck by a car with enough speed to propel his body into the ditch. The body had suffered various degrees of lacerations, shattered ribs, and more than enough blunt-force trauma to kill the man twice over.

"I sure hope you can find some tangible evidence," Izzy said. "I didn't find a thing when I looked at it."

"I'll do my best." Andrea set her little toolbox on the concrete in front of the car's black honeycomb grille. She shined her flashlight on the hood, fenders, and bumper. "You're right. Someone has given this car a good scrubbing recently. Not one insect." She then slipped on a magnifying headband and spent a few minutes examining the grille. "Oh, here's something." She waved Izzy over. "See that there?"

Izzy knelt beside Andrea. "Where?"

"Here, put this on." Andrea handed Izzy her headband and pointed with a gloved finger. "See inside, there? The little brown thing lodged in that hairline crack?"

With the small honeycombed rectangle now the size of a toaster, Izzy saw what Andrea was talking about. "And that's what?"

Andrea pulled a pair of tweezers from her toolbox then slipped the magnifying headband back over her own short, graying hair. She then reached those tweezers into the little grill hole and came out with her prize pinched between the tweezers' narrow hand-filed tips.

Izzy bent over it. "Cool, a piece of yarn. But what's it from?"

Smiling, Andrea dropped the little brown yarn fiber into a two-by-two plastic evidence bag. "Of course. You only saw the body when it was covered with mud." She tucked the bag into her coat pocket. "But beneath all that mud was a cardigan sweater. A brown cardigan sweater. With a tear on the sleeve."

Chapter 42

IZZY

IZZY WAVED GOODBYE as Andrea Muncy drove away. It would take Andrea an hour to get back to her lab in Dalton, but she had assured Izzy that comparing the fiber to the sweater Earl Benson was wearing when he was struck should only take a few minutes. In the meantime, Izzy returned to Rudy's Tavern.

As usual, the place was dimly lit except for a bright lamp over the pool table. The bartender, a young tattooed man a few years older than Izzy, stood behind the far end of the bar. In front of him sat a handful of retirement-aged men watching a baseball game.

Steeling herself, Izzy stepped to the nearest barstool, dragged it out a few inches and hopped on. As she expected, the scraping sound got their attention, and all five men—bartender included—looked just a little bit confused at the sight of the small pony-tailed young woman who had entered their domain.

Smiling a what-the-hell-are-you-doing-here smile, the bartender sauntered over as the group chattered away behind him. "Afternoon. What can I do for you?"

"Are you Eddie?" Izzy asked.

"That's right. Who's asking?"

She placed her badge on the bar between them. "I'm Detective Isabel Santos," she said so all the bar could hear. "I was told you were tending bar here Saturday night, the last time Earl Benson was seen alive."

"I knew it." A squat old fellow sporting wide, red suspenders slapped the bar. "Didn't I say that was Earl they was pullin' outa that ditch yesterday?"

"So, what happened to the old guy?" a lanky fellow wearing a sweat-stained trucker cap asked. "Did the Taker get him?"

Now, the focus of everyone's attention, Izzy cleared her throat and tried to ignore the blood thumping in her temples. "Gentlemen, Mr. Benson's body was discovered in the drainage ditch about a quarter mile up the road.

According to the medical examiner, he died from internal bleeding after being struck by a vehicle."

The men responded with a burst of comments and exclamations.

"Were any of you here Saturday night?" Izzy asked.

Suspenders, Trucker Cap, and Eddie raised their hands.

"And did Mr. Benson speak to anyone that night?"

"Sure," Eddie said. "Mostly with these two. Like every other night with baseball on the tube, they drop their cans in front of the TV and drink their way through all nine innings." He seemed to remember something. "There was another guy with them that night. Never seen him before."

Suspenders elbowed Trucker Cap. The two slid off their stools and strolled over. "That's because you're new here," Suspenders told the bartender. He looked at Izzy. "In the old days, Grizzy used to come in two, three times a week, regular."

"Grizzy?" Izzy couldn't believe her luck. "Are you talking about Alvin Griswold?"

"That's right." Trucker Cap pointed. "He sat right there."

Izzy tried not to show her excitement. "And Mr. Griswold and Mr. Benson appeared to know each other?"

"Hell, yeah," Trucker Cap said. "Those two were thick as thieves back before Grizzy got his DUI and he quit coming here. Wife threatened to leave him if he didn't."

"And that was twenty years ago," Suspenders added. "So imagine our surprise when Ol' Grizzy showed up. Must have sucked down at least six boilermakers."

"Wrong," Eddie said. "All I served that fella was beer."

"Uhhh . . ." Trucker Cap exchanged knowing glances with Suspenders, then gave the bartender a rueful smile. "Alvin poured whiskey in his beer when you weren't looking."

"Seriously?" Eddie said.

"So, was Mr. Benson happy to see Grizzy?" Izzy asked.

"Sure was," Eddie told her. "Bought the man his first beer."

"And who left first?"

Eddie looked at the other two. "Earl?"

·The others nodded their agreement.

"Yeah, I remember," Suspenders said. "When the game was over, Earl said he was ready to hit the hay. Griz even offered to buy him another beer, but he refused."

Izzy didn't get it. Who runs over their friend and leaves him lying in a ditch like that? "So, how much later did Mr. Griswold leave?"

"Not long after," Eddie told her. "He finished his last beer and cashed out, so . . . I don't know. Five minutes?"

It made sense. The road was narrow and curvy. A guy as sloshed as Griswold could have taken a corner a little bit too wide, and if Earl Benson happened to be there . . .

Since Vega had only shown her the part of the CCTV video in which Earl Benson was leaving the bar, she watched what happened after that, too. And there it was, Alvin Griswold's white Chrysler. And there was Alvin. She watched him back into the big garbage dumpster, then weave off down the road. The same direction Earl Benson had taken five minutes earlier.

A FEW MINUTES later, Andrea Muncie phoned. As Izzy had expected, the fiber on Griswold's car grille matched the sweater Earl Benson was wearing. She phoned Fulton, who offered to meet her at Griswold's place. Izzy agreed, and fifteen minutes later, they were both standing in front of Alvin Griswold's front door.

Since first hearing the man's name, she'd envisioned an angry get-off-my-yard type with stubbled cheeks and baggy, beer-stained khakis. Except for the man's temperament, she was right. Finding two police officers at his door, Alvin Griswold seemed more stunned than angry.

"What's going on?" he asked as Izzy and Fulton flashed their badges. "You catch that kid who's been stealing all the catalytic converters?"

"No, sir," Izzy said. "May we come in, please?"

"Sure, sure." Brow creased, Griswold stepped aside, and as he ushered them into his living room.

The empty beer cans on the coffee table reminded Izzy of her first big case. Much messier than this, that living room had been owned by Nicky Bass, a man who murdered his wife for burning his dinner. Alvin's wife had also passed recently, but unlike Bass, Griswold was grieving, evidenced by the open wedding album on the TV tray and the sepia-toned eight-by-tens on the mantel.

Griswold attempted to remove a full laundry basket from the sofa, but Fulton told him not to trouble himself.

"Sir, are you familiar with a man named Earl Benson?" Izzy asked him.

"Earl?" Griswold blinked at one, then the other. "He okay? Fella's not as old as me, but he's up there too."

Was Griswold for real? "Excuse us a moment." Izzy took Fulton aside. "What do you think?"

"I don't think he knows."

Izzy agreed, and that seemed to make it worse. Her throat tightened as they approached the old man.

"Sir," Izzy began. "Mr. Benson is dead.'

Griswold grimaced, his crow-footed eyes welling with tears. "I was afraid you'd say that. But why are you telling me this?"

"You were drinking with him at Rudy's Tavern, Saturday," Fulton said, "and five minutes after Mr. Benson started walking back to his hunting shack, you left too. In your Chrysler."

"What are you saying?"

"That Chrysler's got quite a bit of damage," Izzy told him.

"No, I . . ." He swatted away Izzy's words. "I . . . I hit a deer that night—and I didn't stop because . . ." He cursed under his breath. "Because I had to use the toilet."

"It wasn't a deer," Fulton told him softly. "It was your friend, Earl Benson."

Chapter 43

GABE

EVEN THOUGH GABE hadn't found one twig of Aconite that morning or any other, his future still seemed brighter. Almost a whole day had passed since Angie was taken off her coma meds, and she still hadn't opened her eyes. And now, he was free of Tonya, having just dropped her off at the Dalton airport.

He got back to town around three, dropped by the hospital, and on his way to Angie's room, ran into Fulton. Didn't he say Maggie was supposed to be having surgery soon? Was that today? Not sure, Gabe tested the waters.

"Hi, Chief. So . . . what's the deal with Maggie's surgery?"

"Oh, it went great, thanks." Fulton continued to share, and Gabe learned far more detail than he cared to hear. "She'll probably be sent home in a few days. I sure would love to hear those words from you one day."

"I can only hope," Gabe said, hoping he looked solemn enough.

But Angie's condition hadn't changed. Thrilled, Gabe played a few hands of blackjack on his phone, then headed over to O'Malley's to celebrate with a burger. While searching for a place to park, the sight of his wife's Honda surprised him. He strolled to the front of the building and found Kylie sitting outside at a table next to a window eating an ice cream cone. Also eating ice cream were her best friend Addison and a good-looking boy Gabe had never met. Probably that Ryan kid she'd been seeing. All three were laughing, engrossed in watching Ryan shine a little red laser pen through the window.

"Can I try it?" Addison asked.

He handed her the pen, and, like him, she held it against the glass.

"What's going on?" Gabe asked.

"Gabe!" Kylie leaped to her feet and raced over. "What are you doing here? Did Mom wake up?"

"No, not yet." He put on his happy-dad-face and returned her hug. "But she will, honey. She will. What's with the laser?"

Kylie grinned. "Mr. O'Malley's cat's inside there. We're exercising him."

"I see. And who's this with you?"

The boy stood and offered Gabe a firm handshake. "Hi, Mr. Fox. I'm Ryan Lanister. Kylie was just telling us what happened with her mom yesterday. I'm sorry Mrs. Fox didn't wake up."

"Thank you, Ryan. But we're still hopeful. So, what are you celebrating? Good scores on that big Spanish test?"

Ryan raised an eyebrow at Kylie, who grimaced.

"Yeah . . . about that test . . ." She returned to her seat beside Ryan. "I got a B . . . and then . . . I kind of freaked out."

Gabe stared in disbelief. "You're kidding, right? Hell, I'd have been thrilled with that grade."

Kylie winced. "I know, but if I'm ever going to get into an Ivy League school . . ."

Right, Kylie and Angie's crazy elitist fantasy. Kylie was smart, but to get a scholarship to one of those joints, her grades needed to be perfect. "Okay, so ask for some extra credit work."

"She did," Addison said. "I made sure of it."

Kylie's expression hardened. "Yeah, but even if I completed every assignment, my final grade would never be higher than an A-minus. I think Mrs. Del Campo hates me."

Sure, you do. "And that means no scholarship?"

"Exactly." She noticed her ice cream was melting and gave it a maintenance lick.

Gabe took in Kylie's demeanor. "Well, you look reasonably calm now. She told you that? What did you do then? Cry? Shout?"

The girls shared a wistful smile.

"That and more," Addison told him.

. "At first, it was all about the extra work, but then Mrs. Del Campo said that if her grade was so important, then she should have studied harder. You should have seen her." She chuckled. "Kylie jumped up so fast her chair fell over. Mrs. Del Campo looked petrified. I was too, kinda."

Chin quivering, a flush crept across Kylie's cheeks. "I-I guess the stress finally got to me."

Addison smiled at Gabe, her dark eyes gleaming. "She got right in that woman's face, shouting, 'You have no right to say that. I studied for this test every single day, even with my mom in a coma!'"

With a pained smile, Kylie raised her gaze to Gabe's. "If you think that's crazy, *after that,* I dragged Addison out of the classroom and down the hallway— of course, I was still crying."

"That's when she ran into me. Literally." Ryan took Kylie's hand and laced her fingers with his.

"But that's not even the best part," Addison said. "Mrs. Del Campo followed us out into the hallway. She probably thought you were having a psychotic break."

Kylie grimaced. "Oh, come on. I wasn't acting *that* crazy."

"You screamed that she'd just ruined your life. Outside. With all those people watching." Smiling, Addison turned back to Gabe, chin raised. "And all that without using one single cuss word."

Gabe felt a headache coming on. Was it from hunger or this foolishness? He looked the trio over. Ryan and Addison seemed perfectly relaxed as they finished off their ice cream cones, but was Kylie? He wasn't so sure.

"So, are you still angry?" he asked. "I can't tell."

"About Mrs. Del Campo's grading system? Definitely. But I'm over the Ivy League thing. These guys convinced me I don't need to go to that kind of school."

"Oh, really?"

"Yeah, Addison Googled it. Did you know that before George Lucas got into USC, he went to a junior college? And since I'm probably going to be a kindergarten teacher, what's the point? I just hope Mom won't be too disappointed."

Chapter 44

ROSA DEL CAMPO

FORTY-THREE-YEAR-OLD Rosa Del Campo prided herself on her flat tummy as well as her firm thighs and calves, all of which she attributed to her building obsession with exercise.

After cleaning up the dinner dishes, she went into the bedroom to change into her running clothes, a habit she and her husband Chad had developed ever since they moved into the house almost a year ago. She'd just pulled her shoulder-length brown hair into a ponytail when Chad clunked into the room on his crutches. Struck by a car while biking the day before, he sported a full cast on his leg and a frown on his face.

"Poor baby," she said, giving the road rash on his cheek a gentle pat. "I'd go nuts if I had to sit on my butt for eight weeks."

"That's not what's bothering me." He dropped onto the bed and propped his leg on the stack of pillows Rosa had made for him. "It's those killings." The light creases on his forehead deepened as he watched her pull on her running tights. "There have been two in just over a week, Rosie. I don't like you running around in that park by yourself. Especially after dark."

Chad had a point. It had been easy to ignore the first killing, and even though she didn't know Lexi Siegel personally, the girl had attended her school. But the rain had kept Rosa away too long. Plus she'd spent half the day before hanging out with Chad in the emergency room. "You know the park has plenty of lights, and"—she tapped the pocket on her sweatshirt— "I've got my trusty cell phone." She slipped on her running shoes. "Watch that movie you recorded. I'll be back before the closing credits."

"Fine, but don't leave the park, okay? I can't stand the idea of you running out by that creepy old barn."

"Deal." Grinning, she straightened his pillows. "You're lucky I'm a sucker for guys with leg casts." With a quick peck to the forehead, she handed him the remote and dashed out the bedroom door.

Rosa loved the location of their new home, just a block from Stafford Park. Most nights, she and Chad would follow the jogging trail along the edge of the creek until it met Fry Road, which they would continue running on until it dead ended at the old barn. Up and back, the five-mile journey normally took about fifty minutes, but without her trip to the barn, she'd be cutting off at least a mile.

Well, if it makes Chad happy, Rosa told herself and stepped out onto their front yard. After doing her usual stretches, she headed down the street. The clear sky was a welcome change, even though the evening was cool and breezy. She'd started out a bit late tonight, but that was okay. Like her mom always said, there was nothing in the dark that wasn't there when it was light. Still, it was smart to stay aware of one's surroundings.

At the entrance to Stafford Park, Rosa crossed paths with another regular, the fellow she and Chad referred to as the German Shepard Guy because he always ran with his dog. Seeing they were on their way home, she scanned the park for anyone else she knew, but with the sun starting to drop behind the hills there wasn't another soul in sight.

Normally, Rosa enjoyed the sound of decomposed granite beneath her shoes, but tonight the familiar crunching seemed far too loud, drawing attention she didn't want.

She chuckled at her silliness. Right, like the killer's going to magically appear at the sound of my footsteps. And why on earth would he be here anyway?

On Fridays and Saturdays the picnic area could get rowdy, but this was Monday.

Just because Chad's paranoid doesn't mean I have to be. Light or dark, this is just a another run through the park.

She spotted some broken glass on the trail ahead and frowned. Someone had broken the globes on two lampposts. The bulbs too. Probably kids. Plenty of them were capable. Avoiding the glass, she passed through the darkened area and continued on her way, but when she reached the Fry Road entrance, she paused and jogged in one place.

What was the difference between a run out to the barn and an extra lap around the park?

Chad wouldn't know. She jogged a slow circle as she considered. Yeah, but you will.

Keeping her promise, Rosa was about to begin a second lap when she noticed one of her shoelaces had come undone. As she crouched to tie it, a gust of wind struck her, chilling the thin layer of sweat that glazed her skin. Shivering, she zipped her sweat jacket all the way up as the mostly bare tree branches swayed. Geez, all this place needs is some tombstones. With a nervous giggle, she double-knotted her laces and turned toward home.

Relax, she told herself. Focus on the path or better yet, look at the sky and the blanket of stars above you. It was nice. Restful, and after a bit, she even managed to enjoy the rhythmic crunch of her footsteps. Soon, another set of crunches joined hers, several yards back but keeping the same pace. She smiled, relieved she was no longer alone. Most likely it was the old guy who sometimes jogged at this hour, the one with the ridiculously short shorts. She smiled, remembering how the skinny eighty-year-old's gym shorts barely covered his privates.

And if it wasn't the old guy? She considered turning to see. No, after all she'd gone through with Chad about jogging alone, she would not turn paranoid now. Still . . . there had been two murders.

The sound of their footsteps in union did nothing to ease her mind, and the stars had lost their magic. Who was running behind her? With no adjustment to her pace, Rosa did a three-hundred-and-sixty degree turn.

Well, that sure didn't tell her much.

With a black hoodie shading his face, she had no idea who he was. The only thing she did know was that it wasn't the old man. But did that matter? People took up running all the time. He was probably laughing at her right now, thinking, That woman's scared to death. She probably thinks I'm The Taker.

For the next several minutes, the man kept pace, always keeping the same thirty or so yards between them. He was staring at her. She knew it because the space between her shoulder blades was itching. She reached back for a scratch, then, realizing she'd slowed, picked up her pace, and the steps faded. See, silly? He wasn't going to kill you.

But then, he picked up his pace.

Rosa considered shifting gears again, but hesitated, deciding he was probably just messing with her. Anyway, what if she sped up and he did too?

Crunch, crunch, crunch.

The pair continued their faster pace and had reached the far end of the park where a line of tall slender cypress trees edged the right side of the trail.

Was it her imagination, or was the guy slowly creeping up on her? Uncomfortable with taking another peek so soon, she kept going, her breathing starting to strain. She wouldn't be able to run this fast much longer, but for now, the thought of the guy trotting by as she grabbed her knees, an embarrassed, wheezing idiot, was all the motivation she needed.

Crunch, crunch, crunch.

A tiny river of sweat snaked down between her shoulder blades. The steps were louder. She confirmed it with a quick over-the-shoulder glance. Damn it, the son-of-a-bitch was barely twenty paces behind her. Maybe less.

Why was this guy messing with her? He seemed normal enough, but who knew, with that hood shading his face? And his hands. Something was strange about them.

Rosa's fear, which until now, had been jogging alongside her, now leaped onto her back. It was time to leave this guy in the dirt. But an increase of speed would likely gain her another hundred yards, max. After that—a sudden clatter of steps roused her from her thoughts, She glanced back. He was coming for her. Breath coming in quick gasps, she ran for her life. Now she understood why his hands had seemed so strange. They were covered with nitrile gloves.

Chapter 45

THE TAKER

HAVING BURST INTO a sprint, he closed the gap between himself and the teacher quickly. A hard shove from behind sent the woman skidding face first across the crushed granite trail. Like a runner stealing second base. Was that a simile? A metaphor? Whatever, he was having fun.

Del Campo had started to rise, so he pressed his foot to her back until she collapsed.

"Where do you think you're going?" Acting on lifelong curiosity, he pounced onto her back with both feet, emptying her lungs with a *whooosh.*

He smiled as Del Campo gasped, eyes bugging like a fish out of water. Since that was pretty much what he expected, he stepped over to the nearby bushes and pulled out the Louisville Slugger he'd stashed. To his surprise, he turned back to find her crawling down the trail.

"Aren't you the sneaky one." He pressed the fat end of the bat to her ribs and pushed. She went over like a three-legged table and lay on her back, gasping. Eyes already wide, they doubled in size as he raised the bat. The dull thump it made was different from when he'd killed Lexi, but hey, he'd used a tire iron on *her.*

Victim subdued, he scanned the park, ready to use his bat again. But there was no movement, and the only sound was the nearby croaking of the frogs. Slightly disappointed, he shoved the bat between the line of skinny cypress trees that paralleled the trail, then dragged Kylie's Spanish teacher with him into the darkness beyond.

Behind the trees, the grass was tall, over a foot near the small creek which currently flowed ankle deep with fast-moving water. He used the light of the nearly full moon to collect the bat, then looked at the unconscious woman at his feet. Initially, he'd planned to continue the strangling thing, in keeping with the first murder. But he'd really enjoyed swinging that tire iron, and especially the bat. Never one to deny himself, he brought it down hard. And more than once.

Wow. Was this how O.J. felt when he killed that whoring wife of his?

Feeling more alive than ever, he dropped the bat and crept back to the tree line where he parted a tiny space between two of them and shoved his head through. Finding the trail empty, he collected the hacksaw he'd hidden nearby. He then pulled a mini flashlight from his pocket and knelt beside the body. This part he didn't like.

With his back to the trees, he clicked on the flashlight and held it between his teeth to light his work as he guided the hacksaw blade between the little carpal bones in the wrist and the two bigger bones in the lower arm, the ulna and radius. It was funny how the names returned to him. He'd learned them in his freshman year, Anatomy and Physiology. The memory brought a smile. A skilled teacher could make even the most boring subjects interesting.

After a few minutes, the first hand came off. He retrieved a plastic bag from his back pocket and dropped the hand inside, smiling at how his skills had improved. Encouraged, he'd stepped over the body to start on the second when his shoe rolled across the baseball bat. Off balance, he dropped the saw, the hand, *and* the flashlight. With a loud grunt, he landed on his butt near the water's edge.

Damn it. The bag had landed on top of him, but the hacksaw and flashlight were in the water. Realizing he'd been lucky not to cut a gash in his own arm, he sat there a few moments listening to the night. All he could hear were frogs and a slight breeze rustling through the trees.

That and footsteps. Crunching down the path. Had some jogger heard him fall? What if they decide to peek through the trees?

One hand would have to do. The bat was only slightly cracked, but he'd planned to leave it anyway, knowing he'd never be able to clean it well enough. But the hacksaw and flashlight were another story. He grabbed them both and splashed through the water and into the woods. In a few seconds he had vanished in the shadows.

Chapter 46

IZZY

AFTER A NICE dinner at The Fish Market, Brody suggested he and Izzy stop and see Maggie at the hospital for a few minutes. They had only been chatting with Maggie and Fulton for ten minutes when Izzy's phone rang. A third body had been discovered. This one at Stafford Park.

"Okay . . . I'll tell the chief." Frowning, she turned to Brody. "Looks like this visit's going to be cut short." She climbed onto the bed beside her aunt. "Sorry we have to leave so soon, Tita."

"Yeah, this sucks." Brody patted Maggie's new leg brace. "But I am happy you're doing so well after your surgery."

"Yes, the nurses have had me up and walking with crutches twice today."

"Sounds like they want you out of here almost as much as we do." Izzy kissed Maggie then hopped down to kiss Fulton too. "So, when do you think you'll be able to join me?"

"Doc Pierce said he'd stop by around nine-thirty, so, let's say an hour."

"Sounds good." Izzy took Brody's hand and they went to the door.

"Hey, uh. Who took the call, anyway?" Fulton asked.

"Gabe Fox."

"Oh. Okay."

What was that look? Izzy wondered. Had Brody seen it? She waited until the elevator doors closed behind them. "Did you notice the way Fulton looked when I said Gabe Fox had taken the call? What was that about?"

"What do you mean?" Brody asked. He pulled her close, and she wrapped his arms around her.

"That look." Izzy rested her cheek on his chest. "Like it surprised him or something. You know, Fox was first on the scene at Darcy Callahan's killing too."

The elevator opened, and they stepped into the lobby, now empty save the security guard seated behind the circular information desk. They answered the man's goodnight with their own and stepped out into the night.

"I can see my breath," Brody said as they strode through the parking lot to his car. "You better take your heavy jacket. I'd take gloves, too. You can pick them up at your place once I drop you off." He opened the passenger door for her, and Izzy climbed in.

She waited until he started the car and backed out. "But what do you think about Fulton's expression?"

"I think you're making too much of it. For all we know, it was indigestion. What's wrong with Fox showing up first?"

"At two murders? Quite a busy little bee, don't you think? I mean, for a guy with his wife in a coma."

"Being a little judgy, aren't you?"

Wasn't judging part of the job? But Fox hadn't committed a crime—at least none that she knew of, and who was she to decide the amount of time a man should spend at his injured wife's beside? "You're right. It's just that Fulton had that funny look, so . . ."

"Made your spider senses tingle, did he?" Brody turned onto Marina Road.

Down at the end, Salty's, his poplar burger joint, now sat dark, having been closed at eight by the newly hired manager. With a quick glance at the structure, he turned down the little gravel road that led to the docks and parked alongside Izzy's SUV. They strode down the ramp to Izzy's houseboat, and Brody waited on the dock as Izzy climbed onto the boat, lighting the way with her flashlight.

Izzy threw on her coat and climbed back off. The boat was still rocking as she reached under his jacket and wrapped her arms around his waist. "Man, I was really looking forward to you staying over with me tonight."

They shared a heated kiss as the boat settled in the water beside them.

"I can stay, keep the bed warm for when you get back." Grinning, Brody pulled down on the boat's railing, making it rock again.

"Oh, you." Izzy took his hand and led him back up the ramp to the parking area. "It could be morning before I get back." She kissed his cheek and pulled away. "Guess I'll have to rely on my coat and gloves to keep me warm."

OTHER THAN LAST year's weirdness, Rocky Harbor rarely had one murder per year, and this new victim was the third in just one week. Would its hands be missing too? Izzy pulled her SUV into Stafford Park. Designed for day use, the place wasn't well lit, but she spotted an unusually bright light and followed the narrow road in that direction. Apparently Gabe Fox had aimed his cruiser's spotlight toward the entrance. A thoughtful gesture from good old Gabe Fox.

So, why had Fulton looked that way? It wasn't like Fox had taken *all* the murder calls. She herself had been first on the scene after the discovery of Lexi Siegel's body, although Fox did arrive soon after. She recalled his shock at the sight of the girl's missing hands. Poor guy. Lester Mathis took it as a dad worried his own daughter could end up like that. Unless . . . no, that was crazy. Did Fox think Kylie had killed Lexi? It would explain his extreme reaction, and the girl did have a motive. But *Kylie?* And how often did kids kill their bullies anyway? She should Google it, but right now, she had a crime scene to process. Tired of looking at grass, trees, and shadows, Izzy pressed down on the accelerator.

There he was, talking to a stocky, middle-aged black man wearing a Seattle Seahawks jacket and beanie. She parked alongside Fox's cruiser and zipped her jacket against the wind, happy she'd taken Brody's suggestion to wear gloves. Flashlight in hand, she got out as Fox and the Seahawks fan strode over.

"I haven't been out here in years," Izzy told Fox. "Thanks for the spotlight."

"Yeah, well, it is pretty dark back here." He shined his own flashlight at the line of darkened streetlamps and the scattering of broken glass shards beneath each of them. "Kids, maybe."

"Ahem." Hands stuffed in his pockets, the Seahawks fan raised an eyebrow.

"Sorry, Mr. MacPherson." Fox looked sheepishly at Izzy. "Detective Santos, this is the gentleman who discovered the body. Mr. Jacob MacPherson."

Izzy nodded. "Pleased to meet you."

MacPherson nodded back, but his focus seemed to be on the row of Italian cypress trees to his left.

"I'm guessing that's where you found the body?" Izzy asked softly.

"Yeah, I was expecting to see a deer, but instead . . ." Again, his gaze drifted back to the closely planted row of trees.

"Ready to go back?" Fox asked her.

No, Izzy thought. But looking at dead women had become her thing lately. She turned to MacPherson, who seemed unable to stop staring at the tree line. "Sir, we're going back there now." She pointed her flashlight at a nearby bench. "Would you please sit over there for a while? I realize it's cold out, but I may have some questions afterward."

"Fine with me." MacPherson shook his head as he plodded toward the bench. "I didn't want to see that again, anyway."

Izzy followed Fox over, then stopped him as he was about to step onto the jogging trail. "This looks pretty normal," she said, thinking out loud.

"Yeah? So?"

"So, there's no sign of struggle."

"Oh, yeah, huh."

Since Fox didn't appear to follow, Izzy elaborated. "I'm just wondering how the victim ended up back there. I mean, most women aren't into creeping around in the dark." Eyes on the path, she took a few strides, paralleling it, and Fox joined her.

"Just as I thought. See those shoe prints? They're all the same, coming and going—except for those there." She pointed. "They're on top of the others and turn off into the trees."

"MacPherson's?"

"Yeah, I think the guy subdued her out here, smoothed the trail somehow, then dragged her behind those trees for privacy. But MacPherson came along and—"

"Chased him off."

"Exactly." She gestured to their right. "Maybe we shouldn't disturb this area."

Fox nodded and gave that part of the trail a wide birth as he lead Izzy to the body. Following procedure, he pushed his way through the trees, forearms crossed, flashlight hand bracing his gun hand. Chest tightening, Izzy drew her own weapon and followed.

"As you can see, the city doesn't mow back here," Fox said softly. "But even with knee-high grass, she's pretty easy to spot."

Izzy agreed. Dressed in blue with red and gray splatters, the dead woman lay on her side, facing them, one arm extended—hand included. And why was that? Because MacPherson had chased the guy off before he could finish? She hoped so because otherwise, they'd have two nutjobs running around.

"Think MacPherson did it?" Fox asked her.

Izzy shrugged. "Maybe, but why call it in?"

"I don't know. Maybe he wanted to . . ."

A twig snapped somewhere in the darkness.

Like Fox, Izzy swiveled left then right, gun and flashlight raised and pointing. "See anything?" she whispered.

"No, nothing."

Because a smart killer would be long gone. Comforted by her logic, she focused her attention on the shallow creek a few feet beyond the body. The grass was matted there too, and a cluster of deep shoe prints cast shadows in the muddy earth. The CSI team would get excited, but Izzy doubted anything would come from them. Even OJ Simpson knew enough to ditch his size-twelve Bruno Maglis.

Fox stepped over to something poking out of the ankle-deep water, half hidden by the grass. He shined his light on it. "Baseball bat. Probably the murder weapon. Maybe forensics will find some prints on it."

"Stranger things have happened." Hoping Andrea Muncie and her CSI team would find some fibers on the body, Izzy shined her light on the woman's face. "She looks asleep, doesn't she?"

"Yeah, except for the little trickle of blood on her forehead."

Izzy circled around to look at the back of the woman's head. "And definitely not from this angle."

The top and backside was a disgusting mess. Squinting in concentration, Izzy cast the flashlight beam slowly down the length of the body and over the grass surrounding it. What she needed was concrete evidence. Like what, the killer's wallet? No, that kind of luck only happened once in a lifetime.

"Any identification?" she asked.

"None that I could find."

"That's okay, I think I know who she is." She pulled a printout of Rosa Del Campo's driver's license from her jacket pocket and held it for Fox to shine his light on. "That's her, isn't it?"

"Looks like," Fox said. "Let me guess. She went out jogging, and the husband got worried when she didn't come home."

"Pretty much. Her name's Rosa Del Campo. If the name's familiar, that's because she was a Spanish teacher over at the high school."

"Oh, man. Kylie was just talking about her."

Izzy was stunned. "Kylie knows this victim too?"

"Uh, yeah. She's in fourth-year Spanish."

"I see." Well, Rocky Harbor only had one high school. Not sure what to think, Izzy cast her light along the body again. Maybe it wasn't the same killer. The woman did have her hands—at least the right one. "Hang on." The woman's left arm was tucked beneath her. Izzy pulled on some gloves and rolled Rosa Del Campo over just enough to see that the left hand was indeed missing.

"Humph." Fox bent to look. "MacPherson probably spooked the guy before he could take the other hand."

"Looks like." Izzy eyed the man, wondering what possible reason he or Kylie could have for killing this woman. "Okay, well, anything else I should be aware of?"

"Just the shoe prints." He moved his flashlight beam, first right behind Izzy, then a step to the right. "They're all over that area."

Izzy nodded. "Probably a match to the ones on the jogging trail." She looked at her watch, then Fox. "The CSI team should be here in thirty minutes. Let's go talk to MacPherson."

GABE

HAVING GOTTEN NOTHING useful from MacPherson or the crime scene, Gabe regretted taking the call. The CSI bunch had plenty to do back behind the trees, and Santos could watch them work, but all Gabe had to do was stand around on the jogging trail making sure nobody got past the police tape. Even MacPherson had gone home, so who could he talk to? A few restless squirrels?

He zipped his jacket up to his neck. Cold, bored, and with nothing to do but watch the vapor from his breath float away in the breeze, his fears deepened.

Since Santos didn't act any different, there was no way to know if something incriminating had been found at Darcy's. She could be building a case against him right now. And if she suspected him of killing Darcy, wouldn't she also suspect him of killing Lexi *and* the Spanish teacher?

He imagined himself standing trial for all three killings with Angie wide awake and laughing her ass off. God, could that really happen?

Off in the darkness, headlights drew his attention. A late-arriving CSI tech, maybe, or—Gloria Gomez. The hot little number sure had a nose for news. As the bright yellow KDMC News van rolled to a stop behind the coroner's van, Gabe imagined Gomez asleep in her bed, a police scanner tucked beneath her arm like a teddy bear.

Naturally, Gloria would portray the situation in the worst possible light. She might even claim the teacher had been killed by a serial killer. Gabe didn't care if Santos pinned the title on Kylie, but what if she picked him instead? He turned at the sound of someone pushing their way through the trees. There was Santos. Hands stuffed into her jacket pockets, she strolled over. She didn't look like she suspected him, but she wouldn't, would she?

"You okay?" she asked as Gomez climbed out of the van. "You look a little pale."

"Yeah, I'm fine." Gabe offered a weak smile. "Just worried about what's going on in this town, you know."

"Sure, who wouldn't be?"

Along with her trusty cameraman, Gloria Gomez now stood behind the crime scene tape recording her next installment for the eleven o'clock news. As Gabe expected, she was talking serial killer.

Great. The more pressure she put on the police force, the more she put on him, because if Santos caught the guy before Gabe did, she'd find out he hadn't killed Darcy just by asking a few questions. And she would, wouldn't she? Well, maybe a little curiosity would help.

Since Santos was nearly a foot shorter, he leaned down and whispered, "What do you think the killer is doing with those hands?"

"I don't know," Santos whispered back. "But Gloria's right. This makes three murders with similar MOs, and that means serial killer. Too bad MacPherson didn't show up a couple of minutes earlier. He might have caught the guy in the act."

"Yeah, or he'd have gotten his own melon bashed in."

Chapter 47

IZZY

THE FAMILIAR SOUND of Malcom Dillbeck revving his engine woke Izzy with a start. Boat pitching, she jumped up and caught a sleep-blurred glimpse of him through the porthole above her bed just as his old Boston Whaler disappeared around the large sailboat tied to the end of the dock. Doubting the man would hear her shouting—or heed her if he did—she turned off her alarm. She had set it for nine, and it was almost that, anyway.

Having spent most of the previous night at Stafford Park, Izzy was only slightly less tired than when she went to bed. She skipped her morning jog and phoned Erina instead. "I know it's early into the investigation, but I was hoping you might have news on the Del Campo case."

"Okay, let me think." Erina took a moment. "First of all, the missing hand appears to have been removed by a hacksaw. Andrea says it's probably the same one used to cut off Lexi Siegel's."

"Yeah, she told me that last night."

"Okay. Did she tell you the shoe prints were a size eleven with very worn soles?"

"No. Got a brand for them?"

"Yes, New Balance. And she found wood slivers in the wound, proving the baseball bat was the murder weapon, not a tire iron as in Lexi Siegel's case."

"So, nothing earth shattering, huh?"

"Sorry, no."

Izzy ended the call disappointed and frustrated, and as she picked out her clothes for the day, focused on something her father, a well-respected member of Rocky Harbor PD, had always told her. "First, you focus on what you believe. Then you focus on what you know and how you're going to prove it."

"Fine," she grumbled and climbed into her boat's tiny shower stall. But what *do* I believe? That Kylie McKenna is a serial killer? She imagined the girl hacking away at Darcy Callahan's wrist and winced.

At that point in her investigation, Izzy had no strong opinions on Mr. MacPherson, unlike Rosa Del Campo's husband who she'd also interviewed last night. Not only was the man a puddle of grief and guilt, he was also sporting a full-leg cast. Even if he *had* managed to make his way to the jogging trail—an achievement she found highly doubtful—Stafford Park would be covered with little round crutch marks.

But it wasn't. "So, what else do I believe?" She poured shampoo onto her hand and considered the question as she worked the suds into her hair. "I *believe* Darcy's husband has an airtight alibi." She turned her face up to meet the spray. Also, that Lexi probably wished she had different parents.

Did she believe the same person had killed all three women? Maybe, maybe not. Scowling, she rinsed the suds out of her hair and picked up the conditioner.

If Izzy were to believe Kylie, the girl hadn't seen her former babysitter in years and had no motive for killing the woman. Of course, that didn't apply to Lexi Siegel, but was getting conked in the head with a volleyball enough reason to kill a person? For some, maybe, but why kill Rosa Del Campo, and why cut *any* of their hands off?

She would speak to Kylie again, but before that, she would learn all she could about bully killings. Izzy finished her shower, and as she was starting to dress, a text message from Fulton got her blood pumping. The FBI was coming, and Fulton wanted as many officers there as possible.

Feeling more than a little defensive, she responded with: *So, you don't think I can solve this?* Then, immediately deleted it. Three murders meant serial killer, and that always brought the FBI.

As if reading Izzy's mind, Fulton's text was soon followed by: *Don't take it personally.*

Fine. The meeting was at two, so she still had time to come up with something useful.

Izzy grabbed her laptop, poured herself a cup of coffee, and took a seat at her little kitchenette table, ready to see what she could learn about the five men Darcy Callahan had dated with the help of her dating app, Between You and Me. Since the worst any of those guys had done was miss a couple of child support payments, she moved on to the man who discovered Rosa Del Campo's body, Jacob MacPherson. An accountant, MacPherson turned out to be just as boring as Darcy Callahan's husband since all their records revealed were a few parking tickets.

Lexi Siegel's parents were slightly more interesting, with the mother's record sporting two shoplifting arrests and the stepdad having spent a week in jail for disorderly conduct. Remembering Lexi probably had a biological dad, she located the man in Wisconsin where he was serving time for car theft.

Having failed to come up with one person of interest with a violent background, Izzy poured herself a second cup of coffee and Googled *Victim kills bully.*

"Holy crap." She sipped her coffee and scrolled.

Chapter 48

GABE

GABE PARKED IN the station's back lot just as four teenagers climbed out of the day-shift cruiser, all wearing uniforms similar to his, minus the gun belt and badge.

Then he remembered. The Junior Police Academy had started their new Ride Along Program that day. He opened his car door as a familiar black SUV pulled into the parking spot beside his. Isabel Santos waved. Although Gabe managed a smile, his stomach clenched a little as he waved back. He got out and looked at the cadets again.

The tall dark-haired boy seemed familiar. Was that Kylie's friend, Luke Manetti? As if on cue, the boy bent to tie his shoes. Yup, that was Luke. The kid standing alongside Luke, also tall and athletic looking, was chatting with Officer Hanley Andres. Finished with his shoes, Luke locked eyes with Gabe and jogged over.

"Mr.—I mean, Officer Fox!" Grinning his dopey Luke grin, the boy offered Gabe his hand.

Reluctantly, Gabe shook it. "Hey, Luke. I didn't know you were into this stuff."

"I joined the Junior Police Academy last month. Kylie didn't tell you?"

She probably had, but since Gabe had never cared for Luke, it must have gone in one ear and out the other. "Oh, yeah." He pulled off his sunglasses and checked them for smudges. "Sorry. Hey . . ." Gabe decided to share his misery with Santos and waved her over. "Luke Manetti, I'd like you to meet Detective Isabel Santos."

Luke smiled broadly as the two shook hands, then suddenly went somber. "Oh, hey. I forgot." His expression turned somber. "Sorry about Mrs. Fox not waking up. Kylie told me."

"Thanks, man." Gabe cut to his go-to response of, "What are you gonna do?"

"So, how long have you wanted to be a cop?" Santos asked. Her warm tone drew another goofy grin from Luke.

"Oh, man, since forever." He threw out his chest and waved his friend over. "Me and Jeff watch all the cop shows. Mr. Fox, you remember Jeff, don't you?"

"Jeff . . . ? Should I?"

"Of course, he does." Santos chuckled. "Hi Jeff, I hear you want to be a cop too?"

Like Luke, Jeff also puffed up. "Yeah, hopefully, here in Rocky Harbor."

"That's very admirable." Santos shook Jeff's hand, followed by Gabe who was ready to dump this bunch and get inside.

"Thank you, ma'am." The boy swept his blond shaggy hair away from his face. "Hey, what's up with these murders, huh? I didn't know the first lady or Mrs. Del Campo, but I did have a few classes with Lexi." He turned back to Luke, eyebrows raised. "You knew Mrs. Del Campo, didn't you?"

"Uh-huh. Back in ninth grade. She was a good teacher." Luke shook his head sadly. "Man, Rocky Harbor used to be a safe place before this. Now, it's like we're living in a slasher movie."

Gabe agreed, then decided to mess with the boys. "Hey, I hear the six of you have rented a limo for prom. Why? You kids plan on doing some drinking?"

"Drinking?" Jeff shook his head. But Luke actually looked hurt.

"I would never compromise my chance of joining the force," Luke assured Gabe. "Plus, we'd get kicked out of the dance, and I sure don't want that, especially now that Addison's going to be my date."

"Oh, yeah. Kylie mentioned that." Addison was a good-looking little hottie. But the girl must be even more brain damaged than Angie to date this moron.

"Hey, what's this I hear about making it a costume ball this year?" Santos asked.

"That's kind of half right," Jeff said. "No costumes. Just prom clothes and masks."

"To go with the Mardi Gras theme," Luke added. "But not just regular tuxes. This year, the guys are wearing white tie and tails. I already got mine."

"Well, this was fun"—Gabe took a step toward the building—"but Detective Santos and I have a meeting to get to."

"Oh, we understand." Luke, tossed them each a sloppy salute. "Who knows? Maybe we'll be partners someday."

"Maybe we will." Fat chance. Gabe chuckled to himself as he and Santos walked toward the building. Kylie had shared a few of the stupid things Luke had done over the years. Jumping off a house into a swimming pool . . . zip lining between two pine trees. He'd rather have Bozo the Clown as his partner.

As soon as they stepped through the main conference room doors, Gabe spotted the new additions to the bulletin board that took up the entire back wall of the room. Crime scene photos of Lexi Siegel and Darcy Callahan had filled the left two thirds of the wall, and now, Rosa Del Campo's pictures occupied the empty space. He turned to find Santos heading for the adjacent glass-walled meeting room. Normally a fishbowl, today, someone had lowered the blinds. Probably Chief Fulton who held the door open until Santos had made her way inside. Gabe wondered what they were doing in there, then scanned the main area for a place to sit.

The conference room had nine two-man tables arranged in three rows. A larger rectangular table stood between them and what Fulton referred to as the Murder Board. Most of the two-man tables were already filled, probably since the chief was being mysterious about why he had called this meeting. Since the only open seats were at the front, Gabe made his way over, chatting as he went. He soon learned that some of the guys had been held over after their shifts, and some, like him, had been called in. Even the evidence room manager, Gordy Lytle, was there. Knowing he would expect it, Gabe asked Gordy about his belly.

"Lot's better, thanks. The doctor gave me some pills."

Gabe nodded. Gordy's new security cameras were all up and running, so if he wanted more drugs, he'd have to look someplace else. Not one to cry over spilt milk, he gave Gordy's shoulder a quick squeeze and took a seat at the center front table with Vega, right in front of Lester Mathis, the old guy responsible for the Botox bust.

Lester cocked one bushy grey brow at Gabe. "Any idea what this is about?"

"Don't you? You're the senior man."

"Shit, that don't mean nothin'." Lester gestured toward one of the two female officers seated to Gabe's left. "Wilson says she saw two suits in Fulton's office. Thinks they're FBI. Hope she's right. Maybe they've figured out who the killer is."

Was he kidding? "Lester, they haven't even been here one day."

"Yeah, well . . ." Lester bobbed his grey head from side to side. "I thought with the Internet and all . . ."

"Sure, why not?" Vega said. "On TV, everything falls into place in an hour."

"Well, this isn't TV," Gabe said, recalling the hours he'd spent scrubbing down Darcy's house. "If it was, the star of our show would be Izzy Santos, and right now, she can't even say if this perp is male or female." He tipped back in his chair and crossed his arms. "Sure wish things would get going."

All heads turned, and the room filled with the sound of chairs being repositioned.

The chief was coming out, and walking behind him were two very different people. The first was a stocky, balding black man in a dark blue pinstripe. Gabe guessed that as a boy, the man had worn husky jeans.

"Nice to know the FBI doesn't have height restrictions," Vega joked, who was no giant himself.

"Why's that?" Gabe asked. "You thinking of—"

Lester let go a wolf whistle, cutting Gabe off and earning loud groans from the female officers. A young Asian woman appeared from behind the black guy, petite, with that beautiful dark hair most Asian women seemed to have. Santos brought up the rear.

"That's the hottest FBI agent I've ever seen," Vega said. "She reminds me of that actress . . . uh . . . what's her name?"

"Cindy Chan," Lester chimed in from behind them.

"Yeah, that's the one." Vega raised his chin to Lester. "You know Cindy Chan?"

"Well, not personally."

Chapter 49

IZZY

WITH THE BULLETIN board at his back, Fulton positioned himself between the rectangular table and the police officers. Izzy and the two agents stood beside him. In moments, the room was silent. "Folks, we have two members of the FBI with us this afternoon. Please welcome Special Agents Darrell Starling and—"

The group's applause morphed into laughter due to a jarringly creepy "Hello, Clarice," from Lester Mathis.

"Okay"—Fulton seated himself on the table—"settle down, people."

Smiling, Starling nodded. "I get it. Hannibal Lector . . . *Silence of the Lambs*." He gave Fulton an I've-got-this gesture and, with a little hop, settled himself on the opposite end of the table. "As Chief Fulton *was* about to say, with me today is Special Agent Nancy Kawata."

The woman stepped forward. "Good afternoon. We just got into town, so we haven't had time to do much. After we finish up here, we're scheduled to meet with your forensics team to examine their findings."

"Well, that shouldn't take long," Lester piped, earning a raised brow from Fulton.

Ignoring Lester's remark, Kawata continued. "Afterward, we'll head out to the most recent crime scene and see the other two tomorrow" Kawata continued, ignoring Lester's remark.

Kawata's voice faded into the background as Izzy noted Gabe Fox's interest in the bulletin board. Seated in the front row, he appeared interested in the far left of the board, the section with all the Callahan photos. But was Fox looking at Darcy's post mortem pictures or those of the woman in life, with her sparkling eyes and full red lips? It was bad enough she'd been strangled, but did the killer really have to scrub her naked body down with drain cleaner? She noticed the odd look on Fox's face. Maybe that's what he was thinking too.

"Your CSI team isn't totally empty-handed," Kawata continued. "Chief Fulton mentioned the various weapons used and that several footprints were collected at the latest crime scene. These things help to build a profile."

Fulton took over. "Our guests have suggested we hold a town meeting, and I agree. It's a good way to quiet down the gossip, curb panic in the community, and convince folks we're not just sitting around with our thumbs up our butts like some of the old farts down at Kirby's Coffee Hut told me this morning."

Several officers chuckled.

"We'll be holding it in the high school auditorium, tomorrow night at seven. Detective Santos just posted it on department's social media page, and the radio and TV stations are already announcing it." Fulton stood, a sign Izzy took to mean the meeting would soon be over.

"One more thing." Agent Kawata took a step forward. "There is a good chance that the killer might show up for this meeting, so everyone needs to be on the lookout for suspicious behavior."

Chapter 50

GABE

HAVING BEEN SCHEDULED to work security at the FBI's town meeting, Gabe's day was free to search for Aconite again. He pushed his way through an especially thick clump of shrubs, frustrated by his lack of success and wondering what he should do about it.

It would be easy to shake down an addict for some street drugs, but dosing Angie with those would produce overdose symptoms. Pinpoint or dilated, Angie's pupils would be a big red flag. And with the fat life insurance policy he had on her, even a whiff of suspicion would be dangerous.

He looked around a small clearing. A few madrones had squeezed their way in between the redwoods, and there were plenty of ferns. But where the hell was all the Aconite? Scratching an itch on his left hand, he turned a circle.

Oh, crap. What had he been walking through?

He scratched it again with no relief. Poison ivy. It had to be.

Great.

Robby had used aloe vera when he got poison ivy last summer. Pretty sure there was still half a bottle left, Gabe drove home with nothing to show for himself, unless he counted the little itchy patch on the back of his left hand. After a quick shower, he tracked down the lotion and slathered some on. Then, he got dressed and headed to the kitchen.

He'd just finished building himself a fat ham sandwich when the garage door rumbled open. What was Kylie doing home when it was barely past noon? Expecting the worst, he took a big bite of his sandwich and leaned on the counter in front of the sink, eyes on the door to the garage. What came through it was a shock.

"What on Earth?" Had Kylie been shot? She didn't act like it. Maybe someone standing beside her had. Wait, was that spaghetti dangling from her hair?

"My God!" he said, trying not to laugh. "What happened to *you*?"

"What *didn't* happen?" Kylie whimpered. Cheeks smeared with tomato sauce and tears, she shrugged out of her ruined jacket, exposing an equally-ruined green blouse slopped top to bottom with what Gabe guessed was marinara sauce. "Ask Ryan. I'm taking a shower." She tromped up the stairs.

A moment later, Ryan stepped into the kitchen bearing only a few red smudges. "Hi, Mr. Fox. Kylie was pretty upset, so I, uh . . ."

"You drove her home? Thanks, Ryan. "That was nice of you." Figuring it wouldn't look right to eat alone, Gabe gestured at the sandwich stuff on the island between them. "Looks like you're going to be here for a while. Want a sandwich?"

"Thanks, I did miss lunch." Ryan raised his sauce-dabbed hands. "Mind if I . . . ?"

"No, go ahead." Gabe stepped aside, and Ryan took his place at the sink. Hands clean, he explained what had happened while the two of them made sandwiches, Ryan his own, and Gabe one for Kylie—a burden he wouldn't have considered if Ryan wasn't there.

"Sounds like an accident," Gabe said, plating Kylie's sandwich.

"That's what Jesse and Lance told Principal Peabody, but Kylie doesn't believe it." Ryan followed Gabe over to the kitchen table and they sat down to eat.

"Now, let me get this straight," Gabe said. "The boys were arguing, it escalated into pushing, and one of them stumbled into Kylie just as she was walking past with her spaghetti. Why doesn't she believe them?"

"Because Lexi was a good friend of theirs."

"Hey, wasn't Lexi your girlfriend at one time?"

Ryan heaved a frustrated sigh. "I never said one word to Kylie until long after I broke up with Lexi. But that didn't stop her from calling Kylie a boyfriend thief. And when Lexi disappeared, her friends started these crazy rumors. The first was that Lexi had been kidnapped by Kylie."

Gabe chuckled through a mouthful of sandwich.

"Ridiculous, right?"

"Yeah, but there's a lot of stupid people out there."

"Exactly. And now, with Lexi dead . . ."

"They're saying it was Kylie who killed her?"

Ryan nodded.

The idea of Kylie sawing though a human wrist was ridiculous, but since it wouldn't look right to laugh, he frowned. "That's the stupidest thing I've ever heard."

"And you guys don't even know the half of it." Kylie scuffed into the kitchen in her fuzzy pink slippers and wrapped in a powder-blue bathrobe belted at the waist. Her rust-colored hair was combed, but still damp.

"There's more?" Ryan asked. He blinked up at her. "Why didn't you tell me?"

Gabe was surprised too, considering how quick she'd been to complain when Lexi hit her with the volleyball. Something had changed in his stepdaughter. Along with the tomato sauce, Kylie's little-girl poutiness had been replaced—at least temporarily—by steamy frustration.

"I'm sorry," she told Ryan. "I was still too upset to talk." She rested a hand on Ryan's shoulder and looked at Gabe. "Did he tell you he almost got in a fight with one of those boys?"

Gabe shook his head.

"Mr. Peabody got between them and talked Ryan out of it. A good thing too since anyone who gets in a fight this month can't go to prom."

Too bad Ryan didn't, Gabe mused. Kylie's fancy dress had cost him an arm and a leg. A refund would be sweet. "You mentioned something else happened . . . earlier in the day?"

"Yeah, it started when Mrs. Sheraton announced the school had gotten this big equipment grant."

"I don't get it," Gabe said. "What can new basketballs have to do with you being a serial killer?"

"Not basketballs. Archery equipment." She took a bite of her sandwich, making them wait. "And not just bows and arrows. Mrs. Sheraton got us everything. Arm shields . . . targets. Even a big wall of hay bales stacked behind the targets."

Like Ryan, Gabe's eyes narrowed. He'd have heard if someone had tried to put an arrow through her.

As if reading his mind, she cracked a half-hearted smile. "No, nobody tried to shoot me. I'll just start at the beginning. We were all pumped up and eager to start shooting, right? Especially when we saw the targets lined up out in the field and the big table stacked with bows and stuff. But before Mrs. Sheraton would let us touch anything, she had the class sit down on the grass so she could go through all the safety rules.

"Luke and Jeff asked a few of their usual stupid questions, and then, it was time to demonstrate the proper firing stance. I don't know why, but Mrs. Sheraton picked me to demonstrate, and the moment she put that bow in my hand, Jade Moon started in. She was like: 'You sure you want to give her that, teacher?'"

"Didn't Sheraton tell her to shut up?" Ryan asked.

"Sure, and Jade did for a while. But then, I got to shoot." Her lips curled into a satisfied smile. "Bullseye. Right down the middle."

Gabe caught himself scratching the back of his hand and stopped. "But you've never shot a bow before."

"Guess I'm a natural." Her smile dropped away. "Ugh. That's what Jade's friend Eden said too, only she added the word killer."

"A natural killer?" Ryan said. "You?"

"Yeah, then, Jade started up again." Fingers splayed, Kylie held her hands in front of her face, reminding Gabe of some silent movie heroine. "She was like, 'Run, everybody! Run, before Kylie puts an arrow through your chest!'"

"What happened then?" Gabe asked.

"People started laughing. Eden screamed. One guy shouted, 'Murderer!' I think it was Jamari Stewart."

"No surprise there." Ryan looked at Gabe. "That's Jade's boyfriend."

"Exactly," Kylie said. "I didn't know what to do. Thankfully, my friends were there to help Mrs. Sheraton shout them all down. Luke got right up in Jade's face and said, 'Knock it off! Acting like an idiot is my job!'"

"Ha!" Ryan leaned back in his chair. "That sounds like Luke."

"Yeah, it was crazy." Kylie was putting on a strong front, but her eyes were rimmed with tears. "Mrs. Sheraton pulled Eden and Jade out of the group to yell at them, and the class settled down." A tear rolled down her cheek.

Wishing he could have seen it, Gabe patted Kylie's hand. "I guess you were pretty upset, huh?"

"I was a mess. Addison must have thought so too, because she asked if she could take me to the bathroom." She dabbed the tear with a paper napkin. "I think Mrs. Sheraton was happy to get rid of me."

"Those damned girls," Ryan said. "What did they think they were doing?"

Thankful he wasn't in high school anymore, Gabe sighed and rubbed the back of his itchy hand on his pant leg. "Sounds like one of those old cowboy movies where somebody tries to start a lynch mob."

"I don't get it." Kylie groaned. "Why are people saying those horrible things about me? I would never do anything like that." She slipped one hand beneath the collar of her robe and pulled out her mother's locket.

Had she worn the damned thing in the shower? Gabe tried not to roll his eyes as Kylie rubbed her thumb over the locket's shiny silver surface.

"Who knows why people do what they do?" Ryan said. "Lance had a crush on Lexi last year. Maybe he never got over her."

Nodding, Kylie popped the locket open, and as she studied the tiny photos inside said, "Addison heard Jade and Eden won't be allowed to participate in the archery unit."

"Good," Ryan said. "They deserve it."

"They sure do." Gabe raised his brow at Kylie. "But you're not satisfied with that, are you?"

"No." She snapped the locket shut. "Expulsion would be nice."

Gabe chuckled. "Well, don't hold your breath for that to happen. But, if you want, I can talk to the principal about it. Maybe he can put the fear of God into those little *bitches*."

Kylie giggled the way she always did when he used profanity, but she also shook her head. "No, don't do that. They'll just say I went whining to my dad. Then I'll be a murderer *and* a crybaby."

Since Ryan's opinion of Gabe might help if he actually did kill Kylie for the insurance money, Gabe reached across the table and took her hand. "Honey, I hate seeing you like this. Would you like me to arrest them?"

Chuckling, she pulled away, and then tipped her head to the side. "What would you arrest them for, exactly?"

"Oh, I'd think of something," he said, trying not to scratch his hand.

"How about we wait on that. With any luck, that Taker guy will get caught and all of this will blow over." She sat back, eyes on the ceiling. "Oh, man. Look at me, pouring out my heart." She looked at Gabe. "I'm sorry. You're always so strong, I forget you're suffering too."

Oh, he was, just not for the same reasons.

Thankful he'd taken that one semester of drama back in community college, Gabe dropped his gaze. A heavy sigh would go well here, but then, what would he say? As if trying to contain his emotions, he drew in a deep breath and took his time blowing it out. "Yeah, I'm suffering." He put a little crack in his voice. "Seeing your mom in that bed every day, and me not able to do anything for her . . . I-I mean . . . damn." He slumped back in his chair. "Enough about me. What's that scent you're wearing, honey? I noticed it when you came down."

"Oh, this?" She sniffed the inside of her wrist and smiled. "It's Cypher. Ryan gave it to me."

"That's your favorite, isn't it?" Gabe looked admiringly at Ryan. "How'd you know to get her that?"

"Addison told me. I was going to give it to her on prom night, but she was so upset this morning . . ."

"Well, that's very thoughtful of you." Having switched the conversation away from himself, Gabe moved to keep it that way. "I have some news."

"Is it good?" Kylie asked. "I could use some right now."

"Well, I don't know if it's actually *good* news, but the FBI is having a town meeting tonight over at the high school auditorium. That's why I didn't go in earlier. The chief wants me to work security later."

"The FBI?" Ryan looked more gloomy than surprised. "Watch everybody in town show up."

"We do expect a big crowd." Gabe gave Kylie a wisp of a smile. "I just hope they can figure out who's *really* been doing these killings so Lexi's buddies can leave you alone."

"Wouldn't that be nice," Kylie said. Then she noticed him scratching the back of his hand.

Chapter 51

GABE

PREFERRING NOT TO explain how he'd ended up with poison ivy on his hand, Gabe offered to pay for Ryan and Kylie to go bowling. As he expected, Kylie forgot all about his itchy hand as he passed her a twenty.

Alone, finally, Gabe got ready for work. His plan was to watch a little TV then pay Angie a quick visit before heading to the high school auditorium.

Delighted to find the TV already set to his favorite movie channel, he dropped into his recliner just as a young shaggy-haired John Voight arrived at a VA hospital after being wounded in Viet Nam. Ever the war buff, Gabe watched for a while, then lost interest at the sight of Jane Fonda cuddling on Voight's paralyzed lap. The bitch's husband was still in Nam, and here she was making out with this hippie. Could the guy even do it?

Never one for love stories, he set the alarm on his cell phone and stretched out to take a snooze. He was just starting to nod off when the movie's plot started to get interesting.

Voight's sad-sack buddy, Bobby, had just sneaked an empty syringe off a tray and was locking himself into some sort of window-lined storage room. What was he up to?

Voight seemed to know. Suddenly horrified, he started thumping on the glass and shouting for help. Was the kid going to hang himself in there? And why take the empty syringe?

At the sight of Billy stabbing the needle into his arm, Gabe lurched forward. The guy was shooting air into his veins.

Unable to get into the room, John Voight pounded the glass with all his strength. The camera didn't show what Voight was seeing, but from his facial expression, Billy's suicide attempt had worked. Done with banging the glass, Voight slumped back in his wheelchair looking shaken and exhausted.

Air, Gabe mused. All it took was air. Like John Voight, he slumped back in his own chair, but unlike Voight's character, Gabe was feeling happier than he had in weeks. Smiling, he clicked off the TV and headed into the garage where he kept his old footlocker tucked below his workbench. He dragged it out and unlocked the padlock.

At first glance, the stuff inside was boring enough. A few old car magazines and Chilton manuals. He kept the more interesting stuff tucked beneath the lift-out tray. He set aside the *Hustler* magazines and travel brochures and drew out two of the syringes. He didn't bother with the wadded-up paper napkin tucked down into the corner. He didn't expect to get a fair price for Darcy Callahan's wedding ring in Mexico, but it would have been a waste to dump it with the rest of the evidence.

GABE STEPPED INTO Angie's hospital room. With Tonya gone, it would be much easier to try his new trick on Angie. Finding a nice little clearing in the forest of scabs spotting the flab on her upper arm, he stuck the needle in and pushed down on the plunger, ready to pin her to the bed if she started to spaz out.

But she didn't. Angie never moved a muscle, and the only sounds were the same old wheezy respirator noises. Had he done something wrong? The guy in the movie had barely pushed down on the plunger, and he was flopping around like a landed trout.

Having moved the little plastic pulse monitor from her fingertip to his own, he clipped it back on Angie's and tucked the syringe safely up his shirtsleeve.

Okay, what went wrong this time? He replayed the movie scene in his mind but found no fault in his method.

Was the syringe bigger? Maybe, but not by much.

Ready to give it another try, he sneaked a quick peek down the hallway before injecting Angie with three more rations of air, but, to his undying frustration, neither Angie nor her monitors showed any reaction.

What was he doing wrong, this time?

He pocketed the syringe and was heading over to check the hallway again when the door flew open, striking him on the forehead.

"Ow! What the hell?" Gabe staggered back as a perky young candy striper followed a food cart into the room.

"O-M-G!" The girl took in Gabe's police uniform. "I hit you, didn't I? I am so sorry. There was a mix-up with the food carts. The cook said this was supposed to be delivered like thirty minutes ago, so I rushed it right over."

Feeling the lump rise on his forehead, Gabe frowned down at the cart. "Meatloaf?" He swiveled his gaze back at Angie before cocking an eyebrow at the girl. "Did that cook also tell you to chew it and spit it down her feeding tube?"

Eying Angie's formidable setup, the girl gave her head a hard shake. "All he said was to bring it to room 327."

"This is 372."

"Crap!" She stumbled back into her cart.

"Yeah, crap. 327 is down the hall to your left." Fuming, he stood in the doorway watching the candy striper hustle back the way she'd come.

Enough of this.

He marched over to Angie and gave her another shot of air, but again, nothing happened. By this point, Gabe was through fooling around.

Damn it, I am going to keep doing this until she dies, or the needle breaks off in her arm, whichever comes first.

He selected a different injection spot a few inches over. When nothing happened, he did it again.

And again.

And again.

Was it the needle?

"Excuse me, sir."

Startled, Gabe almost dropped the syringe. Having remembered to keep his back to the door, he slipped the hypodermic up his sleeve, threw on his "Poor Angie" face, and turned. A slender male orderly stood in the doorway holding a stack of pale green linens.

"Sorry to interrupt. I'm here to change the sheets."

What was next? A marching band? Knowing it would look weird if he said no, Gabe waved the guy in and stepped outside. A few minutes later, he was back at Angie's side, needle in hand, but he hadn't even filled it with air when the door swung open. Again.

This time, it was a little Asian guy with a clipboard. "Hi, I'm supposed to take Mrs. Fox down for an EEG.

"Sure. Knock yourself out." Gabe stood against the wall, arms crossed, as the man got Angie ready to be wheeled out of the room. Once the creak of the bed's wheels faded in the distance, he pulled the syringe out of his sleeve and slipped the cap back into place. *Stupid movie.*

Chapter 52

JADE

EVEN IN SIX-INCH heels, Lexi's friend Jade was still shorter than many of her peers, a fact she was reminded of as she and her classmates made their way into the high school auditorium. Wondering if Kylie McKenna would have the guts to attend the memorial, Jade gripped her boyfriend, Jamari's arm for balance and gave a little hop to see past all the bodies. Impossible.

Although Jade would never say it to Eden's face, she considered her friend's six-feet-two-inches excessive. But today, Eden's height was a good thing, and Jade spotted her easily as Eden was being escorted to a seat directly in front of the stage. Having volunteered to speak, Eden had been allowed to leave her last class early to change clothes. The dark blue dress Jade had helped to pick out suited her friend and the occasion perfectly.

After a few hops and waves, Jade caught Eden's eye, but when she tried to join Eden, a stern head shake from her ceramics teacher, told Jade she wasn't going anywhere.

"Everyone stays with their class," Mr. Anderson told her. Grunting in frustration, Jade dropped her jacket on the seat she'd been assigned. It would have been nice to sit beside her friend, but at least Jamari was here. He was hot, and they *were* going to prom together.

Not ready to sit yet, she stood in front of her flip down chair and scanned the auditorium. "Jamari, did you see Kylie McKenna come in? I can't find her."

"Sit down!" a boy barked two rows back. Several others joined in, as well as Jamari and another member of her ceramics class, Luke Manetti, who she'd also ended up sitting beside. She ignored them all until her teacher, Mr. Anderson, called out from his spot three rows down. "Jade, you can either park it now, or come down here and sit next to me." He gestured at an empty seat beside him.

Ninety percent sure the man was gay, Jade grumbled, "bitch" under her breath and flopped into her chair. Up on the stage, Principal Peabody, dressed in a dark suit and tie, had just taken a seat beside Lexi's volleyball coach and some other equally well-dressed people, three fiftyish men and two women even older.

Jade waited until Mr. Anderson's focus had turned toward the stage, then knelt on her seat in order to see over the taller heads in front of her. She didn't find Kylie, but she did locate Lexi's family hunched in the front row. At the sight of Lexi's crying mother, a lump rose in Jade's throat. She turned her attention to the strangers on the stage. Who were they, school board members? Those old bastards definitely didn't know Lexi.

The big clock on the auditorium wall told her it was nearly two. Since school let out at two thirty, that left just thirty minutes to celebrate Lexi's life.

With a motorized hum, the newly installed projection screen scrolled down behind the folks seated on stage. Jade scanned the program she'd been handed at the door and found Lexi's memorial would begin with some sort of PowerPoint presentation. The room darkened and pictures of flowers and sunrays breaking through clouds flickered across the screen as the music teacher played "I Believe I Can Fly" on the piano.

Stupid song. Jade swallowed hard, forcing back the tears. When she was sure her voice wouldn't crack, she turned to Jamari and whispered, "Lexi hated that song."

Never much of a talker, he rolled his eyes and slumped further down in his seat. To her right, Luke was even less helpful. Sleeping? Really? She jammed him with her elbow. "So . . . where are *your* friends?"

"My friends?" Eyes wide, he sat up blinking, as if unsure how he'd gotten there. "Sitting with their own classes, I suppose."

She ignored his logic and plowed ahead. "But where's Kylie? I can't see her anywhere."

"That's because she's not here," Luke said through a yawn.

"Oh, really?" Before she could ask another question, the music stopped and Principal Peabody stepped to the microphone. She bumped Luke's leg with her own. "It's getting to her," she whispered. "All that guilt."

"Give it up, Jade." He closed his eyes and rested his head against the back of his seat. "Kylie doesn't feel guilty because she didn't *do* anything wrong. She went home this afternoon because Mr. Peabody asked her to. Smart, considering everything you and your buddies have been up to."

"Whatever." Kylie was such a little suck-up. It was no surprise she'd gotten Peabody on her side. Mrs. Sheraton too, since the PE teacher had given Eden and Jade two days of lunch detention. And for what? Trying to save their classmates from getting arrows through their heads? So unfair.

Finished with the boring introductions, Peabody finally called up the first speaker, a man about the age of Jade's dad. The program said he was Rabbi David Bitterman, but except for the little black beanie thingy on his head, he was dressed like all the other men on stage. Never having discussed religion with Lexi, it surprised Jade to learn she had been Jewish.

As the rabbi led the assembly in a generic prayer, Jade focused on the three-foot-high poster resting on the easel beside him. Lexi's graduation portrait. Jade had been with her the day it was taken. The poster showed a somber Lexi wearing a simple green dress and leaning against a huge redwood tree. Ironic, since the tree was probably less than a quarter mile from where Lexi's body had been found.

Jade looked back at Luke, now engrossed in some stupid cell phone game. She jabbed her elbow into his arm and giggled when the avatar on the screen flopped over dead. "What did you mean? How could it not be Kylie's fault? Lexi's dead, isn't she?"

He shot her a look as if she were retarded. "You don't seriously think Kylie's the one who killed Lexi?"

Before Jade could reply, Mr. Anderson twisted back in his seat, giving them an emotionless "Shut up or else" look. Unnerved by the man's continued stare, Jade returned her focus to the stage. Lexi's little brother, Jacob, was walking up the steps toward the podium, a sheet of binder paper clutched in his right hand.

Good for him. There was no way Jade could get up there. Just thinking about it rose a lump in her throat.

With Mr. Anderson's attention now on Jacob, Luke leaned closer, his hot breath battering Jade's ear. "I always thought you were a little slow, but if you think Kylie killed Lexi, you really *are* an idiot."

Had he really said that? "Screw you, Luke." She punched him in the shoulder, prompting a loud groan and raising giggles from those nearby. Of course, Mr. Anderson had to check what all the fuss was about. Thankfully, Luke wasn't a snitch, and all the teacher saw was a bunch of kids applauding the next speaker, Lexi's volleyball coach.

Satisfied Anderson had been properly conned, Jade grabbed Luke's neck and brought his ear closer. "Obviously, I don't believe Kylie's the killer. But it's definitely her fault Lexi's dead." She pressed her long nails into Luke's skin, and as he tried to pry her fingers away, Jamari leaned closer.

"What the hell is going on with you two?"

"Shut up. This is a private conversation." Jade spotted the detective woman who had interviewed her. "Look at that." She pointed her chin at the cop. "On TV, the detective always goes to the victim's funeral to see if somebody looks guilty. I bet she's looking for Kylie."

Since neither Luke nor Jamari took the bait, Jade focused back on the stage where Coach What's-Her-Face was reminiscing about Lexi's amazing athletic skills, racking up win after win for the good old orange and black.

Irked Lexi wasn't there to enjoy the praise, Jade turned back to Luke. "Look, fool. If it wasn't for Kylie moving in on Ryan, Lexi wouldn't have been given that detention. And if Lexi hadn't had to stay after, she wouldn't have had to walk home by herself." Her lips formed a bitter smile as she allowed the words to sink in. "See? Kylie *is* responsible. She needs to pay."

"I guess you forgot what you did to her in PE."

Her smile widened as she remembered Addison dragging Kylie away from the archery range in tears.

"Wasn't that enough, Jade? I guess it doesn't matter that Ryan broke up with Lexi long before he ever spoke to Kylie."

Why did Luke have to be so logical? "It's only fair," she muttered as Lexi's volleyball coach returned to her seat behind Principal Peabody.

"Oh, so now it's about what's fair," Luke whispered. "So, what do you think is fair, Jade? Are you going to kill Kylie and chop *her* hands off?"

"Jesus, I never said anything about killing her."

She shifted away from Luke and opened the program. All that was left was Eden reading her poem and the closing benedictions. They'd be dismissed, and everyone would forget about Lexi until the last week of school *if* they noticed her picture in their new yearbooks. After that, they might bring up her name on camping trips. At night. Sitting around the fire. Eventually, she'd just be that girl who got murdered back in senior year.

Jade pinched her eyes shut in frustration. One of her two best friends in the world was dead, and as far as she was concerned, it was Kylie's fault, but what could she do about it?

Jamari squeezed her hand, bringing her back to Earth. "Girl, you need to relax. How about we go down to the creek when this is over and spark one up?"

"Sure," she replied, not bothering to open her eyes. Even though relaxing was the last thing on Jade's mind, smoking weed was a good idea. She did her best scheming when she was high. She settled back in her chair, ready for Eden's speech.

Chapter 53

GABE

BUILT THE YEAR after Gabe graduated, the high school auditorium was a little worn around the edges, but still nicer than the local movie theater. The thick red velvet curtains had been pulled wide for the event. A battered podium stood in the center and behind it, several empty folding chairs. As assigned by Chief Fulton, Gabe stood near the steps leading up to the left side of the stage with Adrian Vega guarding access to the right. The place was filling up, and Peabody, that pudgy little principal fellow, stood alongside Gabe, nervously shifting his weight from one foot to the other.

"There's even more people here than for our *Cats* performance last year," Peabody said, his eyes flicked from the seats to the high windows on both sides. I hope it doesn't get too hot. There's no air conditioning, and people get irritable when they're too hot."

The man was right. Gabe eyed the constant stream of humanity pouring in through the main doors. "How about opening some of those windows?" He pointed at the pull-down things high above them.

Peabody dropped his arms. "I bet they're painted shut. I'll see what the janitor says."

Gabe smirked as Peabody snaked his way through the incoming crowd. Whatever the headcount, he doubted the auditorium could hold many more. Townspeople were already lining the walls, and the back of the room was ten deep, reminding him of the few times his mom had dragged the family to Christmas services. Just below the stage, a cluster of media folk had wedged themselves into the tiny orchestra pit. He counted reporters from three area newspapers and two television stations. Cameras too, with Gloria Gomez right in the thick of things.

Fire Marshal Burt Mendes sat in the main seating area, front row center. To the evident annoyance of his wife, Burt got up every minute or so to gaze around the room, his seventy-two-year-old face pinched up like a worried basset hound. Probably because the auditorium was at least a hundred souls over fire code. But who was going to tell those people to go home? Not Gabe, and from what he could tell, not Burt either.

Santos had mentioned something about the Spanish teacher's husband having a broken leg, so Gabe doubted that guy had shown. He spotted Lexi's mom and dad seated right behind Burt, and a few seats over, Darcy's friend, Monica Curtis, making him think the skinny old goat beside her might be Darcy's husband, Patrick. Humph, no wonder Darcy had needed banging that night.

The din created by so many people reminded Gabe of the football games he'd played in high school. When the rumble turned to grumble, he turned toward the stage. A handful of people were marching out from behind the red velvet curtains. In the lead, Chief Fulton got a decent amount of applause, as did the mayor. But it wasn't until the two FBI agents appeared that the place really shook.

Gabe turned back to the audience, a sea of familiar faces. Their emotions, which were almost palpable, ranging from anger to relief with everything else in between. Most of them were parents, people he'd gone to school with, and every one of them was worried that either they, or worse, their child, might become the next victim of the new local boogeyman, The Taker. Yes indeed, that nutjob might very well be seated there with them.

IZZY

SEATED ON THE stage between Principal Peabody and Agent Kawata, Izzy looked out over the crowd, worried about how unrealistic her fellow townspeople's expectations had become. Many thought the FBI's arrival meant The Taker was as good as caught. The idea was comforting, but also naïve. There were plenty of active serial killers running loose in the country, a fact that, if advertised, would cause those same locals to barricade their doors and order all their groceries through Instacart.

"Here we go," Fulton murmured.

He stepped up to the podium. Along with the school's microphone, each of the TV crews had added one of their own, giving the tall skinny piece of furniture an imposing presidential look. After another round of applause and a few scattered boos, a tide of anxious silence spread toward them from the back of the room as Fulton slipped on his reading glasses. He unfolded a sheet of lined paper and began by offering condolences to the families of the victims.

"To assist us in bringing their killer to justice," Fulton continued, "we are fortunate to have obtained the services of the Federal Bureau of

Investigation. Here with us today are Special Agents, Darrell Starling and Nancy Kawata."

With the mention of each name, the agents stood up and acknowledged the crowd's enthusiasm with somber nods, maintaining the professional bearing fitting the occasion. Agent Kawata traded places with Fulton. Shoulders back, she lowered the microphone with a look of quiet confidence. "Thank you, Chief Fulton." She scanned the audience, which had quickly quieted. "We realize that the people of Rocky Harbor have been suffering these last few weeks. We also know you want answers."

A murmur swept through the crowd.

"As you might imagine, it's a challenge to determine what information should and should not be released."

Yeah, yeah, Izzy thought as Kawata prattled on. How many times had the agent spoken those same words? Did everything blend together for people like her? The towns? The bodies? The grieving relatives?

"Skip the salad and get to the steak!" a man shouted.

The exclamation inspired both laughter and more grumbling, but Kawata plowed on, her raised voice overpowering their impatience. "Yes, we get it. But I can't stress enough how important it is that the investigators not tip their hand."

The crowd seemed to understand and quieted.

"Sadly"—Kawata lowered her voice—"those efforts have been hampered by certain media personalities who have circumvented the process."

Although no names were mentioned, Izzy, and probably everyone else within eyeshot, turned their attention to the orchestra pit to see how Gloria Gomez would respond, but the woman didn't flinch. Eyes glued to the laptop computer in front of her, only her fingers moved as they danced across the keyboard.

"Furthermore . . ." Kawata continued.

GABE

"SO, DO YOU have a suspect or not?" an angry female shouted. Several others echoed her question. In moments, the auditorium was like a giant hive buzzing with angry bees. Gabe looked across the room at Vega, who acknowledged his concern with raised eyebrows.

Kawata took a deep breath and lifted both hands in a lets-keep-it-down gesture, and for the moment, it worked. "At this point, we still don't have any—"

"Sounds like you're all chasing your own tails!" Darcy's prune-faced husband shouted.

An echo of agreement surged through the masses, which Kawata ignored. "That's not to say there are no persons of interest. We have several leads, but if our investigation is to be successful, that information must remain confidential."

Leads? That was new. Were these FBI people keeping secrets, or just serving up bullshit to calm a surly crowd?

"An area of great concern is the amount of rumors that are being spread here in Rocky Harbor. Fake news, we can't simply blame on journalists." Agent Kawata looked back at Agent Starling, who nodded, as if giving her permission to continue. "We believe the suspect is a white male, reasonably attractive, and somewhere between the ages of twenty and forty years old. We also believe he's local, intelligent, and well organized."

"That's it?" Andy Perski hollered, owner of two of the town's three gas stations. "Twenty to forty? That's half the guys in the county!"

Kawata leaned into the microphone. "I apologize, but that's all the information we can release right now."

Annie Stanton, Kirby's Coffee Hut waitress and mother of five, was chugging up the center walkway toward the stage, her bleached ponytail flapping. Gabe tried but failed to hold back a smirk. Annie never knew when to shut up back in high school, and apparently, she still didn't.

"How am I supposed to keep my kids safe if you people can't even tell me what the guy looks like?" Annie bellowed.

Worried the linebacker-sized woman might charge the stage, Gabe raised one arm, blocking her progress. "That's close enough, Annie."

Scowling, Annie stayed put. A relief to Gabe since his bucket list didn't include hugging a woman who looked like she was hiding a half-dozen bicycle tires under her blouse. But the entire assembly had risen in support, and the TV cameras had already turned to watch.

Gabe shot a look over at Vega, who shrugged as if to say, "Better you than me."

Annie seemed to blossom with the media attention. She pointed a pudgy finger at Gabe's nose. "Funny *you're* here, because I heard it's *your* daughter who's been doing all the killing!"

The crowd roared, reminding Gabe of every gladiator movie he'd ever seen.

Gabe lowered his face to hers. "Annie, are you nuts? Who—?"

"Mrs. Stanton!" The chief used her last name, even though she'd been filling his coffee cup down at Kirby's for the last dozen years. "I understand your frustration."

Fed by the crowd, Annie's cantaloupe-sized breasts heaved as she split her attention between the chief and Gabe. "How come his girl hasn't even been questioned? Huh? Why not?"

"She has, Annie." Fulton stepped to the edge of the stage above near where Gabe and Annie stood him. "Just like everybody else who knew the victims."

"Stop the cover-up!" a man in the back shouted. The crowd picked up the chant, rattling the painted-shut windows as they pounded their feet to the beat.

"It's a coverup *and* a conspiracy!" Annie shouted.

"Oh, come on," Gabe said, trying not to laugh. "Annie . . ."

"Enough!" Fulton moved to the front of the stage, arms raised. "Everybody quiet down!"

Annie had done a great job of rousing the crowd, making Gabe wonder if a modern-day lynch mob was in the making. But Fulton had his own skills, and for the moment, the look of determination on his face stalled the rebellion. Instead of heading back to the podium, he stayed where he was and pulled out a slice of Juicy Fruit which he calmly unwrapped and tucked into his mouth. Hands on hips, he stood there chewing until every voice was silent. "Now, most of you have known me your whole lives. And hopefully, you consider me a straight shooter." He scanned the audience as if daring anyone to say otherwise. "I don't know what you've heard, but I promise you the department has treated Kylie McKenna like any other person of interest. If there was evidence against her, we would act on it. But there isn't any." He scanned the crowd with a stern gaze. "So, let's stop accusing innocent kids, shall we?"

A far cry from the heated mob it had just been, the crowd grumbled their response.

"Good." Fulton nodded sharply. "And when we have a *real* suspect, we'll announce it. No matter who they are."

Gabe marveled at the man's control.

"These past weeks have been scary for everyone," Fulton continued. "Me included. But there are things we can do."

Once rebellious faces turned up to him, eager for guidance, and as Fulton spoke, Annie blessed Gabe with an eye roll worthy of any teenage girl, but he paid her no mind and kept his arm raised, forcing the woman to stand on tiptoes to see over it.

"Keep your kids in at night," Fulton continued. "Make sure they walk to school with a friend, better yet, two friends. And for gosh sake, keep your doors and windows locked."

Wow, Gabe thought. He's sure got this bunch where he wants them.

"And the same goes for the grownups," Fulton added. "Until this thing is over, don't go out walking by yourself—especially to someplace isolated. With any luck, whoever is doing this will make a mistake, and Rocky Harbor can get back to being the normal, safe town it's always been."

All good stuff, but for The Taker to make that mistake, he'd have to strike again, wouldn't he?

Chapter 54

IZZY

FINALLY, THE DAY had come. Maggie had been discharged from the hospital and was keen to get going.

"Are you sure everything has been taken care of?" she asked Izzy.

"Yes, Tita. As soon as the nurse brings you a wheelchair, we're out of here."

Eager to leave her hospital gown behind, Maggie had instructed Fulton to bring her not just a tee shirt but also a pair of skinny jeans. With the help of Izzy and two nurses, they got Maggie into her jeans, then slipped the big leg brace over the top and adjusted all the Velcro straps. All packed and dressed, she lay on the bed, staring at the ceiling.

"What's Sean doing?" she asked.

"Fulton?" Izzy chuckled. "He's pacing up and down the hallway, just like you'd be if you didn't have that big brace on your leg."

"If I didn't have this brace, I wouldn't be in this hospital." She raised up on her elbows, giving Izzy a clear view of the *Real Men Love Cats* tee shirt Fulton had surprised her with that morning. "How long does it take to find a wheelchair, anyway? I'd like to get home before my pain meds wear off."

"Relax," Izzy told her. "The nurse barely left five minutes ago."

With the hospital room door wide open, the sound of approaching voices drew their attention. Fulton stepped into the room.

"Hey, look who I just ran into," he told Maggie.

Behind Fulton stood Gabe Fox. Although sharp as always in his black uniform, the man looked a bit tense as he waved at Maggie from the doorway. "Hey . . . I hear you're going home. Congratulations." He nodded to Izzy.

"Yes, finally." Maggie beamed. "I've been lying in this bed for nearly . . . oh. I'm so sorry. Here I am complaining and you with your wife still . . ." She winced. "Has there been *any* sign of improvement?"

"No, ma'am, but Angie will come around, eventually. I love that woman to death, but punctuality has never been her strongpoint. Oh, hey." Fox seemed to remember the decorative tin in his hands. "I didn't know what she'd like."

He shifted from one foot to the other as he passed the tin to Fulton. "Ma'am? Do you like coffee cake?"

"Certainly. Oh, isn't that nice." Maggie raised her arms to him. "Come here. You deserve a hug."

"Better not." Fox tapped his chest. "I think I'm coming down with something, so . . ." He looked to his right and grinned. "Hey, here comes your wheelchair." Taking that as his cue, Fox said his goodbyes and left.

Following the nurse's instructions, Fulton picked up the house plant a friend had dropped off, grabbed Maggie's overnight bag, and a bouquet of Get Well Soon balloons and dashed downstairs to bring the car up. Izzy collected an armload of magazines and flowers, and when the nurse delivered Maggie to the loading zone, Fulton was already there to greet them with the car's passenger door open wide. With some helpful suggestions from the nurse, they stowed Maggie's things and maneuvered her into the passenger seat.

"That's fine," Maggie huffed as Izzy reclined the seat for her. "Just take me home. I'm worried about my Diego."

"I'd worry about that cat too," Izzy teased. "Fulton's been feeding him ice cream for dinner."

"¡Ay, Dios! Really, *hija*?"

"He ate a whole cupful the last time I was over," Izzy teased. Smirking, she helped Maggie with her seatbelt as Fulton reached for his own.

"Diego weighs thirty pounds now," Fulton added and slid behind the wheel.

"At least, that." Izzy climbed into the back seat. "If he could talk, he'd say, 'Maggie who?'"

"Oh, you two." Maggie closed her eyes. "*Bueno*, take me to him."

"You don't have to tell me twice," Fulton said.

In a few moments the Nissan was headed for Blackberry Lane, the private road leading to the riverside property he and Maggie had moved onto only a few months past.

"Poor Officer Fox." Maggie's voice was wistful. "You know, he caught a shoplifter for me a couple of years ago."

"The big guy who stuck the fish sculpture down his pants?" Izzy asked. "Fox arrested *him*?"

Maggie chuckled. "He sure did. I hope Officer Fox doesn't think badly of me after that thoughtless comment I made."

"I wouldn't worry about it," Fulton said. "What happened to that guy's wife is terrible, but I doubt he expects the rest of the world to suffer along with him."

Izzy thought back on Fox's brief visit. Was he really getting sick, or had he refused the hug because he'd heard about Maggie's powers? Having stopped at a light, Fulton glanced over his shoulder at Izzy. "Speaking of Fox, the guy sure seems to attract trouble these days, doesn't he?"

"I know, right? Bad enough that his wife's in a coma, but that stuff they're saying about their girl. You've known her longer than me. Do you think she's capable?"

"I suppose that's possible with Lexi and the teacher, but—"

"Sorry to interrupt." Maggie touched Fulton's arm. "But would you pull in there, please?" They were approaching Dawnview Estates, and Maggie motioned at the dirt-caked entrance road.

"There?" Fulton asked. "But that's where we—"

"—found that poor girl's body. Yes, I know."

"Then, why go in there?"

"*Por favor, cariño*. Humor me."

Spanish. Along with Maggie's adorable accent, it was Fulton's kryptonite. Izzy chuckled as he slowed and guided the Nissan off the main road. Although recently paved, the streets were more brown than black, due to all the rain and police activity.

Curious what Maggie was up to, Izzy sat forward, her gaze swiveling from one side of the street to the other. Why would Lexi come here alone? And if she was killed somewhere else, why dispose of her body here?

"There." Maggie pointed. "Stop there."

Fulton rolled over a muddy strip of police tape lying in the street and pulled to a stop behind a dumpster overflowing with soggy carpet scraps.

"Okay, Señorita Margarita. What are we doing here?"

Maggie's eyes flashed with annoyance. Then, she winced. "Looking for evidence?"

"Seriously?" Izzy said.

"To be honest, I just felt the need to see this place."

Not sure what to think, Izzy looked out the window. The house they'd found Lexi's body behind showed no modifications. Were the employees too superstitious to work there? "Sooo, do you want us to get out or something?"

"Please," Maggie said. She rolled down her window as Izzy and Fulton climbed out. Following Maggie's request, they ambled around the car to Maggie's now open window. She pointed. "You found the body behind that house there."

Izzy nodded. "Don't tell me. You know because Lexi's ghost is standing on the front porch."

"No, smarty pants. Because of the police tape. Most of it is still hanging there."

"So, there's no ghost?" Fulton asked.

"None that I can see. I just . . ." Maggie slumped down in her seat. "Please . . . look around, would you? I'd do it myself, but as you can see . . ."

Izzy shared a look with Fulton and shrugged. She trusted her aunt, but what could they possibly find now that a dozen police officers hadn't? Hoping for the best, she turned a slow circle, in an effort to see the place with fresh eyes. Two more foundations had recently been poured, their wooden frames still in place.

"I thought I'd sense more once we got closer," Maggie said. "But here we are, and I don't feel anything. Maybe if I walked around a little." She opened the car door. "Izzy would you help me, please?"

"Tita, no." Izzy ran over. "It's too muddy to use your crutches here. You could fall. Fulton, I think it's time we head home." She looked around. "Fulton?" Her pulse raced. Where'd he go? He was right there a second ago. "Fulton!"

"What?" His head popped up from behind the dumpster. "Geez, I'm right here."

Izzy raced over. "What the hell, boss. Why didn't you answer me? I thought—"

"You thought The Taker got me? Ha! Good one. I was just looking at this." He dropped a sludge covered object into Izzy's palm.

She rubbed her thumb across it, removing some of the mud. "This isn't evidence."

"But it's a button. If Lexi struggled, she might have pulled it off the killer's shirt."

"Not possible."

Fulton frowned. "Don't tell me you've got psychic powers too."

"No." Izzy pulled a scrap of carpeting from the dumpster and wiped the button off with it. "See? This button came off a cop's shirt."

Fulton held the button up to the light. "Damn it, you're right."

"Yeah, and there were probably a dozen cops out here wearing shirts with those same buttons."

"Sean!" Maggie shouted through the open window. "Whatever you found, please bring it to me."

Fulton strode to the car and placed the button on Maggie's open hand, which she closed over the thing.

"Anything?" Izzy asked.

"Anger . . . fear . . . jealousy. About what, I don't know." She opened her hand.

With a nod, Fulton took the button and tossed it over his shoulder. "Home?"

"Yes, and I'm sorry for wasting your time," Maggie said.

Izzy climbed into the back seat, and Fulton walked around the car, but as he opened the driver's side door, he froze.

"Something wrong?" Izzy asked.

"Depends."

Chapter 55

GABE

GABE STOOD IN front of the large bulletin board with its growing array of crime scene photos. For the last five days, the ones taken at Stafford park had been the most recent, but this morning, they'd found Darcy's car. Arms crossed, he studied each of these new images, basically, four angles of the same blackened husk.

He'd done an excellent job of destroying evidence, and these new pictures proved it. Fire had destroyed most of Darcy's hands, eliminating all remnants of her fingernails and Gabe's DNA beneath it. Like the few charred bones that remained, they found nothing helpful in Darcy's Audi. And as for the bedding and towels, a combination of heat, smoke, and fumes had destroyed any possibility of getting useful DNA from the tiny scraps that hadn't burned to ashes. The same went for the vacuum cleaner, probably because of Gabe's generosity with the gasoline.

With no new leads, Agents Starling and Kawata had said their goodbyes and had flown back to Quantico, and as far as Gabe was concerned, they could stay there.

He studied the photos of Darcy's bathroom then moved on to the ones of Lexi Siegel and Rosa Del Campo. Like every day since they discovered Lexi's body, Gabe asked himself the same questions? Who was The Taker, and what was their game plan, because he wasn't trying to pin the killings on Gabe—or at least, Santos wasn't acting weird around him. But she wouldn't, would she? Not until she'd gathered enough evidence. And what was with that Spanish aunt of hers? If he believed the chatter around the station, Maggie Fulton was a witch who could tell what a man had done just by touching him. And not just people. Things too. He cursed under his breath, worried Santos hadn't believed his off-the-cuff justification for turning down Maggie's thank-you hug when he'd re-gifted that home-made banana walnut cake some moron had left for Angie yesterday. Seriously? Coma patients can't eat cake.

Oh, well. At least Angie was cooperating. Off her coma meds for nearly a week, the woman was still as lifeless as a sofa cushion, and her doctor didn't expect things to change. Gabe had kept that happy news from the kids, but according to her surgeon, Dr. Jennings, if Angie was going to rally, she'd have done it by now.

But.

There was still a chance. So, if he was going to get himself to Mexico, and from there, Belize, it was time to get going on that life insurance. Should he do both kids at once? More money was definitely a talking point, but wouldn't it draw suspicion? And how would he kill them? Cutting the Honda's brake line? Why bother? The insurance company would figure it out. They always did.

Maybe he could fake Kylie's suicide. The girl had been under a lot of stress lately.

Oh, yeah. Insurance companies don't cover suicides.

Gabe flopped into one of the conference room's many empty chairs, annoyed by his own stupidity. But what if they both overdosed . . . like accidentally? People died from Fentanyl all the time, but would anyone believe the kids had taken the stuff voluntarily? Still mulling his options, he rose and turned. There stood Izzy Santos.

"Hungry?" Santos held up a half-eaten maple bar. "Donut Barn just sent a whole box over." Smiling, she waved him over to the coffee table and flipped open the lid of a pink card stock box. "See? Must be three dozen in here."

Looking like the last thing on her mind was arresting Gabe, Santos munched her maple bar as Gabe selected an apple fritter.

"Let's go into my office," she said. "There's something I'd like to discuss with you."

Holy cow, was this it? Gabe tried not to show his alarm as Izzy held her office door open for him. Once inside, they sat down, Santos on one side of her desk, Gabe on the other. Stacked in the center of the desk were three file folders. He couldn't make out the names on the tabs, but he could guess what they were.

Elbows on her desk and still smiling, Santos rested her chin on the heel of one hand. "So, you've been keeping up with the killings?"

"Easy enough. The CSI folks didn't find a thing on the Callahan car."

"Yeah, but you've watched the news . . . heard how Gloria Gomez is still making us look like a bunch of inept hicks?"

"Sure, but what can we do?" He took a bite of his fritter and chewed slowly, hoping to appear nonchalant. "Even those two FBI agents got bored."

Nodding absently, Santos flicked the edge of the top file with her finger. "I spoke to Fulton, and there's something we need you to do for us."

The vein in his left temple started pulsing as it always did when he was stressed. "Sure." He smiled. "Anything to find the killer."

"I appreciate that, because this needs to happen. Some might even say it's overdue."

Had Andrea Muncy turned up something new? Nah. If she had, he and Santos sure as hell wouldn't be here eating pastries. So, what was Santos up to?

They munched away in silence. Finally, Santos stuck the last remnant of maple bar into her mouth and chewed it thoroughly, as if putting off something distasteful. Eventually, she swallowed, then licked her fingers. "I need you to bring Kylie in for questioning."

Gabe barked a relieved laugh. "What the hell for?"

"Honestly, it's politics. You saw what happened at the town meeting. The public needs to know we aren't playing favorites."

"Did this come from the chief or the FBI?"

"Does it matter? The fact is, a lot of people think Kylie's involved."

"Yeah, like the parents over at Center Elementary who forced the principal to fire Kylie from her volunteer job there. They were afraid she might strangle their kid with a jump rope or something."

"See? That's what I'm talking about."

Now that Gabe knew Santos didn't suspect him, the vein stopped its pulsing. "Oh, come on." He sat forward, ready to feebly defend his stepdaughter. "Kylie's just not the killing type."

"I won't argue that, but you know the old saying. The squeaky wheel gets the grease. A lot of folks have been squeaking, Gabe, and—stupid or not—the chief can't have folks think we're playing favorites. Plus, you probably never realized this, but Kylie is probably the only person in town with connections to every single victim."

Faking his indignation, Gabe crossed his arms over his chest and sat back to consider what he'd been told. Okay, so Kylie knew all three, but could the FBI really pin these killings on *her*? He would continue with the shock and bluster, but no way would he disrupt an investigation that took the focus away from himself.

"I don't know," Gabe said, milking it. "If you call her in, people will think it's because you've found something to prove her guilty. Hell, the day she and her friends went shopping at the Dalton Mall for prom dresses they overheard some old biddies talking about how if her dad wasn't a cop, she'd already be locked up."

"You're just proving my point."

That's why he said it. Gabe heaved a frustrated sigh. "If they knew Kylie, they'd know it was crazy." Hoping to look like a good dad but not sound too convincing, he added, "You know, these rumors were all started by Lexi

Siegel's friends. And they haven't stopped messing with Kylie, either. When she was paying for her prom dress, she spotted two of those girls hiding behind a rack of clothes, watching her."

"That's why Kylie needs to come in. I ask her a few questions, she goes home, folks hear we let her go, they say, 'Okay, so it wasn't her.'"

"Or, they just keep believing there's a coverup."

Santos tipped her head from side to side. "Yeah, I suppose that's possible, but I still need you to bring her in." Finished with her maple bar and apparently, the conversation, Izzy stood and looked Gabe straight in the eyes, then opened the office door. "How about noon tomorrow?"

For such a cute little thing, Santos had a real icy stare. "Okay, she'll be here." Gabe stood. "But you do know tomorrow night's prom?"

Chapter 56

IZZY

WITH MAGGIE STILL struggling with her crutches, Fulton was nervous about leaving her alone, so Izzy was more than surprised when he showed up an hour before Kylie was scheduled to be interviewed.

"Oh, my gosh. I can't believe you're here." Izzy resisted the impulse to jump up and hug him, sticking to their agreement to keep their interactions professional in the office.

"Maggie's at the physical therapist," Fulton said, chuckling. "I wanted to stay with her, but she insisted I drop her off."

Izzy took in Fulton's jeans, sneakers, and paint-spattered sweatshirt. "I assume you're not staying for the interview?"

"No, no. There's something I need to share with you, and Maggie thought I should do it in person." He dropped into one of the chairs across from Izzy's desk and rested his right ankle on his left knee. "Have you looked at those articles Agent Kawata sent us?"

"I have." Izzy already had the folder in front of her. She sat down and flipped it open. "Apparently, there's no common profile for serial killers. No single cause, no single motive, no single profile. Most offenders are loners, but others have full-time jobs and families."

"Sounds right," Fulton said. "Anything stick out?"

Izzy didn't have to think. "Women. They only make up ten percent of the total serial killer population."

"And?"

"Well, at first, I thought that made it very unlikely for us to have one here in Rocky Harbor. But now . . . I'm not so sure."

"Oh? Why's that?"

"Motivation." Izzy sat back. "I mean men usually kill because they get off on it, but for women, the motive is usually revenge. Someone wronged them and they want paybacks."

"Exactly." Fulton offered a stick of Juicy Fruit to Izzy, then took one for himself. "And you're thinking Kylie fits right into that description because all three of those dead women had wronged her in one way or another."

"I do—not that their punishments matched their crimes." Izzy frowned. "Wait a minute. You said all *three*."

Fulton smiled. "That's what I wanted to tell you. Ever heard a name but couldn't place where you'd heard it before?"

"Yeah, like an itch you can't scratch."

"Right, well, I've been trying to scratch that itch for nearly two weeks, and as I was reading through your interview notes, I finally did." Fulton's smile was not a happy one. "About ten years ago, there were rumors going around that Gabe Fox was having an affair. At first, that was all anyone in the station could talk about, but after a week or so, Gabe and Angie were still together, and our fellow officers had moved on to some new scandal. In fact, I forgot all about that mess until today."

Izzy shook her head. "And?"

"The reason I couldn't place the name was because it was different when she was having her little fling with Fox. Back then, her last name was Prescott."

"Holy . . ."

"And guess where she and her first husband, Ronny used to live."

"Where?"

"Right next door to Gabe and Angie Fox."

HAVING COMPLETELY BLOWN her mind, Fulton left Izzy seated quietly behind her desk, thinking. Gabe Fox had sworn he didn't know Darcy Callahan was his old flame, and that made sense. Not only had her last name changed, but with all the chemical burns, her body was unrecognizable. Of course, once he did figure it out, he'd kept his mouth shut. But that seemed more like the actions of a guy protecting his reputation than those of a killer.

Kylie seemed surprised about the affair, but she could be lying. If so, she might consider Darcy responsible for nearly destroying her family. There was her motive.

Izzy opened her notebook and read one of the quotes she had highlighted out loud, "Revenge is an excellent motivator for people with mental disorders." *Did* Kylie have a mental disorder? Izzy didn't think so, but she also wasn't a psychiatrist.

Although Fulton had expressed his confidence in her before he left, Izzy didn't share it. Of course, she'd researched plenty of serial killers, but she'd only spoken to one. At the time, she thought Dylan Coates was just a shy nineteen-year-old gardener concerned for the welfare of his clients' missing daughter.

Izzy couldn't help but shudder. What if Kylie had similar acting skills?

At the sound of three quick raps, Izzy looked up at the wood-framed smoked-glass door. She recognized the broad-shouldered silhouette of Gabe

Fox immediately. Hoping Kylie was right behind him, she tucked the papers into their folder and stood. She'd always liked Kylie, but a lot of people had felt the same about Ted Bundy, hadn't they?

Shoulders back, she stood. "Come in."

The door swung open. There stood Fox, and beside him, Kylie, barely two inches taller than her own five-feet-one. The only person Izzy didn't see was a lawyer.

"Sorry to put you guys through this today." Hoping her smile was pleasant, she waved them into her office. "Have a seat." Izzy settled into her own chair, then quickly sprang back up. "Oh, can I get you anything? Water . . . ? A soda?" They shook their heads, and she sat back down, fingers laced in front of her. "So, your prom is tonight, huh?"

Fox grunted. "It is, so let's get to it. Kylie needs time to get herself ready."

Attitude but no lawyer. Interesting. Izzy locked eyes with Fox. "As a policeman yourself, you know I couldn't avoid this. Your stepdaughter is connected to all three victims. If you know anyone else who fits that bill, give me their name, and I'll interview them too." Afraid she may have come off too strong, Izzy shifted gears and smiled at Kylie. "So, ready to answer a few more questions?"

Kylie shrugged. "Ask whatever you like."

"Thank you, and don't worry. I'll have you out of here in plenty of time." Izzy pulled a pen and legal sized pad from her drawer and flipped to the list of questions she and Fulton had come up with. "So, how long have you known Lexi Siegel?"

Kylie blew out a long thoughtful breath. "Since fifth grade, I guess."

"Were you two ever close?"

"Not really. We were in the same classes, sometimes, but she had her own friends."

Nodding, Izzy scribbled some words on the blank lines she'd left between the questions. "Okay, now tell me about the conversation you had with Lexi back on . . ." She opened the folder and scanned the top page. "March tenth."

"You mean the day she threatened me and hit me with a volleyball?"

"Yeah, tell me about that."

"There's not much to say." Kylie sat forward. "I was in the girls' locker room dressing for PE when Lexi came up to me. Jade and Eden were right behind her, and they sort of cornered me. I didn't know what their plan was, so I was scared, especially when Lexi got all up in my face. She said something like, 'Stay away from Ryan . . . or else.'" Eyes moist, Kylie sat back, her arms crossed high over her chest. "Not that she had any right, because Ryan broke up with her like two weeks earlier."

"So, you figured you could see him if you wanted to."

"Well, at that time, it was just for math tutoring, so, yeah. A few minutes later, she slammed a ball into my head."

Izzy frowned. "Sounds embarrassing *and* painful."

"Sure was. Everyone was laughing, plus I almost got a concussion."

She gazed into Kylie's soft green eyes, remembering all the articles she'd read in the last few days. The girl had motive, and she was probably strong enough, but damn it, Kylie just didn't look like a killer—of course, neither had Althea Mikos, the subject of one of Agent Kawata's articles. Three years younger than Kylie and quiet as a dead mouse, the bashful Greek girl had stabbed three neighbor kids to death for teasing her about her cleft lip.

Izzy refocused and jotted down Kylie's last answer. "And when did you last see Lexi?"

"That was it. She hit me with the ball, and Addison took me to the nurse's office."

"You'll be happy to know that Addison's story syncs with yours."

Kylie nodded, and for a while, they sat in silence as Izzy wrote.

"As I recall, your stepdad picked you up early from school that day," Izzy said.

"That's right."

"And you stayed home the rest of the afternoon with your brother?"

"Yeah, you asked me that in your first interview."

Fox took Kylie's hand. "Don't take it personally, kiddo. She's just doing her job."

"He's right," Izzy said. Then, why did she feel like such a jerk? Because she didn't think Robby had lied about Kylie staying home that afternoon?

She glanced down at the next question on her list. "What about Rosa Del Campo? She was your Spanish teacher, right?"

"You know she was."

Izzy noted the defensiveness in Kylie's voice. "Tell me about the exchange you two had outside the classroom. I hear you got pretty upset."

Kylie looked at Fox, who waved his hand.

"Go ahead," he told her. "You've got nothing to hide."

"Okay," A bit of color rose in Kylie's cheeks as she turned back to Izzy. "It all started when I got a D on this really important test. I asked Mrs. Del Campo for extra credit assignments, and she said yes. But she also told me that no matter how much work I completed, my final grade would never be higher than a B—and before you say it, I know. A B isn't a bad grade, but it did blow my chance of getting the type of scholarship I want."

"And that's why you went off on Mrs. Del Campo?"

"Yeah, she said I should have studied harder, but I did. I studied a ton. I'm just terrible at foreign languages."

"I can understand why you were so frustrated."

"Yeah, I was angry." Kylie sat forward. "But not anymore."

"Because Mrs. Del Campo got what she deserved?"

"No, nobody deserves that." Kylie looked a little hurt. "I'm not mad because Addison and Ryan told me that if I chose a state college, we could all be together next year."

"I see." If Kylie believed Rosa Del Campo had ruined her life, she may have told her friends what they wanted to hear, all the while, planning her vengeance on the woman.

Another topic she and Fulton had discussed was the possibility that Kylie hadn't been working alone. "Remember that button I found at Lexi's crime scene?" Fulton had asked her. "It could have fallen off Fox's shirt."

Izzy agreed it was possible, but even if that was true, it didn't mean he'd killed Lexi or assisted in any way. As she'd expected, Fulton agreed. "The possibility of a family coverup is a little farfetched, but since we don't have anything else to go on, keep it in mind. And I'm not just talking Kylie and her stepdad, but the brother, too. Even if it was just giving his sister an alibi."

Freshly reminded of Fulton's family revenge theory, Izzy moved on to her next question. "Mrs. Del Campo was killed around seven o'clock that night. Do you remember where you were then?"

"At seven?" Kylie uncrossed her arms. "That was the night I worked at the library from six until eight," she said, sounding more confident. "Ryan met me for math tutoring after."

Gabe tapped Izzy's desk with his finger. "See, she has an alibi."

It was possible. Hopefully, also true. "I'm sure lots of people saw you there that night?"

"Some. It was a Tuesday."

"The library is only a few blocks from Stafford Park, isn't that right, Gabe?"

"Yeah, so?"

"So, it might be possible for someone to slip out a side door and head on over there . . . if they had planned it all out in advance." Or, if Fox did it himself. He was first on the scene, after all.

"Seriously?" Tears welled in Kylie's eyes. "You-you think I . . . that's ridiculous."

"This is all speculation." Gabe scowled. "You've got no evidence."

Fox was right. The last thing Izzy wanted was to railroad an innocent girl, but she had to be sure. "Folks have been convicted for less."

"Yeah, yeah, but unless you plan on arresting Kylie now, we're leaving." Fox started to get up.

"Please"—Izzy motioned for Fox to sit—"stay for just a few more questions."

Kylie grabbed Fox's arm. Like Izzy, he seemed surprised by her sudden burst of assertiveness. Fox sat back down.

"Ask me whatever you want," Kylie told Izzy.

"Okay." She pulled out the notes Fulton had given her and read the first question. "Kylie, aren't you wondering why I just skipped over Darcy Callahan?"

Kylie looked puzzled, but from the way Fox's eyes narrowed, he probably guessed where Izzy was going. Kylie also saw her stepdad's change. She looked warily at Fox, then back at Izzy. "Okay, why?"

"Darcy was good friends with your mom back when you and Robby were little, wasn't she?" Izzy asked. "In fact, she spent a lot of time at your place, babysitting you and your brother."

"Exactly, so why would I want to kill her? I loved Darcy."

Now came the hard part.

"I bet you were shocked when she and her husband suddenly split up and moved away."

With Fox avoiding all eye contact, Izzy plowed on. "How old were you when this went down, Kylie? Eight? Do you remember how your folks were getting along at that time? Maybe Gabe wasn't coming home when he should?"

Fox glared. "Damn it, Santos. You have no right to bring this up now."

Kylie looked up from her clasped hands. "W-wait, a-are you saying Gabe and Darcy—?"

Izzy put her pen down. "Do you remember your folks arguing a lot, maybe about something to do with Darcy and your dad?"

From the look on her face, Kylie did. She pressed her fingertips to her now closed eyes. "Gabe, please tell me that's not why Darcy took off the way she did."

"Are you saying you had no idea your dad caused Darcy's marriage to break up?" Izzy asked. "Half the town knew about it."

As if seeing him for the first time, Kylie stared at Fox, her soft green eyes overflowing with tears. If Kylie was faking, she was awfully good at it.

Exposed, Fox's jaw sagged open. "Kylie, I—"

"You . . . and *Darcy*?" She turned from Fox and plucked a tissue from the box Izzy had slid across the desk to her. "Okay, Detective. What are you implying? That my folks weren't getting along, and *that* caused Gabe to have an affair with Darcy, or they weren't getting along because he *was* having an affair with Darcy?"

"What do you remember?"

Dabbing her cheeks with tissue, Kylie sat back. "You know . . ."

The sudden edge in her voice surprised Izzy.

"I think I must have blocked that from my memory, but now that you mention it . . ." She shifted and looked at Fox head on. "*That's* why Mom quit her job, isn't it? She didn't trust you."

"Kylie"—Fox looked whipped—"that was years ago. You've seen your mom and me these last few months. Things have been good between us."

Not sure who, if any, was acting, Izzy pressed on. "That's a very good reason to be angry."

Kylie groaned. "Oh, I get it. You think I killed Darcy because she tried to break up my family. Then, why didn't I kill Gabe, too?"

"Yeah." Fox stared Izzy down. "Why am I still standing? And why wait ten years?"

"She was only eight when you had your affair. Kids block things they don't like thinking about. Kylie could have spotted her in the mall one day, and it all came flooding back. Or, Lexi found out and decided to rub it in Kylie's face. She didn't kill you because you're family. But Darcy wasn't family."

"That's stupid, I-I'm not a killer!" Face contorted, Kylie hugged herself, a silver locket clutched in her fist.

Izzy had seen that locket before. Kylie's mother had worn it to Chief Garver's retirement party last year, and soon after to Fulton's promotion ceremony when he became chief. And hadn't all these killings happened *after* Angie fell? Maybe the accident put Kylie over the edge. She would run it past the department's psychiatrist. But why cut off their hands?

In an effort to calm Kylie down, Izzy sat back and sighed. "Yeah, it does sound crazy, but, like I said, those FBI folks wanted me to talk to you about it. By the way, do you remember where you were the night Darcy died? I know it's been a couple of weeks."

Izzy's new tone seemed to relax Kylie. "I'm not really sure," she said, lowering her arms. "I think Gabe was working and Robby was playing games in his room, s-so no, I don't have much of an alibi." Hand still gripping the locket Kylie looked apologetically at Izzy, who made a note to check Fox's work schedule.

Fox stood. "Okay, Detective, Kylie's been more than cooperative. Yeah, she knew all three of the victims, and no, she doesn't have a rock-solid alibi for any of them, but you know as well as I do the forensics people didn't find one thing they could link to her or anyone else. You can't arrest her, so what's your next move?"

Izzy also stood, her eyes on Fox. "Relax, Gabe. We're just talking, remember?"

"Oh, so, we can go, then?"

Izzy stepped out from behind her desk. "Of course, you can go. And Kylie, I'm sorry you had to learn about this . . . this Darcy thing the way you did."

Kylie frowned. "Yeah, me too." She stepped out of the room and headed off down the hallway, not bothering to check if Fox was following.

Izzy offered him her hand. "No hard feelings?"

Fox took it. "No, no hard feelings. It all seems so unbelievable—I mean, Kylie . . .?"

"Yeah." Izzy wondered what, if anything, Maggie would have gotten from the handshake. There were a few more things she'd have liked to ask, but the questions about Darcy had really shaken the kid. That wouldn't matter if Izzy was sure Kylie was the killer. But she wasn't sure. Not by a long shot.

Alone again, Izzy looked back at the list of life events serial killers have in common. The first was exposure to alcohol early on in life. But from what Izzy remembered from Garver's retirement party and the last Christmas party, neither of Kylie's parents were drunks. Still, who knew what happened behind closed doors?

She moved down the list. Head trauma was a big one. One article had stated that seventy percent of all serial killers had suffered from some kind of knock to the head at one time or another. Well, Lexi did hit Kylie with that volleyball, and hadn't Fulton said something about Fox rushing Kylie to the emergency room when she was little? Maybe she'd hit her head then. A look at her medical records would answer that question, but it would have to wait. Suspicions wouldn't earn her a warrant.

Many serial killers had also experienced psychological abuse, often because of their bed-wetting. Maybe Kylie's parents had gone ballistic over too many wet sheets. School files might hold the answers, but she'd need a warrant for them too.

Chapter 57

GABE

GABE STOOD BY as Kylie primped in front of her mother's full-length mirror. With her friends' help, she'd managed to pick out a pretty nice dress. Emerald green and strapless, it had a bunch of those shiny little sequin things sprinkled all over the bottom half. Topped off with a pair of matching elbow-length gloves, spiked heels, and the thick waves she'd put in her short auburn hair, the image was striking.

"You're a knockout," he told her.

Kylie glanced over her shoulder at him, but said nothing, obviously still irritated over what that nosy bitch, Santos had told her. For Gabe, his affair with Darcy was ancient history. But it was fresh news to Kylie, and apparently, the wound was deep. Why did women have to be so damned emotional?

He checked his watch. "Leave your hair alone. It's perfect, and Randy will be here any minute."

Her back was to him, but he could see her face in the mirror, and Kylie wasn't smiling.

"I get why you like him," Gabe continued. "All that wavy hair, those golden highlights . . ."

"Seriously?" She turned to him, eyes narrowed.

"Let me take some pictures." He picked up Angie's camera from the hall table and cradled it with both hands, ready to shoot. "If . . . *when* your mom wakes up, she'll want to see."

Kylie looked at the camera and grimaced. "There'll be a professional photographer at the prom."

He nodded. Taking pictures had been her mom's job, and like Angie, Kylie probably expected he'd screw them up. Not sure what to say next, he was relieved to hear the doorbell ring.

"I'll get it," Gabe said, but before he could take two steps, Kylie grabbed his arm.

"Look, Gabe. I just learned about you and Darcy a few hours ago. I'm not over it, so stop acting like things are okay between us. They're not, and I don't know if they ever will be. But with Mom in a coma, I'm stuck with you." She pushed past him and out the bedroom door.

He trailed behind, smirking at the way she shambled down the steps in those six-inch heels, then stood behind her as she threw open the front door. Even through the screen, the boy looked impressive in his white tie and tails. White gloves, too. Crouched on the curb behind him, the sleek white limo he'd been guilted into chipping in for waited, door open, and beside it, a black-suited chauffeur. Kylie pushed open the screen door and stepped outside.

"Wow, you look awesome," Ryan said, left hand behind his back.

"So do you," Kylie said. "Like Leonardo DiCaprio in *Titanic*, but better."

"Thanks, and you look even more beautiful than . . . that girl in *Titanic*."

Gabe held back a yawn. Clark Gable he wasn't, not that Kylie seemed to notice.

Ryan noticed Gabe standing in the doorway and offered his hand. "Good to see you again, Mr. Fox." He eyed Gabe's uniform and smiled. "So, Kylie wasn't kidding about you joining us at prom tonight."

"Yeah, kind of a last-minute thing. With what's been happening lately, my boss thought we should have some extra eyes out there." Gabe chuckled. "No worries. I'll stay out of your way as much as possible."

He tapped Kylie's shoulder. She turned and discovered Gabe holding the three things she'd forgotten upstairs: some sort of mask, the white rose boutonniere she planned to pin on Ryan, and a green purse barely large enough to hold the cell phone she'd already stuffed inside.

"Forget something?" Gabe asked.

Her chin dipped. "Thanks, Gabe."

Yeah, she'd better thank him. Cheater or not, he'd paid enough for that outfit she was wearing. Gabe passed Kylie her things then looked back at Ryan. "You know, Kylie thinks you're really something."

"Gaa-abe!" Hands full, she bumped him with her shoulder.

Ryan laughed. "Well, that's nice to hear, because I feel the same way about her." The hand he'd been hiding swung forward, revealing a white rose wrist corsage.

Smart choice. Gabe remembered how flustered he'd been while trying to pin flowers on his own prom date's chest with her daddy looking on.

As the kids took care of the flower business, one of the limo's windows slid down, and an irritatingly familiar voice erupted from inside. "Helloooo! We're getting hungry in here, Ky-leeeee!"

"Sounds like Luke wants his pizza," Ryan said.

Gabe smiled and nodded, having decided not to comment on the group's choice to eat their pre-prom meal at Saltini's Pizza House.

"Ready?" Ryan offered Kylie his arm.

She nodded and never looked back as she walked off down the driveway.

Chapter 58

GABE

ON HIS THIRTY-MINUTE drive out to the recently built Pinecrest Hotel and Resort, Gabe recalled his last conversation with Chief Fulton.

"This event couldn't come at a worse time," Fulton had told him. "Normally, I'd be okay with just Vega backing up the hotel's two security guards, but the Pinecrest is a big place, and since I've got no idea where the killer will strike next, I'd sure feel better knowing you were there with him. I might send someone else, too."

Of course, Fulton knew Kylie's connection to all three women, so why pick Gabe to be his extra set of eyes? Did he expect Gabe to make some special effort to stop his stepdaughter from killing again? The idea of Kylie attacking someone at the dance was ridiculous, but wouldn't it be great? He imagined catching her in the act and being forced to shoot her down in front of a hundred wide-eyed teenagers. Interesting, but if he were responsible for Kylie's death, could he still collect the insurance money?

Once at the hotel, Gabe put aside his fantasies and tracked down Vega. After instructing the rookie to patrol the outside of the building, he was on his way to the main entrance when the kids' limo glided under the hotel's carport which had been decorated with purple, gold, and green balloons, the theme of Mardi Gras.

Gabe watched from behind a tree as the six masked prom-goers piled out of the car, the girls squealing their delight over all the balloons and the lengthy purple carpet runner leading up to the big redwood doors. Like her friends, Addison and Chelsea, Kylie had selected a gold half-mask decorated with colorful silk and feathers. The boys had settled on different versions of the jester theme.

Once the girls checked each other's hair and Luke had tied the laces of his shiny black dress shoe, the group entered the building and Gabe followed them from a distance across the crowded, voice-filled lobby. He arrived at the open ballroom doors just as the kids passed beneath an archway of balloons,

Diana Corbitt

a nice frame for the ballroom's open doors and the gilded scroll work bridge beyond.

Seemingly unaware of her stepdad's presence, Kylie accepted Ryan's hand and they led their group through a white vapor that rose from beneath the bridge, concealing their feet, and, supposedly, creating a mood of mystery and romance. Gabe hesitated outside the doorway, in no hurry to torture his eardrums with the annoying teen music blasting at the far end of the ballroom.

He watched as groups of masked kids poured into the big rectangular room. The night would be long and probably uneventful. But what if it wasn't? In his new, slightly more realistic dream scenario, The Taker would attack a girl at the dance—Kylie, of course. Cornered, he would use Kylie as a human shield. With so many students in danger, Gabe would be forced to take the guy out, and sadly, one of his bullets would stray, striking Kylie right between the eyes.

That wasn't likely to happen either, but wouldn't it be great? With the killer dead, all three murders would be lumped onto that one guy, Gabe could wash his hands of Darcy forever and he might even collect a nice chunk of life insurance money for accidentally shooting his stepdaughter.

He noticed some of the kids in the ballroom were staring upward. Having heard about the amazing domed-glass ceiling, he took a peek. The whole room was covered in wood, with paneling on the walls and ceilings. Fancy enough, but it was the center of that coffered ceiling that had gotten the whole town buzzing. He moved further into the room, head tipped back to take in this new Eighth Wonder of the World.

A big glass igloo.

Humph. That must have cost a shitload. With a snort, he ended his brief art critique and looked for Kylie, who he located just as Ryan was going in for a kiss. From Kylie's reaction, it wasn't their first.

But their lips barely touched as Luke tapped Kylie's shoulder. He pointed out some empty tables, and the group split up. Girls, to claim a table, boys to get some snacks at the buffet.

With the kids all occupied, Gabe strode across the bridge. The walls, strung with vertical green, purple, and gold streamers, were also decorated with several Mardi Gras themed hangings. Satisfied with the location of an extra-leafy potted palm, he took his position beside it. Hidden by big floppy leaves, he could keep a discreet eye on things with the added bonus of Kylie's table being just a few feet away. If she left the room, he would follow, and if everything looked good . . .

Having only a cursory idea of how the hotel was laid out, he grunted. Fulton should have told him he'd be working this assignment last week. Then, he could have checked the place out beforehand, and he would already know where the security cameras were located. He might even have found a blind spot he could lure Kylie into.

He peeked through the palm fronds and found the girls focused on the elevated stage where a purple-tuxedoed DJ was throwing bead strands into a large crowd of kids.

"Don't forget to fill out your ballots!" the DJ shouted. "They're right there on the table."

Some things never changed. The popular kids get voted Prom King and Queen, and everybody else is a loser.

Chapter 59

IZZY

AN ATTRACTIVE MULTI-FLOORED combination of stone, glass, and pinewood logs set against the backdrop of Atherton Lake, the Pinecrest Hotel had quickly become a popular vacation destination, and part of its fame came from the amazing glass dome. Eager to see what all the fuss was about, Izzy pulled her SUV onto the side of the road and climbed out to look at the resort from a distance.

A fifty-foot-wide half-hemisphere, she found the dome was best viewed from directly in front of the hotel since the ballroom was closed in on three sides by seven floors of guestrooms, all with open-air walkways that look down on the dome.

It was stunning. She and Brody might spend a weekend there one day, but tonight, she was supervising the prom. Hoping the evening would end without incident, Izzy strode into the lobby and spotted Gabe Fox standing in the ballroom doorway. She tapped his arm.

"Surprise, I'm here too," she told him, expecting at least a smile. What she got was a squinty stare. "Hey, it wasn't my idea. I know you can handle things. You've got Vega and two rent-a-cops. Plus, I'm sure Peabody's got a few chaperones wandering around."

Fox grinned. "No, no. The more the merrier. Maybe I'll ask you for a dance, later."

"Sure, I'd love that." Izzy returned his smile with one just as insincere. Man, was Fox really that misogynistic? "Okay, uh . . ." She fumbled for an excuse to leave. "I'm gonna check out that dome from the inside." With a wave, she strolled over the mist-covered bridge, confused about what had just transpired. Like the group of kids she was following, she looked up.

Since it was dark out, what she saw was a little disappointing compared to the selfie Maggie had sent her last month when she and Fulton had driven down to the hotel for lunch. At high noon, the clear, triangular panes had been lit up by the sun, a stunning sight with the bright-blue sky above.

Enough of that. There was a killer out there, and she was on duty. Having done a little online research, Izzy knew the ballroom had one main entrance and two fire exits which opened onto a hallway. She located the latter and smiled, impressed by the colorful balloons and streamers that had been used to frame those doors. She located the chaperones standing around talking. After a little chat, she'd stationed some by the exits and buffet table and the rest out by the restrooms.

Besides the emergency exits, the bridge was the only way to get in and out of the ballroom. She decided that she and Fox would patrol the ballroom then directed the two security guards to oversee the lobby. That done, she got herself a glass of punch.

As Izzy sauntered the perimeter of the dance floor, she noticed one of the junior police academy kids Fox had introduced her to was piling his plate with cheese and crackers. Tall and fit, the guy filled out his white tie and tails well, but the silly big-nosed jester mask he'd pushed back on his head diluted the classiness.

She was still trying to remember the kid's name when two more boys arrived. Of similar stature, they busied themselves by filling several glasses of punch. She recognized one of the boys as Kylie's hunky boyfriend, Ryan Lanister. A gold and white jester mask covered the third boy's face. With white-gloved hands, they carefully picked up the six glasses they'd filled and headed off, accompanied by the junior policeman/cheese lover who, along with all the cheese and crackers was carrying a second plate heaped with tortilla chips and guacamole. Their journey ended at a table where Kylie McKenna and two other finely dressed girls were seated. Of the three, Izzy liked Kylie's gown best, the stunning, floor-length green frock accented by white elbow-length gloves.

The three couples laughed and joked, all seemingly having fun. But why was the goofy, cheese-eating boy—Luke, yeah that was his name—why was Luke staring so intently at the two couples making their way across the bridge? All four were masked, but from the look on his face, he knew who they were.

An impressively tall and attractively dressed couple led the way, followed by an equally attractive, yet much shorter pair. The short girl's thigh-length black hair swayed as she model-walked across the bridge on six-inch spiked heels. No wonder Luke was staring. If that was Jade Su, then the tall girl was Jade's buddy, Eden Hendrix.

Izzy glanced back at the door and found Gabe Fox was also watching Jade. But why the smirk on his face? And then she understood. Except for the wide, sequined belt encircling Jade's waist, her dress looked exactly like the one Kylie was wearing.

GABE

ONCE THE GROUP had stepped off the bridge, Miss Spikey Heels pulled off her mask and scanned the room. That's when Gabe put two and two together. The little one was Asian, and the other was black and tall enough to dunk a basketball flatfooted. If he remembered the names correctly, he was looking at Jade Su and Eden Hendrix, Kylie's tormentors, and Lexi Siegel's besties.

Fighting to hold back his smirk, Gabe found himself a spot beside a potted palm. So, Kylie hadn't exaggerated. Jade and Eden really had spied on her when they were shopping for prom dresses.

Although he could only see the backs of Jeff and Chelsea, he had a pretty clear view of the other seated at Kylie's table. Luke was the first to notice the new arrivals, followed by Addison. She whispered something to Chelsea who reached behind Ryan and tapped Kylie's shoulder. Likely a warning since Jade was heading their way. If Gabe didn't know better, he'd think little Jade was dashing over to greet an old friend. But, of course, they weren't friends, something anyone could tell from the look on Kylie's face as Jade arrived at the table.

Little or not, the chick had balls.

As Jade looked Kylie up and down, her happy expression vanished. "I can't believe it!" she bellowed. "You copied my dress!" She tossed up her hands like some flustered southern belle, then quickly engaged in a shouting match with everyone at the table.

Then, something Kylie said appeared to hit a nerve. Gabe couldn't hear, but it was enough to make Jade lunge for the closest glass of punch.

Anticipating a cat fight, Gabe perked, but Jade's date quickly removed the glass from her hand and pulled the little hellcat away, ruining things.

Since Jade continued to spew cuss words, Santos looked at Gabe. He waved her off and was about to step in himself when Principal Peabody appeared. Half the room watched as Peabody huddled with Jade's crew, then found them a table as far from Kylie's as possible. Was Miss Spikey Heels done for the night? Gabe hoped not. Watching the girls tussle would be a nice break from babysitting these spoiled teenagers.

Hey, what if he killed Kylie and made it look like Jade did it? After that show, even the busboys would think Jade was guilty.

Wondering how he might pull that off, Gabe turned his attention back to Kylie's bunch, whose expressions ranged from angry to stunned. And then there was Luke, who threw his head back and laughed. "Forget that loudmouth," he seemed to tell Kylie. Still grinning, he flipped a double-handed bird in Jade's general direction then stood and motioned at the busy dance floor.

Good idea, Gabe thought. You can't be angry if you're dancing.

When Addison shook her head, Luke did a little jig. His friend, Jeff, joined him in an improvised square dance and soon, all three couples were out on the floor, laughing and dancing.

Chapter 60

JADE

SEEING RYAN LEAD Kylie onto the floor, Jade grabbed Jamari and pulled him out there with her. "I'm keeping that bitch on my radar."

No big sacrifice, since Jade adored dancing. Her favorite TV show was *Dance Night,* and she loved watching the couples glide across the stage, the ladies' brilliant white smiles proving to the world how fun it was to tango in six-inch heels. But after hours of nearly constant dancing, Jade knew how far from reality the show actually was. Heels blistered and arches cramping, Jade took Jamari by the arm and dragged him back to their table.

"So, take off the damned shoes," Jamari said, dismissing Jade's problem with a flap of the hand. "Eden took hers off a long time ago."

"Yeah, but she's super tall. If I take mine off, I'll look like a little girl dancing with her father."

Jamari shrugged, and they sat in silence while their sweaty classmates gyrated in front of them. "Hey." He rested his hand on Jade's. "I've still got that joint. Wanna go find someplace to smoke it?"

They'd had a little weed and vodka before the prom, but she'd come down from that a while back. "Okay, but I need to use the bathroom first."

The two made their way down the crowded hallway to the restrooms. Both lines were long, but the line for the ladies' extended far out into the hall, and then some.

"You gonna make it?" Jamari asked.

Chapter 61

GABE

AFTER WHAT MUST have been his tenth tour of the ballroom, Gabe checked the time and was delighted to see it was nearing eleven. He looked up from his watch in time to notice the Asian girl and her boyfriend were crossing back over the bridge. Bored, he followed them into the lobby and traded places with one of the two rent-a-cops as the couple wove their way through the through the crowd to where the main restrooms were located. A line of gabby teenaged girls snaked out of the ladies' room and down the hall. Gabe smiled as the scowly faced little Asian girl took a spot at the end. A few moments later, Kylie also crossed the bridge. He moved to greet her.

"Hi, honey."

"Hi, Gabe."

She tried to get around him, but he blocked her path. "Having a good time?"

"Yeah." She sighed. "*Now.*"

"So, what did you say to that Jade Su girl?"

"Nothing, I just . . ." Kylie looked away.

"Oh, come on. Please? What did you say to piss her off like that?"

Kylie motioned for him to move in closer. "I told her that the belt made her look like a hooker and that if she didn't leave me alone, I would punch her in the face."

Gabe chuckled. He would pay money to see that.

"I just hope she's finished with me tonight." As if to show she was mad at Gabe, Kylie backed away a few steps. "So, anyway . . . where's the ladies room in this place?"

"You should probably look somewhere else. This one here has a big line, and Jade just got in it."

"Oh, great." Having abandoned her high heels a while back, Kylie raised up on her bare toes and took a look for herself. A passing bellhop noticed.

"Yeah, that line is pretty long." He pointed in the opposite direction. "There's another restroom out by the pool. At this time of night, it can't be very busy."

Interesting.

Gabe watched Kylie trot off down the empty hallway. This could be the opportunity he'd been looking for. A lot can happen in a swimming pool, especially at this hour.

Chapter 62

IZZY

AS A FAMILIAR hip-hop tune blared from the nearby speakers, Izzy stood by the food table, scanning the crowd for suspicious behavior and finishing up a glass of fruit punch. So, was The Taker here? For all she knew, he was one of the busboys or even the janitor who had just mopped up a spill. Maybe he was one of these kids on the dance floor, or for that matter, sitting at home watching TV. She prayed for the latter and that the worst injuries suffered here tonight were a few blistered feet.

Jade and Kylie's little dustup had been interesting. It would be sweet if that ended up being the highlight of her evening. As she poured herself another glass of punch, she noticed Fox cross the bridge and disappear into the crowded lobby. A minute later, one of the security guards crossed back into the ballroom. Apparently, the two had traded places.

Well, maybe Fox needed a change of scenery. She remembered the man's annoyance when she popped up in front of him—not that Izzy blamed him. Other than Lester Mathis, Fox had been on the force longer than anyone. If he'd felt slighted when she was promoted to detective, that was understandable. But hadn't she deserved that promotion? Izzy had solved two murder cases in just over a week. Could Gabe Fox say as much?

Then again, what if he'd reacted the way he had for a totally different reason, like concern that Izzy was onto him? In Kylie's last interview, she'd said her stepdad had been working the night Darcy Callahan was murdered. But Fox was also the one who'd taken the call the next morning, so did this guy *ever* sleep? She took out her pad and made a note to confirm Fox's schedule with Sergeant Peterson Monday morning.

Until then, Izzy would do her best to maintain the safety of her charges and behave as if Fox were totally innocent, which, as far as she knew, he was. That settled, she ditched her empty cup and picked up a plate. A ham and cheese sandwich wasn't much, but a peace offering might help to smooth any bad feelings Fox might be holding against her. It might also lower his defenses. Sandwich assembled, she added some olives and chips, then headed out to the lobby. But Fox wasn't there.

She approached the doorman. "Excuse me. The cop who just came out here. Did you notice where he went?"

"That way, I believe." The man pointed down an empty hallway.

"Anything down there besides guestrooms?"

"The pool, if you walk far enough. And another restroom." The doorman eyed the long lines of kids leading to the restrooms. "Maybe he couldn't wait."

GABE

PROMISING HIMSELF THAT he wouldn't touch Kylie unless the situation was perfect, Gabe moved through the shadows of a small grove of birch trees, trailing Kylie as she walked the length of the fence surrounding the now-darkened pool enclosure. She found a gate and jiggled the door handle. Locked.

Aw. Can't get in? Read the sign, dummy. It closed ten minutes ago.

Now less than a dozen steps away, Kylie growled the angry-puppy sound she often made when frustrated.

What? Afraid you'll wet your panties?

Gabe looked around as she pressed her face to the bars. Shadow-filled and desolate, the area was made for murder. Adrenaline surging, he was about to make his move when Kylie scampered off around the pool's shrub-edged perimeter. What the heck?

Keeping to the shadows, he followed her around the corner. No Kylie. A few strides later, he understood. The enclosure had two gates and this second one was propped open with a chair. He stepped through the open doorway just as Kylie disappeared into the restroom.

IZZY

IZZY FOLLOWED THE dimly lit path between the various buildings with growing concern. Where was Fox leading her? What she wasn't concerned with was leaving the dance short two officers. Because she'd gotten that weird feeling again, back in the lobby. To be honest, she still had it, and that feeling was telling her to stay on Fox's tail. Why? She had no idea, but the sensation hadn't misled her yet. A moment later, she arrived at the pool and a few steps later, its entrance. But the sign said the pool was closed.

Okay, so where was Fox? Izzy tried the gate with no luck. Maybe Fox had headed back to the men's room via another pathway.

A flash of light on the far side of the pool area caught her attention. She peered between the fence's long vertical bars and found the pool and hot tub area empty. Also dark, was the swim-up bar on the far side of the pool and the two restrooms beyond. What if that flash she'd seen had been one of the restroom doors opening and closing? Maybe Fox had found a way inside. Wishing she hadn't drank so much punch, Izzy continued around the fence's perimeter, hoping to find out how.

Chapter 63

JADE

WHEN JADE FINALLY left the ladies room, she expected to find Jamari slouched against the wall. But he wasn't. She looked up and down the hallway. No Jamari.

Had he tired of waiting for her? As she imagined him outside smoking the whole blunt himself, a jingling sound caught her ear. Way down the hall in the opposite direction from the lobby stood a masked man in white tie and tails. Feet set apart and gloved hands pressed to his hips, he reminded Jade of Superman.

Jamari. There was no mistaking him. He'd chosen the coolest mask in the store. A sexy gold face topped with a three-horned jester hat. She grinned.

"There you are." Mimicking his hands-on-hips stance, she called down to him. "I thought you were going to wait outside the door."

Jamari raised and dropped his shoulders dramatically.

"What are you doing down there?"

He gestured for her to join him then pranced around the corner, jester bells jingling.

What was he up to? Ignoring her aching feet, Jade trotted down the gaudy floral carpeting and paused at the corner. It would be just like Jamari to hide around the bend, ready to pounce. She edged her face around the bend, fists clenched.

Nothing. Just a short, empty hallway and the jingle of bells fading in the distance as Jamari ran down the next hall. Well, he better not expect her to run. Not in these shoes.

But she did walk fast. She found him down at the end, frozen in that ridiculous Superman pose of his.

Had he found a good place to smoke while she was in the bathroom?

"Jamari, where are you taking me?"

This time, he pointed upward with one hand, his white gloved hand flashing beneath the harsh fluorescent lighting. The other hand, he rested on the door separating him from the emergency staircase behind him.

Oh, no. Not stairs. "Hey! Don't open that. You'll set off the alarm."

Jamari responded with a theatrical don't-worry-about-it wave. He pushed the door open then raised a gloved hand to his ear, head cocked, as if listening. Nothing happened.

"How did you know that?" Jade asked as she approached.

Jamari shrugged and disappeared through the doorway, bells jingling.

Heels already blistered, Jade hobbled over and peeked through the long window slit in the door where one fluorescent light bulb glowed dully. Finding the staircase landing empty, she pushed the metal fire door open slowly and checked the corners.

No Jamari.

The door snicked shut behind her, the sound echoing off the glossy-white cinder block walls, along with her footsteps. She peered up the stairwell and groaned at the sight of seven more sets of steps, all of them empty. "Jamari, you said you wanted to smoke, so let's do it. What's wrong with right here?"

The tinkle of distant jester bells told Jade her crazy boyfriend was at least two floors up and still moving. After a few moments, a golden face grinned down at her over the top railing.

"Jamari, this is bullshit. I'm not walking up seven flights of stairs in these shoes."

Gloved hands clasped together, his exaggerated begging kept the bells tinkling.

Damn it. Why did he have to be so adorable? "Oh, all right!" Jade slipped off her heels and as she trudged barefoot up the hundred-or-so steps, a joyful Jamari skipped around the top landing, urging her on. But just as she reached the final flight, the jester face disappeared and the sound of another door clanging shut echoed down to her.

What was that boy up to?

With one shoe in each hand, Jade forced herself up the last few steps. As she expected, all she found was a door. Screwed onto it was a small metal plate with the words: TO ROOF.

Jade stood there, catching her breath. Well, at least Jamari couldn't climb any higher. She imagined the two of them, alone, smoking out there under all those stars. It would be nice. Romantic even. Smiling, she slipped her shoes back on, adjusted her bra and ran her fingers through her long black hair. Ready as she'd ever be, she pushed the door open and gasped.

What faced her might one day be a lovely rooftop bar, but right now, all Jade saw were piles of building materials, tools, and rolled-up extension cords. But where was Jamari? Pea gravel crunched beneath her shoes as she passed by a waist-high stack of two-by-fours.

Finally. There he was by the far wall, peering down at something. Above, a million stars twinkled. Maybe coming all the way up here *was* a smart idea.

He turned to her, hands on hips. Damn, he looked good.

She felt a light breeze lift her hair. Hoping it made her look hot, Jade sauntered over slowly, swaying her butt the way he liked. "Okay, you got me here. Now take off that mask and kiss me."

He pulled her to him, but the golden-faced jester mask remained.

"Come on, Jamari, stop fooling around." She reached up and pulled the mask off.

It wasn't Jamari.

Chapter 64

GABE

THIS POOL RESTROOM was actually a great location to kill Kylie. She would come out of the stall, and Gabe would be waiting. Surprise! Strangling her wouldn't be easy, but even if she managed a scream, no one would hear it with the outside door closed.

Ready to get it over with, he stepped into the pool area. And then, he noticed the many landscaping rocks in the flowerbeds. The smallest was the size of a potato, so any of them could kill a man. Probably with just one blow. So, should he strangle her like Darcy, or bash her head in like the other two victims?

He would strangle her, of course. Why risk getting blood on his shirt? That settled, he approached the ladies room door. Hoping the hinges didn't squeak, he reached for the door handle, then stopped, realizing he should be wearing gloves.

"What's wrong? Men's room locked?"

"Holy crap!" Heart in his throat, Gabe couldn't have pulled his hand away faster if he'd been burnt. Fucking Isabel Santos. What was she doing here? He turned, lips forming what he hoped was a pleasant smile. "You following me, Detective?"

"Sorry, Fox. I just wanted to bring you this sandwich." Santos offered him a plate. "I thought you might be hungry, so when I couldn't find you in the lobby, I asked around, and the doorman pointed me this way. Hope you like ham and cheese."

"I do . . . thanks." Gabe took the plate, amazed his hand wasn't shaking.

"So, is the men's room locked?"

Men's room? What was she talking about?

The sound of a flushing toilet turned their heads.

"Someone's in there?" Santos asked.

Gabe nodded, and a few moments later, they heard water running, followed by the woosh of a powerful hand dryer.

"But this is the ladies room. Do you know who that is?"

"Oh, sure. It's Kylie. I was just, uh . . ." Gabe shook his head.

The door opened, and Kylie stepped out, mouth wide and trout-like. "What the heck?" Her wide-eyed gaze bounced from Gabe to Santos and back to Gabe. "You . . . you followed me?"

"No. I mean, I-I was just—" He looked at Santos for help, but all she did was shrug.

"I was just being a caring dad. I mean, look at this place." Gabe gestured at their sinister surroundings.

Kylie shoved past them and dashed out of the pool area. Fox followed.

IZZY

FOX'S RESPONSE HAD seemed sensible, and, seriously, what was that girl thinking? Wishing she hadn't drank so much punch, Izzy rushed inside the restroom and after a few minutes, stepped outside and checked the time. Excellent. There was less than an hour left and—thank God—nothing much had happened. Eager to wrap this party up, she started for the gate, then stopped.

Hang on, now. If the men's room door was locked, and Fox knew Kylie was in the ladies', why did he reach for the door handle? She strode back and pushed on the men's room door. It swung wide easily.

GABE

IN NO MOOD to deal with another of Kylie's temper tantrums, Gabe didn't bother to keep up and soon lost sight of her. He followed the trail back to the main building, and as he approached the door, his blood ran cold. A security camera was mounted six feet above his head.

Christ on a cracker. Was he a complete moron? He'd been so intent on looking out for two-legged witnesses that he'd forgotten all about Big Brother. If Santos hadn't brought him that sandwich . . .

Gabe realized he was still holding the plate and tossed the whole thing into the nearby trash bin. Jesus, how many cameras had recorded him prowling through the bushes? Plenty, but since he didn't kill her, no one would bother to look at the recordings before they self-erased. He threw the door open and retraced his steps, grateful for how lucky he'd been, but not ready to give up on the life insurance money.

Chapter 65

GABE

ALTHOUGH THE HOTEL had plenty of signs directing guests out to the pool, the return trip wasn't as well marked, and Gabe found himself walking past the main restrooms and the never-ending line of girls waiting to use them. With traffic stopped temporarily for a room service cart to pass in the opposite direction, he noticed Jade's boyfriend slouched against the wall outside the ladies' room, his suit coat slung over one shoulder. Curious how long the boy had been waiting, he checked his watch.

The kid had spent twenty minutes standing outside the ladies' toilet. Well, it couldn't be any more boring than how Gabe had spent his last five hours. He entered the ballroom and found Kylie sitting with Ryan at an otherwise empty table eating what looked like cake. Like most other boys this time of night, Ryan's jacket was now draped across the back of his chair, and his white bow tie hung loose around his neck.

Resigned that he wouldn't be murdering Kylie anytime tonight, Gabe returned to his spot beside the potted plant and surveyed the room. Not long after, Isabel Santos arrived and found a place against the opposite wall. She spotted him and waved. He waved back, remembering the sandwich he'd thrown away. Hopefully, she'd assume he'd already eaten it—not that Gabe would lose any sleep over it.

By now, the crowd on the dance floor had thinned. He noticed Luke and Addison slow dancing near the DJ's stage and steps from them, Jeff and Chelsea. On the opposite side of the room, Jade's gangly girlfriend and her equally-gangly date were sharing a kiss at their table.

As Gabe wondered how Jade could possibly still be in the restroom, her date crossed back over the bridge. At the sight of him, the tall girl trotted over. Probably to ask where Jade was.

And then, the music stopped, and the DJ took the microphone.

Was prom over? Gabe hoped so.

"Okay, people. Gather around." The DJ raised both arms, gesturing for everyone to move in beneath the huge dome. "Come on, now,!" he shouted into the mic. "Don't you want to know who our prom king and queen are gonna be?"

The crowd whooped, and to Gabe's disappointment, Principal Peabody and one of the chaperones lifted a small folding table onto the stage. On the table lay three bouquets of flowers and two crowns. Peabody took over the microphone. "Okay, everybody, I'm going to announce two sets of runners up, and then your new king and queen. Are you ready?"

Another cheer, even louder than the first.

Along with the crowd, Gabe moved in closer, as did Kylie and Ryan who made their way to the base of the stage to stand next to Luke and Addison. Chelsea and Jeff squeezed in behind them.

Once everyone had found their places, Principal Peabody squinted down at the slip of paper he'd been holding. "Okay, here are the second runners up. Let's give a big round of applause to . . . Amanda Bosworth and Damian Pardini!"

The crowd clapped and cheered as the smiling couple made their way onto the stage. Peabody handed Amanda some flowers and shook the boy's hand as everyone clapped their approval.

Smiling and nodding, Peabody looked back at his notepaper. "Okay, on to the first runners up. Let's hear it for . . . Jade Moon and Jamari Stewart!"

Really? Maybe the votes had been more for Jamari. He was a good-looking guy, and had even looked embarrassed during Jade's earlier rant.

This next ovation topped the first, and Mr. Peabody grinned out at the sea of faces, waiting for the couple to appear. After a while, Jamari came forward, smiling weakly as more than one voice called out asking where Jade was.

By the time he climbed onto the stage, the room had gone silent. "I don't know where she is," Jamari said. "Last time I saw her she was walking into the ladies' room."

Everyone laughed, and Mr. Peabody signaled for quiet. "Okay, well, I'm sure Jade will show up soon. Right now, it's time to crown this year's prom king and queen." Again, the crowd cheered. Peabody eyed his watch, and once the group had settled down, called out, "Ready to hear who they are?"

The crowd responded with deafening applause.

"I can't hear you!" Peabody bellowed into the mic.

Challenge accepted, the room rattled with added whoops and whistles.

"All right. Here we go . . . Rocky Harbor High's new prom king and queen are . . ."

A loud thump turned all eyes upward. Something had struck the glass dome above them.

"What the hell was that?" Peabody cried.

Gabe didn't see anything unusual, but then he saw the cracks. Had an eagle fallen from the sky? But how would that happen if the ballroom was walled in on three sides by seven floors of guestrooms?

Eyes drawn by the groan of metal, Gabe stared as, twenty feet above them, a few of the dome's large glass triangles began to crack, and the soldered joints surrounding one particular piece popped free. Would the rest of those joints also break loose? And what caused those damned cracks? He noticed a dark shape on the other side of the glass. Naturally, there was a kid standing right beneath it.

"Hey, grab that kid!" Gabe shouted at Santos. "Take cover, everybody!"

Santos grabbed the fool's arm, and they had barely gotten out from under when the framework around one of the glass triangles gave way, releasing shattered glass onto the ballroom floor. Terrified partygoers dashed for cover beneath tables and chairs. But all Gabe could do was stare, transfixed by what was caught in the gaping hole above him.

Holy shit. That was no eagle. That was Jade Su. Lodged halfway through the three-sided gap, the girl seemed to have taken a header from a great height, her once green ballgown now streaked with blood and shredded by glass and shorn-away framework. Like her arms, Jade's long dark hair hung straight down, limp and motionless.

"Everyone, stay where you are!" Santos shouted. Like Gabe, she stepped a little closer. "Isn't that . . . ?" Her wide eyes told him she was equally stunned.

"Yeah, it's Jade," Gabe whispered. He moved to her side. "Think it could be suicide?"

Santos stared back at the body. "Not with that belt around her neck."

He edged over for a better look. "Oh, yeah." Heat rose to his cheeks. "I hadn't seen that. So, somebody choked her out, then tossed her?"

"Maybe," Santos whispered. "She's too far away to see much."

True. If the girl was still breathing, Gabe couldn't tell. "She's dead, right? I mean . . . look at her."

Santos studied her. "I'd say so, yes. If her heart was still pumping, that blood would be shooting out in spurts."

"Yeah . . . that's what I thought, too." Not that they were lacking in red stuff. Jade had a lot of cuts, and with the help of gravity, tiny streams of blood had merged into larger streams, all going the same direction: down her arms. The blood dripped from the tips of Jade's fingernails and landed with a splat onto the ballroom floor creating two bright red puddles that would soon merge into one.

Was it The Taker's work? Maybe so, but if it was, the guy had really stepped up his game, because this was the craziest murder yet.

IZZY

SINCE ONLY A small fraction of the dome had been damaged, it seemed sturdy enough. Izzy peered out over what at first glance, appeared to be a roomful of empty tables with knocked-over chairs.

She held up her badge. "Rocky Harbor Police! If you're hurt or see anyone else who's hurt, speak up now!"

Only a handful of kids called out. The worst injury belonged to Kylie McKenna's shaggy-haired friend, Jeff, who raised a bloody hand.

"Okay!" Izzy shouted. "Help is on the way, but if you are injured, grab a napkin or something and apply pressure to the wound until they get here." She turned toward the bridge side of the room, which was only occupied by a couple of dozen kids. "Where are my two security guards?"

The two men appeared in the main doorway behind the bridge.

"Here!" they called out.

"Thank you," Izzy said. "How about Principal Peabody? Where's he?"

"Over here!" Looking a bit frazzled, Peabody poked his head out from beneath a table near the stage. "What would you like me to do?"

"That bridge is pretty narrow. I want you, the guards, and the chaperones to move it out of the way so we have a nice clear pathway when these kids move out to the lobby." She looked from Peabody to the two guards. "But do not allow them to leave. Every person here is a witness, and we need to take their statements first." She turned back to Principal Peabody. "I assume you've got a list of who attended?"

Peabody did have a list, and promised that, once he and his students got out to the lobby, he would station himself by the door where he and the chaperones would check the kids out to their parents as soon as the police had interviewed them.

Fox stepped over. "Nice job. Want me to call it in?"

"No, I'll do it. But Vega's still out patrolling the parking lot. Tell him to come inside. That lobby's going to be crowded." Izzy pulled out her cell phone and made the 911 call. For the most part, the partygoers remained quiet, with only the muffled sound of one girl sobbing off in the back corner.

With the bridge out of the way and Vega present, it was time to transfer the kids to the lobby. Izzy opened her mouth to make the announcement as another shard of glass clattered to the floor behind her.

Chapter 66
IZZY

IF THE PROMGOERS weren't looking at Jade before the glass struck the floor, they sure as hell stared afterward. To everyone's shock, Jade's body slowly slid through the hole, revealing a length of rope tied to her waist. The soft murmur of the crowd splintered into a cacophony of shrieks, cries, and profanity that rose as Jade's slide became a free-fall and crescendoed when she jerked to a stop just five feet from the floor.

"Holy shit!" Fox exclaimed.

Izzy's chin all but struck her chest. "Probably snagged on something," she murmured, still trying to absorb what had just happened. They watched, mouth agape, as Jade's body slowly rotated, her hands now brushing her bare feet.

Jesus. Izzy looked back at the tables where, one by one, the once hidden high school students poked their heads out.

"God, they shouldn't see that," she told Fox.

"Sure, but how we gonna stop 'em?"

Izzy turned her back to the kids. "We're gonna scare them back under. Just follow my lead."

With a nod from Fox, Izzy turned back around. She glanced casually up at the dome then froze. "Fox, look! It's cracking again!"

"God, you're right!"

Eyes wide and terrified, they shouted for the crowd to stay down.

"It worked," Fox whispered.

"Yeah, but it won't last. Someone else will poke his head up. But before that happens, we need to get that body covered. But how?"

"We could throw a tablecloth over her."

"Yeah, but that could compromise evidence." Izzy spun toward the kitchen door where a busboy stood staring. "Get me some clean tablecloths!"

He stared back.

"Move!" she shouted.

The young man bolted into the kitchen.

"Didn't you just say we shouldn't cover the body?" Fox asked.

Ignoring Fox, Izzy peered back at the tables. "Principal Peabody? I need you and your chaperones over here, right now."

Like weary meerkats, four heads rose from beneath the same punch-stained tablecloth, Peabody and three ladies.

"Wh-what do you want us to do?" Peabody asked. Like the others, he eyed the dome as if surprised it hadn't crashed down on them already.

So, it wasn't just the kids she'd tricked. With the help of hand gestures and facial expressions, Izzy convinced the group to join her, but halfway over, two of the woman stopped to stare at the body, tears streaming down their cheeks.

"Don't look." Izzy gathered the group in front of her, their backs to the grisly scene. "I'm sure we all agree that the kids shouldn't see that. A busboy just handed Officer Fox some tablecloths. I want you four to hold them up around the body, blocking it from view. Once you're in place, we'll start moving the kids to the lobby." She looked from one face to the other. "Think you can do that?"

Sniffling, they all nodded.

Izzy peered over her shoulder at Fox. "You catch that?"

Nodding, Fox passed the tablecloths to Peabody who, with the help of the three chaperones, used them to wall in the body, hiding it from view.

Talk about closing the stable door after the horse has bolted, Izzy thought. With a sigh, she turned to Fox. "Let's get these kids out of here."

She looked up at the ceiling, then out at the tables. "Okay, folks. The ceiling looks stable now, so everyone stand up and walk calmly out to the lobby."

"PARENTS ARE GOING to freak," Izzy muttered once the ballroom had been cleared. "They'll probably want another town meeting."

"Yeah, probably."

Not surprised by Fox's honesty, Izzy shut the ballroom doors behind them. Two ambulances soon arrived from Rocky Harbor, followed by three police cars. With everyone crowded into the lobby, she left the EMTs in charge of injuries, then set the cops to taking statements from the kids who hadn't been injured. As promised, Principal Peabody and his crew set up by the main doorway with the list of attendees. She told Fox to also begin taking statements, but not until he'd checked on Kylie.

Once everyone else was occupied, Izzy slipped back into the ballroom for a closer look at the body. Was this The Taker's work, or something else? Jade did still have her hands. And where had she been attacked before plummeting through the dome?

GABE

GABE RAN INTO Luke and Addison first, and alongside them, Chelsea and Jeff, Luke's shaggy-haired police academy friend. The first two seemed fine, but Jeff had that cut on his hand. At some point, he'd wrapped a cloth napkin around it.

"Some jerk knocked him down while we were running," Chelsea volunteered.

Although Gabe hadn't asked for a closer look, Jeff held out his hand. The napkin wrapped around it sported a quarter-sized red stain.

"It probably needs a few stitches," Jeff said proudly, "but it'll be okay."

"*If* it doesn't get infected," Chelsea cautioned.

Jeff said something about broken glass, but Gabe tuned them out at the sight of Kylie and Ryan. Kylie's white gloves were dirty, but to his disappointment, her only injury was a small cut on her forehead. Although he'd have rather found her with a hunk of glass stuck in her chest, he put on his worried-dad face.

"What happened there?" He pointed his chin at the injury.

"Where?" Kylie touched her forehead and glanced at the dab of blood on her finger. "Must have happened when I bonked my head diving under the table." She looked past him at the body. "Is . . . is that . . . ?"

"Jade Su, yeah."

Eyes welling with tears, she rested her face on Ryan's chest, already sobbing.

Seriously? After all the names Jade had shouted at Kylie earlier, Gabe had assumed she'd be happy to see Jade dead.

"I know this is messed up," Addison said, positioning herself so Kylie could see her. "But I just realized something. Kylie was right here when Jade fell, and everyone here knows it." Addison gripped her arm. "Honey, if this was murder, you've got the perfect alibi."

Chapter 67

IZZY

NEWS OF JADE Su's highly theatrical death traveled quickly, and within an hour of her crashing through the ballroom's glass dome, half the promgoers' parents had arrived at the Pinecrest, anxious to collect their kids. Jade's parents had come too, and Izzy had spent several tearful minutes with them. Finally, two of the teachers pulled them away, freeing Izzy to continue her duties.

With the hotel's main parking lot suddenly a backed-up mess, Izzy put Gabe Fox in charge of establishing a pickup area on the back side of the building, leaving the front accessible only to police vehicles and ambulances.

Soon, Izzy had eight Rocky Harbor officers working under her. She put the two security guards in charge of guarding the exits, ensuring that Principal Peabody had an accurate count as to which kids had been released. Four of the officers she sent to secure the roof and the seven floors of hallways that looked out onto the dome. The others, she'd set to interviewing witnesses.

According to Fulton's latest text, the CSI team had left Dalton half an hour earlier, and he himself would arrive at the Pinecrest within the next few minutes. Having spent the last fifteen dealing with the grieving parents, Izzy was exhausted. She checked that everything was under control, then made her way outside to the front of the hotel, eager to hand over the reins of responsibility.

Clear and full of stars, the ink-black sky made a lovely backdrop to the half-moon above her. Lungs filled with the crisp night air, Izzy pinched her eyes shut. "Please, Lord. Help me find this Taker guy before he kills someone else."

"Detective! The chief is here."

About twenty yards away, the security guard manning the main entrance was waving Fulton's silver Nissan into the parking lot. Fulton turned down the nearest aisle and found an empty parking spot near the corner of the building. In moments, he was out and slipping into his suit jacket as he strode her way.

"I don't see Gloria Gomez." Fulton said.

Izzy looked around. "Fox directed the non-essential vehicles to the other side of the building. She's probably there recording kids and their parents as they're reunited."

"Makes sense." He looked up at the hotel. "There's not much to see out here."

Izzy led him up to the main entrance where the large wooden doors were propped open and a table and chairs had been set up beneath the overhang directly outside.

"What's going on there?" Fulton asked, reaching into his coat pocket.

"That's the high school principal and his chaperones," Izzy explained. "Once the kids have been interviewed, these people check them out to their parents. The others are still in the lobby. Come on, I'll show you."

Fulton quickly switching out his old Juicy Fruit for a fresh piece as they entered the lobby. A chaotic mess less than an hour ago, now, half the kids had gone home, and the mood was more like the last quarter of a Superbowl Party with the favored team behind by four touchdowns.

"The ballroom's behind those double doors," Izzy explained. They strode past the remaining partygoers, now huddled in small clusters around the lobby as the various police officers took down their statements.

"So, no injuries besides the dead girl?" Fulton whispered.

"Just a few cuts and bruises." Izzy stopped at the heavy table blocking the ballroom doors. "I had this placed here after I caught some kids trying to sneak back in." They dragged the table aside and headed inside.

"Holy cow." Fulton took in the body which hung motionless from the rope, still held in place by the remaining glass and metal framework. Then, he turned his gaze upward. "It would take a good drop to make a hole like that. How many floors are there above this dome?"

"Seven. I haven't been up there yet, but the two men I sent told me each floor has open-air walkways with views of the dome. They didn't find anything on the guest floors, but according to Vega, up on the roof there's a twenty-foot two-by-four stretched kitty-corner from one railing to the other."

"Oh, really? And how'd he get that up there without raising eyebrows?"

"There's a whole bunch of building materials on that roof. According to Vega, they're getting ready to build some sort of rooftop bar or something."

"I see, well, we can check that out once the CSI people get here." He looked at his watch. "It's almost one. They should be here any minute."

Izzy nodded. For the fourth time, the citizens of Rocky Harbor would rise to news of another grisly murder. But besides canceling prom, what could they have done differently? Other than the belt, the method used to kill Jade had no resemblance to those used in the Taker's prior killings. Realizing her nails were digging into the skin of her clenched fists, she turned away from the scene just as the CSI team entered the ballroom.

Having been roused from their beds, Andrea Muncy and her blue-overalled forensics specialists looked a bit disheveled as they made their way past overturned chairs and tables. Once they met up with Izzy and Fulton, everyone formed a circle around the body.

"The victim's name is Jade Su," Izzy began. "Jade was a senior at Rocky Harbor High, and, as you can see, she's still got both hands." She pointed at the sequined belt, still twisted around the girl's neck. "When she arrived at the dance, this was around her waist."

Glasses pushed down her nose, Andrea Muncie peered up at the damaged dome. "Have you been to the roof yet?"

"Not yet," Izzy said. "I sent a couple of officers up to secure the area, but nothing has been examined in depth. When you're ready, we can all go up. Chief . . . ?" She turned to Fulton. "Just so you know, Jade was one of Lexi Siegel's crew, so . . ."

"Great. I'm sure Gloria Gomez will love hearing that." Fulton glanced back in the direction of the lobby. "I didn't see Kylie McKenna. I assume she's okay."

"Kylie's got a little cut on her forehead, but, yeah, she's fine. She was also standing right here when the body struck the glass."

"So, she's got an alibi?" Fulton nodded thoughtfully, then turned to Andrea. "Ready to see the roof?"

"A soon as I get my people going here, yes."

"Take all the time you need," Fulton said. He pulled Izzy aside. "So, any new suspects?"

She shook her head.

"Too bad, but that's okay. In a way, I'm relieved Kylie's got an alibi." He lowered his mouth to her ear. "How about Fox? Is he clear too?"

"Seems like," Izzy told him. "He and Kylie were both down here before Jade fell through the glass. I saw them myself."

"Well, that's a relief."

"I know, right?" She thought for a moment. "Hey, I still haven't assigned anyone to check the security cameras. Or the perimeter and parking area, for that matter."

"Okay." He peered out through the now open doorway to the lobby where Fox and Vega stood chatting. "Put Vega on the cameras and give the outside job to Fox."

"You're playing it safe, aren't you?"

"I am."

Chapter 68

GABE

HAVING MADE HER assignments, Santos joined Fulton and headed for the elevators, leaving Vega a round-shouldered slouch. The young man looked at Gabe.

"So, you happy with that?" Vega asked him.

Of course, Vega wasn't. Over a week had passed since the kid was tasked with reviewing the security videos at Rudy's Tavern, and he hadn't stopped moaning about it. "I almost died of boredom," Vega had told anyone who listened, and now, he'd been tasked with looking at twenty times as many recordings.

"Happy? No," Gabe answered honestly. "But we do what we're told, right?"

"Yeah . . . we do." Vega looked back and forth between Gabe and the lobby.

Was this a crack in Vega's by-the-book shell? Great, because Gabe really wanted to see those security videos.

"What?" he asked, hoping Vega would voice his concerns.

Vega looked at Gabe, eyebrows raised. "Feel like switching jobs?"

It would be helpful knowing if Santos had seen him stalking Kylie. Plus, if Gabe learned who The Taker was, he could eliminate him. Dead men tell no tales, and the tale Gabe wanted kept secret was that he'd killed Darcy.

"I don't know. Santos wanted you to look at the videos." As he expected, Vega went all puppy eyed. "Oh, okay. I suppose she won't care as long as both jobs get done."

Vega's smile couldn't have been broader if Gabe had handed him a winning Lotto ticket. "Thanks, man." In a few long strides, he disappeared into the night.

No, thank you, Adrian.

Now, to see what those cameras had picked up.

At the front desk, Gabe asked to speak to whoever was in charge of security. The desk clerk made a quick call, and not even a minute passed when the ultimate nerd stepped out from a nearby hallway. Round-shouldered, thirtyish and hair already thinning, he introduced himself as Nelson, the head of security. Once they exchanged words and handshakes, Nelson then escorted Gabe down the same hallway he'd emerged from to a heavy metal door labeled with just one word: SECURITY. He entered a four-digit code into the pneumatic keypad, and with a sour-sounding buzz, the door popped open.

"After you," Nelson said.

The size of an average bedroom, the white-walled room was brightly lit, despite having no windows. Gabe stepped inside, and Nelson led him over to a huge computer station.

"Sweet setup, huh? Go on. Sit."

Gabe settled into the cushy leather desk chair. In front of him were three four-foot computer screens, each surrounded by at least ten smaller ones. A sweet setup indeed, but also intimidating. And how was he going to locate the recordings from the pool area with this guy hanging over him?

"It's a lot less complicated than it looks," Nelson assured him. "All you need is a quick tutorial."

And he was right. After a few minutes, Gabe was ready to rock and roll. He stood and, once again, offered Nelson his hand. "Thanks, man. The department owes you a big one. I apologize, but I need you to leave me to my work, now."

"Dude? Really?"

"Sorry, Nelson." Still shaking the geek's hands, Gabe led him to the door. "It's a need-to-know thing, and God knows what these cameras picked up. You understand."

Free of Nosey Nelson, Gabe pulled on some gloves and got down to work. Although finding Jade Su's killer would definitely contribute to his own self-preservation, his first concern was finding out what Santos had seen before she confronted him at the pool. He scrolled through the list of camera locations and soon found one in the main lobby. The Su girl had fallen through the glass right around midnight, so he wound the recording back to eleven-thirty and hit slow forward until Kylie entered the lobby. Soon, she was trotting down the hallway toward the pool with him skulking not far behind. Damn, what a dope.

He continued watching, and not long after, Santos appeared carrying her ham and cheese. Just as she'd told him, she exchanged words with the doorman who directed her down the same hall Gabe and Kylie had taken.

So where was Gabe at that time?

He searched through the various camera views, and a few minutes later, there he was, creeping along lushly-carpeted hallways and later, shrub-lined concrete paths, his bubble-headed stepdaughter completely unaware that a murderer was just a few steps behind her, sneaking through the shadows like Jack the Ripper. Damn. All he needed was a black cloak and top hat.

Had Santos seen him creeping like that? He gnawed one cuticle and then another as he tracked Kylie's progress. Finally, she found the open gate, trotted across the pool area and disappeared into the restroom. A few moments later, there was Gabe, tiptoeing up to the restroom door.

Jesus.

He paused the recording, curious about Santos. Barely a minute behind him, he found her strolling into the pool area, and soon after, surprising the crap out of him as he was reaching for the ladies' room door.

Man, he had certainly dodged *that* bullet. If the woman had shown up just sixty seconds later, she'd have walked in on him with Kylie's throat in his hands. But was Santos just being thoughtful, or was bringing him that sandwich an excuse to keep tabs? And why do that, unless—crap. They turned up something at Darcy's house.

His heart leaped in his chest. No. If that were true, he'd already be locked up.

Calmed by his logic, Gabe got up and took a closer look at the facility map pinned to the wall behind him. He soon located the building the girl had fallen from. Now, how many ways could a man get up there?

He found two elevators, one for service, the second, a straight shot to that rooftop bar they were building, but that one wasn't operational yet. With no elevators for Jade to ride in, Gabe focused on the two staircases, both of which started on the ground floor and went all the way up with a security camera on every floor. He started with the ground floor recordings and sat back to watch them in slow fast-forward. Vega had been smart to switch assignments. Even at triple speed, the job was like watching ice cream melt.

Having gnawed his right thumbnail down to a nub, Gabe started on his left, but after what seemed like an eternity of staring at empty stairwells, his efforts paid off. A masked figure pushed open the door to the west stairwell and pranced up to the second floor. Heart pounding, Gabe switched the image to one of the larger screens.

Was this his guy? He leaned in to study the new arrival, who, like every other male promgoer, was all decked out in white tie and tails.

At the sight of Jade Su entering the stairwell, Gabe knew he was on the right track. He switched from one camera view to another as the masked fool danced and clapped, coaxing the Su girl to follow him up each flight of stairs. With the guy masked and no sound, Gabe couldn't tell if he was saying anything, but Jade was sure yapping. She kept calling up to him—probably begging him to come back down.

Gabe tracked their progress until they reached the door leading to the roof. All that was left was to follow the pair outside. He scanned the board and found there were two cameras up there, but since the bar hadn't been built yet, they hadn't been plugged in. Damn. It would be nice to know the details.

Chair swishing from side to side, he rewound the last recording and froze the fool in mid-prance, both arms raised and one foot raised.

Damned masks. Why did Mardi Gras have to be the prom theme?

No closer to discovering who the Taker was, Gabe slumped back in his chair. Nothing was going his way these days. Not Angie. Not Kylie. He remembered how badly things had gone by the pool. Had the girl inherited some sort of self-preservation gene from her mother? Well, if not Kylie, then he would kill Robby—and the sooner the better. A gas explosion would work. He'd lose the house, but wasn't that why people bought homeowner's insurance?

He smirked, realizing that by blowing the house up, he might manage to collect on both kids' policies. All well and good, but right now, he needed to ID this jester guy. Those bannisters were smooth, stainless steel. Maybe . . . he looked at the guy's hands. "Well, hell."

Unlike all the other boys, this one was still wearing his white gloves, so finding fingerprints was out. Was there really no way to identify this joker? Again, he looked the frozen figure up and down, and this time, he smiled.

HE FOUND ADRIAN Vega in the back parking lot which was now littered with plastic evidence markers. The kid had placed them beside cigarette butts, a gas station receipt, pretty much anything that didn't move.

Seeing Gabe approach, Vega checked his watch. "Don't tell me you're finished already."

Gabe pressed his lips together, hoping he looked apprehensive. "You aren't going to believe what happened." He must have given off the right vibe, because Vega put down the remaining stack of markers and joined him alongside a gold-colored Buick.

"What? Somebody else die?"

"No, not that bad . . . but it's weird."

"Spit it out, Gabe. If you were my doctor, I'd think you were gonna tell me I have cancer."

He looked Vega in the eye. "Somebody got to the recordings ahead of me."

"What . . . ?"

"I'm saying the recordings were blank. Every single camera view."

"You're shitting me."

"No, Vega, I am not shitting you. And I can't figure out how they managed, because the door's got one of those keypads to get in. I'd have been here sooner, but I was rewinding, checking to see if it had really all been deleted."

"Oh, man." Vega slumped against the Buick, his eyes pinched shut. "I do not want to tell Santos that.

"Neither do I, Adrian. But it's *you* who's got to do it. Not me."

Vega nodded. "You were doing me a favor. I get it." He looked at Gabe. "And what reason would you have to delete that stuff? Everybody knows Kylie was down in the ballroom when that girl fell."

Chapter 69

IZZY

IT WAS BREEZY up on the hotel roof, but to Izzy's surprise, not that cold for April. In the distance, Atherton Lake glistened under a crescent moon. Was that what had drawn Jade Su up there? The view?

She took a moment to take in her surroundings. Once the rooftop bar had been completed, it would doubtless be very nice up there, but now, the amazing lake view was diminished by the building's skeleton-like framework and the various stacks of wood, tools, and sheetrock piled all around them. This new killing had Izzy confused, because other than Kylie McKenna, no lines could be drawn to connect all four deaths. Some victims had hands, others didn't. All had been killed privately, but unlike the first three bodies, which were left out for eventual discovery, Jade's body had been presented to the public and in the most immediate and elaborate method possible.

As Andrea phoned downstairs for two of her techs to come up, Fulton joined Izzy at the wooden railing, and for a few quiet moments, all they did was stare down at the triangular hole in the dome six floors below.

"It's just like Vega described," Izzy said, resting a gloved hand on the end of the twenty-foot two-by-four the killer had hammered onto the railing in front of them. The board ran on a diagonal to the attached wall where it had also been nailed to the railing. In Vega's words, kitty-corner.

"For all this to happen, that door alarm had to have been disconnected," Fulton said. "How did he know how to do that?"

It was a good question. "I don't know. Books, friends . . . the Internet. For all we know, there are five YouTube videos showing how to do it."

"You're probably right."

Finished with her call, Andrea stepped over and squeezed in between them. "Got any more gum?" she asked Fulton.

He shared the pack around. "Ready to tell us about that rope, now?"

"I am." Andrea popped the gum into her mouth then folded the wrapper as she spoke. "The killer looped the rope around the center of the two-by-four, then hammered the board into place on both ends so the knot would be right over the dome, as you can see. Once secured, he then tied the other end of the rope around the victim's waist."

Izzy glanced down at the two-foot stub of rope—three if the knot was counted. "So, he tied the rope here, threw the body over the side, and with the help of the two-by-four, Jade ended up hanging out over the dome?"

"That's right."

Again Izzy peered over the railing, this time imagining Jade's body dangling there with kids dancing far below. "Even if they looked up, the lights would prevent them from seeing her, and at midnight most of the hotel guests would be in bed."

"That's a big risk for the killer," Fulton said, "but you're probably right."

"I agree. And that risk panned out." Having folded her gum wrapper into a tiny foil square, Andrea dropped it into her pocket. "Once the body was in position, all he had to do was rig the timer."

"An amazing little device," Fulton said. "And so simple."

They frowned down at what was left of the rope, and a few feet away, a foot-tall stack of scrap wood. On top lay a small pile of ash and a singed cigarette filter.

"And that's what makes it so impressive," Andrea continued. "He simply collected these little chunks of two-by-four and, like building blocks, stacked them below the rope. Once that was ready, he lit a cigarette, tucked it inside a matchbook right next to the match heads, then placed them on top of the wood stack and directly beneath this rope which, at that point, would have been stretched taught by the weight of the body." She drew an imaginary line from the ash to the top of the railing and the two-by-four nailed there.

Izzy bent over the little ash pile. "And how long would it take a cigarette to burn down enough to ignite the matches?"

"About ten minutes. That flame then burned through the rope, causing the body to drop approximately seventy feet to the dome, cracking a handful of glass panels, shattering one, and eventually falling through."

"Humph." Fulton chewed his gum thoughtfully. "Izzy?"

"It's definitely a neat trick. And apparently, it gives our killer plenty of time to get back downstairs."

Fulton grunted. "So, now we're back to square one, meaning our suspect could virtually be anyone, including Kylie McKenna."

Fulton was right, and, of course, everyone was capable of murder in the right situation, but Kylie just didn't seem capable. Was it just a gut feeling, or could it be more than that?

As Fulton continued to discuss the evidence with Andrea, Izzy strolled the rooftop considering Kylie's reaction when she discovered her dad had followed her out to the pool. Kylie's running off in a huff might have been normal teenaged angst, but what if it was just her way to put space between them? If Kylie was fast, she could have rushed back to the ladies room and taunted Jade into following her up to the roof. Easy enough, especially if it was actually Kylie who had copied Jade's dress. With all the construction material lying around, finding the right board wouldn't be a problem. Hammering it in place, preparing the rope, and the cigarette trick would have only taken a minute or two. And how long would it take a teenager to dash back down to the dance? Two minutes? Three?

She ran it over with Fulton.

"That's a lot of what ifs," Fulton told her. "I thought that little voice of yours said Kylie didn't do it."

"It does." Kylie chewed her lip, annoyed by her indecision. "But how do I know where that voice is coming from? For all I know, there's a demon inside me."

"A demon? Really?" Fulton chucked. "Let's just wait until Vega's finishes with the security cameras. If your theory's true, he'll find something to support it."

"Right." Izzy eyed what was left of the burnt-through rope. "The guy must have experimented, you know? Like burning different types and thicknesses of rope until he knew just what kind worked best and exactly where and how to place his little fire bomb beneath it."

"I would have," Fulton said. "Hell, he might have even used an accelerant to guarantee the rope burned through."

Sure, and Andrea would know soon enough, but why did the killer have to be a he? Izzy shared the story of Kylie and Jade's recent dustup over the dresses.

"So, you're thinking Kylie might have copied Jade's dress?" Fulton asked.

"I'm saying we shouldn't just accept her word about who bought the dress first and why."

But she's innocent, the voice insisted.

Ignoring it, Izzy said, "This was all planned in advance. The killer may not have had Jade in mind, but he sure intended to kill someone. He wouldn't know if there would be rope, so he'd have stashed it ahead of time. With so much stuff lying around, there would be lots of workers. A coil of rope wouldn't stand out."

"Agreed." Fulton opened the nearest toolbox and peered in. "He sure didn't need to bring a hammer."

Eager to hear what the hotel video system would show them, Izzy was about to head downstairs when Vega appeared looking strangely sheepish.

"What's up?" Fulton asked. "Find anything good on those recordings?"

"Chief, I've got some bad news."

"How's that?" Fulton looked at his watch. "You've barely been at it an hour. There's no way you could have gone through all that material." Eying Vega's slouched posture, Fulton sighed. "Okay, Adrian. Spill it."

"Sir, I went into the security office, just like you said to . . ." His gaze dropped to the pea gravel rooftop.

"And?"

"And there weren't any recordings. They were blank. Every one of them. And that door's got one of those keypad things. Only managers who know the code."

Izzy couldn't believe her ears. She glared at Vega. "How many managers are there?"

"I-I don't know."

"Well, crap." Fulton peered out over the lake. "I was really counting on those recordings."

So was Izzy. God, why did everything have to be so difficult? She looked back at the charred cigarette filter and gasped. "Hang on, Chief. The cigarette burned down, but we still have the filter. If the killer put it between his lips to light it . . ."

"True enough," Andrea said. "I'll check it out."

"Good," Fulton said. "There could be DNA on the filter. But even if there is, we'll only get a match if the killer's already in the database."

"But we could test people," Izzy insisted. "Compare their DNA to the DNA on the cigarette filter. People would volunteer."

"Sure," Fulton said. "But who do we test? The staff? The promgoers? What about the hotel guests? At almost two thousand dollars a pop, the department can't afford it."

"What if the security videos can be recovered?" Andrea suggested. "I mean, my people don't have the skills, but maybe I can find someone who does."

"Yes, look into it," Fulton said. "Those recordings were deleted for a reason."

Chapter 70

IZZY

WHILE ANDREA MUNCIE was tracking down someone who could retrieve the Pinecrest's deleted security videos, Izzy worked on background checks. The Pinecrest employed more than a hundred people and had more than as many guests the night Jade Su crashed through the dome. Testing everyone's DNA was a budget buster, but looking into all those criminal records wasn't nearly as pricey. Still, it would take time. Knowing Izzy couldn't do it all herself, Fulton had assigned her five officers, and the six of them spent Sunday morning working through the two lists. When they broke for lunch, she phoned Fulton at home.

"How's Tita Maggie doing with her crutches?" she asked.

"As you know, your aunt's got a strong independent streak. She refuses to sleep in the downstairs bedroom, and when she hobbles up those stairs . . ."

Izzy heard concern in Fulton's voice, but also pride. "Make sure she does it the way her physical therapist taught her. And don't let her overdo it."

"Easier said than done. I should know, since I still haven't found somebody who can retrieve those videos. How are the background checks going?"

Izzy groaned. "Slow. It would have been nice to have found some unexpected fingerprints in the security room. Anyway, since the videos were deleted, we started checking everyone with security access, which is mostly the five managers, and all but two commute from Dalton. There were two here yesterday, but one went home at seven, long before the prom really got going. Neither have high school-aged children, so, on the surface, it's not likely that any of them knew Jade personally. And none have criminal records. There's also the head of security, Dave Morgan, ex-marine in his fifties. Dave has two people working under him, but the hotel manager assured me that all three were well-vetted before any of them got hired."

"Anyone else have access?" Fulton asked.

"Two cleaning ladies. They're let in once a day to empty wastebaskets and such, but they don't have pass codes. I had them checked out too. Both are clean."

"So, of all the people with pass codes, which of them were on duty Saturday night?"

"One assistant manager and one security guy. Like I said, neither had criminal records but during our interview, the security guy volunteered that he'd hacked into his high school database when he was sixteen."

"That was nice, considering minors' records are normally sealed."

"Yeah, I don't think it's him. The guy just doesn't seem the type."

"Was that your gut talking, or that demon you mentioned last night?" Fulton asked.

"Both." Izzy chuckled. "Now, I'm hearing two voices."

"Don't, kid. Hey, how hard was it to delete those recordings, anyway?"

"Not very. The hardest part is getting into the room." She referred to her notes. "That said, everybody with the passcode checked out, but that doesn't mean one of them didn't share it with a friend or one of the other employees."

"No, it doesn't. What's your next move?"

"I thought maybe I'd call Dalton PD and get the details on that rope, see if it's sold here in town."

"Okay, sounds—Maggie, stop! I told you to wait and I'd get it for you."

"What's she doing?"

"Trying to carry a cup of coffee into the den."

"On crutches? I tried that when I broke my leg skiing. Get a mop."

IZZY SAT AT her desk with the burrito she'd sent out for, ready for the Zoom call she and her friend Erina had arranged. Soon, she and Erina were facing each other through their computer screens.

"What have you got there?" Izzy asked. "A gyro?"

"It is." Erina turned her little white bundle toward the screen for Izzy to see. "Looks good, no? A new Greek place just opened down the street." She took a big bite and picked up a stack of papers.

"Is that the autopsy report for Jade Su?" Izzy asked. She bit into her burrito, eager for new information.

Erina nodded. "Andrea finished it this morning." She flipped through the documents, then settled on one. "Like the first murder, she was strangled with a belt."

Still chewing, Izzy nodded and swallowed quickly. "Then, how about prints or DNA? He had to grip that belt pretty tightly."

"No prints. We did find fibers consistent with the tuxedo worn by her date, but apparently, every other boy there was wearing similar clothing, all rented from the same local store. We did find some DNA. Too early to know whose, but you said she had a date, so I'm guessing it belongs to . . ." She ran her finger down the page and stopped. "Jamari Hinkle. Should we gather his DNA for comparison?"

"Well, I considered that at first, and he was wearing a tux, but according to half the people at the dance, he was standing outside the ladies room most of the time Jade was missing. I presume it's also too early for the blood toxicology results?"

"You assume correctly. I find it interesting that Jade still had her hands. Do you have any idea why the killer didn't take them?"

"Not really," Izzy said honestly. "Maybe they worried someone at the dance would miss them. I mean, cutting a person's hands off takes time—plus, there's the blood spatter to plan for."

"Yes, I've only done it in my anatomy classes, but those bodies had been drained. Cutting into a fresh body would be much messier."

Gross. Izzy envisioned Erina smiling enthusiastically as she sawed through a cadaver's wrist. "Fun stuff, huh?"

"More fascinating that fun." Erina took another bite of her gyro, and for a while, they enjoyed each other's company.

"Anything special about the rope?" Izzy asked.

"Nothing. It's sold everywhere. Rocky Harbor, Eureka, Dalton. Even that little forest town, Pembroke sells it in their hardware store."

"You checked?" Izzy asked.

Erina chuckled. "I had a few minutes. There are fifteen stores in a hundred-mile radius."

"Ouch." Izzy could check store videos, but who knew when the rope was purchased? Was it last week? Last month? "That's going to take a while to research. How about the fingerprints your guys found up on the roof? Did any belong to someone who shouldn't be up there?"

Still chewing, Erina held up six fingers, then swallowed. "None were hotel employees, so I ran them through the database for you."

"Aren't you the busy bee. Tell me you got a hit on one of them."

"Actually, no." Erina cleared her throat. "One was employed by Triple-A Heating and Air, the company that installed the air conditioning units. The others worked for Harbor Construction, the company hired to build that rooftop bar. That's out of Dalton. They all live there, and none have a record. Here, I'll email you the report."

"Okay, thanks." Izzy slumped back in her chair. They were no closer to finding the killer and probably wouldn't be anytime soon. "There's going to be another murder, isn't there?"

Still typing, Erina looked glumly up from her keyboard. "I don't see why not. This is just my opinion, but I think they're enjoying it."

Izzy sat back, no longer hungry.

Chapter 71

RYAN

RYAN STARTED HIS shift at Seaside Market on Tuesday evening, three days after the prom disaster. He spent the whole time stocking shelves with everything from canned vegetables to detergent. His boss, a beefy man in his fifties named Tony, stepped over and nodded his approval.

"Nice work. Just like I taught you." Tony looked at his watch. "Oh, time flies when you're having fun, huh?" He pointed at the cluster of empty vegetable cartons at their feet. "Before you go home, I need you to take those out back, break them down, and toss them in the recycling dumpster. It's the—"

"Blue one." Ryan chuckled. "Yeah, you've mentioned it a few times."

"Yeah, well, the last kid should have known, too. Maybe he was distracted. You know, mooning over his girlfriend." He started off down the aisle, then, without turning, added, "Or maybe he was just stupid."

Ryan chuckled, and as he picked up the empty boxes, thought over what Tony had just said. In the past three days since Jade's murder, he'd done quite a bit of mooning. But how could he *not* worry about Kylie after everything she'd been through? Her mom's accident was bad enough, but then all those people she knew got killed, and the cops had actually called her in for an interview.

It was all ridiculous. Kylie, a serial killer? To kill those people you had to be a total headcase—the complete opposite of Kylie. He recalled the way she lit up whenever she saw him, the way her coppery bangs shaded her eyes the first time she bent over his geometry book.

Focus, Ryan told himself. When you finish your work, you can call her.

Arms loaded with empty cartons, Ryan carried them into the dimly lit stockroom. Day shift employees had unloaded a delivery truck that afternoon, and even though he'd shelved quite a few items, there were still several box-filled pallets. He pulled a utility knife from his pocket. But as he sliced through the cardboard, he again found himself thinking of Kylie, and how he couldn't wait to spend more time together after graduation.

Hopefully, the cops will have caught that Taker guy by then.

Ryan had never met the first victim, Kylie's old babysitter, but he did have Mrs. Del Campo back in freshman year, and Jade he'd known from when he was dating Lexi. He sighed, remembering the last time he and Lexi spoke. More of an argument, really. About Kylie.

Yeah, Lexi could be sweet, and she was definitely a pain at times, but she sure didn't deserve what she got.

With a growing guilt knot swelling in the back of his throat, he sliced into the other boxes. Come on, man. Lexi's dead, and it's horrible. But it's not your fault and it's sure not Kylie's.

Like giant playing cards, Ryan shuffled the cardboard into a neat stack which he tucked under one arm and carried over to the big roll-up door on the back wall. With a push of the fist-sized red button, the door to the loading dock rumbled upward.

What the heck? All three of the alleyway's street lights were out.

"Hey, Boss!" Ryan called over to Tony's office, just a few feet away. "The lights in the alley are all broken."

"Again? I should probably get some cameras installed out there." Tony waved Ryan over, and after banging around in his desk, handed him a battered old flashlight. "That should do you." He sat back at his desk. "And when you're done with the cardboard, get the push broom. That broken glass will need sweeping."

Standing out on the loading dock, Ryan shined the flashlight into the darkness. Tony was right about the mess. There were shards of glass everywhere. Stupid kids. He trotted down the four concrete steps to the alleyway below and cast the flashlight beam onto the pavement ahead of him. The area really was creepy without the streetlights. He put the cardboard down and flipped the big blue dumpsters lid open. It rested against one of the many overgrown rhododendron bushes camouflaging the high cinder block wall behind them.

Just toss the stuff in there and leave, Ryan told himself. He set the flashlight down and as he dropped the cardboard into the bin, dead leaves rustled somewhere in the shadows.

Oh, man. He snatched up the flashlight and lit up the bushes, now overflowing with pink and white blooms. Was something back there? Crouching, he cast the flashlight beam along the ground beneath those bushes, but all he could make out was a small black box half buried in the leaves. A rat trap. No sign of rats though.

As Ryan straightened, a pleasant aroma came to him. Musky and sweet, and slightly damp. Was it the flowers? As he stared at the bushes, more crunching came from the darkness beneath them. Loud crunching.

A lot louder than any rat could produce. Imagining one scurrying across his shoe, Ryan stepped away from the bins, flashlight aimed in the direction of the sound. The light caught a small branch bobbing as if something had recently brushed against it.

But that was knee high. Way too high for a rat.

"Somebody back there?" he called out, feeling a bit silly.

No one answered.

But that branch didn't move itself.

After a quick scan of the pavement, he picked up the biggest rock he could find and threw it into the bushes. The stone had barely left his hand when a young raccoon burst out. Ryan stumbled backwards as the animal galloped past him and disappeared into the shadows.

He chuckled at his shaking hands, grateful Kylie wasn't there to see.

"Mystery solved," he muttered and moved to the back of the dumpster to flip the lid shut. As the lid dropped down, a different floral scent came to him. Wasn't that Cypher, the perfume he'd given Kylie after Jessie Ortiz spilled spaghetti all over her?

"Thought you could sneak up on me huh?" Expecting Kylie, Ryan smiled, but before he could turn around, a dark line dipped past his eyes, tightening around his neck. He clawed at the thing, unable to breathe, and as he neared hysteria, managed to squeeze his fingers beneath and caught a quick breath. Relieved and strengthened, he reached back and—his attacker slammed him into the dumpster.

Searing pain radiated from his shoulder, his neck.

Weakened, a hard shove dropped Ryan to his knees and then, onto his face. Bleary-eyed, his heart leaped at the sight of a familiar figure standing in the loading bay doorway.

Tony.

Ryan reached into his right front pocket and pulled out his car keys. But it was the small laser pen he was looking for. He fumbled for the button, and as his eyes closed, a thread of red light shot from his hand.

Chapter 72

THE TAKER

SINCE THE FRONT of the supermarket was mostly windows, it had been easy for The Taker to watch Ryan from a safe distance. He'd sat hunched inside his car, watching Ryan stock shelves. Having assumed Ryan would dispose of the empty cardboard boxes behind the store, he'd snuck back for a look and decided to break all the streetlights, just as he had at Stafford Park.

With no lights, The Taker had snuck up on Ryan easily, but how could he know the guy would pull out a laser pen? He sighed as the thread of cherry-colored light spanned the alleyway between them and the open loading dock doorway.

Unlike his other victims, tonight's plan wasn't to kill Ryan, but to trick him. That's why he'd worn Kylie's perfume. If Ryan believed she'd attacked him, he'd be crazy not to tell the cops about it. But now that it was actually happening, the whole plan seemed childishly overcomplicated.

No, Ryan had to die. That settled, he cuffed the laser pen from the boy's lifeless grasp and tightened his grip on his hand-made garrote. But then, he spotted some fat guy standing on loading dock. And he was looking their way.

"Hey, Ryan, what's with the laser?"

What the hell?

"Ryan?" the voice boomed. "What's going on over there? Somebody with you?"

Damn it. The fat guy was coming their way. Confident his dark clothes and ski mask would make him unidentifiable, The Taker pushed his way through the shrubbery and grabbed the top of the wall, cursing the laser pen as he pulled himself up. From there he could see the entire backside of the store. The big guy, too. Surprisingly fast, the man had already cut the distance between them by half.

Without waiting to see if his pursuer was also good at climbing walls, he dropped over to the other side. The market backed onto Walnut Avenue, a street lined with warehouses and personal storage businesses. He'd never seen many people there in daylight. Now, it was downright desolate. Not ready to pull the mask off, he started off down the empty street at a sprint. Sure, it looked suspicious, but who would see him? He raced for his car, four blocks away. Far in the distance, a police siren wailed and another joined it seconds later.

He'd been stupid to go after Ryan at work. Success with the women had made him cocky, and now he was paying for it. He reached the first corner and peeked around the edge of the high-walled warehouse building. The only thing moving was a gray cat trotting across the street.

He ignored the urge to keep running and strode off down the sidewalk accompanied by the cat which left his side when a gust of wind sent a crinkled candy wrapper tumbling back the way they'd come.

Here began the older, seedier part of town, rundown houses fronted with abandoned cars and overflowing garbage cans. Seeing most of the homes still had lights on, he pulled off the mask and stuffed it into the hoodie's kangaroo pocket. A good thing, too, because not two seconds later, a police car turned onto the street behind him. He finger-combed his hair and kept walking, eyes forward, the urge to bolt mounting inside him.

He would stay cool. Stroll. Just an innocent guy trying not to run into one of the many garbage cans lined up across the sidewalk. But the cruiser stuck with him, and he'd only taken a half dozen steps when he heard one of the car's windows roll down, probably the passenger's side.

A stream of sweat rolled down the side of his face. As he debated whether wiping away the sweat would be worse than leaving it, whoever was driving the police car aimed a spotlight his way, pinning him there like an actor on the stage.

Heart beating its way through his chest, the siren's *whoop-whoop* made him jump. He was about to turn when a disembodied voice burst from a loudspeaker, "Boy, what the hell are you doing here?"

"Just taking a walk, officer. Something wrong with that?"

"In this part of town?"

He knew that voice. Unable to see, he shaded his eyes from the light as the driver's side door clicked open, and Gabe Fox stepped out of the car, gun drawn. "Hands behind your head . . . Luke."

Chapter 73

GABE

THE LOOK ON the boy's face was priceless. Wide-eyed, Luke Manetti blinked rapidly as Gabe strode toward him. "Whoa, hey, what's wrong, Officer Fox? I didn't do anything."

"Of course, you didn't." Gabe had caught Luke just two blocks away from where Kylie's boyfriend had almost been murdered. He aimed his Glock at Luke's chest. "Son, I don't want to hurt you, so do as I say. Lace your fingers behind your head and turn around."

Slowly, Luke followed Gabe's instructions. "You're making a mistake. Please, sir, if you'd just let me—"

"Shut up and step back toward me." He led the boy to the cruiser where he ordered him to rest his face on the car's hood so he could cuff him.

"Hey, uh . . . this is really embarrassing," Luke began. "I was hoping I wouldn't have to tell you this, but—"

Gabe ignored the chatter and kicked at Luke's instep, pushing his feet outward. "Okay, now don't move." Starting at the bottom, he patted Luke down. When he got to the bulge in the boy's sweatshirt pocket, he reached in and pulled out a black ski mask. "What's this for?"

"That's what I was trying to tell you. See, I've got this skin condition. It's really rare, and if my face gets too cold, it starts to itch, so . . ."

Gabe chuckled. "Right, and you've got that on your hands too?"

"Huh?"

Gabe snapped the cuff of one of the blue nitrile gloves Luke had forgotten to take off.

"Yes, that's exactly why. Normally, I wear—"

"Oh, give it up, already." Gabe grabbed Luke by the back of his hoody and pulled. "The grocery store manager didn't get a good look at the attacker because he was all dressed in black. Just like you. Coincidence?" He opened the back door of the car and guided Luke over. "Watch your head."

"Somebody got attacked at the market?" Luke sounded surprised. He continued his yapping even as he lowered himself into the car's back seat.

"Hey, that's just down the street, isn't it? Now, I understand why you're so suspicious, Mr. Fox, but that's okay, everybody makes mistakes. Just let me go, and I promise I won't file charges."

Gabe shut the door and as he stepped around to the driver's side, examined the knit mask. He had the kid dead to rights. With a sigh, he slipped behind the wheel and turned back to regard the infamous Taker, discovering the boy's pleading eyes just inches from the grate that separated them.

"Please, Mr. Fox. I'm in the Junior Police Department. I played Marco Polo in your pool. You know me."

"Yeah, I do know you, Luke. More than you realize, so shut up while I make this call."

As if slapped, Luke dropped his chin and slumped back against the seat, eyes and lips pinched shut.

Silence, finally. Eyes on the rear-view mirror, Gabe reached for the radio. "This is fifty-eight. Still searching the area around the market. Nothing so far, over."

Luke's eyes flew open faster than a zipper in a whorehouse.

"Yeah." Gabe grinned into the mirror. "Didn't expect that, did you?"

Chapter 74

LUKE

LUKE SAT BACK and waited for Fox's next move. It twisted his gut to admit it, but handcuffed and locked into the backseat of the cruiser, it was all he could do.

And Fox turning left at the next corner only confused Luke more, because the police station was in the opposite direction. Unable to meet Fox's eyes in the rearview mirror, he rested his head against the side window. They drove on in silence as houses evolved into pastures and pastures became deep dark forests.

After a while, the car's headlights flashed across a small green road sign. They were headed toward Lake Atherton? But except for the resort area, there was nothing but forest out there. He stared at the back of the man's head, considering the possibilities. Had Fox been friends with Rosa Del Campo? Lovers, even? No, that was dumb. Everybody said she was gay. And if Fox was defending Kylie's honor, then why weren't they heading for the police station?

Luke drew a sharp breath.

"Something wrong?" Fox said, eying him through the rearview mirror.

"No, I'm fine." He stared back.

Did Fox intend to kill him, or was Luke just projecting what he would do if roles were reversed? He closed his eyes, hoping it was the latter.

Just chill, Luke told himself. You do your best thinking when you're calm. He focused on his breathing. Once that was under control, he would work on his story. He hadn't even started on his first goal when his eyes flew open. Fox had turned onto a deeply rutted road. A logging road. Luke sat forward, his face pressed to the grate separating the two. "Excuse me, sir."

"Yes, Luke?"

"W-where are we going?"

No answer.

Luke peered out the front window, but all he could see was a narrow ribbon of copper-colored dirt bordered on both sides by redwoods. He shivered.

"What's the matter, buddy, you cold? Want me to turn the heat up?"

Luke shook his head and settled back in his seat.

After a few minutes, they rumbled to a stop, and Fox pushed open his door, lighting up the car's interior. "End of the line. Everybody out." He opened the back door for Luke.

Blinking against the sudden brilliance, Luke remembered the desolate housing development he'd killed Lexi in and scooted his butt toward the opposite side of the car. Even with his nose crushed against the window, all he could see outside was black and emptiness. Such a lonesome place. Not the kind *he* ever expected to die in.

Bang! Bang! Bang! Fox pounded on the car roof, making Luke jump.

"Come on," Fox said. "Don't you want to stretch your legs?"

The edge in his voice told Luke to stay put. He leaned down to look at Fox's face. "What if I don't want to?"

"Here are your options." Fox rested his right hand on his revolver. The left, he lay gently across a yellow and black taser gun. "I doubt you'll like either of them."

There was that grin again.

Trying not to shake, Luke edged across the seat toward the open door, and Fox helped him climb out. Behind the car, taillights reddened the earth and grass. In front, headlights showed what appeared to be a meadow scattered with tree stumps. Fox took his arm and guided him through the tall grass.

Although Luke had already killed three people, the possibility of his own mortality had never occurred to him. But it did now. He remembered seeing a shovel in the trunk of Officer Andres' car when he and Jeff had gone on that ride along a while back. Andres had told them the shovel was standard issue, so Fox probably carried one too. He tried licking his lips, but found no saliva to moisten them.

"Come on, Mr. Fox. You're making a big mistake."

A light wind chilled his feet inside his grass-soaked thrift store shoes. It also carried the smell of cut redwood along with the more disturbing scent of decay. Luke squinted into the darkness. Was there already a hole out there, waiting for him? No, the guy'd had no reason until half an hour ago.

Urged along by Fox's not-so-gentle shoves, Luke stumbled through the grass, the headlights stretching his shadow out in front of him.

"Wha-what are you going to do to me?" he asked, not caring about the crack in his voice. "Please . . . don't kill me. Y-you're a cop for God's sake."

"Hell, kid, if your voice gets any higher you're gonna sound like Kylie. Relax, I didn't bring you here to kill you. This is one of my favorite spots." Fox pointed into the darkness. "There's a great place to fish back behind those trees."

Finding no reason for Fox to lie, relief flooded through Luke, weakening his legs. If he didn't sit down, he was going to fall over. The handcuffs didn't help, and he staggered over to the closest stump. Hands shaking behind him, he gathered all the nerve he could muster. "I'm glad you aren't going to kill me, but you didn't bring me out here to share fishing stories, either. What do you want?"

Fox smirked. "Well, first, I want to congratulate you. That was some crazy shit you pulled at the prom. It's too soon to know if you left evidence at tonight's screw up, but the CSI team hasn't found one damned thing at any of the other crime scenes. I'd shake your hand, but . . ." Fox glanced down at Luke's bound arms and shrugged.

"Well, if you want to shake my hand so bad, take these cuffs off me."

"Boy, you never know when to quit, do you?"

Gabe's backhanded slap spun Luke's head around. It also pissed him off. "Hey! You're the one who said you didn't have any evidence."

No longer smiling, Fox tisked. "I said the CSI team didn't find any evidence. Remember all those video cameras the hotel has?"

Of course. Luke wasn't an idiot. Hadn't he tricked Jade with Jamari's stolen mask? And the day before that, he'd worn a wide-brimmed hat and dark glasses when he disconnected the staircase alarm and stashed the rope on the roof. Fox had to be bluffing. Any recordings of him and Jade would just show some guy in white tie and tails. The mask would prevent anyone from seeing his face, and with the gloves, no one could say if the guy was black or white.

"Okay, what about the cameras?" he said, not wanting to get slapped again.

Fox crossed his arms over his chest. "You did a great job of luring that girl up to the roof, kid, and using the boyfriend's mask was smart. But you forgot something."

What? He narrowed his gaze on Fox, wishing the guy would get to the point.

"It was so obvious." Fox tapped Luke's shoe with his own. "The evidence was right there for anybody who knows what to look for."

Luke peered down at his scruffy sneakers, their laces now muddy and wet from dragging through the grass. "Are you saying I wore these raggedy old things to prom?"

"Good one." Fox chuckled. "No, no. It was the laces, Luke. The laces."

"What? So, one of my shoe is untied. If it bothers you so much, cut me loose and I'll tie them."

"Bother me? Hell no. You're proving my point."

"I . . . I don't understand."

"Come on, kid. You've been to my house a thousand times, and every time, your stupid laces were dragging. Sometimes one shoe, sometimes on both. That's what I saw in the video, Luke. A guy with his laces dragging. You."

"That's no evidence."

"Maybe not for the FBI, but it's sure enough for me. Don't get me wrong. I admire you. I mean, you may have screwed up with Ryan, but you definitely got away with killing those other three."

What was this guy trying to say? He studied Fox's face, half lit by the car's headlights. "What do you mean, *three*? I killed—"

"Oooh, I was wondering how you'd respond to that. What? Are you trying to take credit for Darcy Callahan?"

What was Fox implying? The Callahan woman was the only victim Luke couldn't claim, but nobody knew that except for him . . . and the real killer. "You mean . . . you . . . ?"

"Bingo!" Half-lit by the headlights, Fox's grin looked demonic. "Yeah, I killed Darcy *and* I cut her hands off. All you did was copy."

"All I did? They must have told you how I rigged Jade to fall through the glass. It was classic."

"Okay, you're right." Fox patted his shoulder. "That was pretty good."

Strangely, the knowledge that Fox was also a killer reassured Luke. In a twisted way, they were brothers. But something didn't jive. The man hadn't brought him out there to share murder stories.

Fox grinned down at him. "I have to admit, when I stuck you in the back seat, I wasn't sure *what* I would do with you. That's why I brought you out here. So I'd have time to think."

"And?"

"And"—Still smiling, Fox gripped Luke's chin in his hand—"I came up with the best plan, ever."

Chapter 75

KYLIE

KYLIE TURNED OFF her alarm and sat up in bed. Where was her cell phone? Not on the charger. Still half asleep, she shuffled downstairs and found it lying on the kitchen table. That solved, she opened the fridge, and had just grabbed a Snapple bottle when her phone buzzed. A text from Addison. Apparently, the third one she'd received in the last ten minutes:

Have you heard from Ryan?

Where are you?

Call me when you see this.

Kylie stiffened. The last time she'd spoken to Ryan was yesterday evening, right before he went to work. Had something happened to him? Heart in her throat, she grabbed the phone and had just started to call Addison when the phone vibrated in her hand.

Startled, she dropped the phone and the Snapple. The bottle shattered on the hard tile floor spraying juice and glass everywhere. She located the phone under the table, dotted with juice and snatched it up, and in the process, cut her palm on a piece of broken glass. "Damn it!" Seeing it was Addison, Kylie swiped the wet screen across her pajama top and pressed the phone to her ear, terrified of what her friend might say.

"What happened to Ryan?" she croaked. "Is he dead?"

"No, honey, no, but somebody did attack him behind the market last night. He's in the hospital."

"I'm heading over." She hung up and grabbed a dishtowel. Wound wrapped, she headed up to change and had just reached the top of the stairs when Gabe stepped out of his bedroom dressed in gym shorts and a tee shirt, his dark hair mussed from sleep.

"Morning." He eyed the blood-stained dishtowel. "What's going on?"

Chapter 76

GABE

WITH ROBBY AT school and Kylie visiting Ryan in the hospital, Gabe took advantage of this rare alone time by making himself some pancakes. To his great disappointment, he had barely eaten half the stack when the front door opened then quickly slammed shut.

Cursing under his breath, he put down his fork just as Kylie stormed into the kitchen and dropped into the chair across from him. Of course, she'd been crying.

"What happened?" Gabe said. "Ryan's going to be okay, isn't he?"

"That's what the cop guarding Ryan's room told me." She sat forward, hands on the table. "Someone strangled him, Gabe. He almost died, and they wouldn't let me see him." She narrowed her gaze at him. "Hey, you were working last night. Why didn't you call me? You must have heard about it over your car radio."

Oh, crap. "Yeah, I did." He threw together a lie. "But all dispatch said was that someone had been attacked at the market." He eyed his pancakes. Worried she'd think him heartless if he dug in, he got up and poured himself a second cup of coffee. "I didn't even know Ryan worked there."

"Oh, okay." Eyes glossy with imminent tears, she opened her mother's locket.

God, how many times did she have to look at that woman's picture?

Kylie sniffed. "All I want is for Mom and Ryan to get better so they can meet each other. Is that so wrong?"

"Of course not." In no mood for Kylie's whining, he racked his brain for a good excuse to leave the room. And then his phone rang. It was Chief Fulton.

"Yes, sir. She just walked in." Gabe looked at Kylie. "The FBI wants to talk to you."

PANCAKES ABANDONED, GABE escorted Kylie into the police station fifteen minutes later. As Chief Fulton had promised, he met them in the lobby.

"Right this way." Instead of leading them to his office, Fulton headed to the back of the building. Kylie gave Gabe a questioning look, but he kept his mouth shut. After a couple of turns, they arrived at a door labeled INTERROGATION. The place they took the real criminals.

Surprising Gabe, Kylie took his hand. "Can my dad come in too?"

Fulton shook his head. "Sorry, honey. The FBI people were very specific about that, and since you're eighteen . . ." He opened the door.

"Don't worry." Gabe told her as he freed himself. "I'll be real close."

She peered in at the near-empty room. "Shouldn't I have a lawyer?" she whispered in Gabe's ear.

"Remember what I told you?" he whispered back.

Looking like a frightened rabbit, she nodded.

"Then, don't stress. Lawyers are for criminals and people who have a lot of money to waste. And you're neither."

Fulton motioned her inside. "Have a seat. Someone will be in soon."

Gabe followed Fulton to the observation room next door. Santos, along with Agents Kawata and Starling, were already there, but instead of waving him inside, Fulton shook his head. "Sorry, man." The door closed in Gabe's face.

So, it had come to that. He strolled off to the coffee station, hoping someone had brought donuts.

Chapter 77

IZZY

IZZY WATCHED AS Fulton shut the door on Gabe Fox. Good. Something was off with that guy. She just hadn't figured out what. He'd signed out a cruiser on the night Darcy Callahan was murdered, but the weird thing was, there was no record of him pulling anyone over or even writing a parking ticket. So, what was Fox doing that night?

From the speakers on the wall came the sound of Kylie dragging one of the two stainless-steel chairs they'd placed in the interview room.

Izzy focused on the large two-way mirror separating the two rooms. On the other side of the glass, Kylie brushed off her seat and sat down, a small red purse on her lap. After a few minutes, she checked the time on her cell phone. Then, her gaze drifted to the mirror. She had to know it was a two-way. Why else would the thing be there? So the crooks could make sure their hair looked nice?

"She's beginning to sweat," Agent Starling said, breaking the silence.

You'd be sweating too, Izzy thought, remembering how warm they kept the interrogation room. She leaned toward Fulton. "What's the usual temperature in there? "Eighty?"

"About," Fulton muttered.

And Kylie was keeping her jacket on—in fact, she'd barely moved a muscle since she sat down. When Kylie did move, it was to look at the pictures inside of her mother's locket. Izzy snuck a sideways glance at the two agents who had huddled together, whispering.

Eventually, Agent Starling excused himself and headed out the door. Izzy and the others watched silently as the door snicked open and the short balding black man entered the interrogation room. He offered Kylie his hand and introduced himself.

"Thanks for coming in on such short notice," he said graciously then took the seat across from her, elbows on the table, he rested his chin on his clasped hands. "I bet you're happy Ryan's going home this afternoon."

"No—I mean, I didn't know that. Thanks for telling me."

"Yeah, he'll be okay. Just a sore throat and a cut on his neck. It'll probably leave a scar, but hey . . ." He leaned back, tossing his hands in a *whatcha-gonna-do?* gesture.

That's a different approach, Izzy thought.

"Want to know the details?" Starling asked Kylie.

Barely breathing, she nodded.

"Well, first, his attacker broke all the lights behind the store so it would be dark when Ryan came out. You know, just like they did with your Spanish teacher, Rosa Del Campo. And when he went out to toss some boxes, they jumped him, choking him with some sort of garrote."

Beneath the tabletop, Kylie had a stranglehold on her purse.

"Yeah, Ryan was lucky. He managed to signal the store manager."

"I-I guess neither of them s-saw who it was," Kylie said, fighting back tears.

"Why do you say that?"

"Because if they did, I wouldn't be sitting here."

She glanced at the mirror. "Agent Starling, I don't mean to be rude, but why am I here? I mean, there's n-no way Ryan identified me as his attacker."

Surprised by Kylie's assertiveness, Izzy smiled.

Agent Starling also smiled. "No, Ryan never saw his attacker's face, but he did notice something interesting." He paused, as if waiting for a reaction.

"What, like a tattoo?"

"Detective Santos was right. You *are* smart." He narrowed his eyes as he leaned toward her. "No, Kylie. Ryan didn't *see* anything. What he did notice was a smell—or should I say, your smell. Cypher, the perfume he gave you as a gift."

"Th-this is crazy," Kylie said. "I love Ryan. Why would I want to kill him?"

"Maybe he wanted to break up. You tell me."

She drew in a deep breath and, as calmly as possible said, "Can I leave now?"

"I'm sorry," Agent Starling said, not sounding sorry at all. "But I still have a few more questions. You see, we also found some physical evidence. Ryan's attacker left this." He reached into his suit coat pocket and pulled out a clear plastic bag. Curled inside was a loop of wire. He pushed the bag across the table at Kylie. "That's a hand-made garrote, and that red stuff on it is blood. Ryan's blood. And maybe . . . his attacker's."

Kylie looked up at the mirror. "Why are you showing *me* that?"

"Because we think that person may have cut their hand on it during the struggle."

"Oh?" Smiling triumphantly, she threw up her hands. "See? Nothing."

But there was something.

"What?" Kylie followed Starling's gaze to the little bandage on her hand. "Oh, hey, this isn't . . ."

Starling stared.

"Look, I dropped a Snapple bottle this morning and cut myself picking up the pieces."

"Your blood was also found on Ryan's cell phone. How did that happen?"

"I—I guess from that cut I got."

"But you said that just happened this morning."

"Not from the Snapple bottle. I was also cut at prom the other night. Want to see?"

"Sure."

She pushed her bangs aside, revealing the small scab on her forehead. "See? I cut my head diving under a table when the dome was cracking, then, later, Ryan asked me to hold his phone while he and Luke moved a table off someone who fell. That's probably when I got the blood on it."

Starling nodded. "I suppose that's possible."

"Yeah, because that's what happened."

UNABLE TO FIND one donut, Gabe grabbed a cup of coffee and took a seat in the lobby. Two cups later, Kylie appeared, looking like she'd been crying. She walked past him and out to the parking lot, not stopping until she'd reached the car. They climbed inside and shut the doors.

"What?" Gabe looked at her, confused. "I said you wouldn't be arrested, and you weren't."

Kylie cut her eyes at him. "They took my blood and swabbed my cheek for DNA."

So? Gabe shrugged.

"They also took pictures of my hand and forehead."

"That's just procedure."

"Are you kidding?" Fists clenched, Kylie looked like she wanted to punch Gabe in the face. "The FBI thinks I'm a serial killer!"

"Nah. If that was true, you'd already be locked up."

"Well, it was still horrible. Damn that Lexi Siegel. It all started when she . . . Gabe . . . ?" She grabbed his arm. "What if I really am a killer and don't even know it? Like I have a split personality or something."

He chuckled. "Honey, you are not a serial killer."

"Then, why do so many people think I am? And why didn't *you* get me a lawyer?"

"Because these people have nothing on you." And lawyers cost money. "Like I said, just tell the truth and you're fine. Only guilty people need lawyers. Trust me." He pulled her in for a one-armed hug. "A month from now we're gonna look back and laugh."

"You really think so?"

"Who's the cop?"

"You are."

"Then trust me." He keyed the engine, but as he reached for the gear shift, she took his hand. "Gabe, what if they call me back for another round? You'll get me a lawyer then . . . won't you?"

Chapter 78

IZZY

OTHER THAN THE desk officer, Izzy was probably the last person left in the station. She slumped back in her computer chair and closed her eyes. Not to sleep or to rest, but to limit distractions as she sorted through the evidence. But what evidence did she have? Over two weeks had passed and she was no closer to finding this Taker guy than when she first saw Darcy Callahan's body lying in that tub. Grumbling, she looked at the window and the rain-whipped bushes swishing against the glass.

Was the killer really Kylie McKenna after all? Izzy didn't think so. But why? Just a cop's gut feeling or was she being coached by some omniscient spirit from beyond? Of course, she couldn't discount Kylie's revenge angle, plus the killer would have to have more than one loose screw to pull that stuff in the Pinecrest's ballroom—and what about attacking Ryan? Well, if Kylie hadn't done it, what about the rest of her family?

Izzy pushed off the desk with the toe of her shoe, considering the question as her chair spun around. All the female victims had wronged Kylie somehow. So, had Fox and/or Robby taken it upon themselves to retaliate? Of course, Fox was big enough, but at five-ten or eleven, Robby wasn't exactly a shrimp. She gave the chair another spin.

In their statements, neither Ryan nor Kylie had admitted to having relationship problems. So were they both lying? Otherwise, why would the girl attack him?

Although warped, revenge against the females made sense for both Kylie and her men folk, but why go after Ryan? Some macho overreaction to the family virgin having sex?

Enough. Izzy dragged her heel along the linoleum, slowing her rotation. She should go home.

Brody had closed Salty's early because of the storm, and he was making her dinner, a nice roasted chicken with vegetables. He'd also picked up a bottle of her favorite merlot. Izzy imagined herself driving to Brody's place where they would cuddle in front of a big roaring fire.

And here she was, spinning a stupid chair.

She grabbed her jacket and was about to turn off her computer when the Evidence Room Officer, Gordy Lytle, burst into her office, out of breath, his bright yellow rainslicker dripping onto the linoleum.

"Oh, thank God! I was hoping you'd still be here."

"Gordy, what's going on?"

"There's something you need to see."

"I was just leaving." Izzy pulled on her jacket. "Can it wait until tomorrow?"

"No, no! You have to see this now." Breathing heavily, Gordy headed for the now-vacant lobby.

Curiosity piqued, Izzy was right behind him as he lumbered down the staircase leading to the evidence room.

"Remember . . . that big Botox bust a couple weeks back?" Gordy asked. He turned back every few moments, reminding Izzy of a fat cat guiding its owner to the food dish.

"Yeah, what about it?"

"Well . . ." Gordy's dark brows pulled together as he unlocked the evidence room door. "I noticed something this afternoon before I went home, but I couldn't stop thinking about it. I don't know if you were aware, but my gut had been bothering me quite a bit that week."

"Yes, I remember." But as her Dad used to say, what did that have to do with the price of crab cakes in Baltimore? She tried to remain patient as Gordy pushed the door open and flicked the nearby light switch. Big fluorescent tubing flickered then flashed on. She trailed the big man inside and over to the wall-to-wall chain-link fence, which secured everything she and her fellow officers had collected as evidence during past arrests. He sorted through his wad of keys and opened the padlock.

"Normally, I'm the only one allowed back here." Gordy gestured at the rows of tall shelving behind the fence, every one of them crammed with blue plastic tubs and other oddities. "But you need to see for yourself, so come on." He led Izzy past two cuckoo clocks and a real-but-stuffed four-foot albino alligator to a heavy, metal door at the back of the room which he unlocked and held open for her.

The door clanked shut behind Izzy as she took the place in. Less than half the size of the main area, the drug room contained smaller shelves holding smaller plastic tubs, these red instead of blue. Gordy located the one he was looking for and carried it to a nearby table.

"Check this out," he said, eyes glued to the tub's contents. "I've been stressing about this all afternoon." Several bundles lay at the bottom of the tub, some of them tiny, individual white boxes, others cartons, all of them wrapped in plastic.

"That the Botox?" Izzy asked.

Gordy nodded.

Izzy looked over the contents, confused. "Am I looking for something in particular . . . ?"

"Yeah, I didn't notice at first, either." Gordy snatched up one of the larger bundles. "I checked my logbooks. This should be a complete case, nothing missing from it."

"Looks fine to me."

"Yeah, well, looky here." He peeled away some of the plastic wrap. "See? That is not the original packaging."

"Are you sure?"

"That the packaging's not from the factory, yes. That something inside there is missing, no."

"Well, then. Let's have a look." With a nod from Gordy, Izzy peeled back the rest of the plastic wrap. Immediately, she noticed several of the tiny boxes within had broken seals. "Crap."

"Yeah, crap." Gordy popped one open. "Empty."

It was the same with the three boxes next to it.

"I count four vials missing," Gordy told her.

"Okay, but if you're the only person allowed back here, who took them?"

Gordy leaned in conspiratorially. "Look, I'm going to tell you what I think happened." A plump man, Gordy's face was normally ruddy, but right now, it reminded Izzy of that albino alligator they'd just walked past. He glanced at the door, then back at Izzy. "But you've got to understand. I can't prove any of this."

"I understand." Worried the man might pass out, Izzy helped him remove his rain poncho and walked him to a nearby chair. "Sit. When you're ready to speak, I'm here to listen."

Once seated, Gordy settled down and explained how two weeks ago, he'd been in and out of the main-floor men's room all day. He was about to race up there again when Gabe Fox showed up.

Really? Gabe Fox of all people? Heart racing, Izzy tried to stay cool. "And what brought Officer Fox down here?"

"Well, I . . ." Gordy squinted, as if thinking hard. "I believe he was picking up something from the supply room and decided to step in and see how I was doing. A good thing, too, because I don't know if I'd have reached the john in time, otherwise."

"How's that?"

"My gut was really churning when Gabe showed up. He knew about my problem, and when he saw me fumbling around with the keys, offered to lock up for me. I know it was against procedure, but I was afraid I might . . . you know . . . so I tossed him the keys and hauled ass upstairs. When I came out of the john, there he was with the keyring. I thought everything was good, but then, today I started the drug room inventory, and when I opened that Botox bin . . ."

He tipped his head at one of the two security cameras staring down at them from the corners. "And before you get too excited, those were installed *after* Gabe paid me that visit."

"Well, that's par for the course." But why would Gabe Fox steal Botox? He was barely into his forties, maybe a little vain, but was he so cheap that he'd risk his job or worse just to save a few bucks?

"I Googled it," Gordy whispered. "Each of those vials contains the maximum prescribed dosage for one office visit. And there's four missing."

Great, but what did that even mean? Irritated, Izzy examined the tub's contents more closely and found something buried under the Botox. She fished out a carton the size of half a shoebox. "Syringes."

"Yeah, Lester Mathis threw those in when he arrested the woman selling the shots."

"Makes sense," Izzy said, but why was the box so familiar? She raised the lid. Apparently, each syringe was wrapped in its own little white and green plastic pouch. She pulled one out, thinking . . . thinking.

"What's wrong?" Gordy left his chair and walked over.

"I don't know about the Botox . . . but this . . ." Izzy stared at the plastic-wrapped syringe. "I've seen it before—or another one just like it."

Gordy reached into the box and pulled out a second syringe. "Looks pretty average to me."

And then, Izzy remembered.

"Not the syringe, the wrapper. Somebody left one just like it in the sink at Angie Fox's hospital room a while back." Izzy saw it all clearly in her mind's eye. How upset Angie's sister, Tonya had been about the mess and the way Fox had talked her out of confronting the nurse over it. At the time, Izzy had respected the man's empathy, but what if it was Fox who'd been using the syringe?

"Is four vials of Botox enough to kill a person?" she asked.

"Hell if I know." His chin dropped. "Hold on. Are you thinking Gabe took the Botox to OD his wife with it?"

"Gordy, I don't know what I'm thinking, but that would explain why those vials disappeared." She took out her cell phone and started tapping. "No signal?"

"No, not here in the vault," Gordy told her. "Let's lock up and go back up to your office. Who are you calling, anyway?"

"The third floor desk nurse at the hospital."

Izzy snapped a few photos of the empty boxes and syringes, and once Gordy had locked everything up, they headed up to the lobby where Izzy called the hospital again. This time, someone answered.

"Hi, Nurse Marisol, this is Detective Santos. I know you're super busy, but this is official police business. What brand of a hundred-unit syringes does the hospital use?" Izzy wrote it down. "Uh-huh, and is that the only brand used by the hospital?" She underlined the name. "Great, and what color is the wrapper on those syringes?" She crossed her fingers. "Hot-pink and white, perfect." She hung up and looked at Gordy. "This could be big."

Chapter 79

GABE

THE WINDS AND rain had intensified in the last few hours, making Rocky Harbor a ghost town. Gabe sat in his police cruiser eating tacos and thinking about everything that had happened since he'd pushed Angie off that cliff. In hindsight, he probably could have picked a more dependable method, but who doesn't die when they fall off a cliff? Especially one that high?

He'd just finished his second taco when his phone rang.

Kylie. At this time of night, she would be working that stupid library job of hers. For a moment, he considered not answering, but even talking to her would be a step up from watching the rain pound his windshield. And what could possibly be happening at the library on a night like this?

"What's up, kid. Somebody refuse to pay their overdue fees?"

"Are you busy?" she asked, sounding like tears were coming.

"A little." He flicked some shredded cheese off his shirt, wishing he'd let the call go to voicemail. "Tell me what happened."

The words spilled out of her like water from a fire hose. "Mr. Dwyer came into the library and called me a murderer. He said the only reason I'm not in jail is because you're a cop and the department protects its own. He also told Mrs. Fontenot that if she likes her hands, she better be nice to me."

"Old Man Dwyer said all that?" Gabe chuckled. "Well, screw that asshole."

His profanity brought a tearful giggle. "Yeah . . . that's sort of what Mrs. Fontenot said."

"Well, then, what's the problem? She didn't fire you, did she?"

"No . . ." Kylie sniffled.

"But . . . ?"

"When I told her I wanted to go home she looked relieved. And Mrs. Fontenot's been like a grandma to me. And now . . . even she . . ." More sniffles. "Damn it, everybody thinks I killed those people. And if that's not enough, when I was walking through the library parking lot, the wind turned my umbrella inside out. I'm soaked."

For a moment, all Gabe could hear was the rain thrumming down on the car's roof. "Hey, where are you anyway?"

"Sitting in Mom's car behind the library. What am I going to do, Gabe?"

"Kylie, listen to me." He imagined her clutching Angie's locket for dear life. "Your friends know you didn't do it, and your family knows you didn't do it. We're behind you, kiddo."

"I know, but now, even Ryan . . ."

Between Kylie's story and Vega's, Gabe had a pretty good idea of what had gone down in Ryan's hospital room the other morning. Somehow, she'd burst in while the FBI was doing their interview, and Fulton had ordered Vega to drag her out. Luke's wearing Kylie's perfume hadn't convinced the boy it was her, but his parents sure hadn't welcomed the girl with open arms.

"Kylie? You still there?"

"Yeah."

"Go home, kiddo. Soak in a hot tub, and try not to worry. Something big is going to happen soon. I'm sure of it. And you know what?" He chuckled. "I'm going to be there to watch."

Chapter 80

IZZY

IZZY PRESSED HER phone to her cheek. Across from her sat Gordy, his pudgy hands gripping the edge of her desk as if for dear life.

Erina should be at home at this hour, so why didn't she answer? Two rings later, she did.

"Good evening," Erina's tone was perky. "To what do I owe—?"

"Girl, I need to know something."

"Okay, what?"

"If someone's been injected with Botox, does it show up in their blood?"

"Izzy, what's going on? Is this about the murders?"

"Yes, but I don't have time to explain. Please, do you know?"

"This is all theoretical, but I suppose it could. Normally, Botox is injected into the skin or a muscle, but if it's injected directly into a vein . . . I suppose it depends on the dosage and how much time has passed."

Izzy thought about it. "How about four hundred units and two weeks ago?"

"Someone's been dead two weeks? Where did you find this body, and what makes you think they overdosed on Botox, of all things?"

"No, Erina, I'm talking about a living being. Would Botox stay in their bloodstream for that long?"

"Your someone had four hundred units injected into them, and they're still alive?"

Izzy remembered the look of surprise on Fox's face when she and Tonya walked in on him in Angie's room. Had they interrupted him mid-murder? "It could be less. But it has been two weeks."

"We might find traces of Botox in a person who had been dead two weeks, but it would probably have flushed out of a live person after that long. What's all this about?"

"I'll explain tomorrow. Thanks, though." Izzy hung up. "Gordy, besides you and Fox, has anyone else entered that vault recently?"

"No, nobody." He shifted in his seat. "I wasn't even supposed to take him in there. Guess I was showing off. You gonna tell the chief?"

"I have to." She punched in Fulton's number. "But I'll also tell him how you brought it all to my attention."

He chewed his lower lip as Izzy phoned their boss at home to tell him.

"Okay," Fulton said. "Let's get some labs going for Angie Fox anyway. I know a couple of admins over there, so let me take care of that, and until we know more, keep your distance from Fox. We don't want to spook him,"

They said goodbye, and Izzy was about to hang up when she heard Maggie's voice shout, "Why did you tell Izzy to stay away from Gabe Fox?"

"Hang on," Fulton told Izzy. He put her on hold, then got back on. "Your aunt wants to talk to you."

After a few moments, Maggie came on the line. "I couldn't help overhearing. So, Officer Fox is involved in these murders you are investigating?"

"I believe so, Tita, yes."

"¡Ay, Dios! And he seemed like such a nice man, too, bringing me that coffee cake—I mean, it's got walnuts, but he didn't know I'm allergic."

"Oh, yeah. He did give you that, didn't he?" Izzy thought for a moment. "Tell me you didn't throw it away."

"Of course not. Sean's not allergic. In fact, he's cutting himself a second slice right now. Why—oh, I see where you're going. Hold on." She lowered the phone. "Sean! Bring me that cake tin, would you? Izzy wants me to touch it."

After a few moments, Izzy heard her thank Fulton. After some muffled fumbling, Maggie got back on, her voice was almost a squeak. "¡*Ay, Dios de me vida!* Hija, you were right."

Since this wasn't a conversation Maggie would want Gordy or anyone else to hear, Izzy put her on mute and turned to Gordy. "Hey, uh . . . this is kind of private. Do you mind . . . ?"

"Oh, sure." Gordy hopped to his feet. "I'll just go sit in the lobby."

"Thanks, buddy." Izzy waited until Gordy was out of earshot, then unmuted her aunt. "Sorry, Tita, so you felt something?"

"Felt, no." Maggie could barely catch a breath. "I saw it. Not a like what I got from that falcon statue last year," she gasped, "b-but enough."

"Yeah, well, that was the actual murder weapon. So what did you see?"

"Just a flash." The words came in bursts. "My hand. It was on Angie Fox's forehead. And she . . . she was way up high."

My God, Izzy thought. Was it the view from the Overlook? "And then?"

"And then I pushed her—he pushed her. And she . . . she . . ." Maggie broke down, and Fulton got on the line.

"Obviously, you can't arrest the man on what your aunt just told you," Fulton began. "But at least we know we're on the right track, and you've got that Botox lead. Go talk to Kylie. See if there's a life insurance policy on Angie."

"I'm on it, chief. And thank Maggie for me." Izzy hung up and joined Gordy in the lobby. "Why do men kill their wives?"

Gordy scratched the back of his ear. "I dunno. Isn't it always sex or money? Like when a guy wants a divorce but doesn't like the idea of paying her alimony?"

"Yeah, that's a big one. Life insurance, too." Izzy dropped into the chair beside him. "Wait. Everybody believed Fox when he said his wife fell off that cliff by accident. But what if he pushed her off so he and his lover could share the insurance money?"

"There you go. And when she didn't die, he tried to finish her with the Botox."

"I need to check on that life insurance. I also need to figure out who the lover is."

"Too bad that Callahan woman's dead," Gordy mused. "You do know about that thing her and Gabe had a few years back?"

"Yeah, but how did you find out?"

"My wife's hairdresser lives on the same street. They talk."

Being back with Darcy would explain why Fox might have wanted his wife dead, but now, Darcy was dead and Angie wasn't. Bad luck? Coincidence? Or did Fox have a hand in both? She thought back on Darcy's murder scene. It wasn't just clean, it was cop clean. But why kill his girlfriend, and what about the other victims? Fox was first on the scene for Darcy and Rosa Del Campo, but not Lexi. And wasn't he right there when Jade Su—?

"So, what now?" Gordy asked.

Izzy looked at Gordy, relieved to see his plump cheeks were back to their normal ruddiness. "Let me think. It would be good to know whether Fox has a life insurance policy on Angie. But without a warrant . . ." She needed to make another phone call.

"So, are you going to arrest Fox?" Gordy's asked.

Noting the man's wistful tone, she said, "That depends," and walked around the desk to shake his hand. "Gordy, I can't tell you how important you've been to this investigation, but I need to make another phone call. Maybe you should go home."

"Oh . . . okay." He looked like a puppy that had been swept out the back door. "I get it. More private stuff." His lower lip jutted. "Well, keep me in the loop, huh? Maybe I can help."

"Of course, of course." Izzy rested a hand on Gordy's shoulder. "And keep this to yourself, okay?"

Chapter 81

KYLIE

KYLIE DROPPED HER phone into her purse and stared out the car's windshield, barely noticing the booming thunder and huge lightning flash that had just lit the sky above of her. Although Gabe's words were a comfort, they hadn't solved anything. Frustrated, she allowed herself a good long cry, then, unexpectedly lighter in spirit, buckled up and started the car. Maybe Gabe was right, and something big *was* going to happen. Hoping it wasn't just BS, she wiped her tears and headed home.

This new rainstorm seemed to be following her, mounting in severity with every house she passed. It wouldn't surprise her if the whole town lost power. She dodged around some garbage totes which had been blown onto the street and was happy to find the electricity in her own neighborhood still flowing and every home on the street with one or more lights on. So, why was *her* house so dark? From what she could tell, the only window with a light was Robby's bedroom, and that was upstairs.

Kylie pulled into the driveway. A real scaredy cat, Robby should have the place lit up like some out-of-control Christmas party. But it wasn't. Not even close.

She grabbed her purse, pushed her hood up on her head, and tried not to let the wind tear the door handle from her hand as she got out. Hood held in place with her free hand, she shivered her way through pelting rain to the relative safety of the craftsman-style porch. No, Robby was fine. He'd been playing online-computer games when she'd left the house, but it was still light out then. With nobody home to say otherwise, he'd just kept on playing, oblivious to the fact that the world was darkening around him.

Once inside, Kylie clicked on a nearby table lamp, enjoying the warm and toasty living room as she hung her raincoat on one of the hooks by the door. She then headed into the kitchen to get herself a drink.

The mess Robby had left there made Kylie want to scream: dishes in the sink, empty soda cans on the table, and a frozen pizza carton on the counter. Who did he think was going to clean this up? Her? Robby needed to be taught a lesson, and pouncing on her unsuspecting brother always made her smile.

Kylie's plan was simple: still wet and dripping, she would sneak upstairs and scare the crap out of her little brother with a big soggy hug. With any luck, he would scream his lungs out. She then would chew Robby out about the mess he'd left in the kitchen, and once she'd driven him downstairs to clean it, Kylie would take Gabe's advice and hop in a nice hot bath. After that, she would try to lose herself in a book. It wasn't the best plan, but considering how things were going, it would have to do.

Switching to stealth mode, she kicked off her wet shoes and headed up, allowing the dim entry light to guide her way. A flash of lightning lit every window, immediately followed by a boom of thunder loud enough to rattle the pictures on the wall. The seventh step always squeaked, and for a moment, she considered stepping over it, but between his game and all that thunder, a herd of buffalo could rumble up these steps and Robby would never notice.

Upstairs, the sound of gurgling gutters competed with the now, torrential downpour, and the overgrown tree outside her own bedroom was scraping the window above her bed. What a racket. If she did manage to fall asleep, she'd probably wake up with rain and broken glass hitting her face.

Smiling, Kylie tiptoed over to Robby's open door. His computer desk faced the window, so he'd have his back to her, the perfect arrangement for sneaking up on unsuspecting little brothers. But as she got closer, other sounds reached her ears. Sounds she hadn't anticipated like grunting and what she imagined to be sheets rustling.

Holy crap, Kylie thought. Don't tell me he's got that Rebecca girl in there.

Another lightning flash lit the house, followed by a thunderous explosion even louder than the last. This time, the lights did go out.

Wait a minute. Rebecca was just as loud and giggly as any other fourteen-year-old, so why hadn't she squealed? To make matters worse, the rustling and grunting hadn't skipped a beat. No longer in the mood for pranks, Kylie hesitated just outside her brother's door. She had to know for sure, because if Rebecca wasn't in there with Robby, then who was? The Taker? Robby would die from embarrassment if she was wrong. But what if she was right?

The open door more than bothered her. If Robby really *did* have a girl in there, wouldn't he have closed it? Her heart filled with dread.

Lean in for a quick peek, she told herself. If it's just him and Rebecca you can slip back downstairs and make some noise. If it's not . . .

Barely breathing, Kylie slid her cheek around the edge of the door frame just as lightning flashed through Robby's open blinds, allowing her to catch the briefest image of two dark shapes thrashing on the bed. Another boom of thunder added to her shock, and she lurched back, suddenly lightheaded. That was not Rebecca.

Chapter 82

IZZY

WITH GORDY FINALLY on his way home, Izzy sat down to think. Tonya and Angie were close. Enough for Tonya to leave her job to fly down and sleep on that pull-out bed for nearly a week. So, what had Angie shared with her sister over the years?

She stared at her cell phone, now lying alone in the center of her desktop. Damn.

An affair. Killing for life insurance. How did a person start those conversations?

She dialed, and Tonya picked up after two rings.

"Izzy, what's up?"

"Hey, remember that syringe you found in Angie's bathroom?"

Soon, Izzy had told Tonya what she and Gordy had just worked out, and if Tonya was hot at finding an old syringe wrapper in her sister Angie's bathroom sink, now, she was boiling.

"Are you *sure* the hospital doesn't use that brand of syringe?"

"That's what the head nurse told me."

"So . . ." Tonya's voice cracked. "So we literally walked in on him shooting my sister up with poison?"

"It looks like it, yeah." Izzy pinched her eyes shut. She should say something comforting, but what? She opened her eyes. "But we messed up his plans, Tonya, and I'm going to get this guy." She said the last part firmly, like it was a proven fact. "But I need some information. Do you know anything about Gabe and Angie having money problems? Like, currently?"

"Currently? How about the last ten years?" Tonya then went on to explain how Angie had caught Fox cheating.

"Yeah, I heard about that," Izzy said, relieved she wouldn't have to share that too. "And it sucks, but what's it got to do with their money problems?"

"Because instead of divorcing him, Angie punished the jerk by quitting her job. He's been working two or three extra shifts a week ever since."

"I'm guessing Gabe resents having to do that?"

"Wouldn't you? But Angie was softening up, lately. At least, she thought so."

Apparently, Fox wasn't on the same page. "Has Angie ever mentioned them getting life insurance?"

"Oh, man, let me think." For a few moments, the phone went silent, then Tonya surprised Izzy with a loud, "Yes, like a year ago. And it was Gabe's idea, too. At first, he was just about getting small policies on the kids. You know, like for funeral expenses. But once he convinced Angie to do that, he suggested they take one out on her too, but she would only agree if they both got policies—which they did. Oh, my gosh, Izzy. This is . . . I . . . I don't know what to think."

"Any idea how much they were for or what company they used?"

"No, but Kylie might know where they keep the paperwork."

"Oh, sure. I'll just call her up and say, 'Hey, Kylie. Any idea where your folks keep the life insurance policies? I think your stepdad may have tried to murder your mom, and that money would make a great motive.'"

"Oh, I see your point." Tonya sounded overwhelmed. "Damn that man. You really think he pushed her, huh?"

"Tonya . . . the only person who knows that for certain is Angie."

"And my ass of a brother-in-law," she grumbled.

"Yeah, we can't forget him. And don't you worry, Tonya. If he did push her, I'll find out. I promise."

"I know you will, and be careful," Tonya cautioned. 'Because if all that's true, then God knows what he's capable of."

After assuring Tonya she would indeed be careful, Izzy promised she would call with an update the following day and signed off. What *was* Fox capable of?

She phoned Kylie's cell, and when she got no answer, tried the family's landline. But nobody picked up there, either. Well, the storm was pretty bad. Remembering she'd copied down Kylie's work schedule, Izzy flipped back through her notebook. That was it. Kylie worked on Wednesdays. She was at the library, and she'd probably left her phone in her purse, most likely tucked away in some employee locker area.

So, Izzy phoned the library.

"Kylie's not here," the woman on the other end replied. "I sent her home. She . . . she wasn't feeling well."

Izzy grabbed her keys.

Chapter 83

KYLIE

KYLIE PEERED INTO Robby's bedroom. Her eyes had adjusted to the dark some, but she still wasn't sure what she was looking at. There was no mistaking Robby's green high-topped shoes, but who was the figure straddling him? Not Rebecca. And Robby was struggling. The stranger was holding a pillow over Robby's face.

Dizzy with fright, she pressed her back to the wall. What should she do? Call 911? But Robby was being suffocated. Across the hall, the door to her parents' bedroom stood open. There was a spare gun in Gabe's closet, but without electricity, how would she ever find it? Gooseflesh pebbled her skin. She wanted to run. Get away. But not without Robby.

Then she remembered the baseball bat Gabe kept behind the bedroom door. "For protection" he'd explained when he'd put it there, years ago. At the time, Kylie had chuckled at the idea, because who was dumb enough to break into a cop's house? Tiptoeing, she crossed the hall and stepped into the depths of her parents' now cave-like bedroom. The bat was still there. Steeling herself, she gripped it with both hands and hurried into her little brother's room.

Hit him, she told herself. Before he sees you.

Arms trembling, Kylie raised the bat and brought it down as hard as she could, striking the man on the side of the head. He vanished over the edge of the bed with a dull thump.

"Robby!" She leaped onto the bed beside her lifeless brother. "Robby, wake up!" She searched his neck for a pulse.

Nothing.

"Come on Robby, breathe!" She slapped his face. "Robby, breathe, damn it!" Terrified of losing him, Kylie started chest compressions. And as she struggled to bring her brother back, the figure on the floor stirred. It rose slowly then fell and rose again just as lightning lit up the sky, illuminating the room and everything in it like the flash from a camera.

Unable to process what she had seen, Kylie froze. Down on hands and knees, her good friend Luke Manetti had just pulled a ski mask off his head.

Chapter 84

IZZY

LIGHTNING FLASHED AS Izzy ran through the rain to her big black police SUV. Thunder boomed as she climbed inside, thankful for both the car's excellent heating system and the Rocky Harbor Police Department's central location. From there, Izzy could get to most locations in ten minutes or less. As a cop, she had never appreciated that more than now, because something bad was going to happen at the Fox house. She knew it, just as she had when she'd told Kylie that things would work out for her and her family. Was she totally off base on both? And what did *something bad* even mean? That their cable would go out? She certainly wasn't confident enough to speed across town, siren blasting—especially in this weather. With visibility greatly reduced, she turned her wipers up to high and pulled onto the road, her headlights illuminating the green leaves and litter tumbling across her path.

Although Izzy wouldn't want her aunt's ability to see ghosts, she had to admit it was much more useful than her own. But even Maggie's gift had its limits. Something—maybe Lexi's ghost—had urged Maggie to enter that construction area, but all they'd turned up was a button. And from a police officer's shirt. Evidence? No, not with all those cops on the scene, but she sure would like to see Gabe Fox's dry cleaning.

Unsure if she jumping to conclusions or finally seeing things for what they were, Izzy thought back to Angie Fox's accident—if that's what it really was, because he could have easily pushed her and claimed she had fallen, especially since the kids hadn't been with them. But Angie had survived, and apparently, Fox had tried to finish her off with Botox. It all made sense if he was dumping Angie for another woman. But Darcy Callahan was dead. So, what or who was the missing piece in this puzzle? And what, if anything, did Fox have to do with the other killings?

Izzy turned into the Foxes' neighborhood. The streetlights were dark. The homes too, mostly. The light she did see, likely created by flashlights and candles. Maybe the power outage was the bad thing she'd predicted would happen. Considering how much the trees were dancing, she'd be surprised if the whole town didn't go black.

She parked on the street in front of the Fox place. No candles here. The house was totally dark. But was it empty? That would explain why nobody had answered the landline, *if* Fox's cruiser wasn't parked in the driveway next to Kylie's Honda. Wishing she were home in front of the fire with Brody, Izzy pushed her RHPD cap firmly down on her head and zipped her jacket. Gusting wind made getting out a struggle, and she almost lost her cap, but after a bit, she muscled the car door shut and trudged up the middle of the driveway to rest her hand on the hood of Fox's cruiser. Still warm. The Honda too.

Chapter 85

KYLIE

"HI, KYLIE." BACK to being a dark shape, Luke wobbled, then sat down hard as thunder rattled the house. "Whoa, you got me good."

Luke killed Robby?

LUKE?

"A little help here?" He raised one shaky hand.

In her confusion, Kylie almost took it. But then, she came to her senses. Heart pounding through her chest, she stumbled off the bed and dashed across the hall to her parents' bedroom where she locked the door behind her. She slumped against it.

This had to be a dream. Luke couldn't possibly have—

Inches above her head, the doorknob rattled, making Kylie jump. Heart in her throat, she grabbed the knob. Gabe always said these inside doors were flimsy. What if Luke broke through?

"You came home early!" Luke shouted through the door. "But that's okay. Just come out, and we'll talk."

She had to call 911. And Gabe. But her cell was downstairs in her purse. Across the room on the nightstand, her parents' old cordless phone was a lump in the darkness. She sprinted over and pressed the receiver to her ear. No dial tone.

"How's it going with that landline?" Luke shouted through the door. "Doesn't work, does it?" He laughed. "Funny how we take electricity for granted. Come on, Kylie, open up. I'll let you use my cell."

Yeah. Right.

She tiptoed over to the French doors.

"Ky-leeee!" The bedroom door shuddered. "Open the damned door!"

Sheets of rain greeted her as she stepped onto the empty deck and pulled the door shut behind her. God, it was dark. When she could make out the railing, she gripped it with both hands and looked down. Man, if she didn't know there was a pool down there . . .

Bang!

Another shriek burst out of her. Luke was throwing himself against the bedroom door.

Bang!

Cowering against the railing, she whimpered with each assault. Stop it, she told herself. If she was going to get out of this alive, she had to be strong. She looked around for a weapon, but unless she she'd suddenly grown strong enough to pick up mom's big redwood chaise lounge and throw it, there was nothing.

And then, the pounding stopped. Even more frightened by the sudden silence, she took a step toward the doors, praying he'd given up.

"Where-arrrre-yoooo-Ky-leee?"

Unnervingly familiar, Luke's hide-and-seek voice sent shivers down her spine. He'd broken through.

She had to climb down. The balcony was high, but once over the side, she could hang down. The drop wouldn't be that far.

A sheet of rain struck her, making her stagger.

"I bet you're squeezing that locket pretty hard now," Luke shouted to the empty bedroom.

Realizing he would find her any moment, Kylie threw one leg over the railing, causing it to creak and shift.

Damn it. Why couldn't Gabe fix this stupid—

Angry hands snatched her back over as another flash of lightning revealed a face she barely recognized. That wasn't Luke, at least not the funny goofy Luke she'd known most of her life.

"You know, I'm a little sad this is going to end." Shoving her down roughly, he kept himself between Kylie and the open French doors. "It was a real kick getting people to think *you* were The Taker." Seeing her eye the dark bedroom behind him, he spread his arms blocking her escape. "You know, this whole thing was your fault."

"M-my fault?"

"Yup. If you had just returned my kiss, none of this would have happened."

"What kiss, Luke?"

"You don't remember?" He slapped his now-wet forehead. "Why am I surprised. I spent years hoping you'd come around. But you never did. Then you fell all over that idiot, Ryan. Seeing you together . . . it made me want to puke." He pressed his hands to his chest. "I offered you my heart, Kylie, and you crushed it like a used Kleenex."

His heart? When did Luke ever . . . ? Her jaw dropped. "That was back in eighth grade."

"She does remember." Arms extended, he lifted his face to the rain and smiled.

"I thought you were kidding, Luke. And don't tell me you killed those people for revenge."

"Why not?" The smile dropped away, and his nostrils flared as he lowered his gaze back to hers. "You have no idea how seeing you with Ryan hurts me."

"B-but you're with Addison now."

"Addison?" He dismissed the notion with an angry wave. "I just wanted to see *you* in your prom dress. I couldn't go to the dance by myself, could I?" His voice hardened. "I wanted you to suffer, Kylie. The way I suffer every time Ryan touches you. And that's why I killed Lexi—which just happened to be the best idea ever."

Luke's cheerful tone had returned, but now it made Kylie shudder.

"You wouldn't believe how easy Jade and Eden were to manipulate—and their friends." He snorted. "Man, I hadn't even planned another murder, but once I heard about that tizzy fit you had over your Spanish test, I said, 'Why not make Kylie a serial killer?' You were asking for it, and I wanted to see how gullible people could be."

"S-so, *you* killed M-Mrs. Del Campo?"

"Your Spa-Spa-Spanish teacher?" He chuckled. "Yup. Jade too, but I can't take credit for Darcy Callahan."

"And now Robby." She slumped. "I-I guess I should be thankful you didn't kill Ryan too."

"Hey, it wasn't for lack of trying." Voice back to its usual happy-go-lucky tone, he adjusted the wrist of one glove.

He was going to kill her now. He had to.

"I-I already called the police," Kylie said, not really expecting Luke would believe her. "Y-you might be able to get away if you leave now."

He snickered. "Well, the landline's not working, so I suppose you used your cell for that?"

"Yeah . . . I did." She could barely get the words out. "Go, Luke. R-r-run."

"Thanks for the advice. Your cell must be in your pocket, then. Show it to me."

Kylie shivered as the rain spattered against his upturned palm.

Sighing dramatically, Luke threw up his hands. "Kylie, Kylie, Kylie. You were supposed to be at the library." He stepped toward her, head shaking. "And after I went to all the trouble of killing your brother and hiding my hand collection in your room for the cops to find." His gloved hands clenched and unclenched. "But that's okay, because I've got a whole new plan. You know what they say, when life gives you lemons . . ."

Feeling more alone than ever, Kylie couldn't help but sob. She was no match for Luke, and soon, she would be just as dead as Robby. She stared up at him, anticipating the inevitable.

But then, the back porch light popped on, followed by the neighbors' lights. And the light in the bedroom. Incredulous, she stared at Luke's outfit. Black pants. Black hoodie. He'd even tucked his signature shaggy hair under the ski mask, which he'd rolled back to look like a beanie.

"What?" He turned a circle. "I was going for a cat-burglar vibe. No good?" In a flash, his hands were on her throat, pinning her to the railing.

Pain stabbed Kylie's back. Her throat. Unable to exhale, her last breath swelled in her chest as he dodged her kicks. Terrified, she reached for his face. When his long reach prevented her from scratching it, she went for the arms. But those were protected by the sleeves of his heavy sweatshirt. Her senses faded. And then, his grip on her throat loosened.

"What am I doing?" Chuckling, Luke slapped his forehead. "There's a perfectly good bed right there, and I'm not taking advantage of it." He gripped Kylie's arm and had just pulled her into the doorway when a deafeningly loud sound made her jump.

Chapter 86

GABE

GABE WATCHED THE boy collapse, blocking the exit. Shooting Luke had been a rush, but now, the kid's blood was leaking all over the deck. He was wondering whether it would stain the wood when Kylie plowed into him, her wet shirt now tie-dyed in Luke's blood.

"Oh, God, Daddy!" Her arms encircled him. "He killed Robby!"

Before she got blood on him too, Gabe pushed her away and hurried over to Luke, who lay on the wood, facing the backyard. Always fascinated by the transition between life and death, Gabe stepped over Luke and knelt beside him.

"Shouldn't we call 911?" Kylie asked, intruding on the moment. "Gabe? Why are you acting so . . ."

He glanced up, then returned his focus to Luke, whose breathing had become raspy.

"You know," he told Kylie, "originally, the plan was for Luke to kill Robby and pin everything on you. But when you told me you were coming home early, I had to improvise." He removed a strand of hair from the boy's eyes. "Actually, this is going to work out even better. With you *and* your brother dead, I can pin all the murders on Luke and collect fifty thousand dollars of insurance money, instead of the twenty-five thousand dollars I would have gotten for just Robby. It's a win-win situation . . . for me, at least."

Luke made a gurgling sound, then went still.

"Guess that's it." Gabe patted Luke's cheek, then straightened. "If I could remember how Darcy died, I could compare, but . . ." Kylie's fish-out-of-water reaction made him smile. "You know, Luke wasn't the only killer."

"What? I-I don't . . ."

"God, do I really have to spell it out?" He gripped her shoulders. "Me, stupid. I killed Darcy. I could have let Luke kill you, too, but why let him have all the fun?"

Would she fight back as he choked her? No, she'd just stand there holding that stupid locket.

"I never did understand why you like that thing so much." Gabe chuckled. "It sure didn't help your mom when I pushed her off that cliff." He bugged his eyes, hoping for a reaction.

"Y-you . . .?"

There it was, that stupid Bambi-eyed stare. Gabe locked his hands around Kylie's throat and shoved her against the railing.

Chapter 87

IZZY

HAVING HEARD ENOUGH, Izzy bellowed, "Police!" guaranteeing she'd be heard above the pounding rain. She stepped over Luke Manetti's body onto the eight-foot-wide balcony. "Let Kylie go, Officer Fox!"

Hair and uniform dripping, Fox let go of Kylie's throat and turned to Izzy as Kylie wilted against him. But instead of lowering her to the wooden deck, he used her as a shield.

"Th-this isn't what it looks like," he stammered. "I was defending myself. Kylie's The Taker. She killed Robby, and then, she killed Luke." He tipped his chin at the lifeless body behind Izzy.

"Save your lies, Officer. I heard your confessions."

For a moment, Fox appeared beaten. Then, he focused on Izzy's taser, and the smile that crossed his lips made Izzy shudder. "Again with the taser? You really are a dumb bitch."

Of course, Fox was referring to the scariest day of Izzy's life. Barely a year ago, she had fired her taser at another killer, Dylan Coates. But that weapon had misfired, giving Coates an opening to charge Izzy with a knife.

Was it a stupid choice? Izzy really did have more faith in her service pistol, but how could she risk the shot with Kylie between them, especially now that the girl was beginning to struggle?

"Let me go!" Kylie shrieked. "Help me, Detective. Please."

But tasering Fox wouldn't be easy. His jacket was thick, and Kylie was really thrashing.

"Hold still," Fox told her.

Arms wrapped around Kylie's waist, he lifted her off her feet, but that seemed to encourage more kicking. Then, as quickly as their struggle began, they looked in Izzy's direction and went still.

What now? Before Izzy could turn, Robby appeared beside her. "Gabe?" His voice cracked. "What are you doing to my sister?"

"Robby!" Still in Fox's grasp, Kylie reached for him. "You're alive."

A thunderous boom rattled the house as lightning lit the deck up like a stage.

"Kylie!" Izzy shouted. "Drop dead."

The girl met Izzy's gaze. Would she understand? Would Fox?

If he did, Kylie was faster. Arms flung upward, she suddenly went limp, her sneakered feet sliding out across the rain-slicked deck. Unable to hang on, Fox caught a handful of her shirt, and with that action, allowed Izzy a brief target. His chest.

Having been tasered as a cadet, Izzy expected Fox to scream. She wasn't disappointed. 50,000 volts surged through him, prompting a high-pitched shriek and stiffening his entire body. Sadly, that included his fingers. With Kylie's shirt clutched in his talon-like grip, Fox's back slammed into the railing, taking Kylie with him. Nails groaned in protest as the wood tilted outward under the combined weight of two people.

Spread-eagle and immobilized on the now outwardly-angled railing, all Fox could do was watch as Kylie, unaffected by the taser, was pulled to safety by her younger brother. After a few moments, Fox managed a slow head turn and peered between the spindles at the concrete below.

"Oh, man." He squinted up through the downpour at Izzy. "New taser?"

"That's right," Izzy said. "And you're under ar—"

With a shudder, the railing tilted out further, prompting a chorus of gasps, none louder than from Fox. "Please." He raised his left hand. "A little help."

"Not from me." Kylie locked arms with Robby.

"But that railing's going to break loose any second, Sis," Robby said. "We can't just . . ."

Although Fox deserved what he got, Robby was right. Izzy swapped the taser for her service pistol, then focused on Fox's, which was still in its holster.

"Take out your weapon," she ordered. "Slowly, and only use two fingers."

"Whatever you say." Fox followed her directions.

"Now, toss it into the pool."

Fox flung the gun behind him. "Now, what?"

"Now, my gun stays pointed at your chest, and Robby lifts you to safety. Okay, Robby?"

Robby agreed. Feet set, the boy started pulling, but just as Fox was getting his feet under him, his right hand disappeared. It reappeared holding a snub-nosed revolver.

"Gun!" Izzy shouted.

On instinct, she fired her own, sparking a pained scream from Fox.

Struck in the left shoulder, he toppled back onto the already-weakened railing, having lost his grip on both Robby and the gun. He'd barely struck wood when the now-familiar sound froze him in place. The nails had broken free.

"No, no!" Eyes bulging with terror, Fox joined the railing as it plunged into the darkness. Even with the heavy rain, the thud was clearly audible.

Kylie looked at Izzy, her expression wary. "My mom survived, and she fell a lot farther than that."

Izzy stepped past Luke's body and, flanked by Kylie and Robby, knelt at the edge of the deck. They stared down at the concrete surrounding the pool area, all of which was now lit up by motion lights.

As if unable to escape his creation even in death, Fox's bottom half lay stretched across the mangled section of rail. His upper half had come to rest on the concrete pool deck, and his head was raised at a strange angle as if examining his shoes.

"Why's his head tilted up like that?" Kylie asked.

"He landed on the cast-iron turtle my mom ordered," Robby said matter-of-factly. "FedEx delivered it this morning."

If the back of Fox's head was bleeding, Izzy couldn't tell. It was raining that hard.

Chapter 88

IZZY

THE KIDS HADN'T shown much emotion when they were looking down from the deck at their stepdad's body. Izzy figured it was because they hadn't had time to process things, to absorb what had happened. Now, they did have time.

Since the living room hadn't played a part in the evening's sad events, Izzy escorted Kylie and Robby there and sat beside them on the sofa as she used her cell phone to report what had just happened. In a few minutes, the house would be swarming with officers and paramedics, but for now, Izzy just let the kids sit.

Also in need of a little quiet time, Izzy slumped back, reviewing the events that had led her to this moment. She'd felt something bad was going to happen at the Fox house, and that sure had come true. But she'd also told Kylie that things would work out as they should. Was this that, with their mother in a coma and their stepdad dead? The poor things were practically orphans. She looked at Kylie and Robby, now huddled shoulder to shoulder across the room from a blank TV screen.

No, not orphans. They had Tonya, they had their friends, and they also had Izzy.

"Feel like calling your aunt?" she asked them.

Although Kylie's response was just a detached nod, it was more than Izzy got from Robby. As Izzy dialed Tonya's number, he rested his head on Kylie's lap and was asleep before Tonya picked up. The news stunned her, but she soon recovered, and Izzy put the phone on speaker so Kylie could join the conversation and share her input. Sadly, Kylie soon became overwhelmed and could barely manage one-word answers. Even with that, her desires were clear, and they settled on a plan. During that time, Robby barely moved. He also slept through Izzy and Kylie's conversations with Addison and Addison's mother and remained asleep until the EMTs arrived, and Izzy asked them to examine him.

HAVING COMPLETED A preliminary tour of the crime scenes with Fulton, he and Izzy returned to the living room where Kylie sat slumped in the corner of the sofa, her cell phone clutched in one hand, the fingers of her other hand mechanically stroking her brother's hair, the only part of Robby that wasn't hidden by the Afghan she had just draped over him.

"Can we get you anything?" Fulton asked Kylie.

Kylie shook her head. "No, thanks, I . . ." Her eyes welled with tears. "No, wait. My mom. Is she okay? I want to see her."

Afraid Kylie might hyperventilate, Izzy bent over her, her lips near Kylie's ear. "Sure," she whispered. "I'll take you there in the morning. But if you want an update, I can call the nurses' station for you. Would you like that?"

"Uh-huh."

Izzy dialed the number, and Kylie took the cell phone eagerly. Assured her mom was safe, she thanked Izzy who dropped an impromptu kiss on Kylie's forehead as she took the phone back.

Surprised by her sudden maternal nature, she waved Fulton to the kitchen to speak privately. "I spoke to their aunt Tonya. She's flying up in the morning."

"Good, but what about tonight? Is there someone they can stay with?"

"Yes, Kylie's best friend, Addison. I thought the kids should stay together, and Addison's mom agreed. I'm sure she's already made up some beds, but I'd feel better if a psychiatrist examined them first."

"I thought the same thing," Fulton said, "so I called Dr. Griffon right after I got off the phone with you. She'll be here any minute."

No wonder Maggie loves him, Izzy thought. The man was one of the most thoughtful people she'd ever met, right up there with Brody and her own father.

As promised, Dr. Griffon arrived within minutes. A sturdy grandmother type, carrying a paper bag, she shrugged out of her raincoat, then turned and announced that the storm was finally weakening.

"Ah, Detective Santos. Chief Fulton described you perfectly. I'm Dr. Griffon." She tucked the bag beneath one arm, allowing herself to give both of Izzy's hands a good, warm squeeze before smiling and turning to the sofa where Kylie had just shaken Robby awake. "Kylie. Robby. I hear you just experienced something terrible. I am so sorry. Life can be so unfair."

They stood, roused either by Dr. Griffon's larger-than-life persona or the alluring scent of cinnamon emanating from the paper bag, which she handed to Robby.

"Obviously, those won't solve anything," she told him, then tugged a thick red beret from her head, releasing a mass of steel-grey curls. "But they won't hurt anything either. Take one, then offer some to the others."

Before Izzy knew it, she was biting into a big, still-warm snickerdoodle and helping Dr. Griffon herd the kids into the kitchen to help her make hot chocolate.

Satisfied Kylie and Robby were in good hands, Izzy strode back into the living room just as Andrea Muncie and her CSI team arrived from Dalton. After a quick tour of the scene, Andrea sent two technicians upstairs to deal with Luke Manetti's body in the master bedroom and one in charge of Robby's room. Out in the backyard, she and another tech busied themselves with Fox's body.

Along with Fulton, Izzy watched from the patio for a while. They were just about to head inside when a somber-faced Adrian Vega appeared. Fulton excused himself, and they stepped away to speak privately. Poor Adrian. Izzy knew how much the young officer had admired Fox. Probably as much as she admired Fulton. Her throat tightened as Fulton pulled Vega in for a hug.

With a nod, Vega left, and Fulton came back and sat beside Izzy at the patio table. "He found the hands."

Izzy sighed. "Hidden in Kylie's room?"

"That's right, three of them." For the third time since Fulton's arrival, he pulled out his trusty Juicy Fruit. "They were in a plastic storage container under her bed." He offered Izzy a piece of gum, but she declined, seeing he was nearly out. "Yeah, Fox burned Darcy's hands when he burned her car and all that other stuff, so a pair and one left hand."

"From Rosa Del Campo?"

"Probably. Andrea's tentatively ID'd the pair as Lexi Siegel's."

"Because of the little heart tattoo on her left index finger?"

"Exactly, and the two left hands are missing their pinky finger. Trophies, I suppose." Fulton peered through the sliding door into the kitchen where Dr. Griffon and the kids sat talking and drinking cocoa. "Kylie's lucky you overheard Luke's confession. A box of hands under your bed normally gets you arrested."

"Yeah, but this is far from normal times." She moved aside to make room for the coroner's gurney as it rolled past them out to the pool area. "So, what do we do about the missing fingers?"

"Vega wanted to search the Manetti house right away, but I decided we give his family some space tonight."

"I suppose, at this point, it doesn't matter." Izzy glanced back at the kitchen window just as Dr. Griffon was pushing her chair back. She noticed Izzy watching and gestured for her to join them.

"Go ahead," Fulton told her. "I should probably head out front and make a statement. The rain has stopped, so Gloria Gomez must to be champing at the bit."

Izzy stepped into the kitchen and found the kids still seated at the table and Dr. Griffon filling their cups with more cocoa. The doctor acknowledged Izzy with a nod then turned to Kylie. "Go on, tell her what you've decided."

Kylie locked eyes with her brother. "We've changed our minds about what the EMTs told us."

"That you should have some tests done to make sure you're okay?" Izzy asked.

She nodded. "We're ready to do that, now. Dr. Griffon's going to drive us to the hospital."

"Smart." Izzy looked at Dr. Griffon. "And thank you."

"The sooner these kids get checked out, the better," Dr. Griffon said.

"And there's something else you should know." Kylie turned to Izzy. "Gabe has a footlocker in the garage. It's got a lock on it, and he's never let me or Robby look inside. I don't even think Mom has. Here . . ." She reached into the bowl of apples in the center of the table, and for a moment, Izzy thought she was going to offer her a piece of fruit. Instead, Kylie handed her a fat ring of keys, several of which had colored rubber caps.

"It's the blue one," Robby added.

HAVING PROMISED SHE would join the kids at the hospital as soon as she finished up at the house, Izzy watched Dr. Griffon's car disappear around the corner, then went inside to see what Gabe had hidden in his garage.

According to Kylie, the footlocker was black and tucked underneath Fox's workbench. Izzy located the small trunk and gloved up. She dragged it out and crouched down in front of the lock which she removed and dropped onto the concrete.

Okay, so what secrets might a murderous policeman keep?

Steeling herself, she threw open the lid. At first glance, the stuff inside was boring enough; a few old car magazines and Chilton manuals. But that was only the first layer. If there was something incriminating in this chest, Fox would have stored it out of sight, and like many footlockers, this one had a shallow tray. Izzy lifted it out.

Girly magazines? That couldn't be Fox's only secret.

She set the *Hustlers* aside. The travel brochures she found beneath were far more interesting. Belize, Costa Rica—holy cow, Cuba? But what really raised her eyebrows were the syringes. There were three, each wrapped in white and green plastic, just like the one Tonya had found in Angie Fox's hospital bathroom, and exactly like the ones Gordy had shown her in the police station's storage room.

She was about to call in Andrea Muncie when she noticed a wadded-up paper napkin tucked down into the corner. Gently, she pinched it between her thumb and forefinger. The object inside was small, round and hard. She unfolded the tiny bundle and stood. From the description Darcy Callahan's husband had given her, this was Darcy's wedding ring.

Izzy's sudden anger surprised her. It hadn't been enough for Gabe to murder Darcy and chop her hands off. He'd stolen her wedding ring too.

"God," she muttered. "I can't believe we trusted that man."

"Ditto." Fulton stepped up beside her. "What have you got there?"

Izzy showed him the ring. "There's some other stuff too." Together, they bent over the footlocker. "The guy sure did pull one over on us."

"That Manetti kid, too," Fulton said. "I only knew him through the Junior Police Squad, but he seemed like a real nice kid during the interview."

"Luke was a psychopath," Izzy said matter-of-factly. "Fox too, mostly likely. And like a psychopath, they only cared about themselves. Kylie and Robby are great kids. They don't deserve what those two did to them."

"No, they don't. But you could say that about the families of all murder victims." Fulton hugged Izzy to him. "They'll be okay with their aunt, and Kylie's eighteen. She'll graduate soon and go to college."

He pressed his last piece of gum into her hand. "Let's go tell Andrea about the footlocker."

They headed into the backyard and found Andrea Muncy looking on as her techs zipped Gabe's remains into a body bag. On the concrete where he had landed, all that was left was a pink puddle, his blood diluted by the recent rain. The iron turtle, small, but sufficient in bulk to have created a baseball sized dent in the back of Gabe's head, was gone.

Spotting them, Andrea held up one hand and they stayed put, giving the EMTs space to lift what was left of Officer Gabe Fox onto a gurney. They watched in silence as the body was wheeled past.

"Well, I sure didn't see that coming," Andrea said, looking from Izzy to Fulton. "You?"

"Not in a million years." Fulton nodded at the puddle of blood beside them. "Somebody should hose that down."

"Once we get out of the way, I'll have one of my techs do it." Andrea held a clear gallon-sized plastic bag, sagging under the weight of the small roundish shape inside it. "The killer turtle." She raised the bag for Fulton to get a better look. "You know, if it wasn't for this little guy, Fox would probably still be alive. Funny how things work out."

Fulton slipped on his reading glasses and leaned in. "Yeah . . . funny."

Chapter 89

IZZY

HAVING PICKED TONYA up at the airport, Izzy drove directly to the hospital and met up with Kylie and Robby in their mother's hospital room. Kylie's boyfriend was there too, and as Kylie introduced Ryan to Tonya, Izzy approached Angie Fox, asleep in the bed behind them. Angie's facial injuries had healed quite well since she was first hospitalized, and she no longer needed the respirator to breathe. All well and good, but from what Izzy could tell, she was still no closer to waking.

"So, where's the doctor?" Tonya asked.

"The nurse said she was running late," Kylie explained. She spotted some folding chairs stacked against the wall. "Want a chair, Auntie?"

Tonya accepted Kylie's offer, as did Izzy and Ryan. Robby posted himself as a lookout in the open doorway.

"So"—Tonya took Kylie's hand—"how come we're just hearing about this Stilnox now? I mean, your mom's been off the coma meds for quite a while."

Kylie smiled sadly. "Dr. Assani said she did tell Gabe."

"And . . . ?"

"Gabe was all over the place. First, shocked, then happy. He said he wanted to do it, but worried it might be too risky—which Dr. Assani said was normal. She printed out a list of side effects for him, and gave him some time to read it. When she came back, he refused the treatment. Apparently, there's a big risk for people with sleep apnea. Their lungs might collapse."

"Oh, wow." Tonya looked thoughtful. "I didn't know Angie had sleep apnea."

"She doesn't." Kylie scowled. "Gabe made it all up."

No surprise there, Izzy thought. The last thing he would want was Angie waking up. "So what changed?"

"What changed is that our story was all over the news yesterday. Dr. Assani heard about what happened, and as soon as she was able, she reached out." Kylie smiled. "God, was I happy. Surprised too, because Stilnox is a lot like Ambien. You know, the sleeping pill? For some reason, the stuff does the opposite on coma patients. A lot of them wake up."

"The doctor's here," Robby announced. "She just got out of the elevator."

Dr. Assani soon entered the room, accompanied by a nurse wheeling a small, silver tray table, in the center of which lay a syringe and a pair of blue nitrile gloves. Once Kylie made the introductions, She slipped the gloves on and picked up the syringe. "Kids, before I inject the Stilnox, you need to understand that it's possible nothing will happen." She looked from one to the other. "Okay?"

Arms looped through Ryan's and Robby's, Kylie pressed her lips together in an anxious smile. "Yeah, we understand."

"Great." Dr. Assani inserted the needle into Angie's IV port. "Now, remember. There's no timetable on how long it will take for her to wake up . . . or, whether she's even going to."

Robby looked at Kylie with hopeful eyes. She nodded back.

"It could take a couple of minutes or several hours."

"That's okay," Kylie told her. "We aren't going anywhere."

Dr. Assani stayed by Angie's side for a few minutes, and when Angie showed no initial signs of reacting badly, announced that either she or the nurse would check back in five minutes, then every fifteen minutes thereafter for the next few hours.

Kylie thanked her then joined her brother at their mother's side.

Robby's mouth twisted into a scowl. "Gabe better be in Hell right now."

"Oh, he is," Kylie said. "Because if Gabe doesn't deserve Hell, nobody does."

Good point, Izzy thought. She marked the time as just past one. God, wasn't the man's autopsy scheduled for that time? She shuddered. Devine justice, irony, or just plain karma, Fox had no one to blame but himself.

Tonya joined the kids by the bed. "I get why you're angry. But anger is neither healthy nor helpful. We have to move on, even if this medication doesn't pan out."

"I know," Robby said. "But Mom *is* going to wake up. She has to."

"I hope you're right," Tonya said. She pulled them in for a group hug, and as she rested her chin on Kylie's shoulder, glanced at Izzy with anxious eyes.

Yeah, I hope Robby's right too, Izzy thought. It would sure fit in with her annoyingly vague prophesy that everything was going to work out as it should.

After an hour had passed, and Angie still hadn't shown any signs of waking up, Tonya slipped Ryan some money to get everyone drinks. Two hours later, all five paper cups were in the wastebasket, and nothing had changed. Besides pacing back and forth, they filled the time by discussing various topics, like how long the kids should continue seeing a therapist, and if things went well with Angie, whether or not they should stay in Rocky Harbor after Kylie graduated. They also discussed the pros and cons of Ryan getting plastic surgery for the scar on his neck. Two topics that never came up were Gabe Fox and Luke Manetti. But regardless of where the conversation went, their gaze always returned to the sleeping form in the bed.

During a brief quiet period, Ryan seemed to have something he wanted to say. He looked at Kylie. "I know you didn't want to talk about this today, but I think you should tell them."

"What?" Seated beside her, Tonya grabbed Kylie's hand. "What happened?"

"No, no," Kylie chuckled. "It's a good thing." She smiled at her aunt, then Izzy. "I wasn't going to mention this today, but I guess I have to now. Thanks to Gloria Gomez, our story has gone viral, and this morning, I got three phone calls: two from TV talk shows and another from a publishing company offering us a book deal. Isn't that great? Because we're broke."

"Don't you worry about money," Tonya assured them. "You can live with me as long as you like." Generous, Izzy thought, but not rational. Tonya's apartment only had one bedroom. But maybe their stepdad could help. Izzy considered telling the kids about the life insurance policies Andrea Muncy had discovered hidden at the bottom of Fox's footlocker. Kylie could probably handle the news, but could Robby?

As if reading her mind, Kylie caught her eye. "So, did you find anything interesting in Gabe's footlocker?"

"Yeah, with so much going on, I forgot to tell you." She took in their fearful yet curious expressions. "There were a few travel brochures, but most of the stuff was car manuals and magazines." Since knowing would only hurt them, she didn't mention Darcy Callahan's wedding ring. "Pretty boring stuff, mostly, but not all of it. Did you know about the life insurance policies?"

Kylie nodded. "Mom mentioned something, but aren't those just for Robby and my"—She scrunched her face—"funeral expenses?"

"Well, they could be." Izzy assumed that once the kids were dead, Fox intended to cash those two policies in and head for Belize, or wherever. She left that conversation for another day. "They also had a policy on your mom and another on your stepdad. That one's worth five-hundred thousand dollars."

"Five . . . hundred . . . thousand?" Robby's eyes were literally saucers. "And we can collect that money?"

"It's in your mom's name," Izzy told him then locked eyes with Kylie, "but since she's still incapacitated, and you're eighteen, dealing with stuff like that's going to be your responsibility—for a while, at least."

"Whoa." Robby elbowed Kylie. "Wouldn't it be cool if Mom woke up and found her car paid off?"

"Hell, yeah. And her credit cards. I mean, with all that money, she could . . ." Kylie looked at Izzy, her expression a mixture of confusion and pain. "And all because Gabe is dead?"

It was, and Izzy was responsible. She must have reacted in some way, because Kylie pulled her to her feet and wrapped his arms around her. "You saved my life, Detective. Robby's too, so don't feel guilty. You're a hero." She turned to look at her mom, still very much asleep in her hospital bed.

Would this poor woman ever open her eyes? For a while, they went silent, and everyone focused their attention on the rise and fall of Angie's chest. Around six, Ryan took Robby downstairs to the cafeteria to buy everyone sandwiches, which they ate in silence.

By the time they finished, it had been five hours since Dr. Assani injected the Stilnox into Angie's IV. As promised, both doctor and nurse had returned, but after a while, the periods between visits grew steadily longer. Angie would still get a flashlight shined in her eyes and her pulse taken, but she was never any closer to waking.

Two more hours passed, and as uncomfortable as their chairs were, eyes were beginning to close. Izzy's too, and on the third time, she got up and stretched, as did Robby.

"I'm going to turn the TV on. Maybe that'll keep us awake." He found the remote and clicked through the dozen available channels, golf, an episode of some Robin Williams sitcom from the seventies, a shopping channel selling cubic zirconium jewelry, and the local news.

"Just leave it on the news," Kylie told him.

Robby groaned. "I hate the news. Why do you always have to—"

"Hey . . ." croaked a frail voice.

Like Tonya and Ryan, Izzy turned toward the bed, but the kids had already reached their mother's side. Tears flowing, they covered Angie's face with kisses, then pulled back, allowing Angie to see the others. She looked questioningly at Ryan's unfamiliar face.

"I'm Ryan," he said. "Kylie's boyfriend."

"Boyfriend?" Eyelids heavy, Angie ran her tongue across her lips, as if tasting the new word. And then, she recognized Tonya and smiled. "Hey, Sis," she rasped. "When did you . . . ?"

As Tonya kissed Angie' cheek, Izzy accepted hugs from Robby then Kylie, whose embrace rivaled Tonya's. "You were right. Things really did work out as they should."

"Yeah, I guess they did," Izzy said, then noticed Angie looking at her. "Hi, Angie. You have no idea how happy you've just made your family."

"Santos . . . ? But why are you . . . ?" Her gaze dropped to the gold detective's badge at Izzy's waistband and the confused smile that had been covering her face hardened. "Hold on." She struggled to sit up. "Where's Gabe?"

Diana Corbitt is a retired elementary school teacher who has lived her entire life in northern California. She has two sons who, although grown up and out of the house, still live nearby. Ever since she was a kid she loved to be scared, either by movies or books. She started writing her first story in sixth grade. That one never got past six pages, but now that she's retired she can't stop writing. When she's not trying to scare herself silly, Diana enjoys travel, and going to the movies. They don't all have to be scary. Just not chick flicks.

Visit Diana's website: http://www.dianacorbitt.com

Detective Izzy Santos goes to Spain
for a birthday celebration/family reunion
and tackles another mystery in
The Black Pig Murders.

Look for it in 2025

⌒⤝

CHAPTER 1
IZZY

The rain had finally stopped, bringing the people of Rocky Harbor its first star-filled night in over a week. To Detective Izzy Santos' irritation, that clear sky was also accompanied by much lower temperatures. Not a fan of numb fingers, Izzy had been ransacking her 40-foot cabin cruiser for ten minutes, and she still hadn't found her gloves. Galley and main cabin scoured, she moved on to the guest area but was still gloveless five minutes later.

"You're a detective," she told herself. "Detect." Scowling, she mounted the four steps to search the boat's tiny galley again. Worried she might have stuffed them in the fridge, Izzy had just opened the freezer when her boyfriend, Brody, poked his head in. "Found them."

"What? Where?"

"In that little cubby above this door." Smiling his typical impish smile, Brody backed out of the narrow hatchway as Izzy burst out of the galley and turned to look.

Her black-leather gloves glared back accusingly. Why would she stow them in the map box? She grabbed them. "Great, let's go. Maggie and Fulton are probably halfway through their salads by now."

Brody chuckled. "I really doubt that, but it's good that new restaurant is only a five-minute walk from here." Green eyes sparkling, he looked Izzy up and down. "Man, that top's really something."

"What? Think it's too lowcut for the occasion?"

"Well, let me see." He moved in until he'd burrowed his lips beneath her dark, shoulder-length hair. "No, no." His warm breath tickled Izzy's chest.

"This is the perfect amount of crevice." His lips moved up to her neck, then her cheek, then…

"You know what…?" Afraid they'd miss dinner completely, Izzy grabbed her hairbrush from the nearby table, putting some space between them. "I think you're so used to seeing me in my work clothes that even a tiny hint of cleavage gets you hot." Senses heightened, she ran the brush through her hair. "Loose or ponytail?"

Brody's lips pressed together as if he'd tasted something bad. "I see enough ponytails when you're working." He grabbed her coat and helped her into it. "Let that gorgeous mane flow, girl."

Grinning, Izzy pulled on her gloves. "Forget me. Look at you." She took in his ultra-sharp dinner outfit: a white turtleneck sweater topped by a gray herring-bone coat, scarf, and, most irritating of all, black-leather gloves. "I suppose that's what happens when you own a walk-in closet."

"Yup, my place has lots of closets." He opened the small door in the port-side railing and they climbed out onto the dock, which they strolled arm in arm. "You know, I've even got a closet just for gloves. Come share it with me."

He was exaggerating, but all that space would be nice. So would coming home to Brody every night. Izzy stepped onto the wooden ramp that would lead them up to the road and turned, her eyes now even with his. She definitely couldn't do any better.

"Marry me," Brody whispered.

She gripped the lapels of his coat and pulled until his wavy blond locks touched her forehead. "I know you love me," she told him. "And I love you too. But that boat was my dream for like ten years."

"Marriage doesn't mean we have to sell the boat. We could take her out on weekends. Cruise down the coast to Shaw's Landing or north to Pleasant Rock and spend the night. You know. Like we did last summer."

Izzy hugged him to her. "That was fun. And the Italian place you found was amazing."

Brody pulled back. "Was that a yes?"

"Let me think about it." She jogged to the top of the ramp and turned. "And no bringing up weddings in front of Maggie and Fulton."

Once they reached the pier, they strode past Salty's, the popular burger joint Brody had inherited from his father nearly two years past. Its multiple picture windows were brightly lit, illuminating the dozen or so customers and making the restaurant a beacon for any fishing boats that hadn't returned to the harbor yet. The couple's destination, Just Hooked, was down at the end of the pier. It too had plenty of lighting.

"For a Wednesday, Salty's looks pretty busy," Izzy said, aware of Brody's constant effort to increase his restaurant's low winter profits.

"I count four cars in the parking lot."

"Sure, but isn't that good for January? I mean…it's freezing out." To prove her point, Izzy waved a gloved hand in his face, but Brody didn't seem reassured. Luckily, they spotted her Aunt Maggie and Sean Fulton, Maggie's husband of more than a year standing in front of the restaurant. Maggie waved.

"There they are!" Izzy tugged Brody along, eager to take his mind off his troubles. "Hey, guys!" She took in the smell of Maggie's signature organic lavender as they exchanged hugs and kisses, then switched over to Fulton, her uncle, boss, and mentor. "I love how close this place is to my boat." She held the door open for the others, eager to get in out of the cold.

Once inside, Brody helped Izzy off with her coat as Fulton assisted Maggie.

"Oh, don't you look fancy," Brody told Maggie. "Did Fulton hide all your jeans and tee shirts?"

Dressed impeccably in black slacks and a cream-colored sweater, Maggie did look out of character. "You talk like that's all she ever wears," Izzy chided Brody. "I remember weeks last year when all she wore was a thin cotton dress."

"Yeah, better known as a hospital gown." Brody chuckled. "And only because her leg was in traction."

"*¡Graciosos!*" Maggie pinched their cheeks. "Don't remind me." She ran her fingers through her long paprika-colored hair and said, "No, nothing has happened, but I do have an announcement to make. Come, let's sit down." Maggie led the way, aided by the hand-carved cat's-head walking stick gifted to her by one of the local artists whose wares she displayed in her downtown gallery.

As the two couples settled themselves into a cushy corner booth and ordered drinks, Izzy speculated about Maggie's announcement. It couldn't be an inheritance. Maggie's closest relative was her mother, Izzy's Grandma, Ofelia. But Grandma was vigorous and barely into her seventies—at least, she'd seemed that way when she'd moved back to Spain with the intentions of traveling Europe with a group of old girlfriends. Four years had passed since then, and Maggie wouldn't celebrate her mother's death with dinner out. So, what could she possibly announce?

"Oh, look. Their specialty is sand dabs." Fulton looked up from his menu. "What are those like?"

"I've never had them," said Maggie.

Brody looked at Izzy. "You like them, don't you?"

"I do." Izzy laced her fingers over her still closed menu and stared at Maggie. "So, what's this big news, Tita?" Auntie.

Unlike Izzy, Fulton had infinite patience. He lowered his own menu and smiled at Izzy with warm, gold-flecked eyes. "Let's order food and get our drinks first, shall we?"

Well, harumph. Izzy scanned her menu, and like the others, ordered the sand dabs. That settled, the arrival of their cocktails drew smiles from everyone.

"Now," Maggie sipped her rum and Coke. "I'm ready to speak." She sat up. Dark, Moorish eyes glistening, she reached into her purse and pulled out what Izzy took to be a wedding invitation. Maggie passed it to her.

"Oh, cool! My Great-uncle Santiago is throwing himself a 76th birthday party-slash-family reunion." Izzy flashed the invitation at Brody, adding, "It's—"

"In Spanish. I figured."

"Anyway," Maggie tucked the invite back in her purse. "All four of us are invited. But it must have been some spur-of-the-moment sort of thing, because the date is next month on February 15th."

"Oh, no." Izzy looked at Brody. "You can't go, can you?"

"Are you sure?" Maggie asked. "Santiago has his own private island."

"Oh, man. I would love to, but…" Brody looked apologetically at Maggie. "My sister is having a caesarian about that time. It's Debbie's first child, and I promised I'd be there."

"I can't go either," Fulton added.

Dark brow gathered, Maggie frowned at Izzy. "He's going to some big police conference in Dallas."

"An event I would happily skip," Fulton said wryly, "But I already accepted their invitation to speak. But hey, just because Brody and I can't go doesn't mean you girls have to stay home."

"Oh, the girls have to go," Brody grinned at Maggie. "I can't even count how many Great-Uncle Santi stories this girl has told me."

"I can imagine," Maggie said. "A lot happened during those two months between the day her mother first received her cancer diagnosis and the day she left us." Izzy's dad barely left Elisa's side those last few weeks." Her eyes became glossy as she spoke, "Our mother was still living here in Rocky Harbor back then, so when we learned nothing could be done for Elisa, we brought her home and took turns tending to her."

"We didn't want my mom to die in the hospital," Izzy explained.

Nodding, Maggie stirred her drink. "Poor Izzy. She was only fourteen at the time."

"And when Tito Santi heard Mom was sick, he dropped everything and flew over." Izzy loosened her tightening throat muscles with several swallows of water.

"Brody, have you seen the photo album he helped Izzy put together?" Maggie asked.

"I sure have. It's amazing." He took Izzy's hand and squeezed it. "Fulton, that man spent days helping Izzy with that album, sorting through photographs, making copies, organizing them. He even brought a few pictures of her mom from when she was a toddler back in that village where she and Maggie were born."

"It was Santi's idea to make it," Izzy said. "He called it my memory book and told me that whenever I got sad, all I had to do was look at those pictures and they would take me back to the good times." She dabbed her eye with her napkin. "And he was right."

"Santi sounds like a great guy," Fulton said. "All the more reason for you girls to take advantage of his offer. You've never been to Spain, have you Izzy?"

"No, never." The thought of seeing her great uncle again was exciting, but so was meeting all those other Spanish relatives. "Should we, Maggie? I would so love to see Tito Santi again." She focused back on Fulton. "How would that work? I mean, what if something happens?"

"You mean, here in Rocky Harbor? As I recall..." Fulton sipped his martini. "Something happened back when I was the detective and down with a nasty flu bug. Remember that?"

"I do," said Brody. Grinning, he took Izzy's hand. "As I recall, some cute little rookie officer did a great job of picking up the slack."

"True, but if you're attending that conference, then we'll both be gone," Izzy argued.

"Look," said Fulton, "The department has lots of good cops. Plus, Andrea Muncie promised to help, and don't forget telephones."

"Fulton's right," said Brody. "He'll cover things just fine while you're gone, and I'm sure my sister will understand you not coming."

"You sure?" Izzy grinned at Maggie, then slumped. "Oh man. At this late date, airline tickets will cost a ton."

"Actually, there was a little note from Santi in that invitation." Maggie drew a sheet of paper from her purse. "He's already reserved first-class tickets to Madrid for February 14th. We'd get there the next morning and stay for a week." She folded the note. "Another example of Santiago's legendary generosity."

"What makes this time different?" Izzy asked. "Santi's offered to pay your way for years."

"Because he's finally convinced me what a fool I've been." Maggie put down her drink. "Look, I haven't seen my mother in four years. My grandmother, even longer. And all because my pride wouldn't allow me to accept my uncle's gifts." She held up the note Santi had sent her. "He says as much right here. He also says that the cost of those airline tickets is like a drop in a bucket to him, and that if I don't get off my high horse and get my butt back to Spain soon, my grandmother might not be around to greet me."

Fulton nodded. "Your uncle is a very wise man," he told Maggie. "I'm glad you've finally realized that."

"So, we're going?" Izzy asked Maggie.

"We're going." Maggie raised her glass. "A toast. Here's to a new adventure!"